S0-ATT-041

THE MONSTER SISTERS

Gaudin, Gareth Kyle, 197
The mystery of the
stone octopus /
2021.

cu   06/03/21

The Mystery of
the Stone Octopus

by GARETH GAUDIN

ORCA BOOK PUBLISHERS

Text and illustrations copyright © Gareth Gaudin 2021

Published in Canada and the United States in 2021 by Orca Book Publishers.
orcabook.com

All rights reserved. No part of this publication may be reproduced or transmitted in any form or by any means, electronic or mechanical, including photocopying, recording or by any information storage and retrieval system now known or to be invented, without permission in writing from the publisher.

Library and Archives Canada Cataloguing in Publication
Title: The mystery of the stone octopus / by Gareth Gaudin.
Names: Gaudin, Gareth Kyle, 1973- author.
Series: Gaudin, Gareth Kyle, 1973- Monster Sisters ; bk. 2.
Description: Series statement: The Monster Sisters ; book 2
Identifiers: Canadiana (print) 20200330756 | Canadiana (ebook) 20200330780 |
ISBN 9781459822290 (softcover) | ISBN 9781459822306 (PDF)
Subjects: LCGFT: Graphic novels. | LCGFT: Detective and mystery comics.
Classification: LCC PN6733.G38 M97 2021 | DDC j741.5/971—dc23

Library of Congress Control Number: 2020944962

Summary: In this graphic novel sequel for early middle readers, two young sleuths must figure out why their sleepy seaside town is being overrun by monsters.

Orca Book Publishers is committed to reducing the consumption of nonrenewable resources in the making of our books. We make every effort to use materials that support a sustainable future.

Orca Book Publishers gratefully acknowledges the support for its publishing programs provided by the following agencies: the Government of Canada, the Canada Council for the Arts and the Province of British Columbia through the BC Arts Council and the Book Publishing Tax Credit.

Cover and interior artwork by Gareth Gaudin
Colors by Jim W.W. Smith

Printed and bound in China.

24 23 22 21 • 1 2 3 4

Dedicated to the following cats: Pushkin, Tabitha,
Audrey Berlin, Orca, Buster Kitten and Hermione Greymalkin.
Special thanks to the real Monster Sisters, Lyra Gotham
and Enid Jupiter, and to their mum, Bronwyn Lee Gaudin.

Welcome back! I'm *still* your host, the Perogy Cat, and this is the second book in the Monster Sisters series. If you've read the first volume, you may remember that the city of Victoria, British Columbia, has been completely overrun by giant monsters, and our two young sleuths are on the case to find out why. The last book left off with them having arrived at their dad's art studio to search for clues. I, for one, certainly hope they find some. Read on, chums!

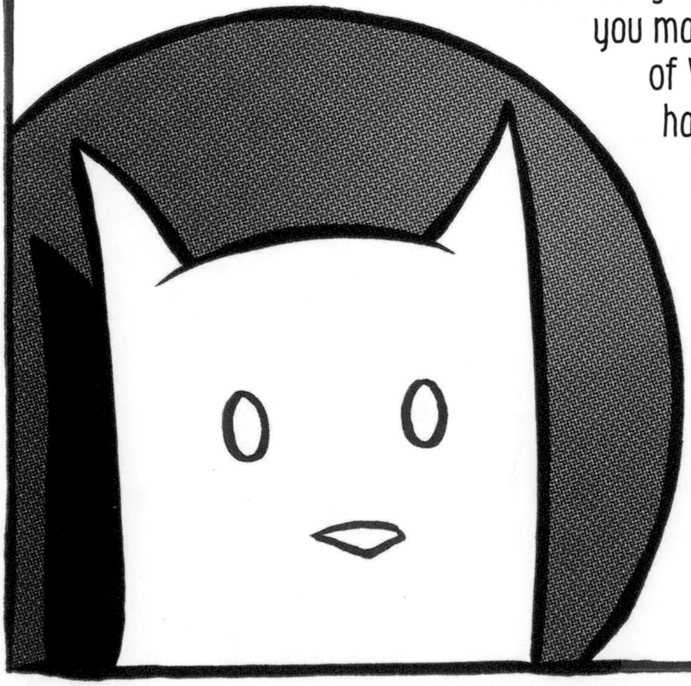

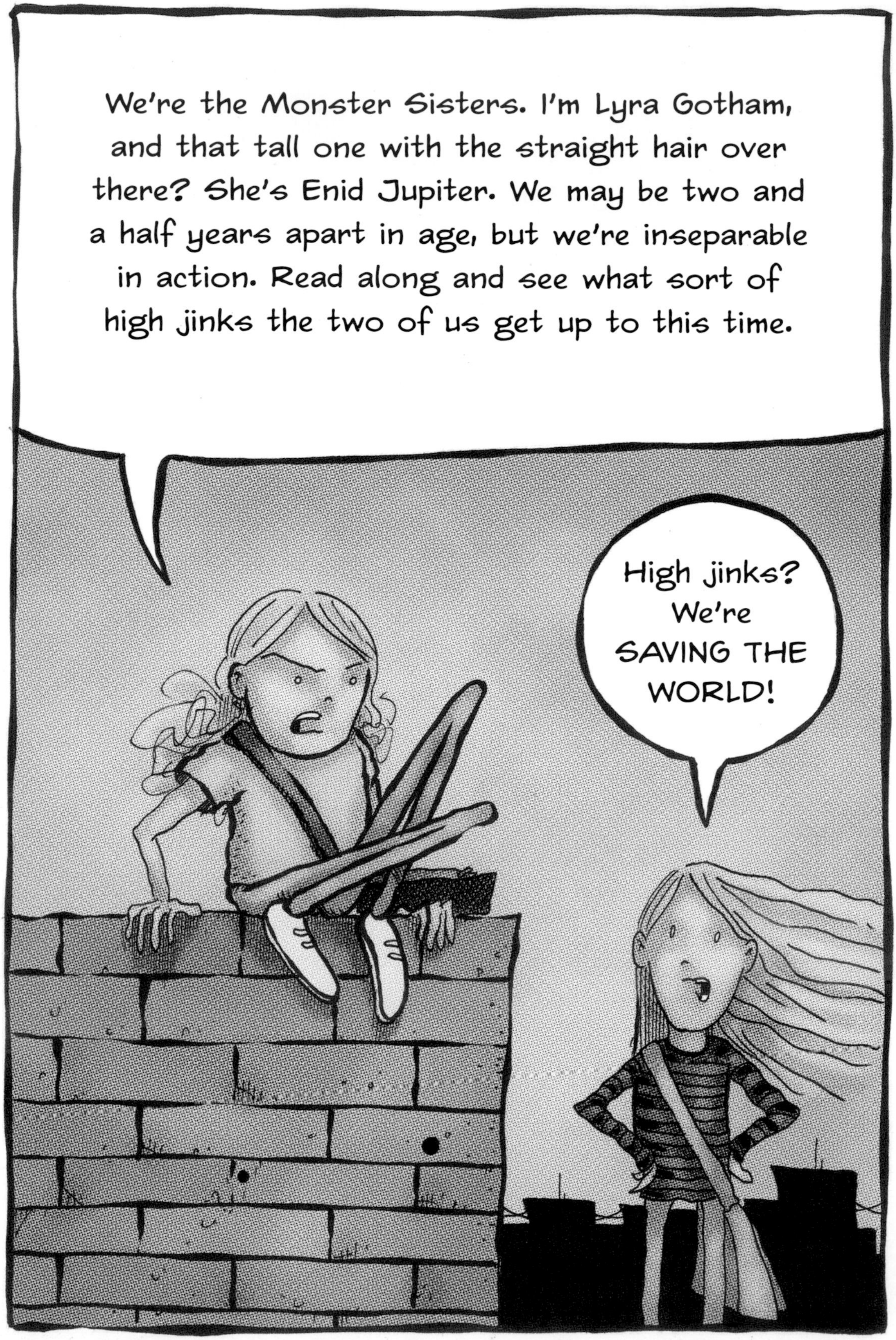
We're the Monster Sisters. I'm Lyra Gotham, and that tall one with the straight hair over there? She's Enid Jupiter. We may be two and a half years apart in age, but we're inseparable in action. Read along and see what sort of high jinks the two of us get up to this time.
High jinks? We're SAVING THE WORLD!

CONTENTS

CHAPTER ONE

INFINITY WITH CHIPS

1

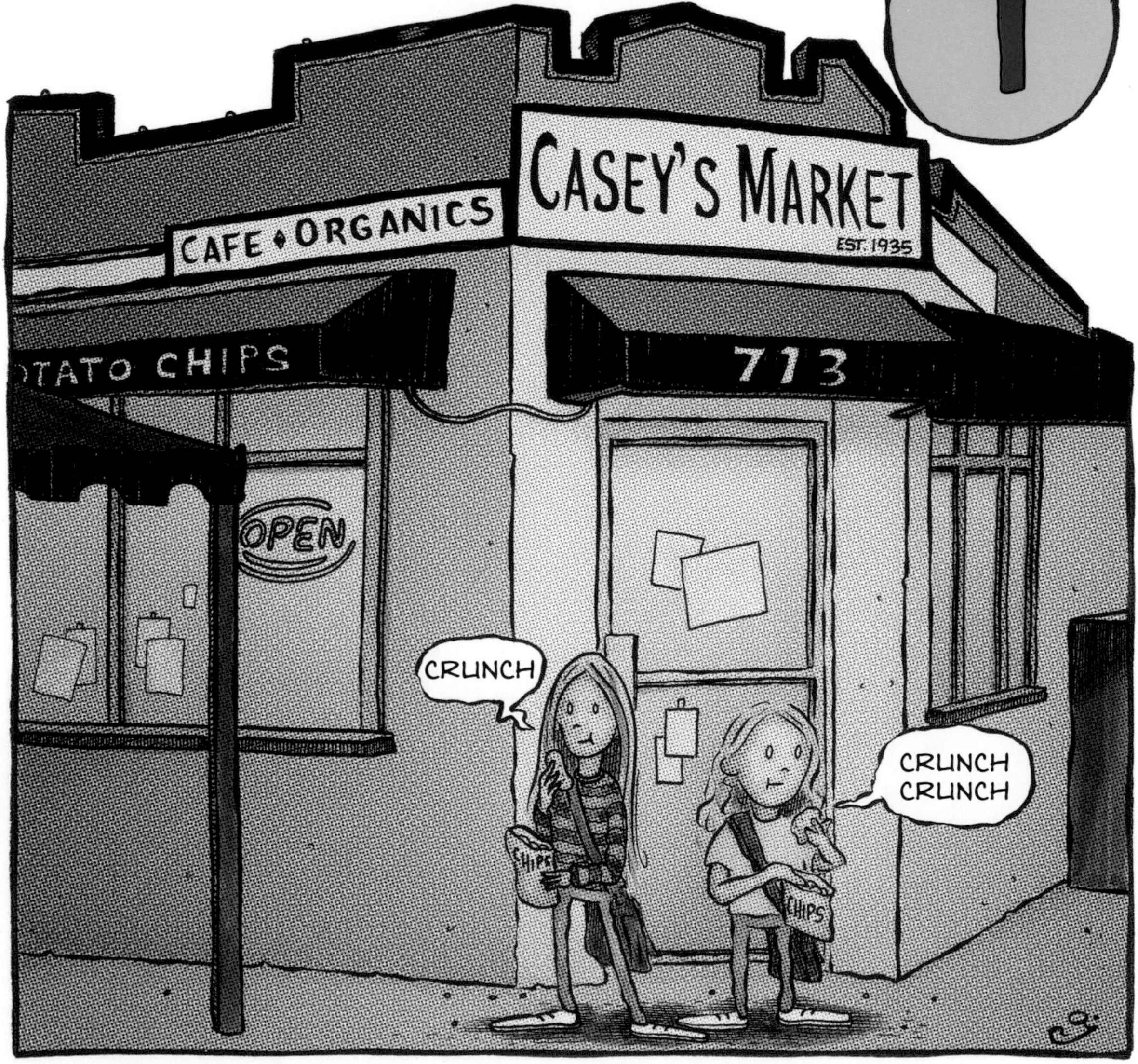
CASEY'S MARKET
EST. 1935
CAFE ◆ ORGANICS
OTATO CHIPS
713
OPEN
CRUNCH
CHIPS
CRUNCH
CRUNCH
CHIPS

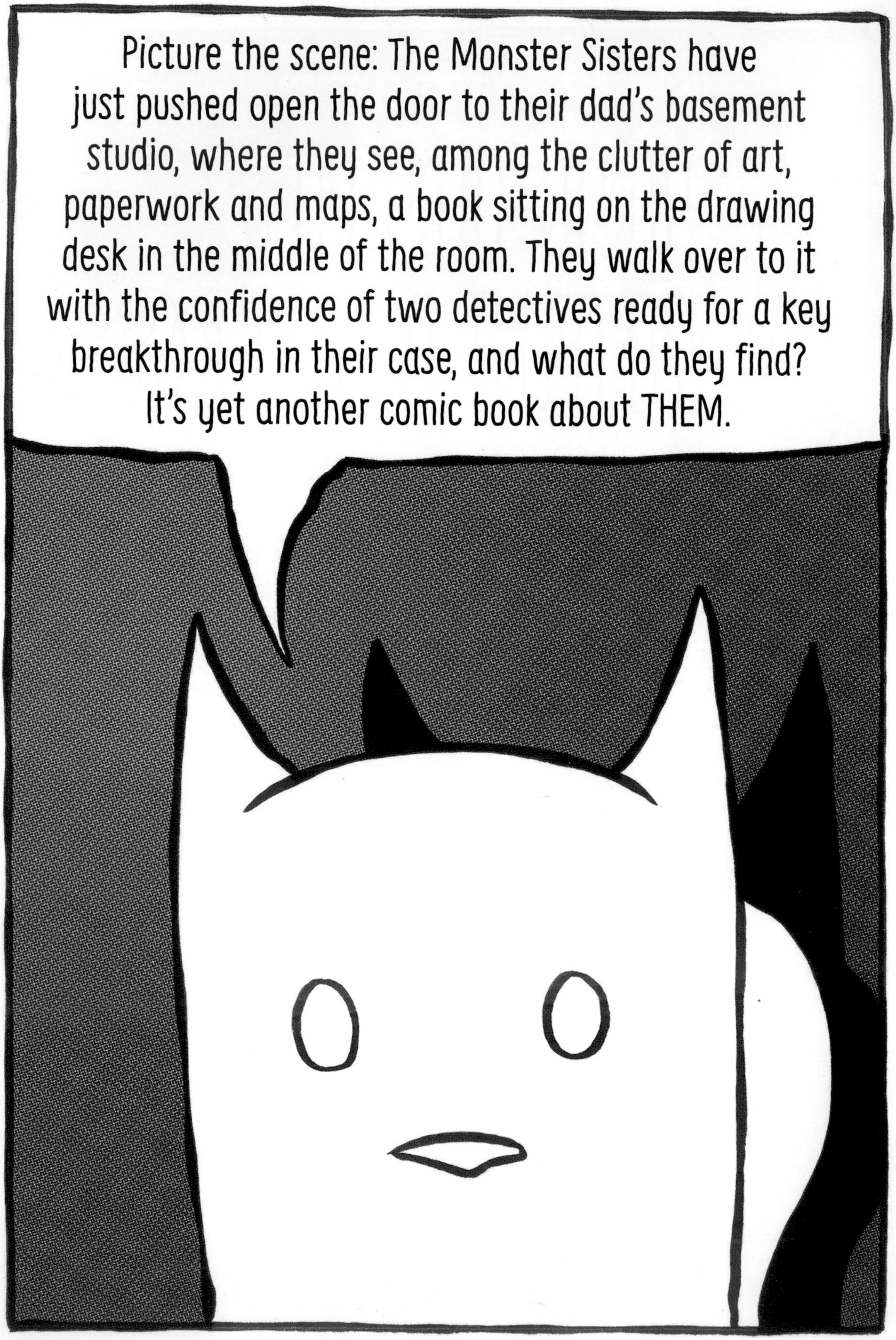
Picture the scene: The Monster Sisters have just pushed open the door to their dad's basement studio, where they see, among the clutter of art, paperwork and maps, a book sitting on the drawing desk in the middle of the room. They walk over to it with the confidence of two detectives ready for a key breakthrough in their case, and what do they find? It's yet another comic book about THEM.

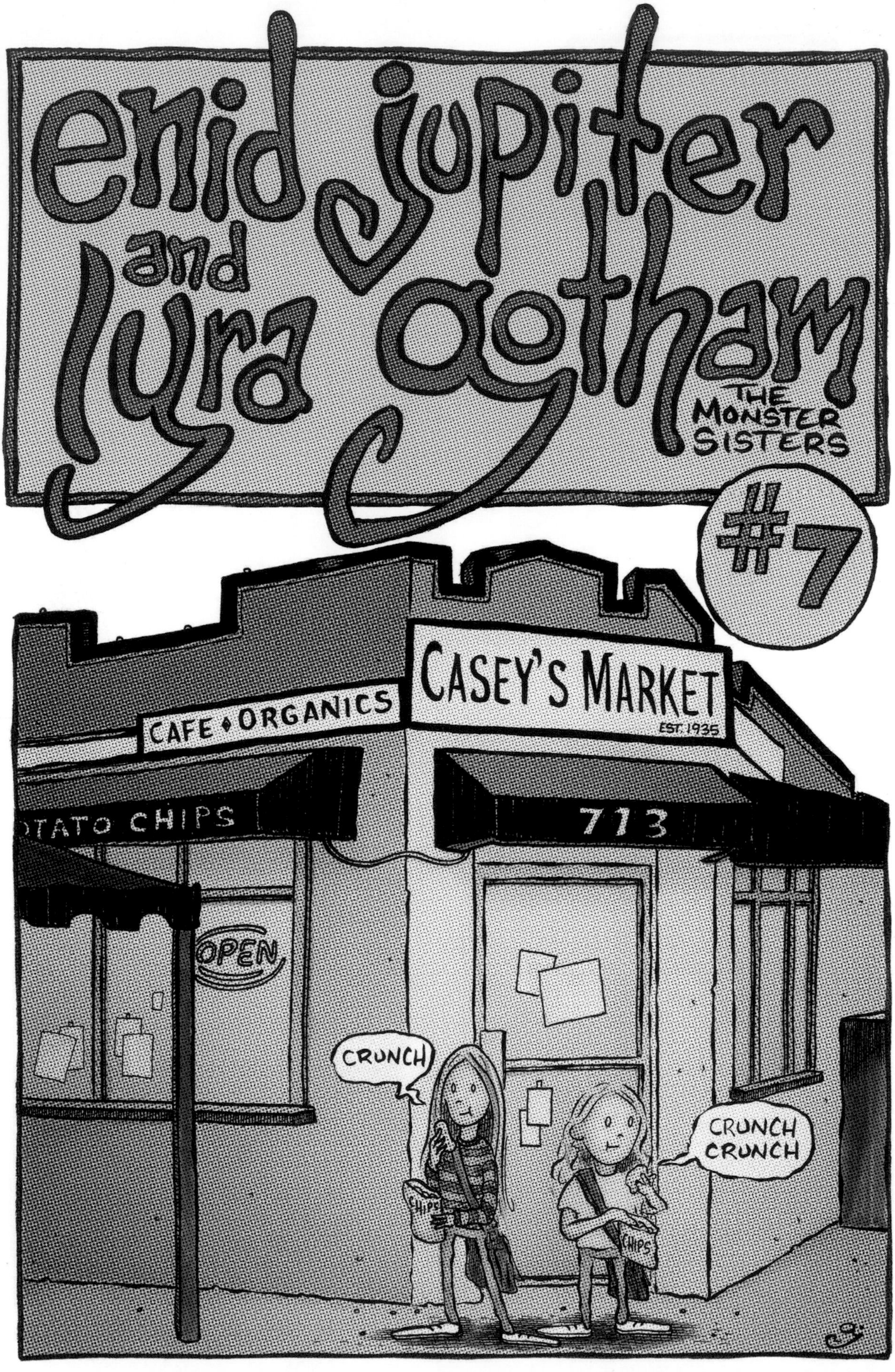
enid jupiter and lyra gotham
THE MONSTER SISTERS
#7
CASEY'S MARKET
EST. 1935
CAFE ♦ ORGANICS
OTATO CHIPS
713
OPEN
CRUNCH
CRUNCH CRUNCH
CHIPS
CHIPS

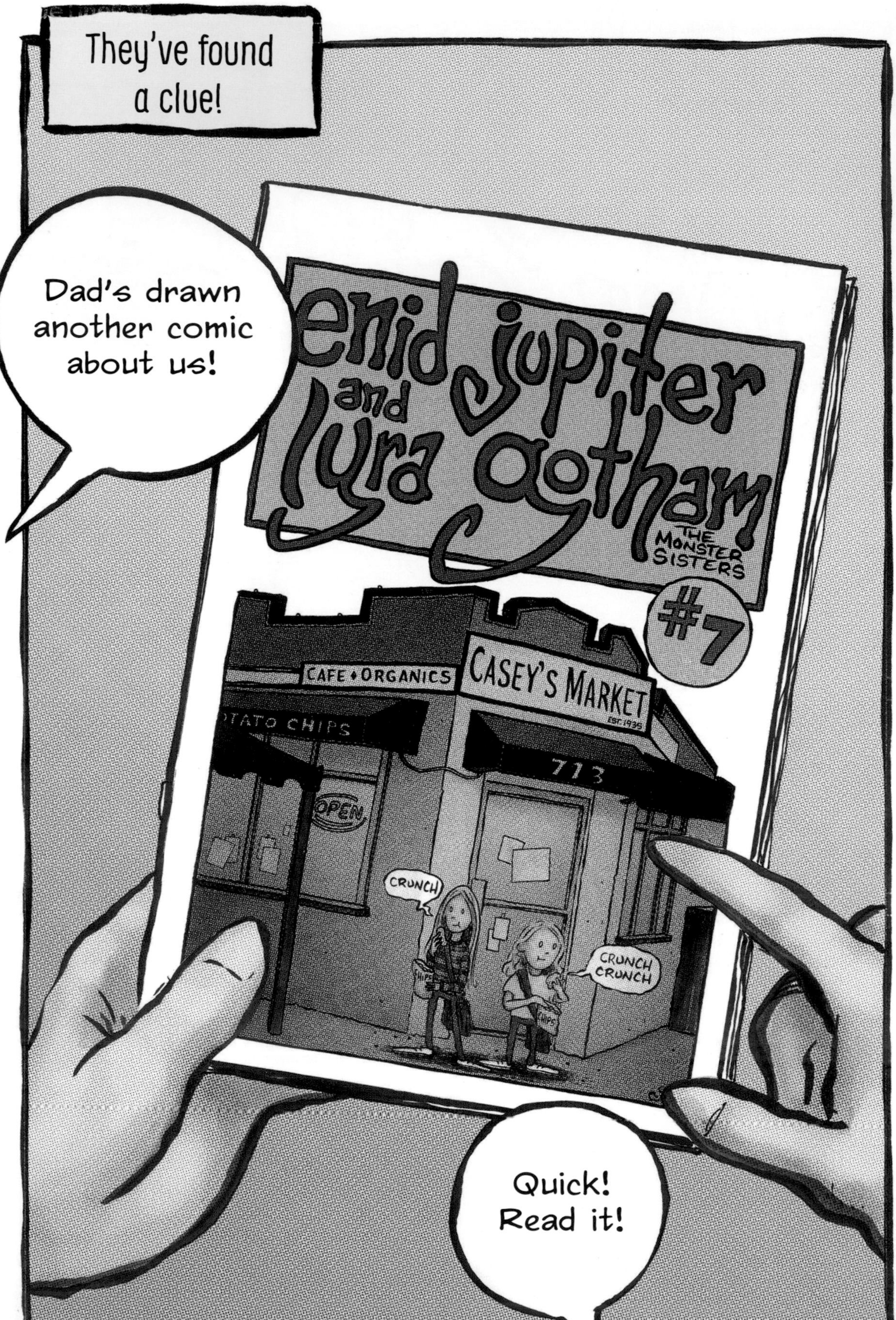
They've found a clue!
Dad's drawn another comic about us!
enid jupiter and lyra gotham
THE MONSTER SISTERS
#7
CAFE + ORGANICS
CASEY'S MARKET
EST. 1935
OTATO CHIPS
713
OPEN
CRUNCH
CRUNCH CRUNCH
CHIPS
CHIPS
Quick! Read it!

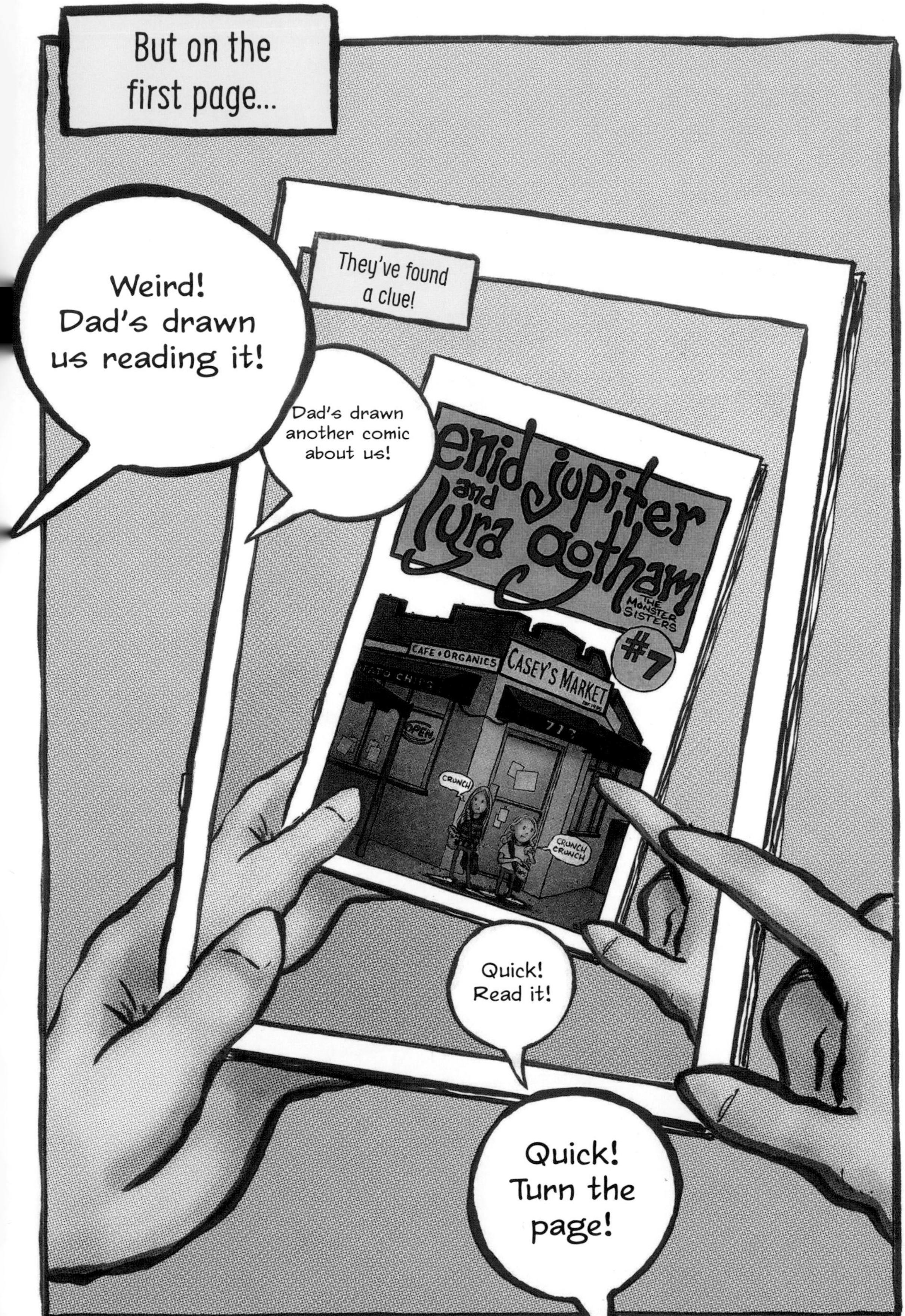
But on the first page...
They've found a clue!
Weird! Dad's drawn us reading it!
Dad's drawn another comic about us!
enid jupiter and lyra gotham
THE MONSTER SISTERS
#7
CAFE + ORGANICS
CASEY'S MARKET
OPEN
CRUNCH
CRUNCH CRUNCH
Quick! Read it!
Quick! Turn the page!

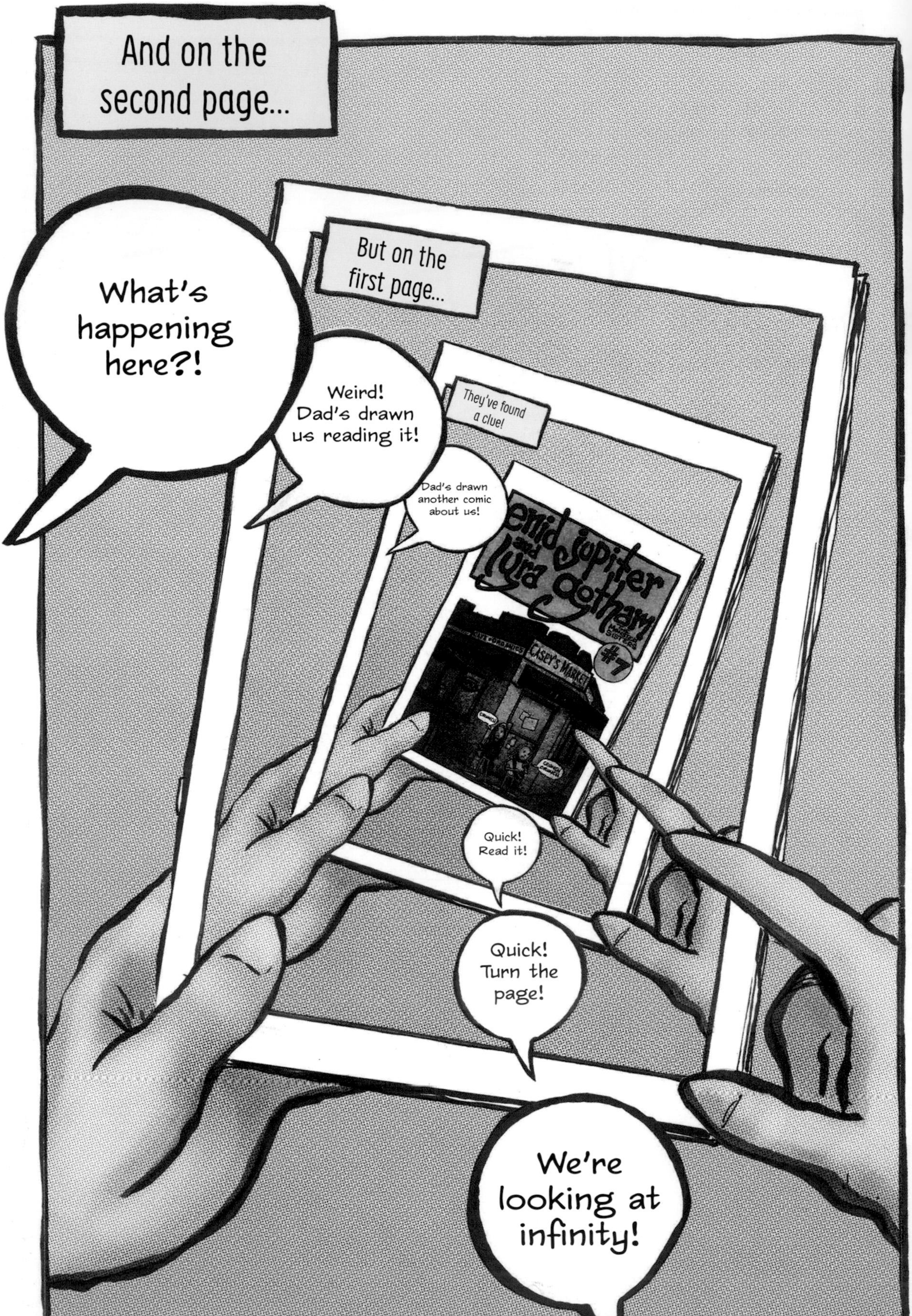

And on the second page...
What's happening here?!
But on the first page...
Weird! Dad's drawn us reading it!
They've found a clue!
Dad's drawn another comic about us!
enid jupiter and lyra gotham
#7
CASEY'S MARKET
Quick! Read it!
Quick! Turn the page!
We're looking at infinity!

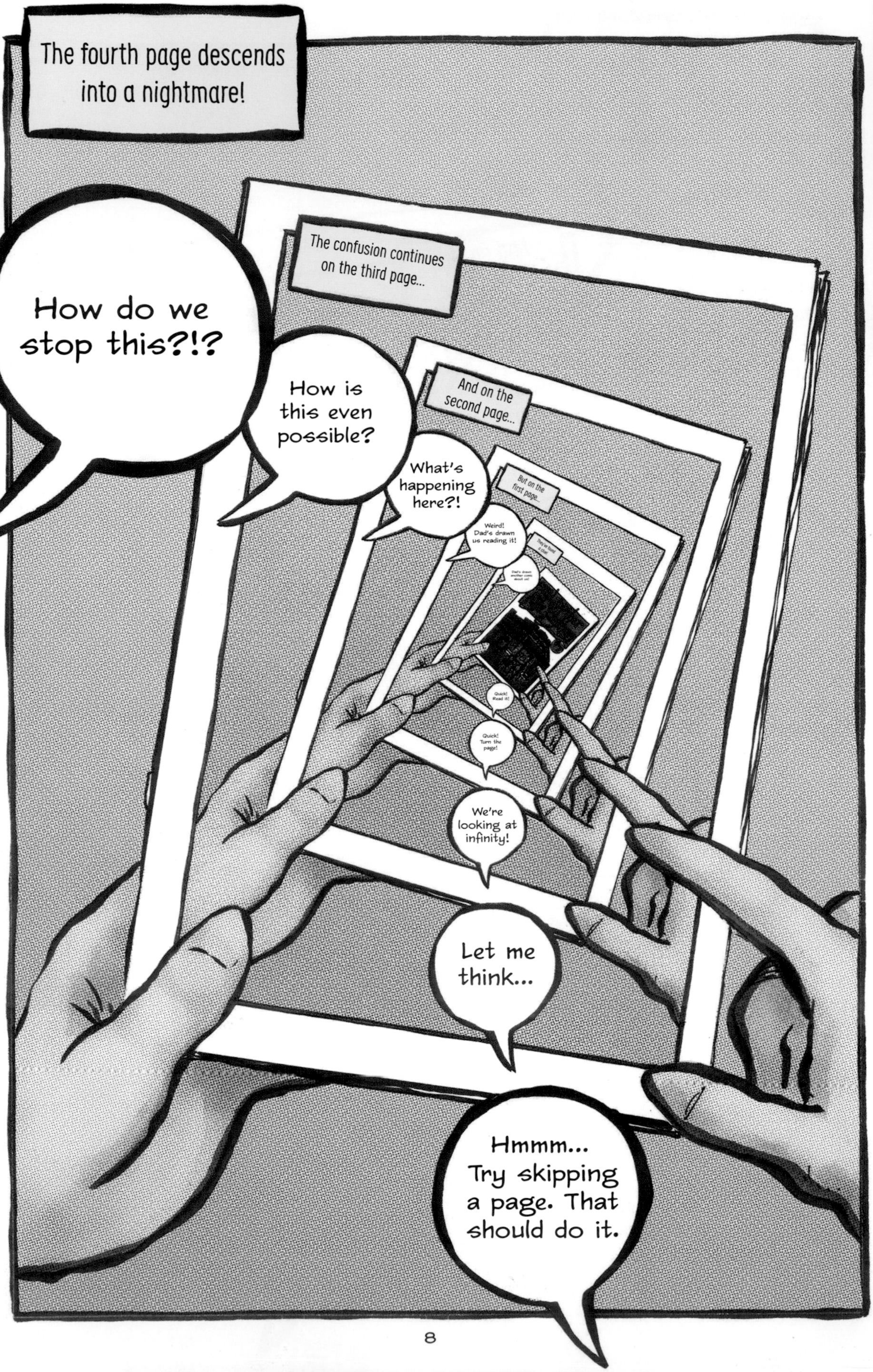
The fourth page descends into a nightmare!
How do we stop this?!?
The confusion continues on the third page...
How is this even possible?
And on the second page...
What's happening here?!
But on the first page...
Weird! Dad's drawn us reading it!
They've found a clue!
Dad's drawn another comic about us!
Quick! Read it!
Quick! Turn the page!
We're looking at infinity!
Let me think...
Hmmm... Try skipping a page. That should do it.

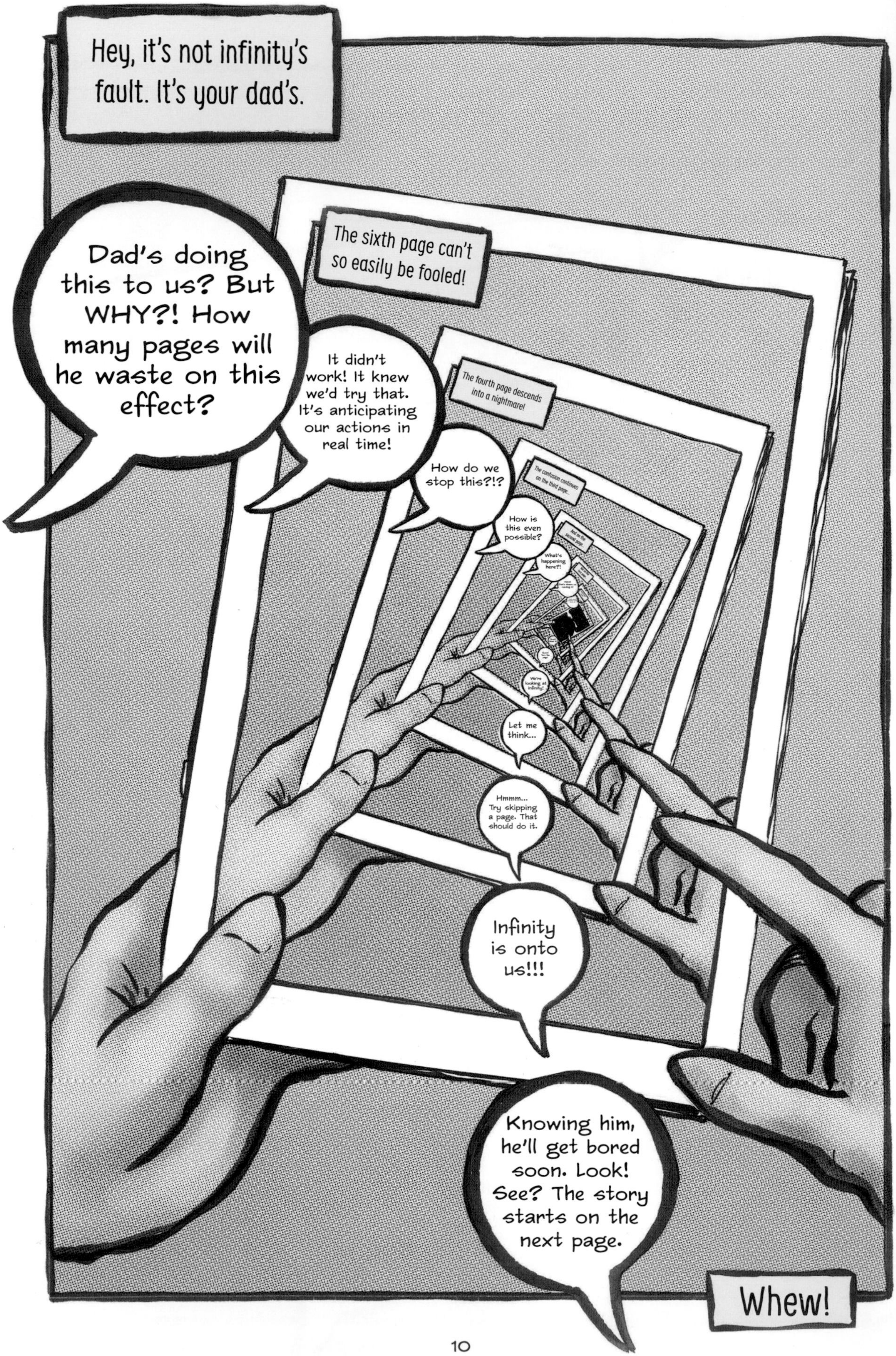

Hey, it's not infinity's fault. It's your dad's.
Dad's doing this to us? But WHY?! How many pages will he waste on this effect?
The sixth page can't so easily be fooled!
It didn't work! It knew we'd try that. It's anticipating our actions in real time!
The fourth page descends into a nightmare!
How do we stop this?!?
The confusion continues on the third page...
How is this even possible?
And on the second page...
What's happening here?!
We're looking at infinity!
Let me think...
Hmmm... Try skipping a page. That should do it.
Infinity is onto us!!!
Knowing him, he'll get bored soon. Look! See? The story starts on the next page.
Whew!

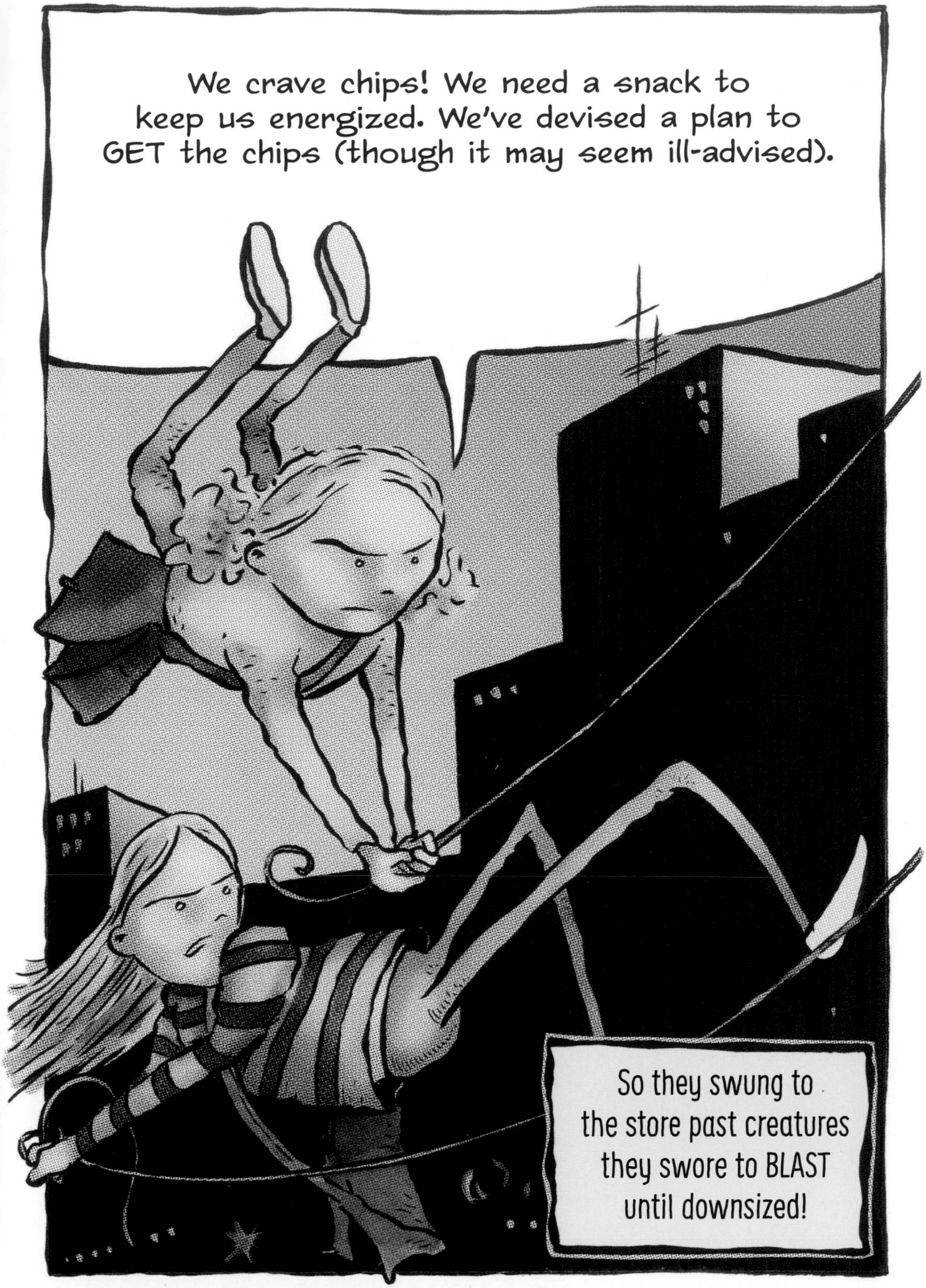
We crave chips! We need a snack to keep us energized. We've devised a plan to GET the chips (though it may seem ill-advised).
So they swung to the store past creatures they swore to BLAST until downsized!

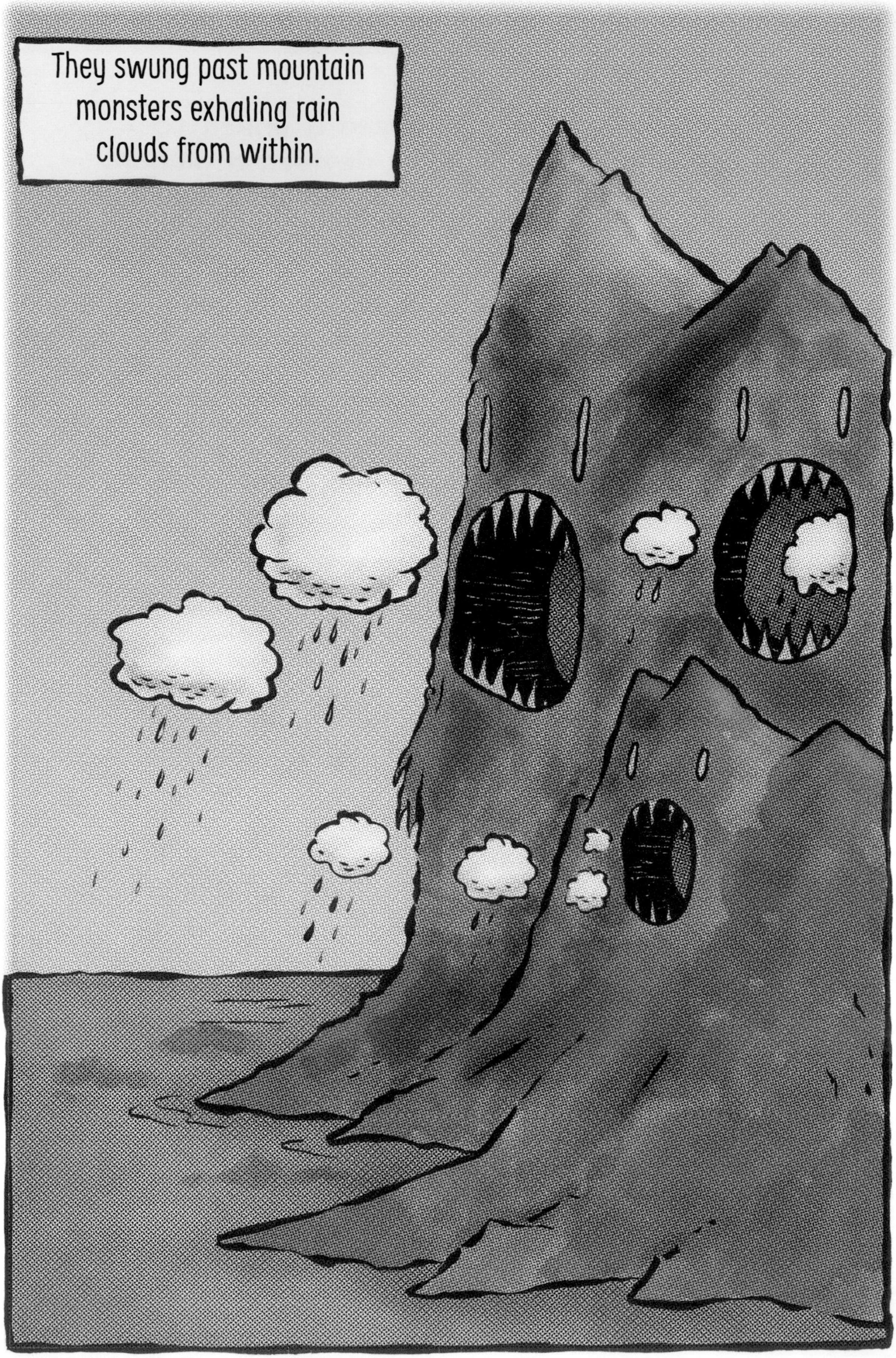
They swung past mountain
monsters exhaling rain
clouds from within.

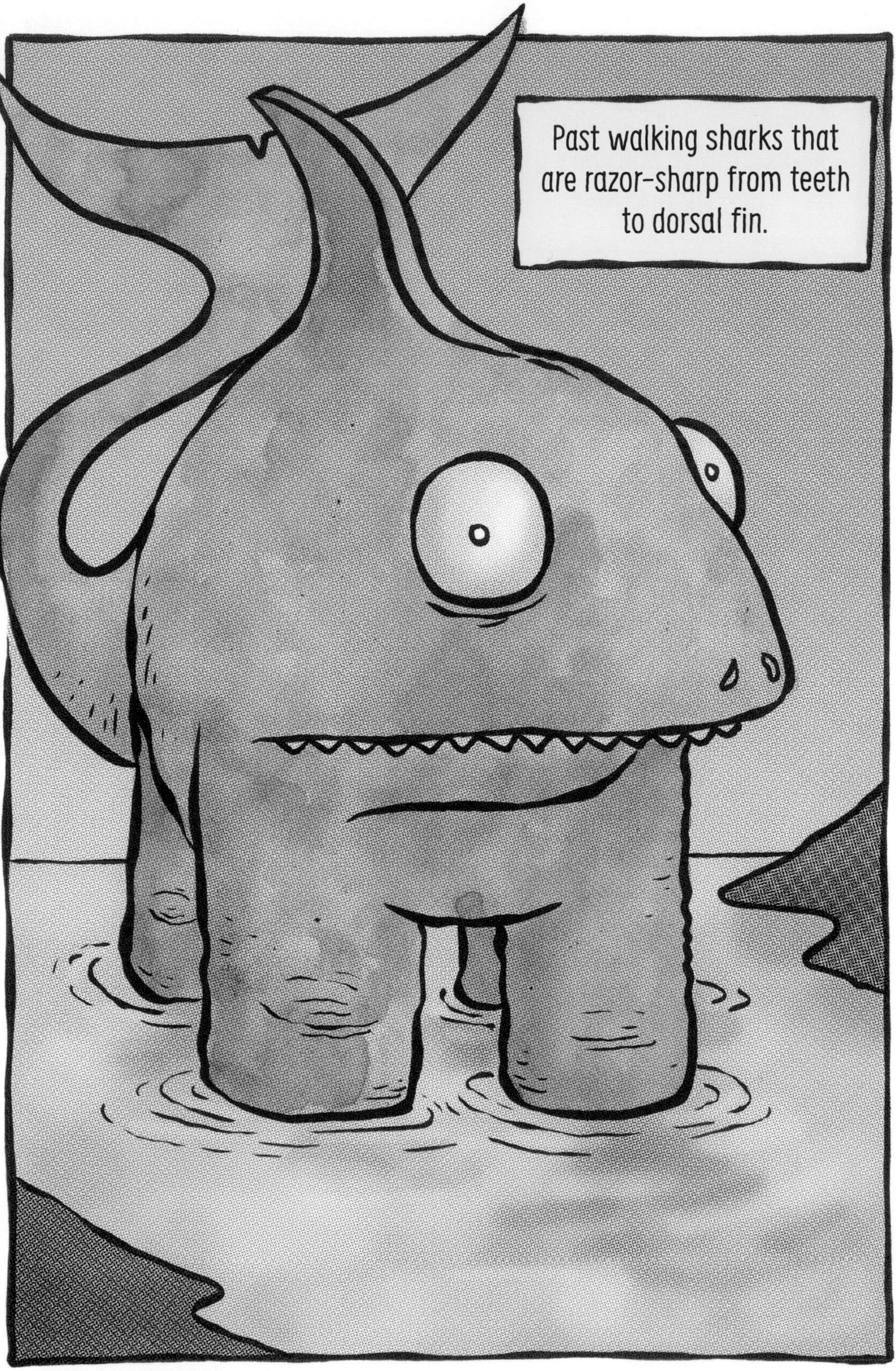
Past walking sharks that are razor-sharp from teeth to dorsal fin.

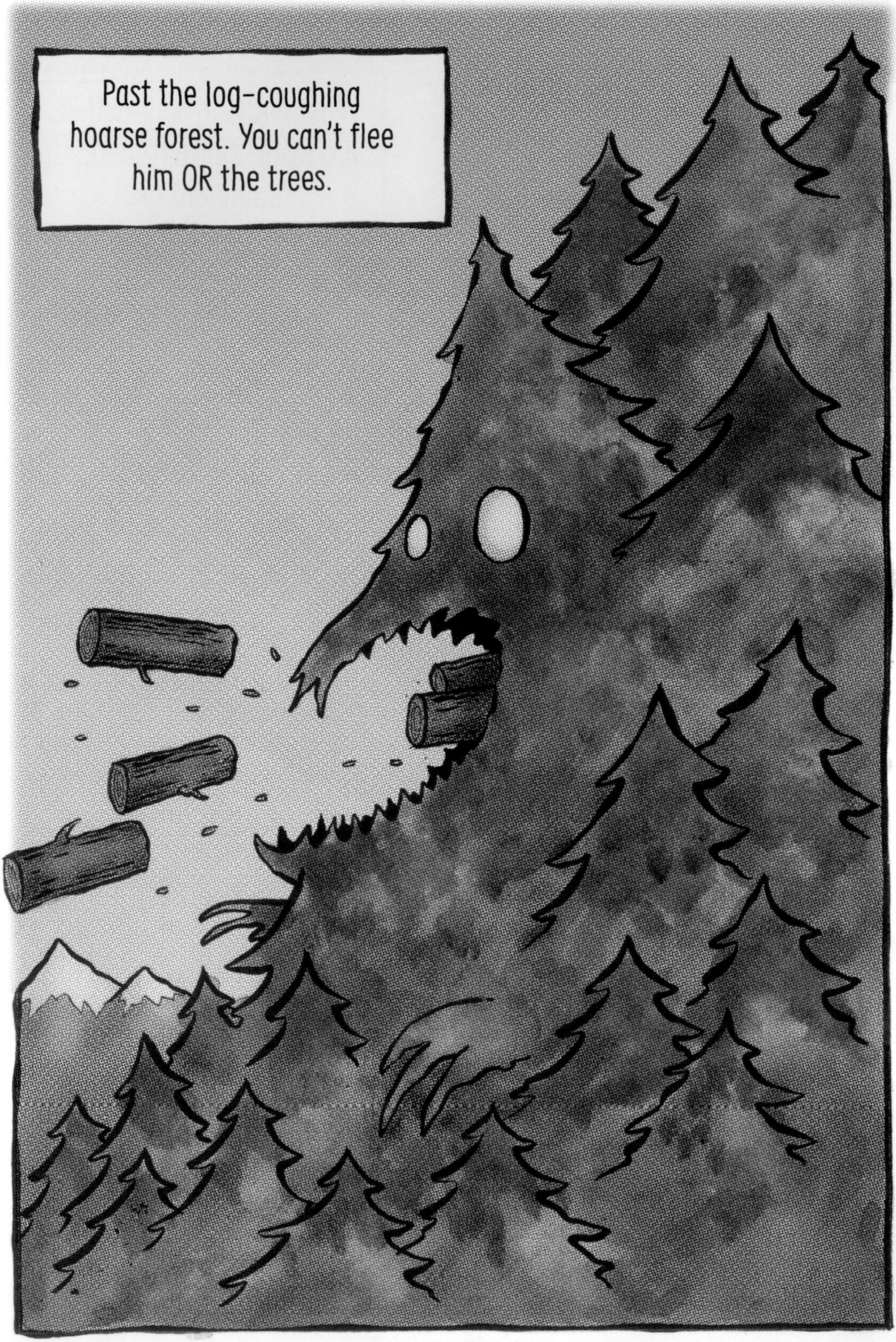
Past the log-coughing hoarse forest. You can't flee him OR the trees.

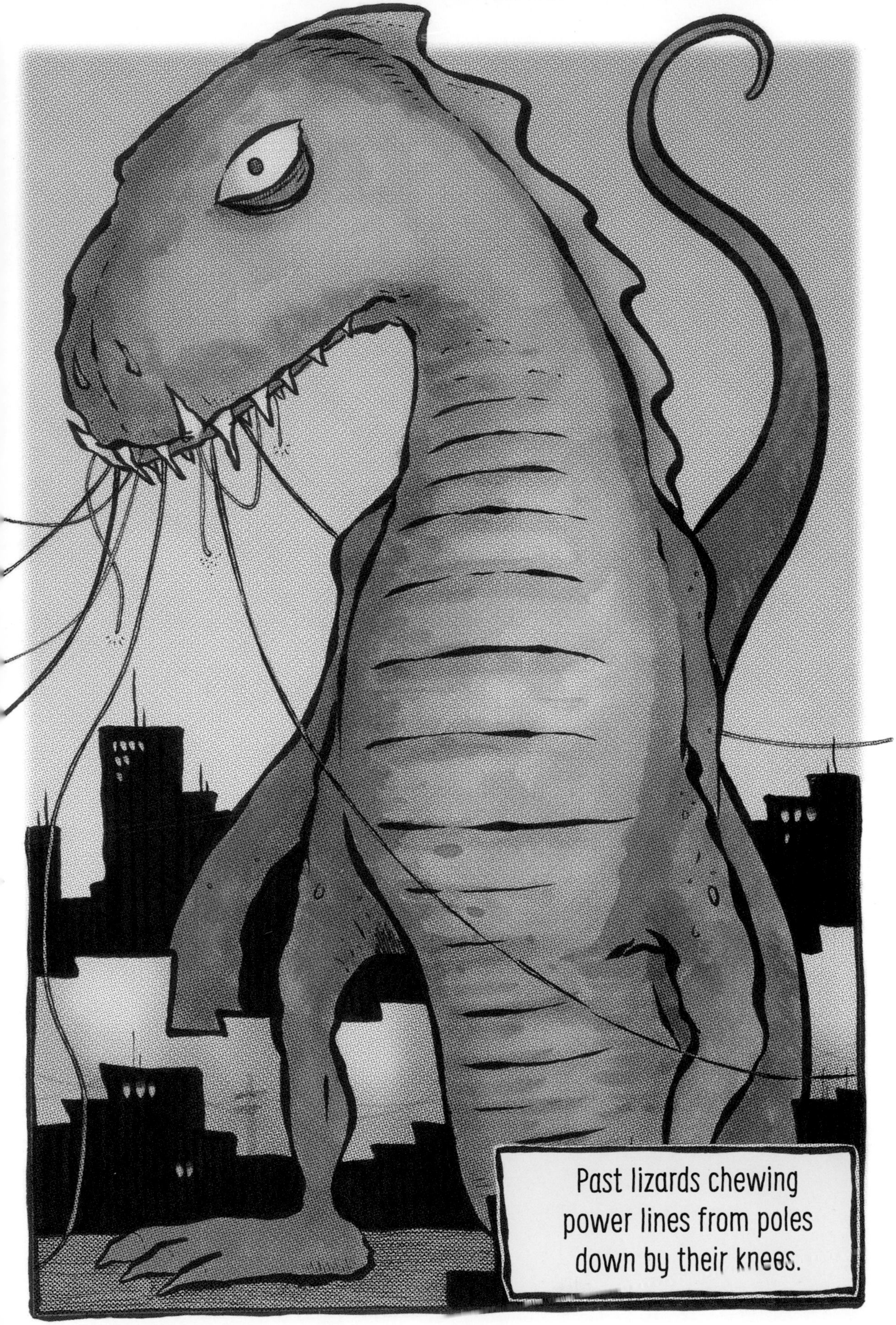
Past lizards chewing power lines from poles down by their knees.

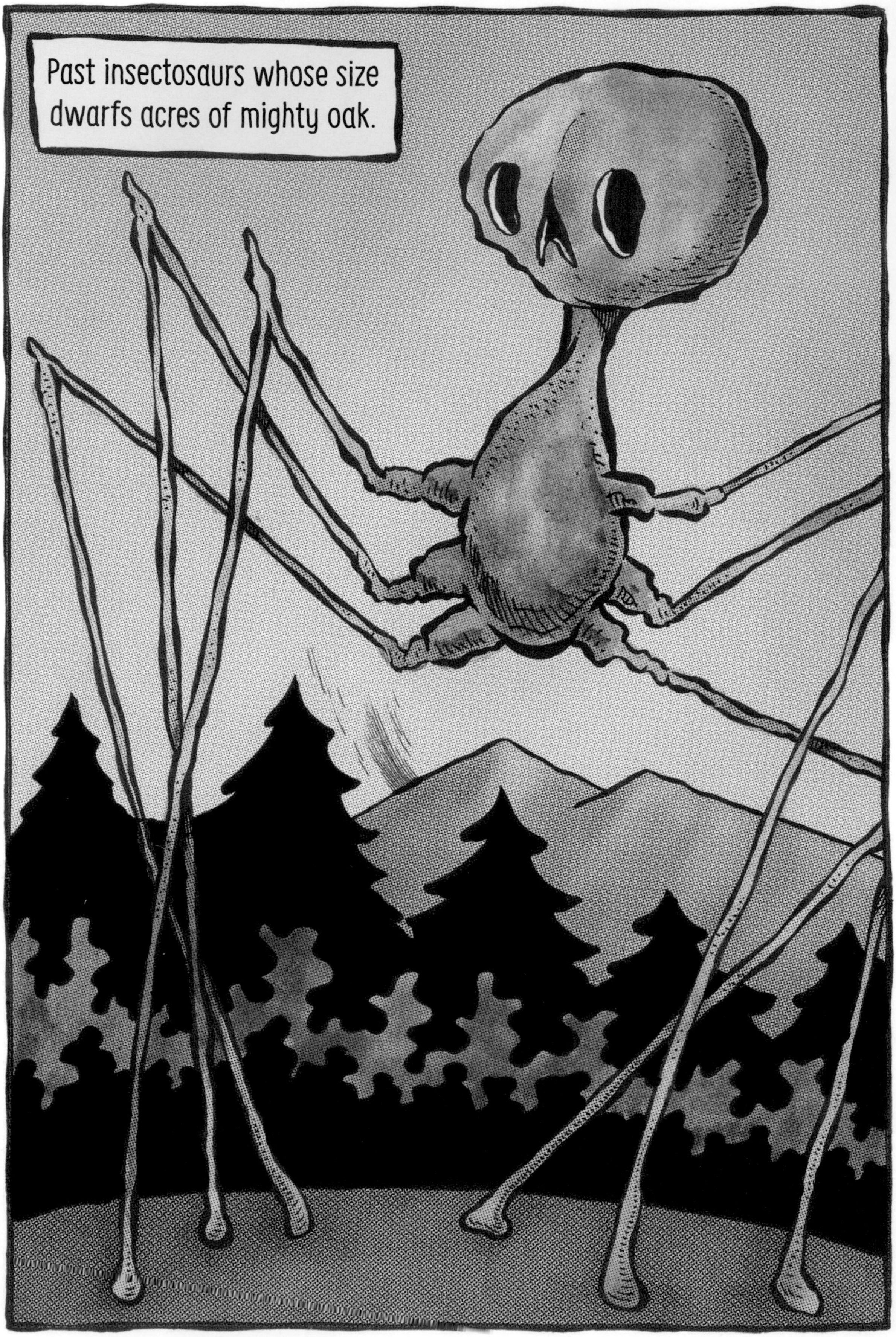
Past insectosaurs whose size dwarfs acres of mighty oak.

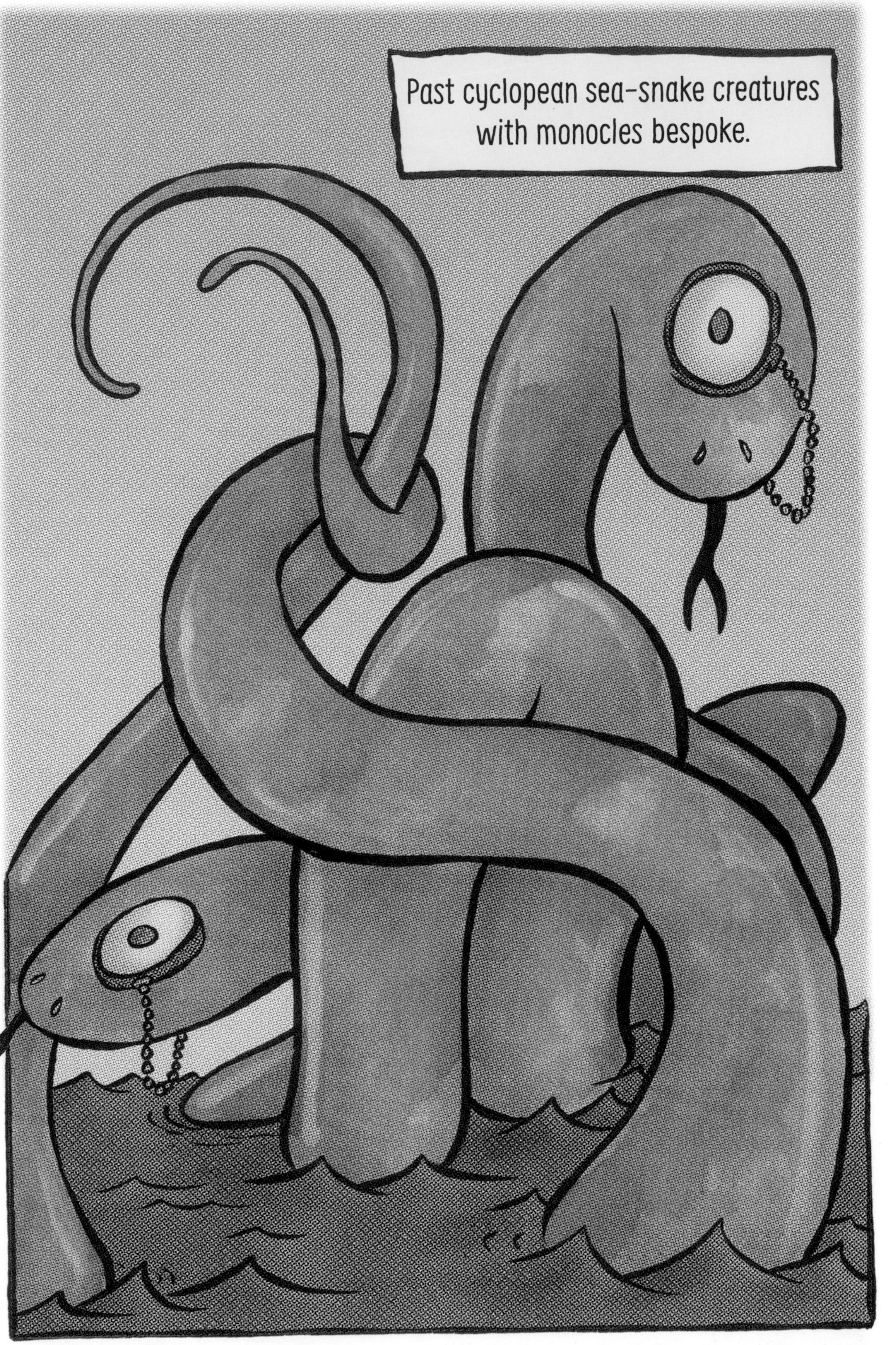
Past cyclopean sea-snake creatures
with monocles bespoke.

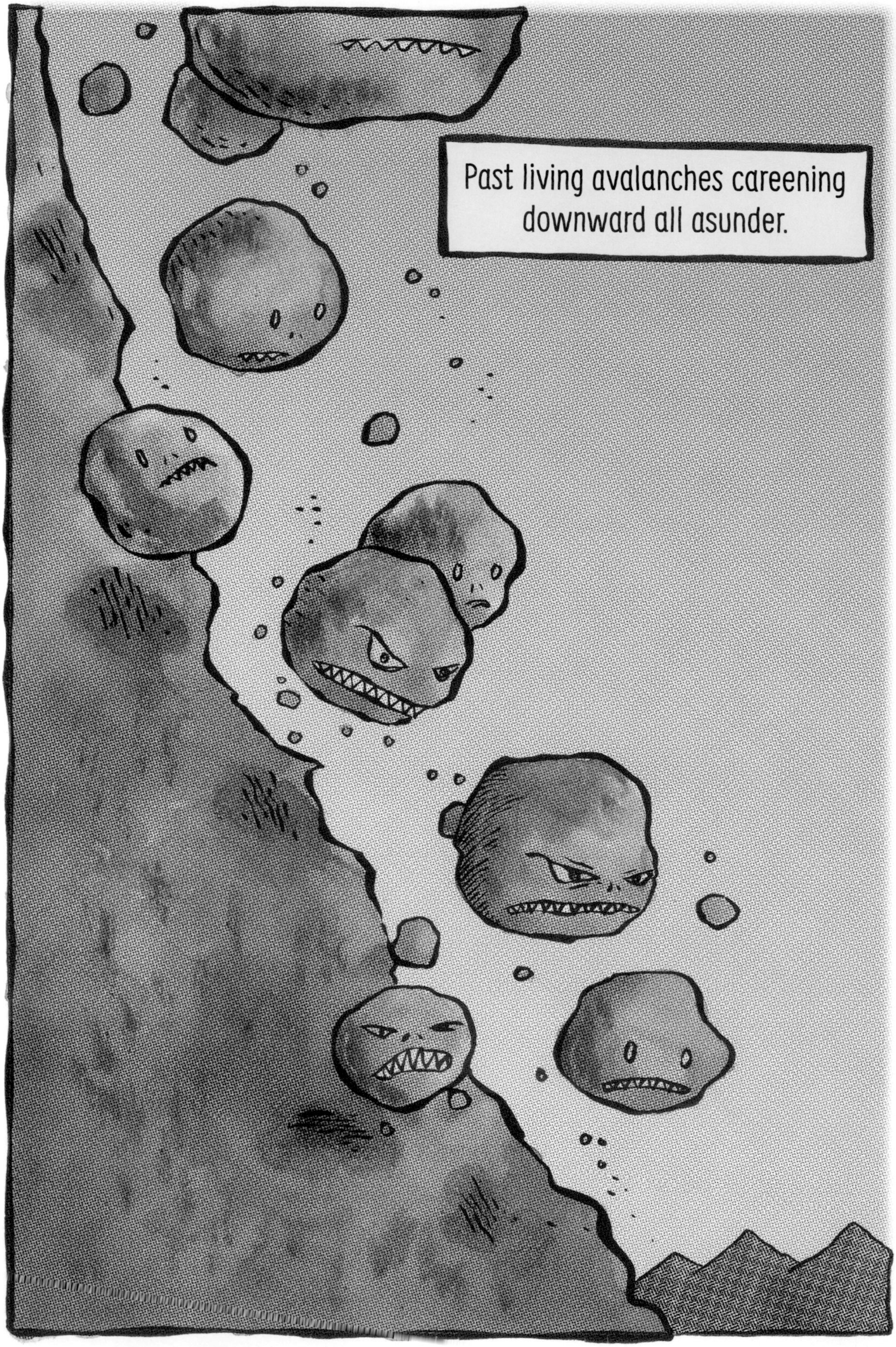
Past living avalanches careening downward all asunder.

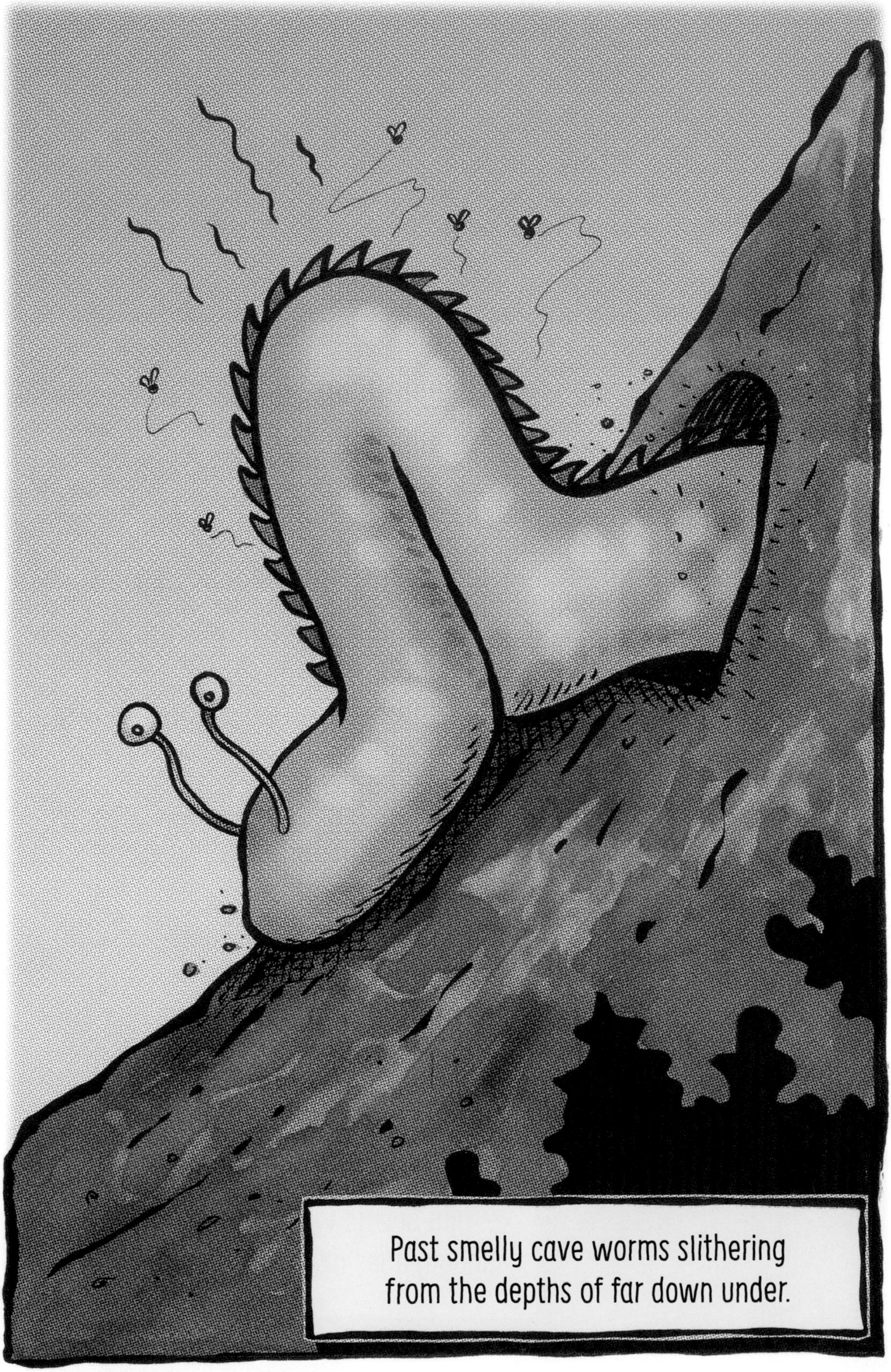
Past smelly cave worms slithering
from the depths of far down under.

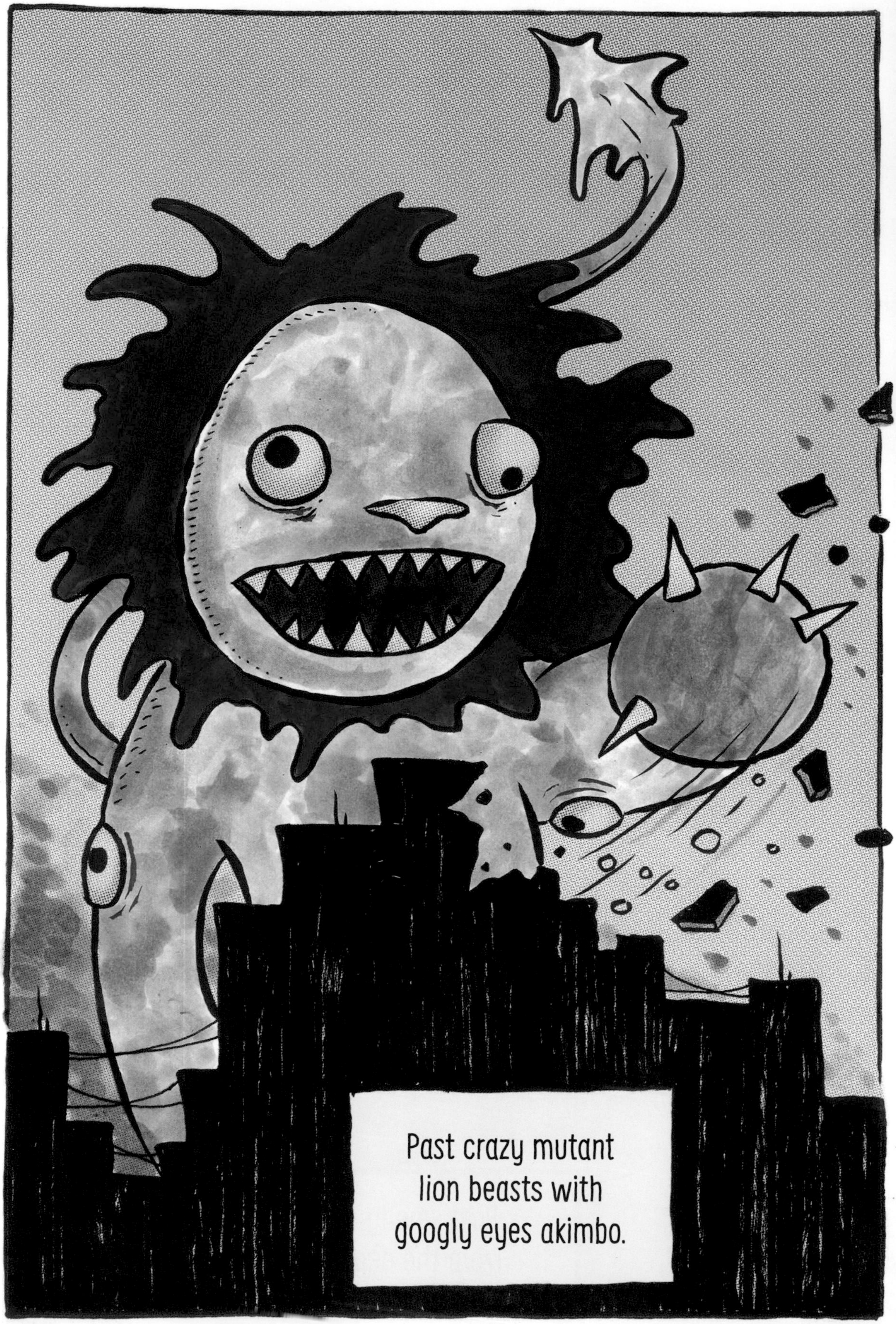
Past crazy mutant
lion beasts with
googly eyes akimbo.

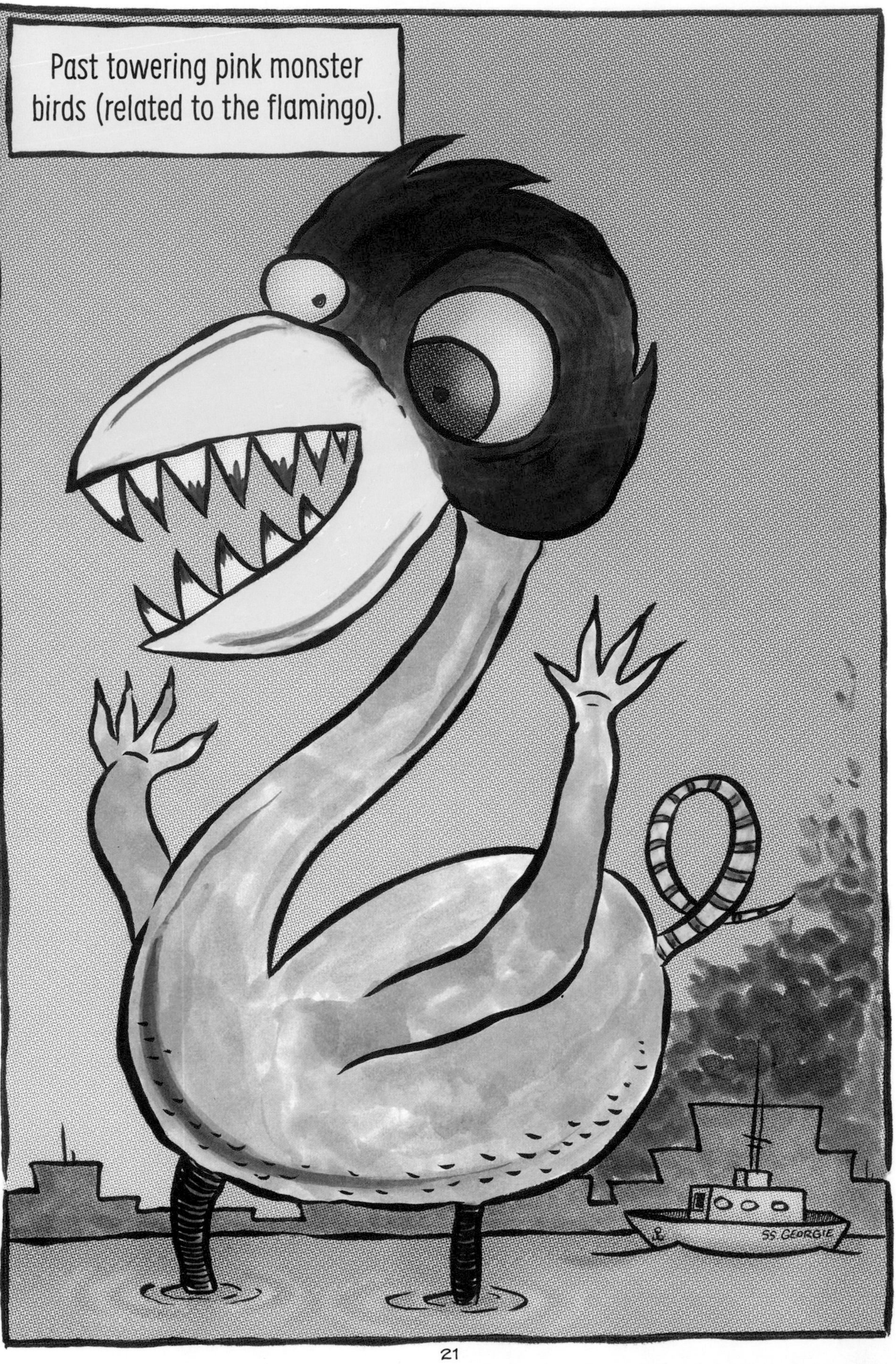
Past towering pink monster birds (related to the flamingo).
SS GEORGIE

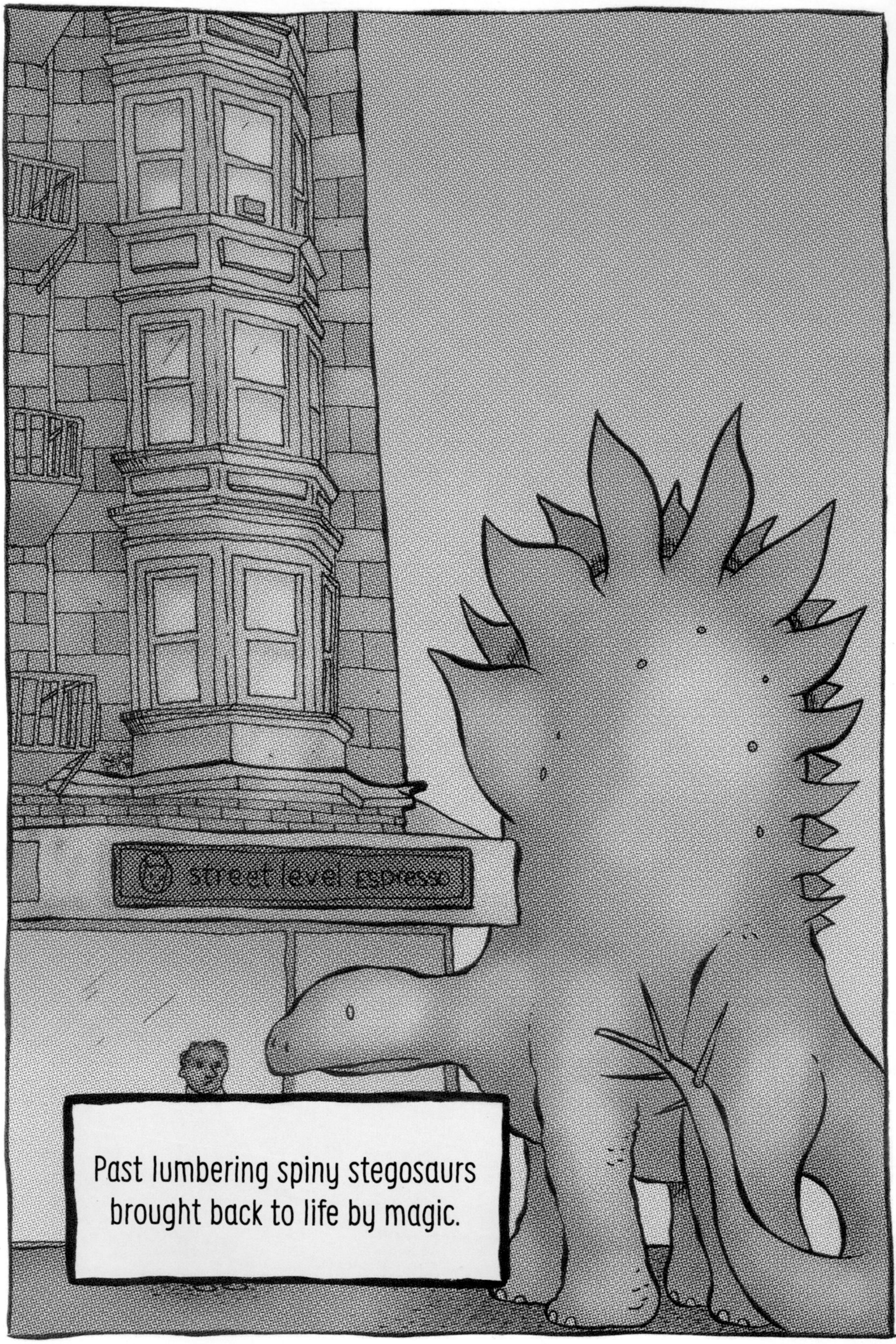
street level espresso
Past lumbering spiny stegosaurs brought back to life by magic.

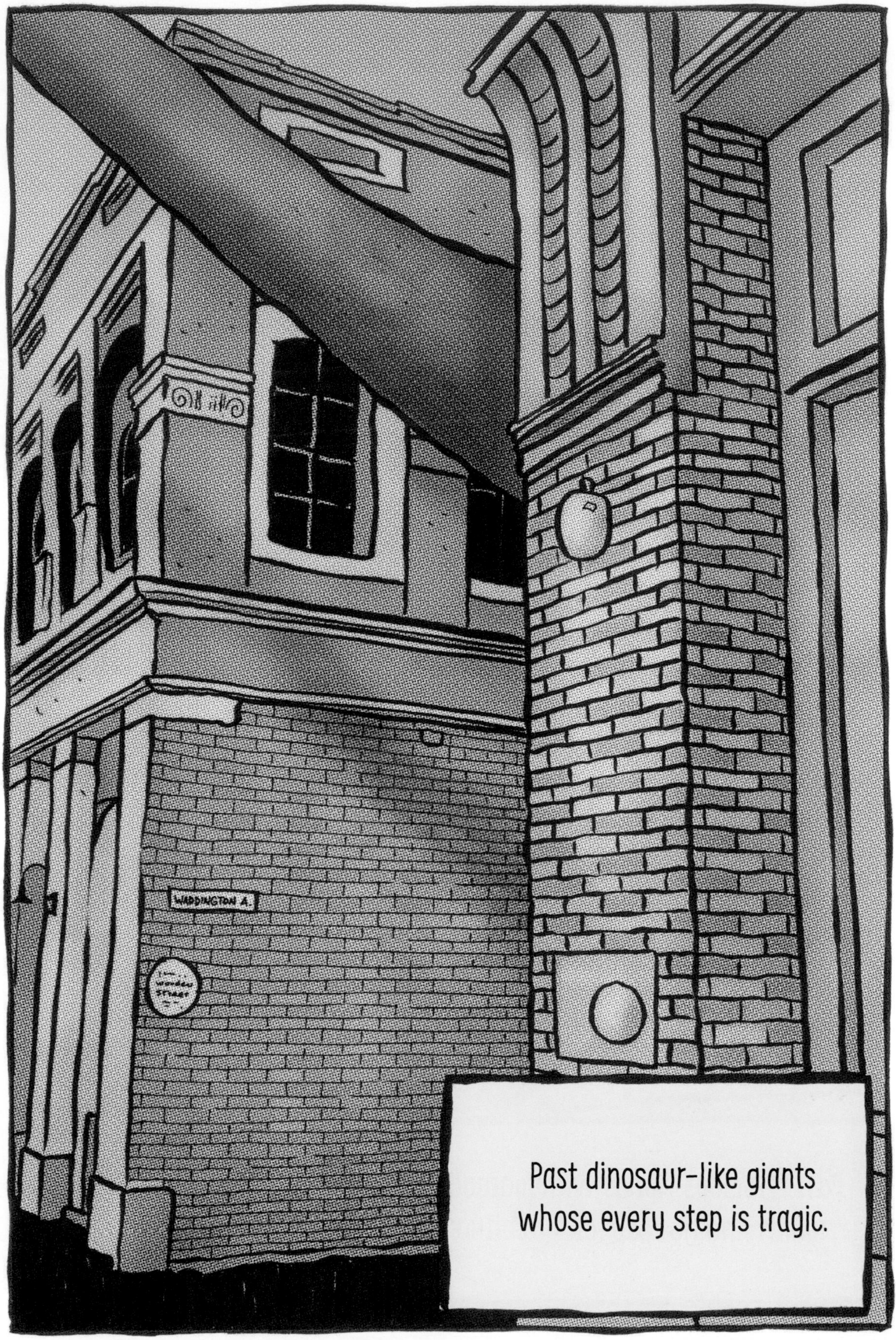
WADDINGTON A.
Past dinosaur-like giants
whose every step is tragic.

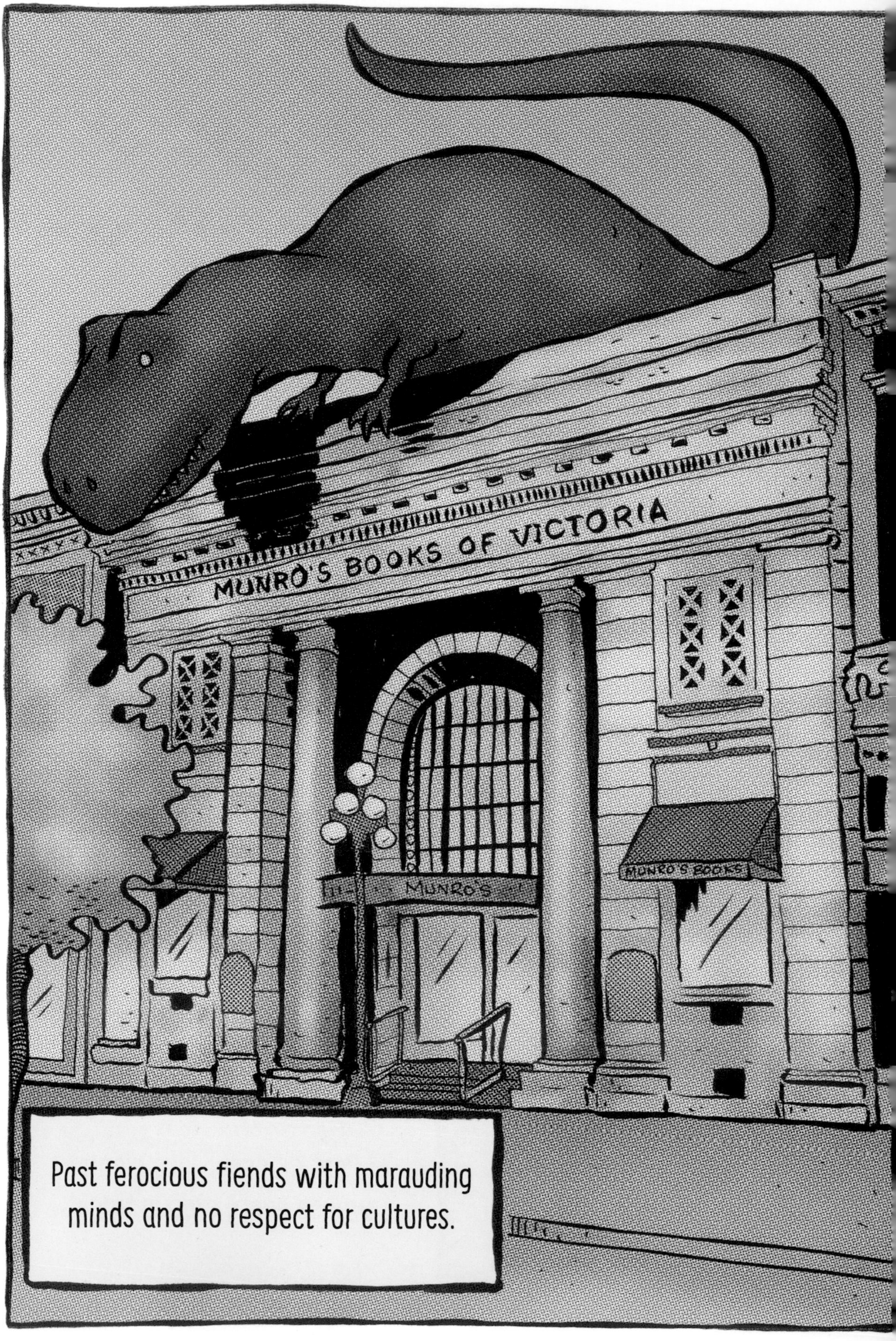
MUNRO'S BOOKS OF VICTORIA
MUNRO'S
MUNRO'S BOOKS
Past ferocious fiends with marauding minds and no respect for cultures.

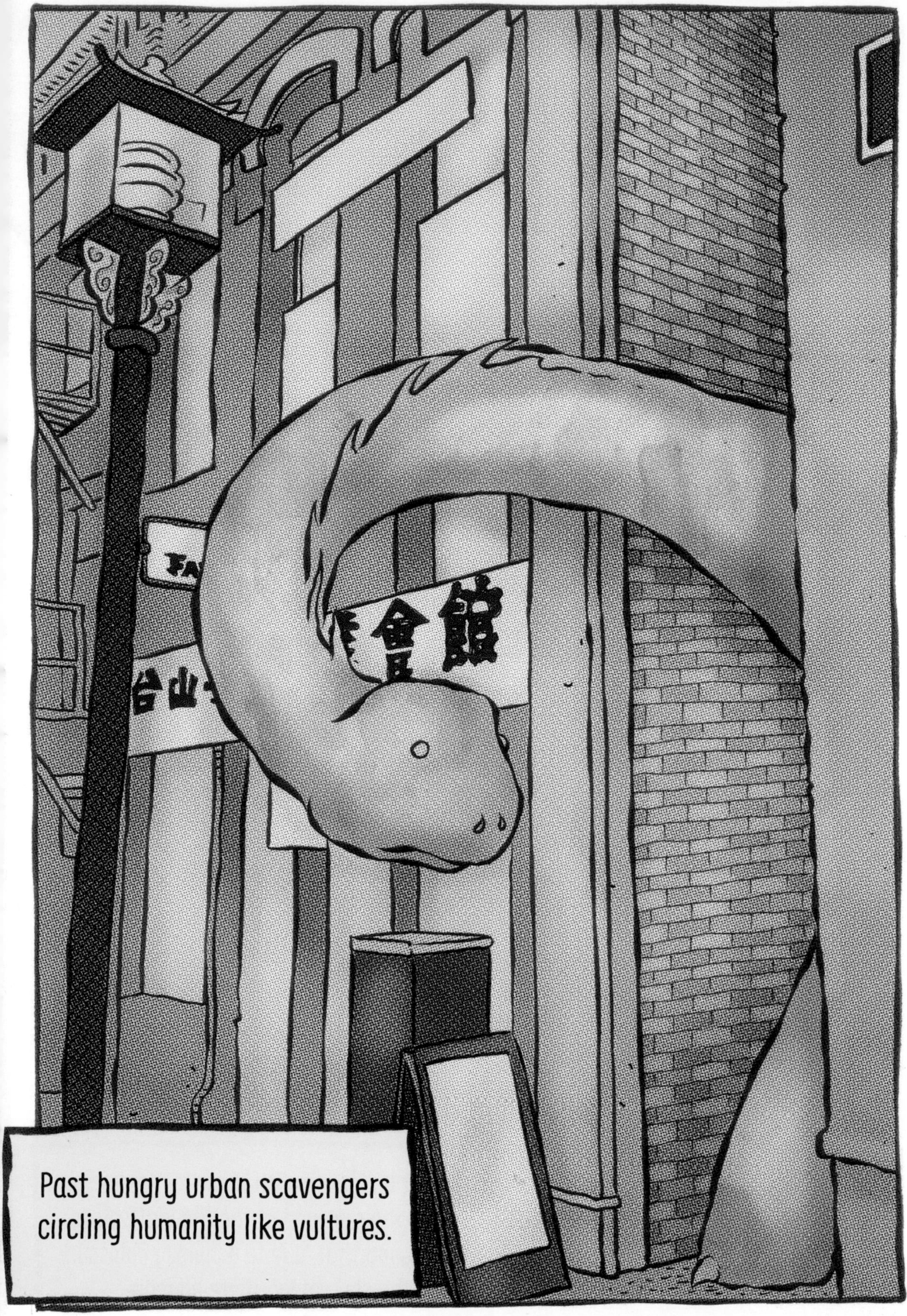
食館
台山
Past hungry urban scavengers circling humanity like vultures.

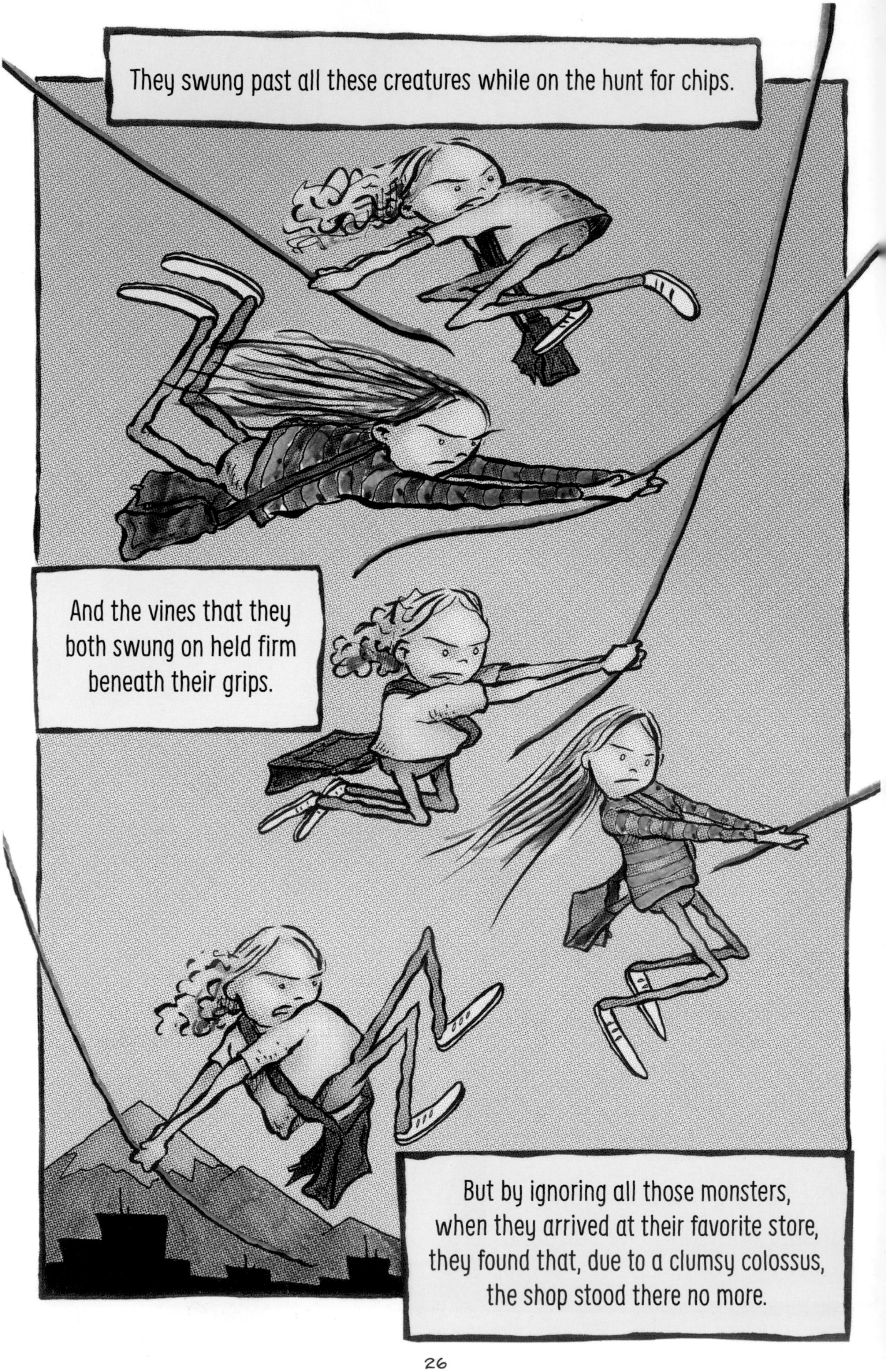
They swung past all these creatures while on the hunt for chips.
And the vines that they both swung on held firm beneath their grips.
But by ignoring all those monsters, when they arrived at their favorite store, they found that, due to a clumsy colossus, the shop stood there no more.

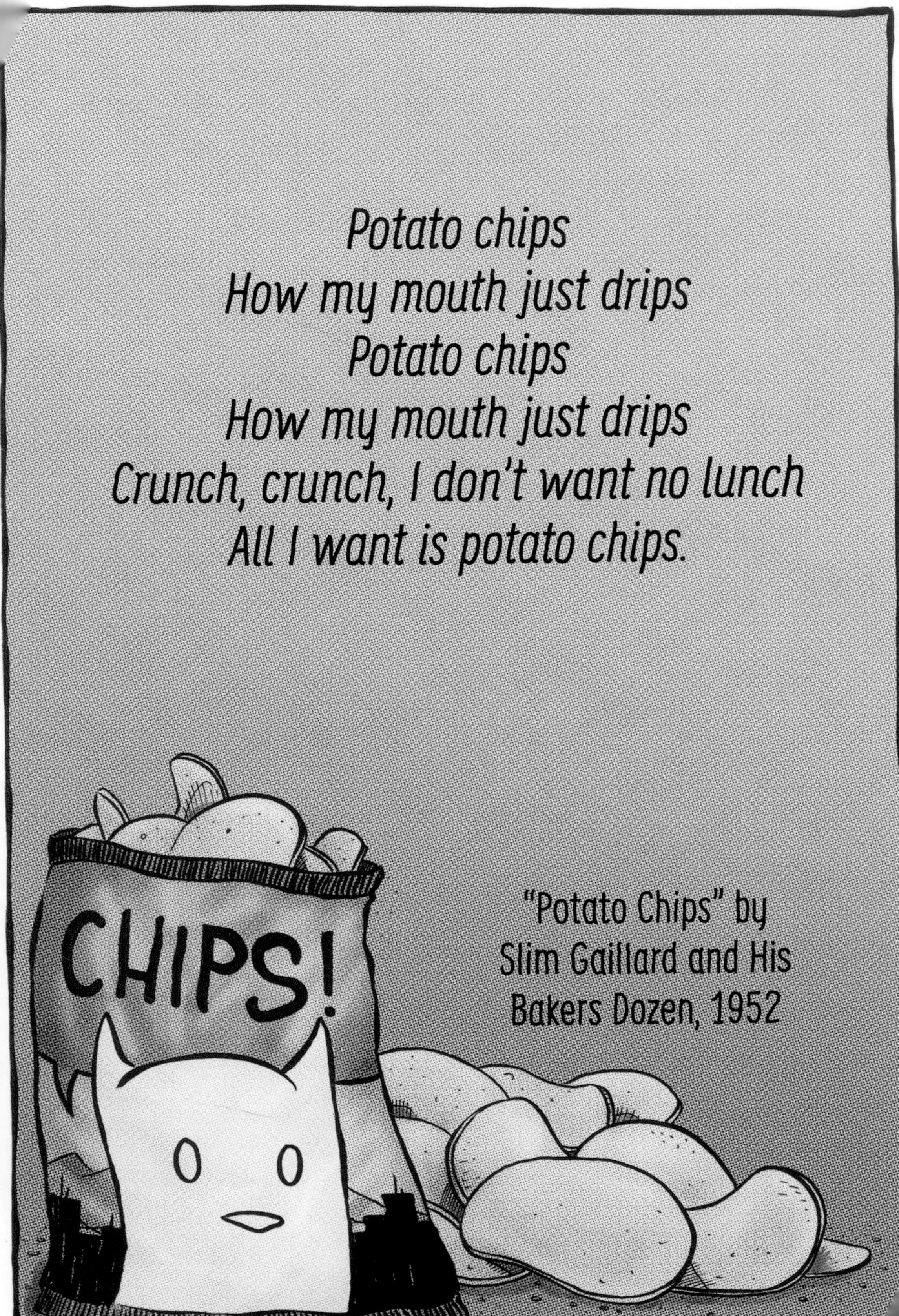
Potato chips
How my mouth just drips
Potato chips
How my mouth just drips
Crunch, crunch, I don't want no lunch
All I want is potato chips.
CHIPS!
"Potato Chips" by
Slim Gaillard and His
Bakers Dozen, 1952

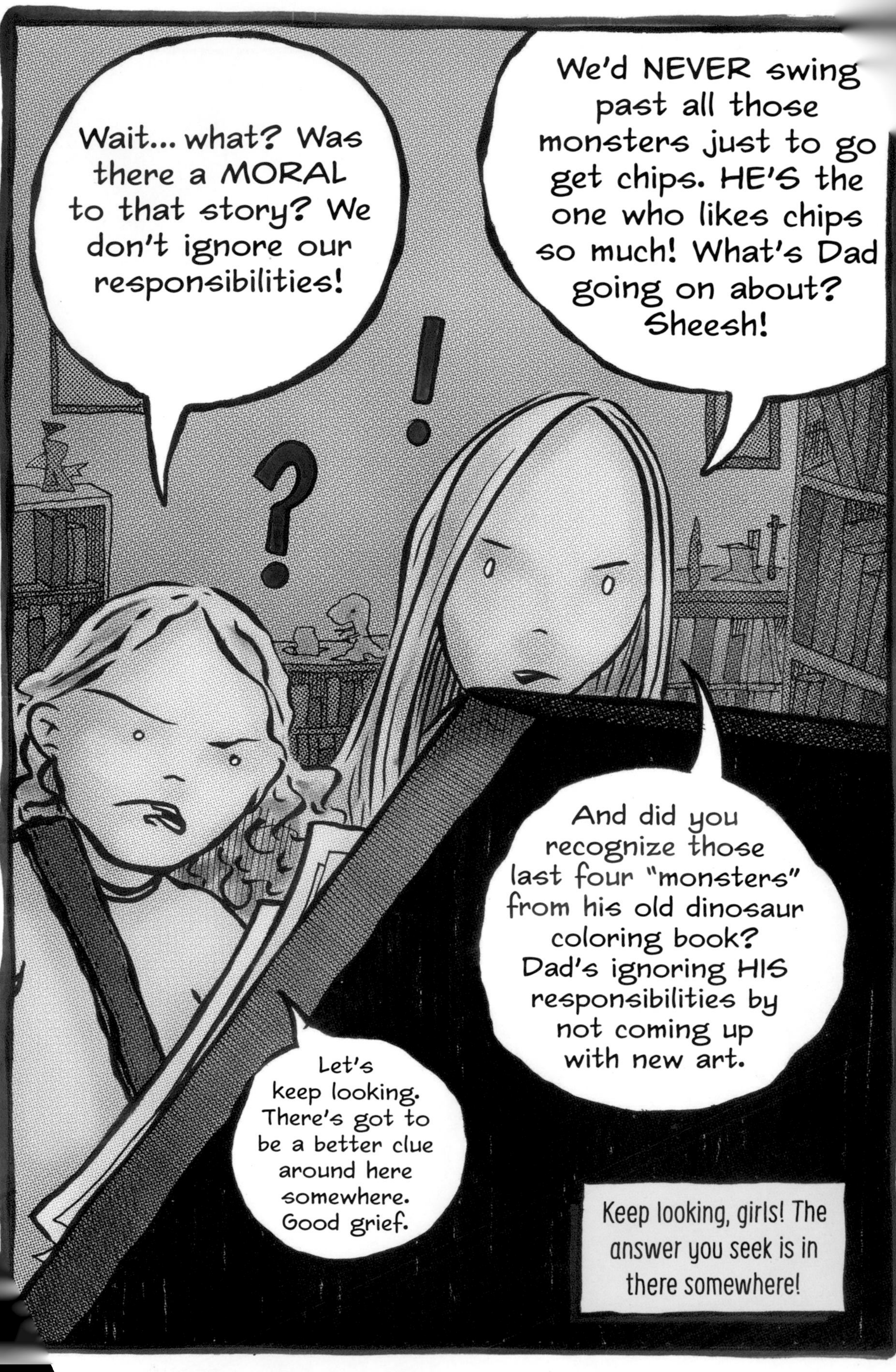
Wait... what? Was there a MORAL to that story? We don't ignore our responsibilities!
We'd NEVER swing past all those monsters just to go get chips. HE'S the one who likes chips so much! What's Dad going on about? Sheesh!
?
!
And did you recognize those last four "monsters" from his old dinosaur coloring book? Dad's ignoring HIS responsibilities by not coming up with new art.
Let's keep looking. There's got to be a better clue around here somewhere. Good grief.
Keep looking, girls! The answer you seek is in there somewhere!

CHAPTER TWO
THE CASE OF THE AUDREY BERLIN
2

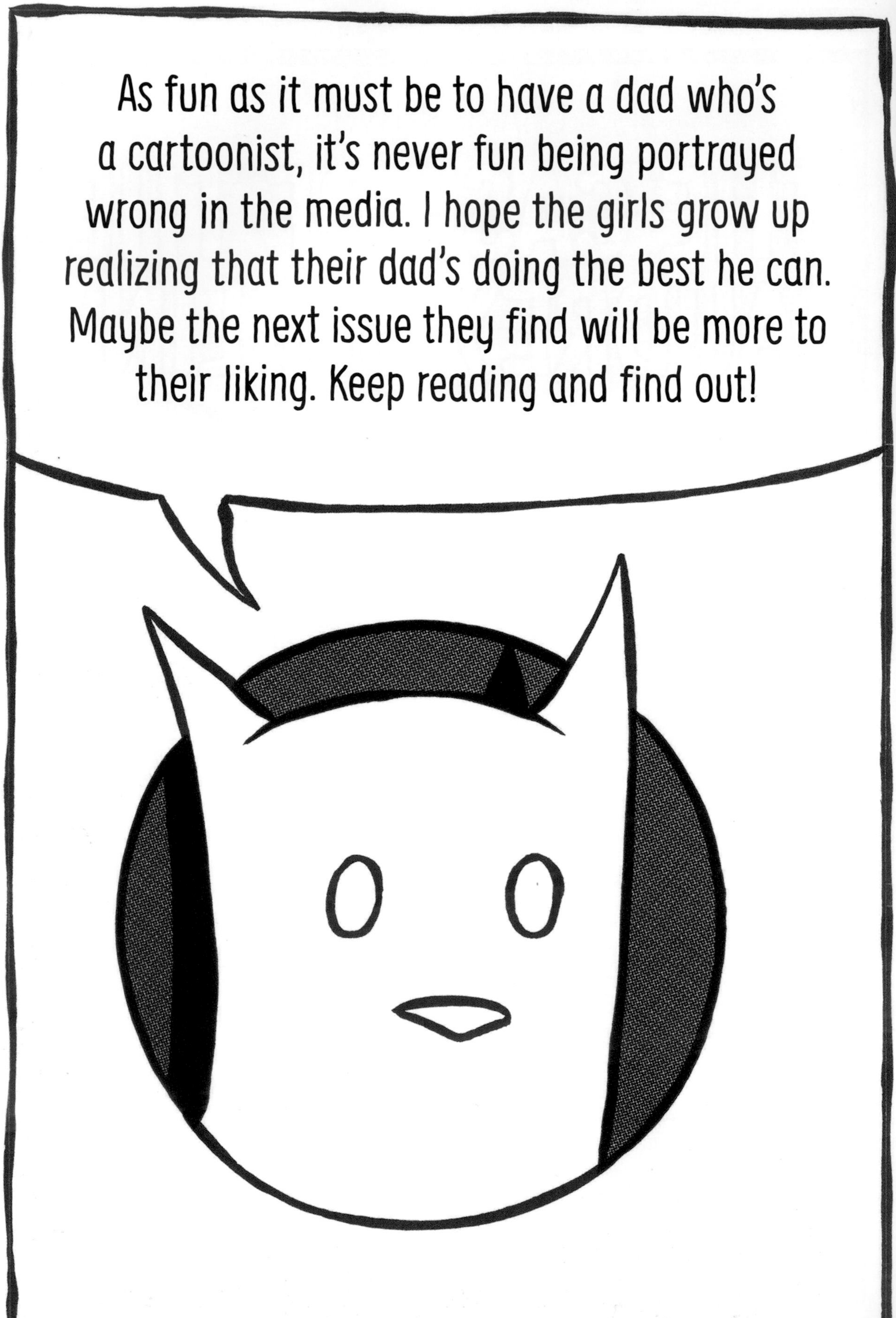
As fun as it must be to have a dad who's a cartoonist, it's never fun being portrayed wrong in the media. I hope the girls grow up realizing that their dad's doing the best he can. Maybe the next issue they find will be more to their liking. Keep reading and find out!

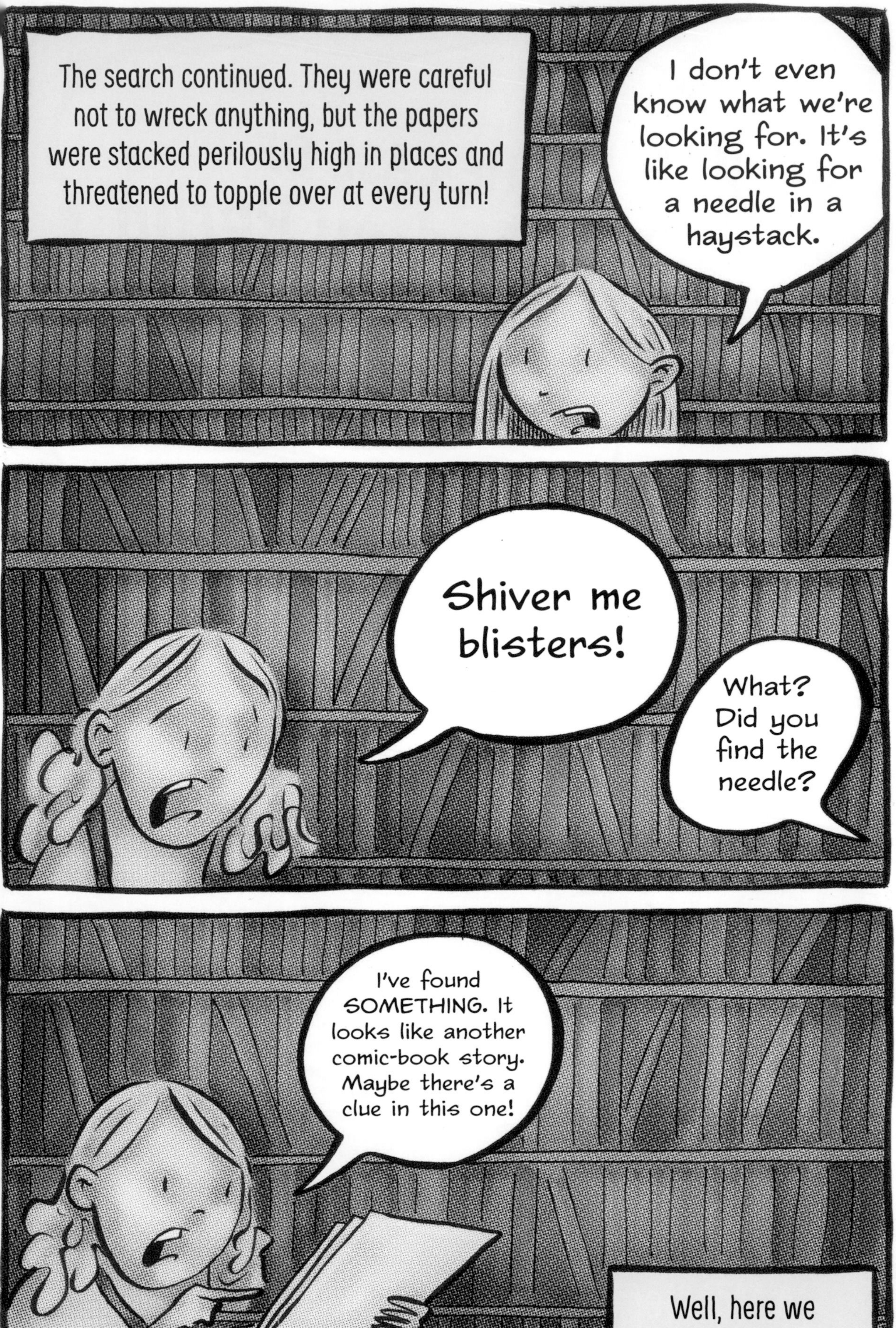
The search continued. They were careful not to wreck anything, but the papers were stacked perilously high in places and threatened to topple over at every turn!
I don't even know what we're looking for. It's like looking for a needle in a haystack.
Shiver me blisters!
What? Did you find the needle?
I've found SOMETHING. It looks like another comic-book story. Maybe there's a clue in this one!
Well, here we go again.

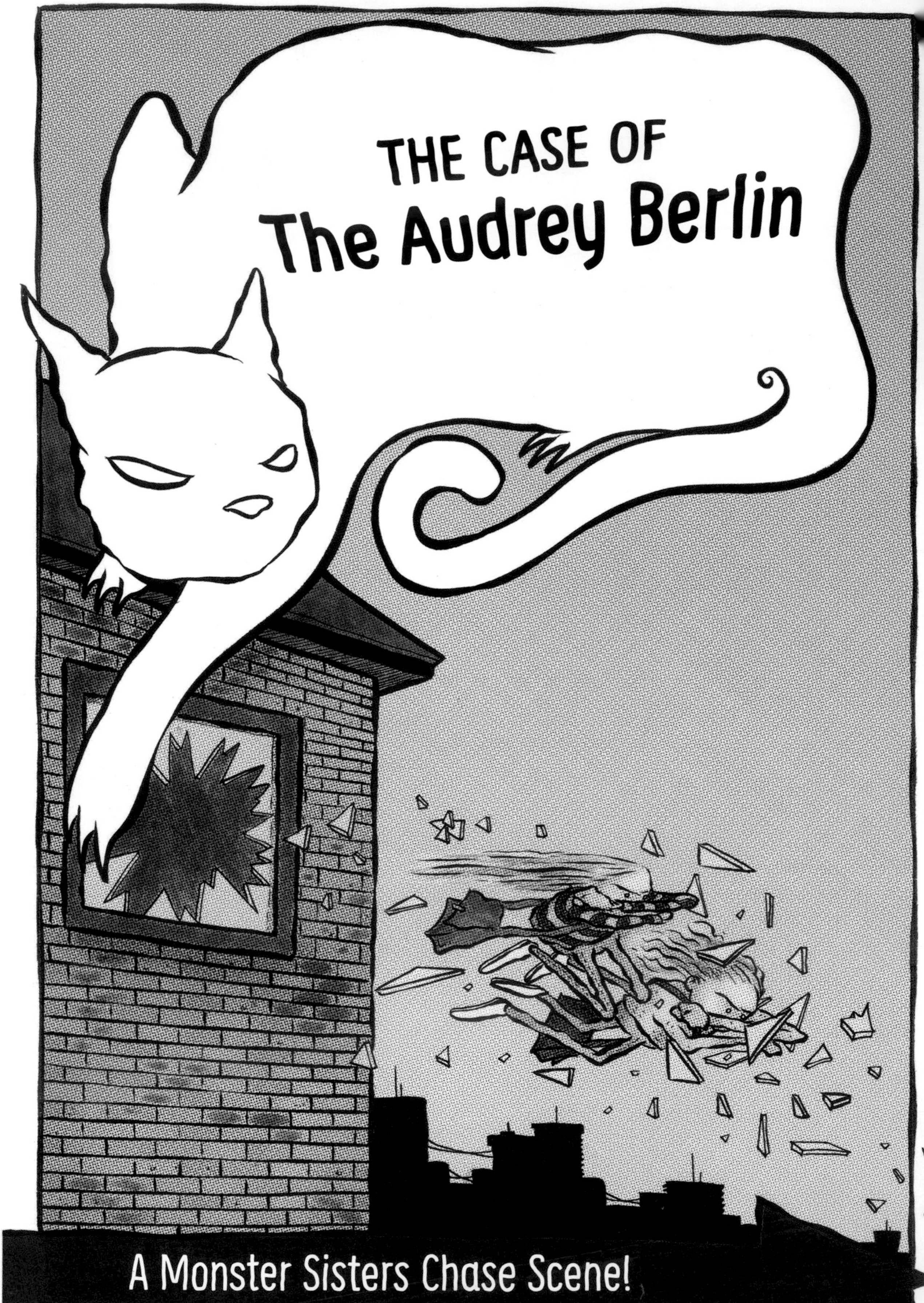
THE CASE OF
The Audrey Berlin
A Monster Sisters Chase Scene!

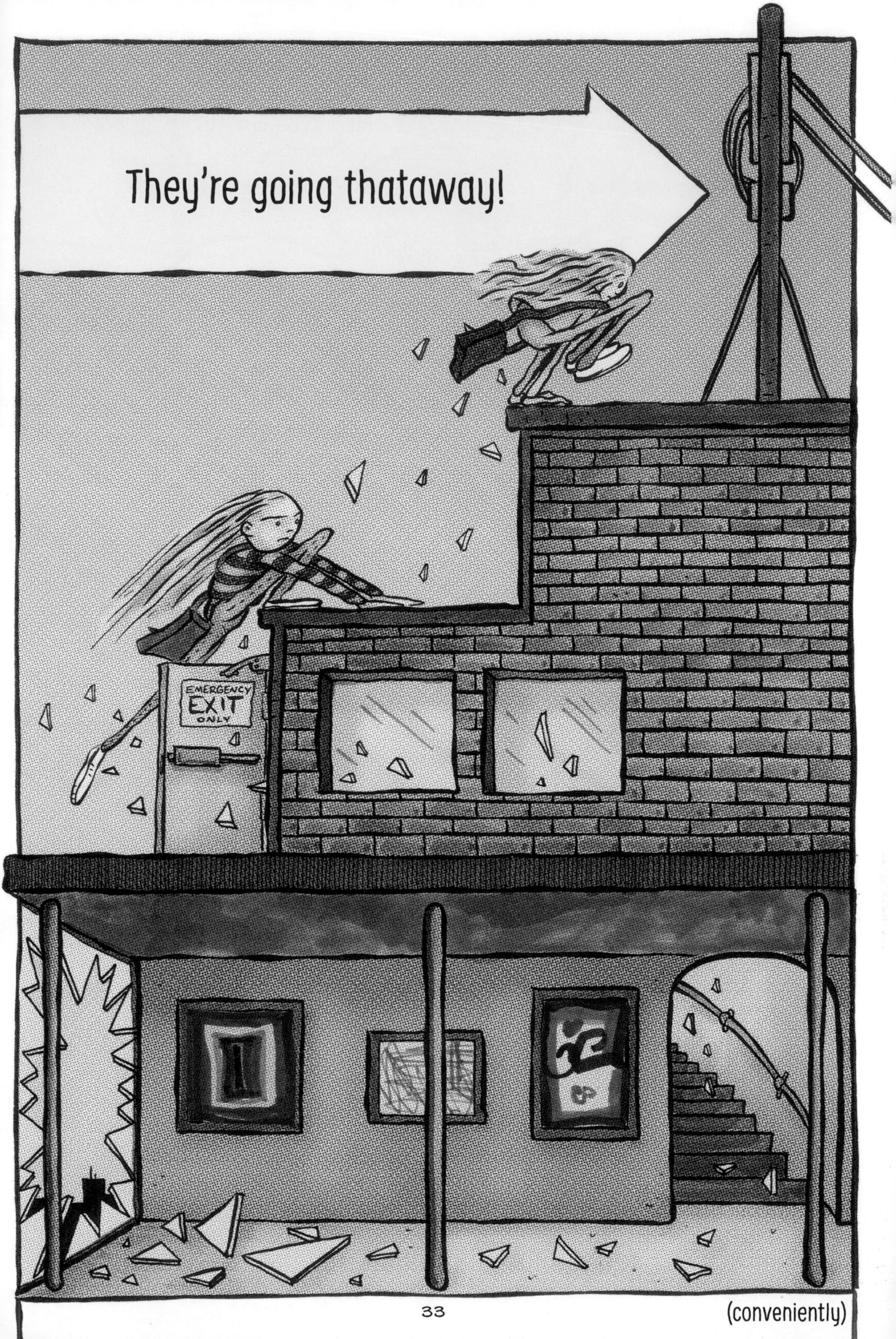
They're going thataway!
EMERGENCY EXIT ONLY

(conveniently)

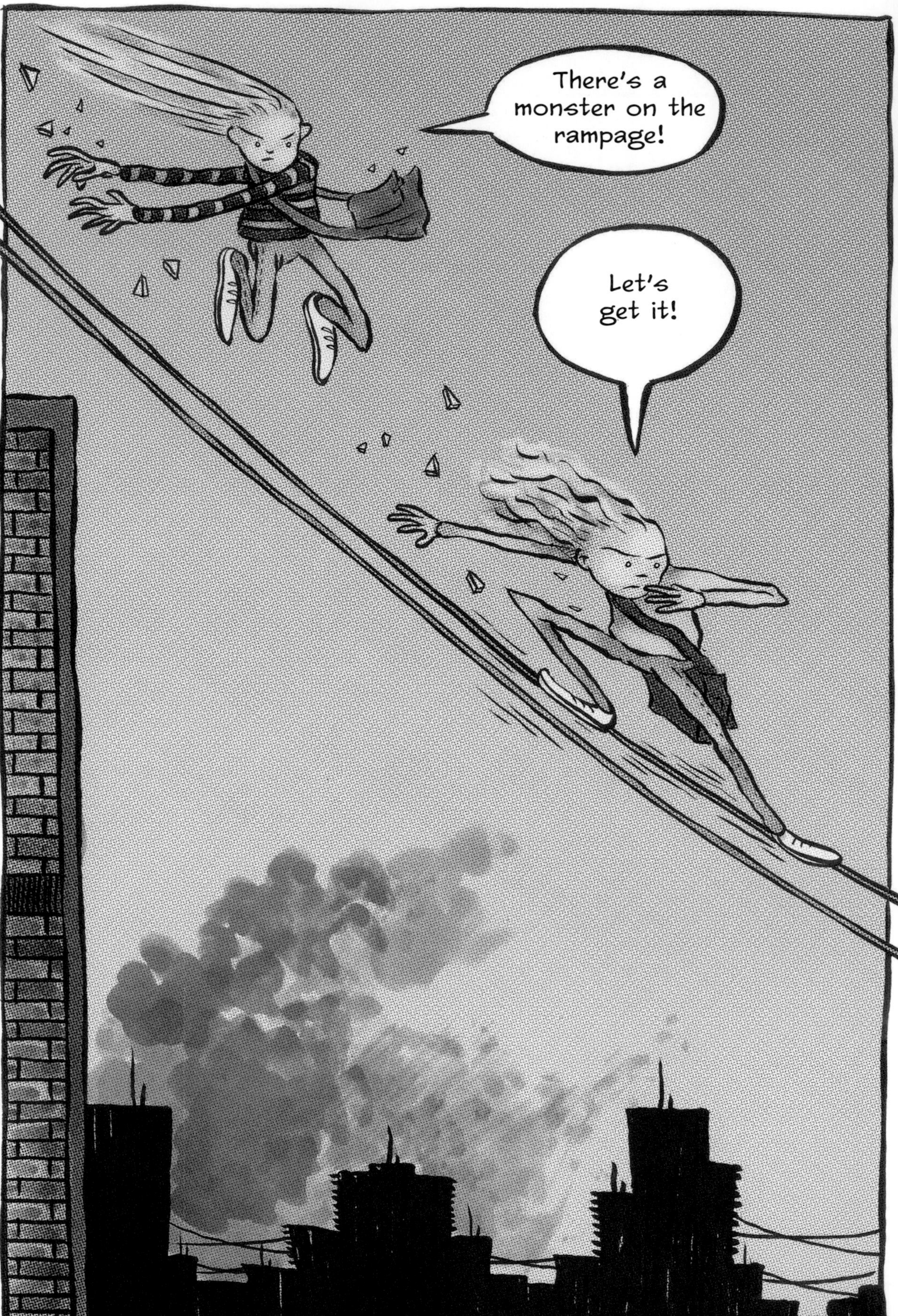
There's a monster on the rampage!
Let's get it!

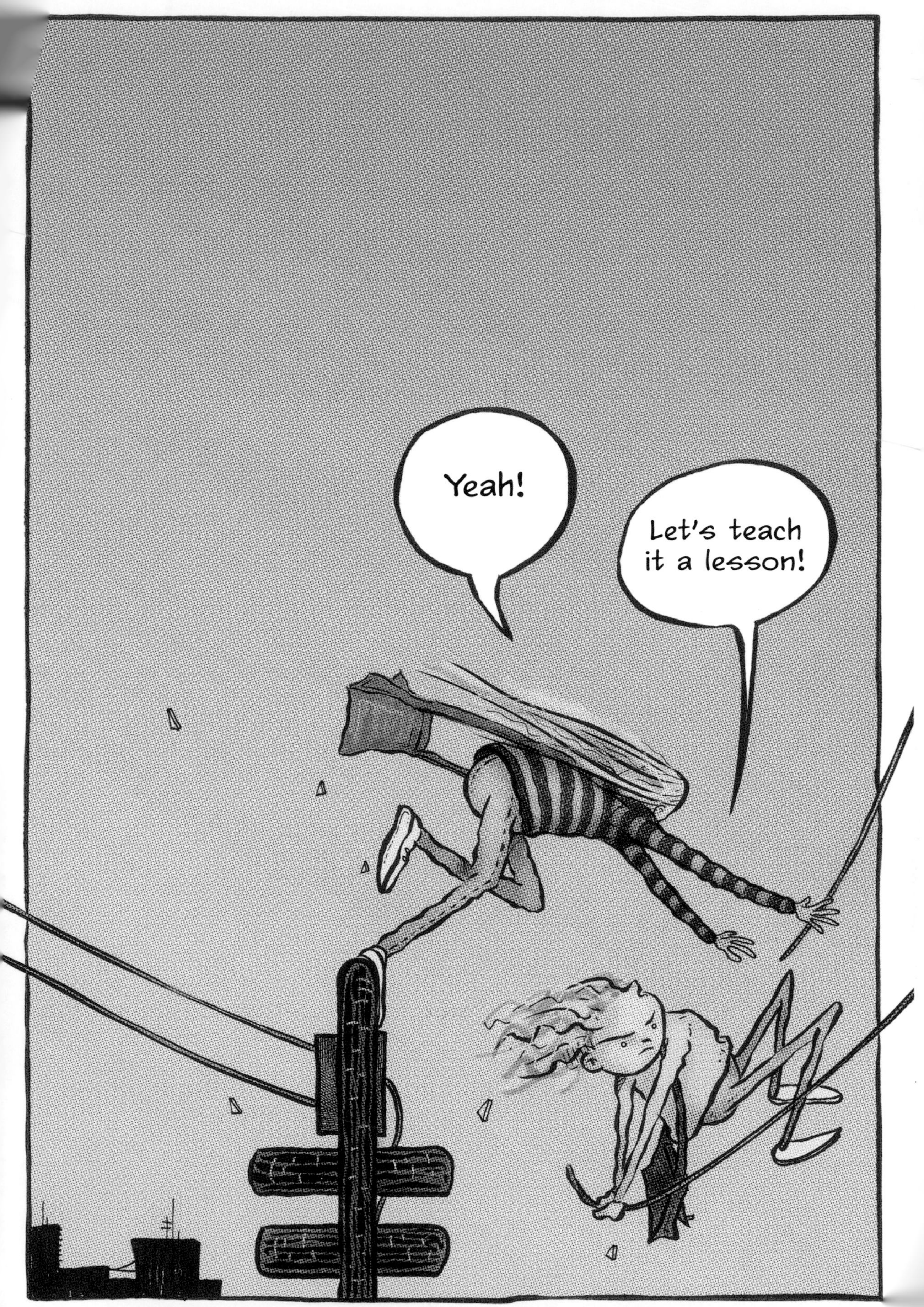
Yeah!
Let's teach it a lesson!

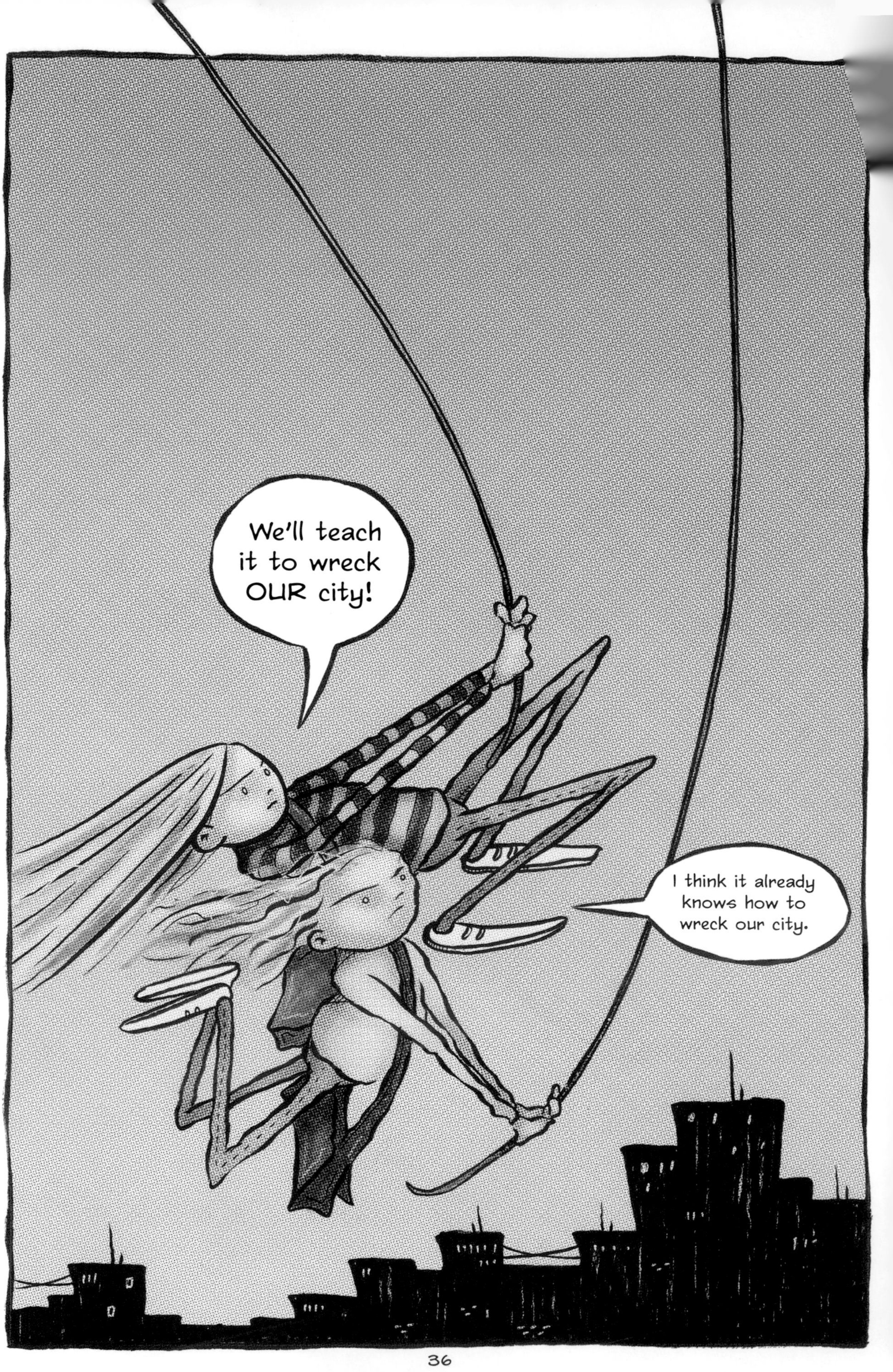
We'll teach it to wreck OUR city!
I think it already knows how to wreck our city.

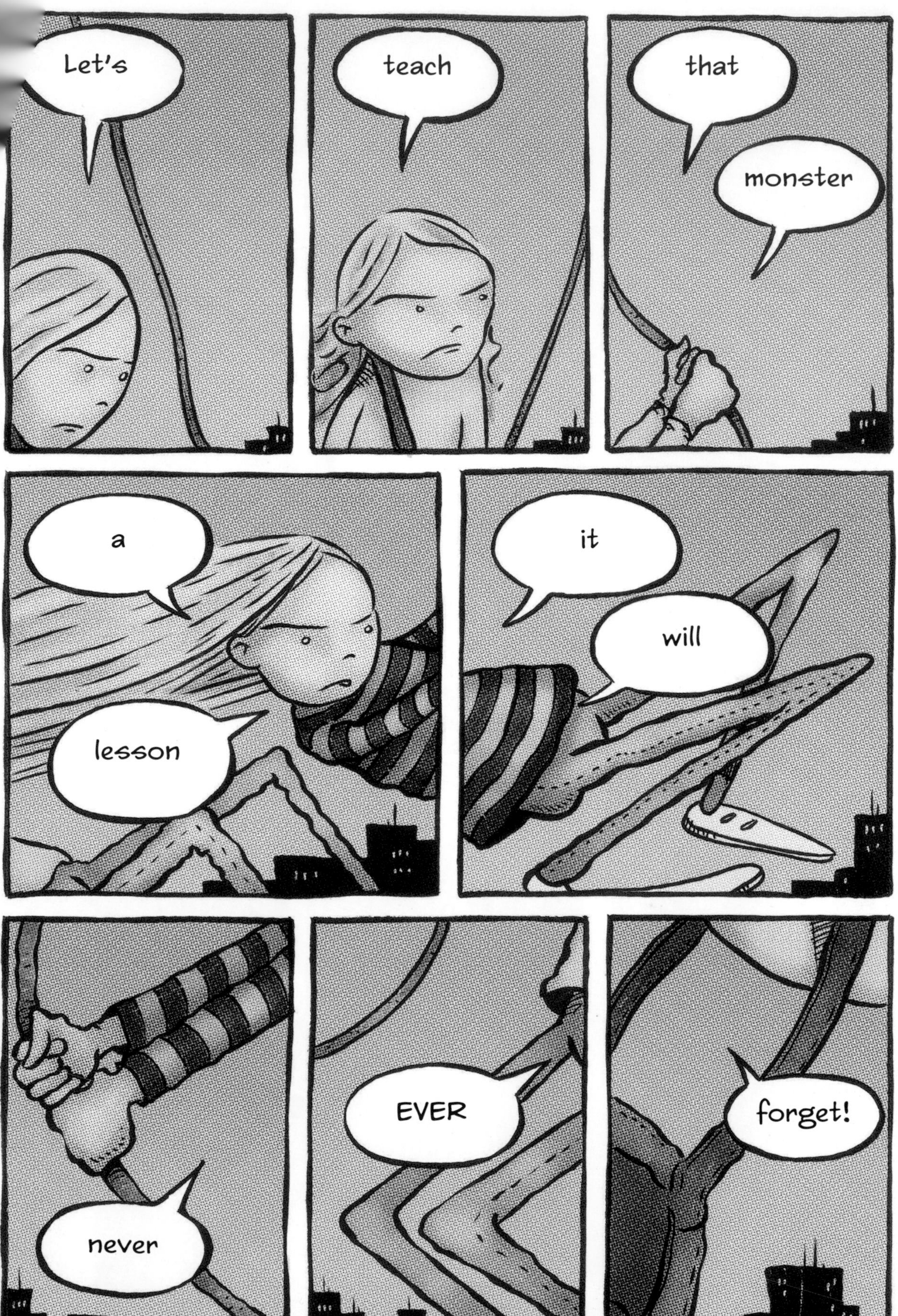
Let's
teach
that
monster
a
lesson
it
will
never
EVER
forget!

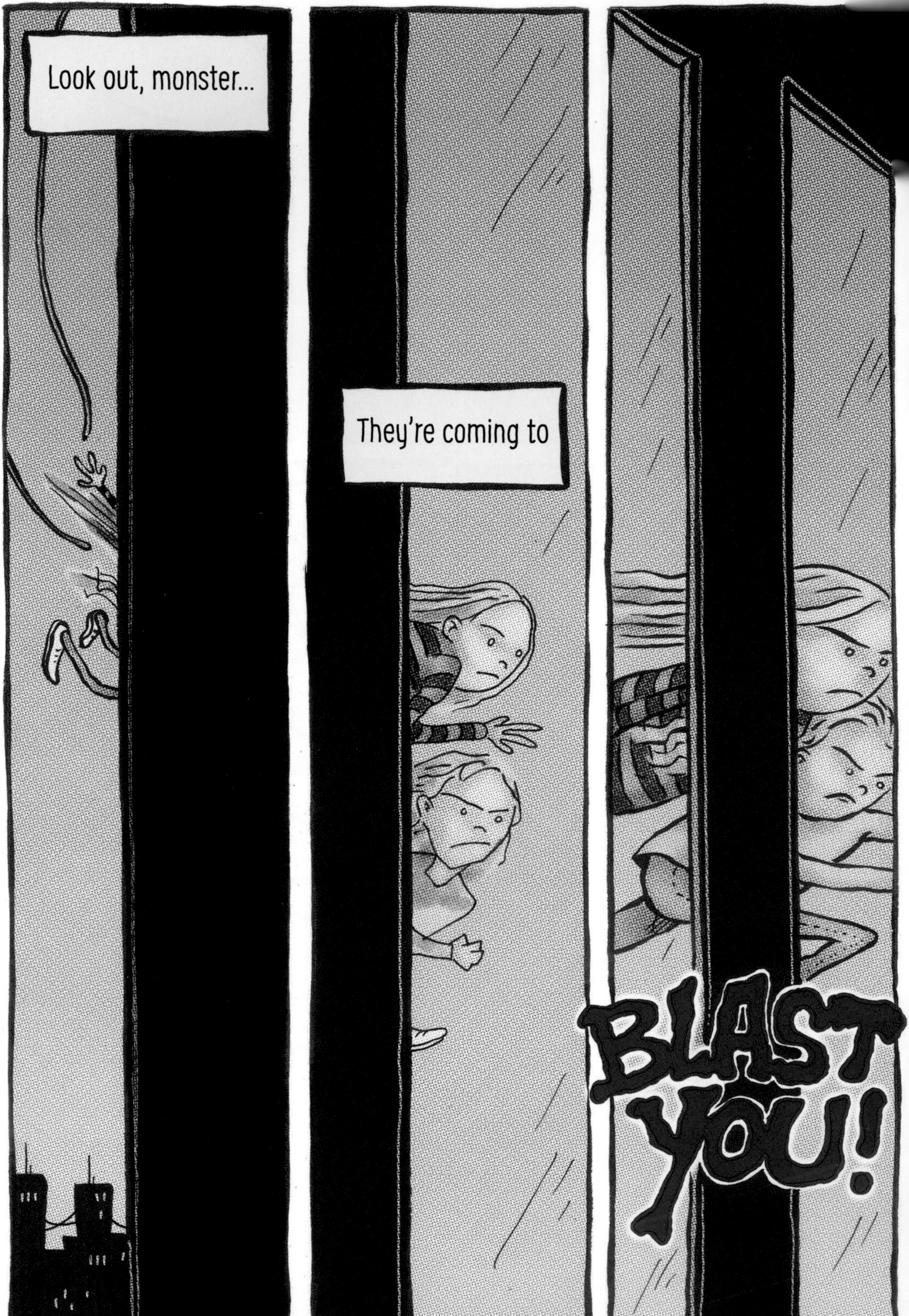
Look out, monster...
They're coming to
BLAST YOU!

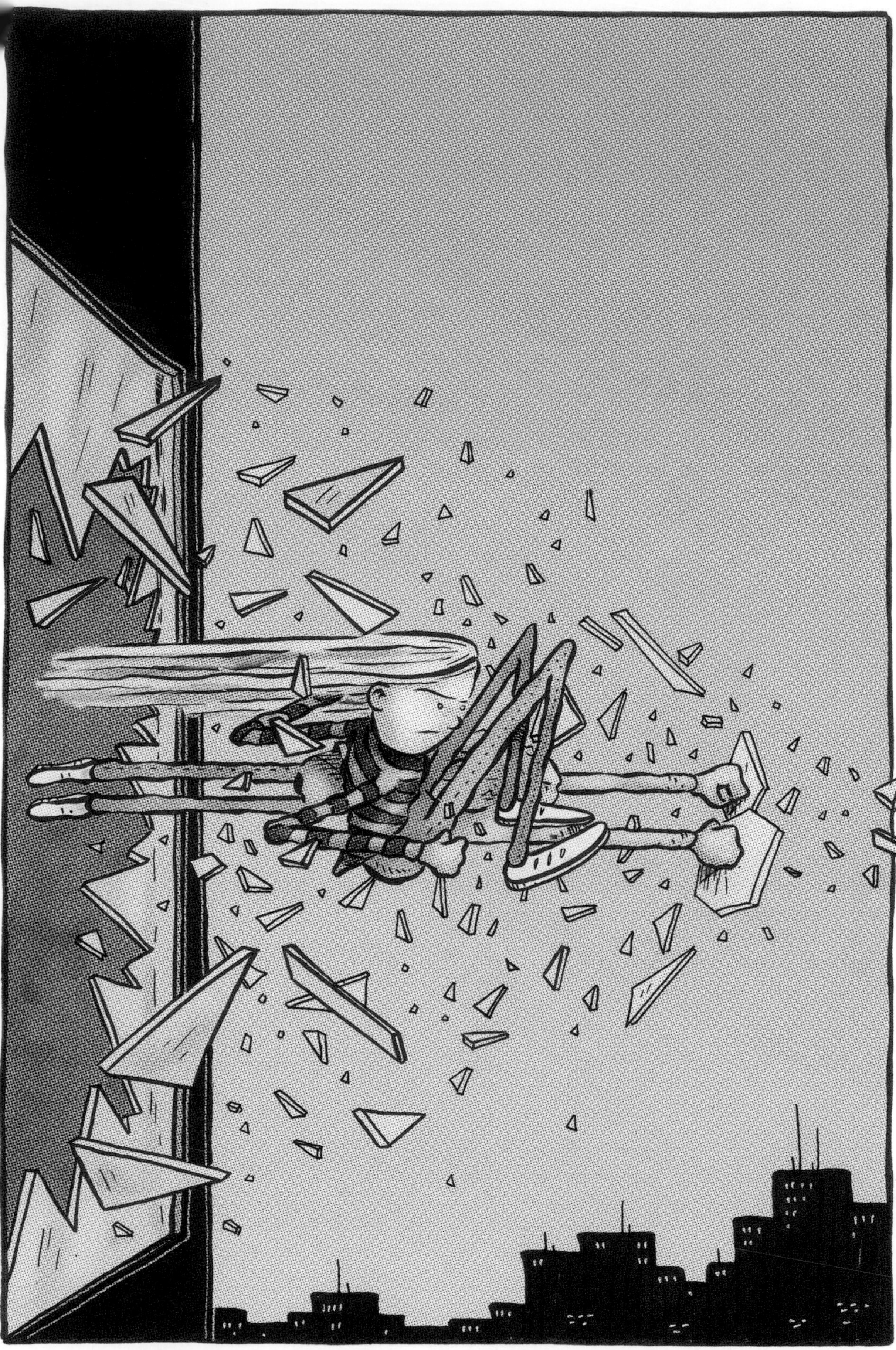

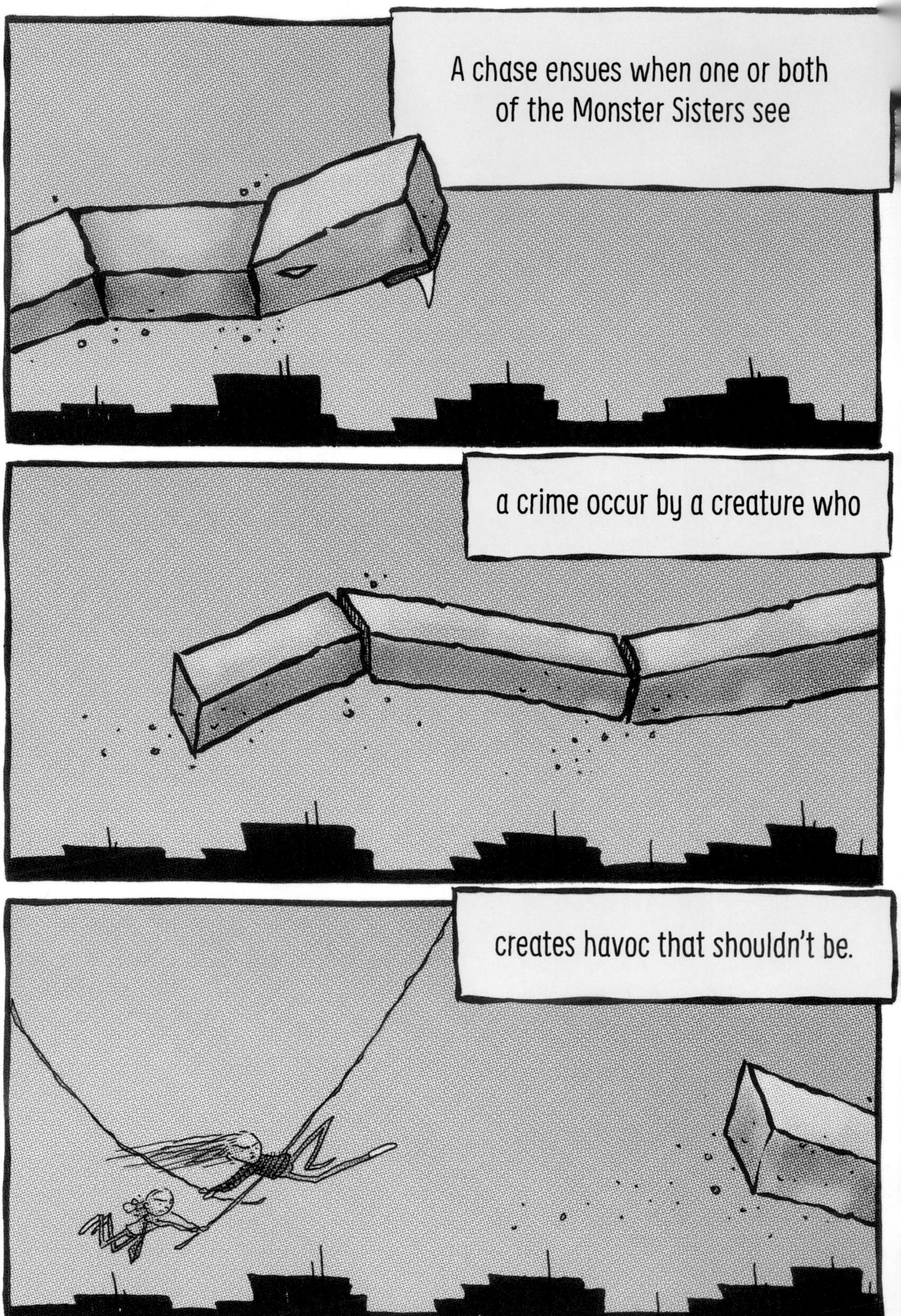
A chase ensues when one or both of the Monster Sisters see
a crime occur by a creature who
creates havoc that shouldn't be.

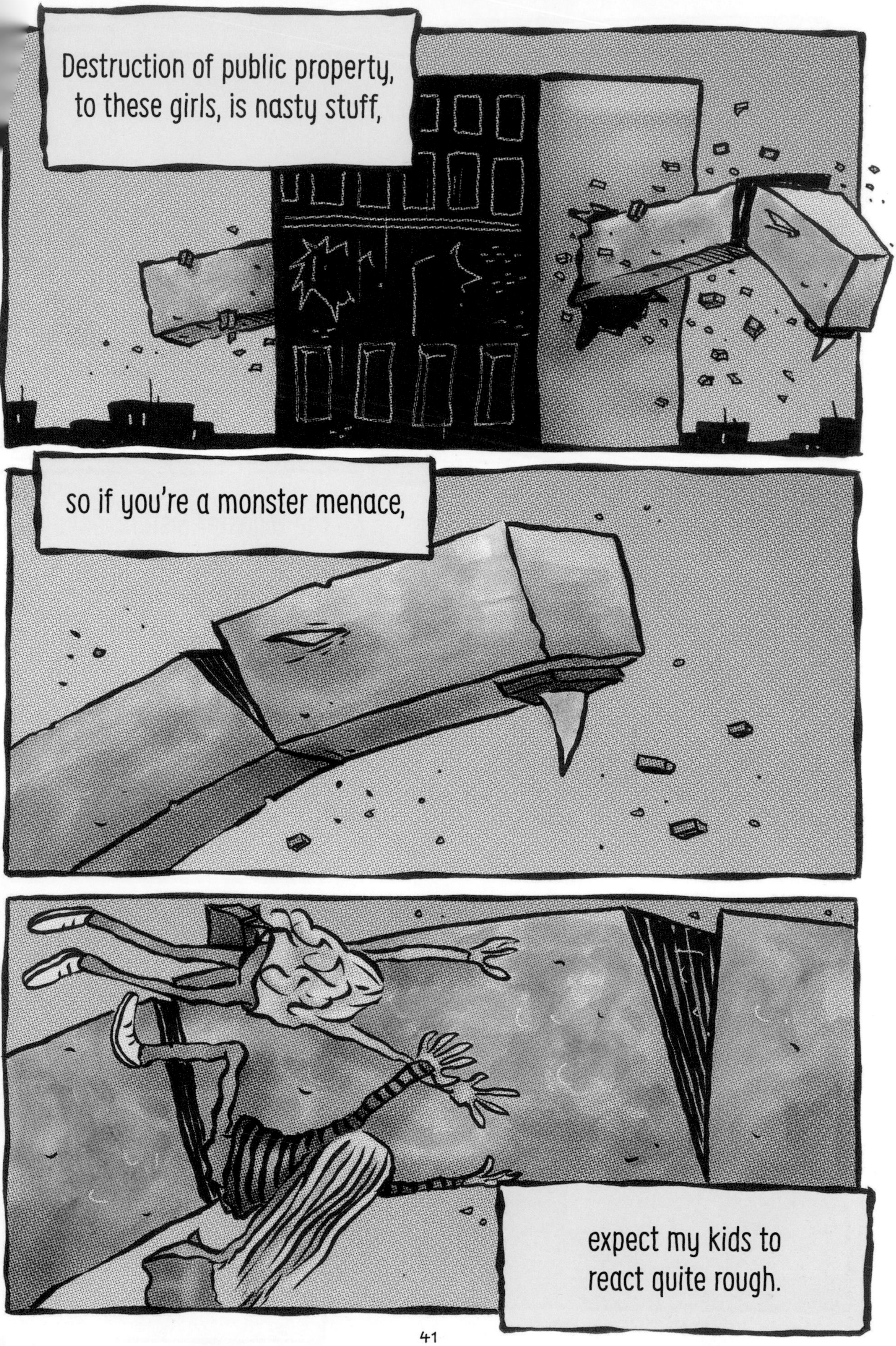
Destruction of public property, to these girls, is nasty stuff,
so if you're a monster menace,
expect my kids to react quite rough.

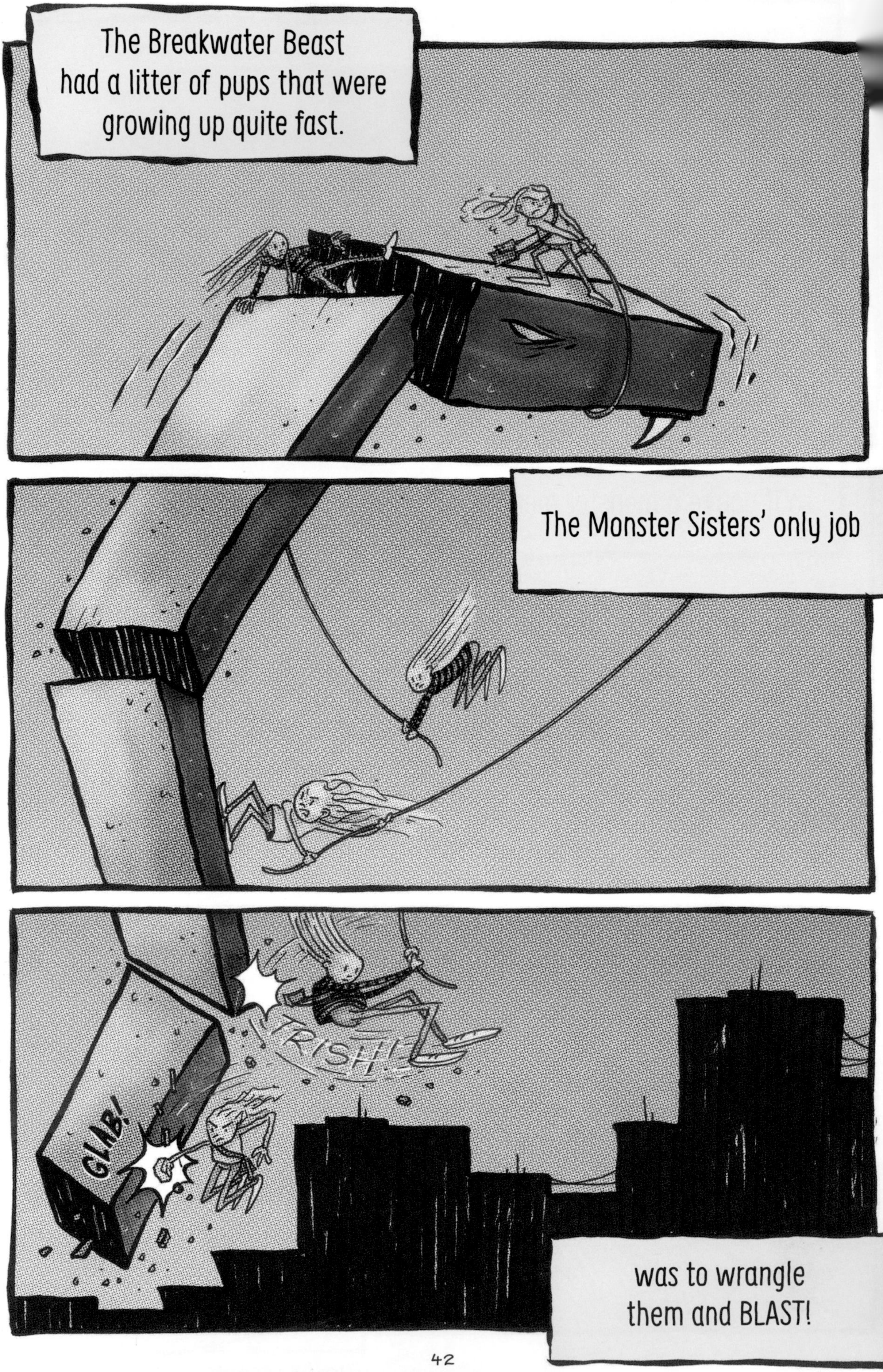
The Breakwater Beast
had a litter of pups that were
growing up quite fast.
The Monster Sisters' only job
TRISH!
GLAB!
was to wrangle
them and BLAST!

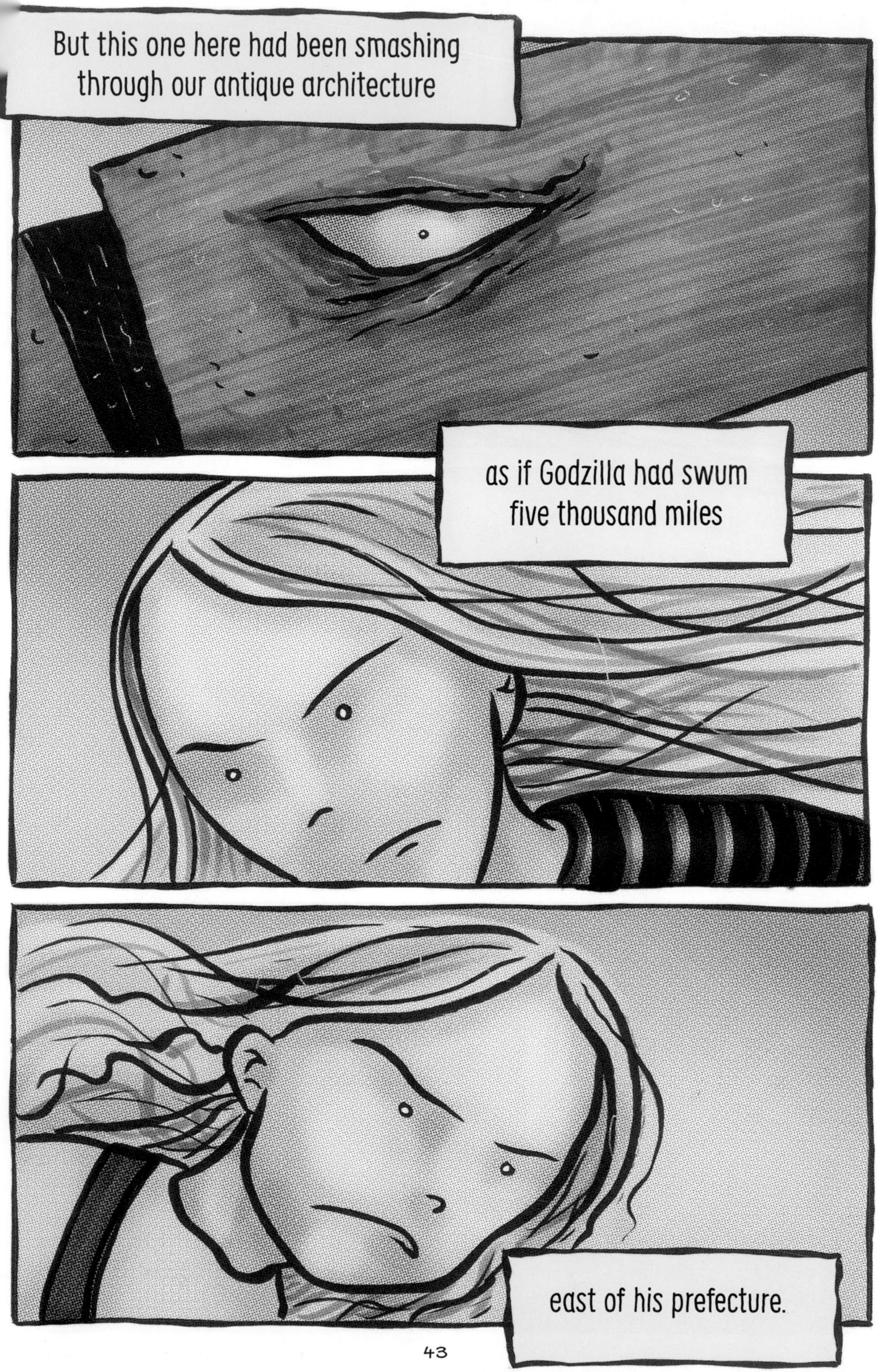
But this one here had been smashing through our antique architecture
as if Godzilla had swum five thousand miles
east of his prefecture.

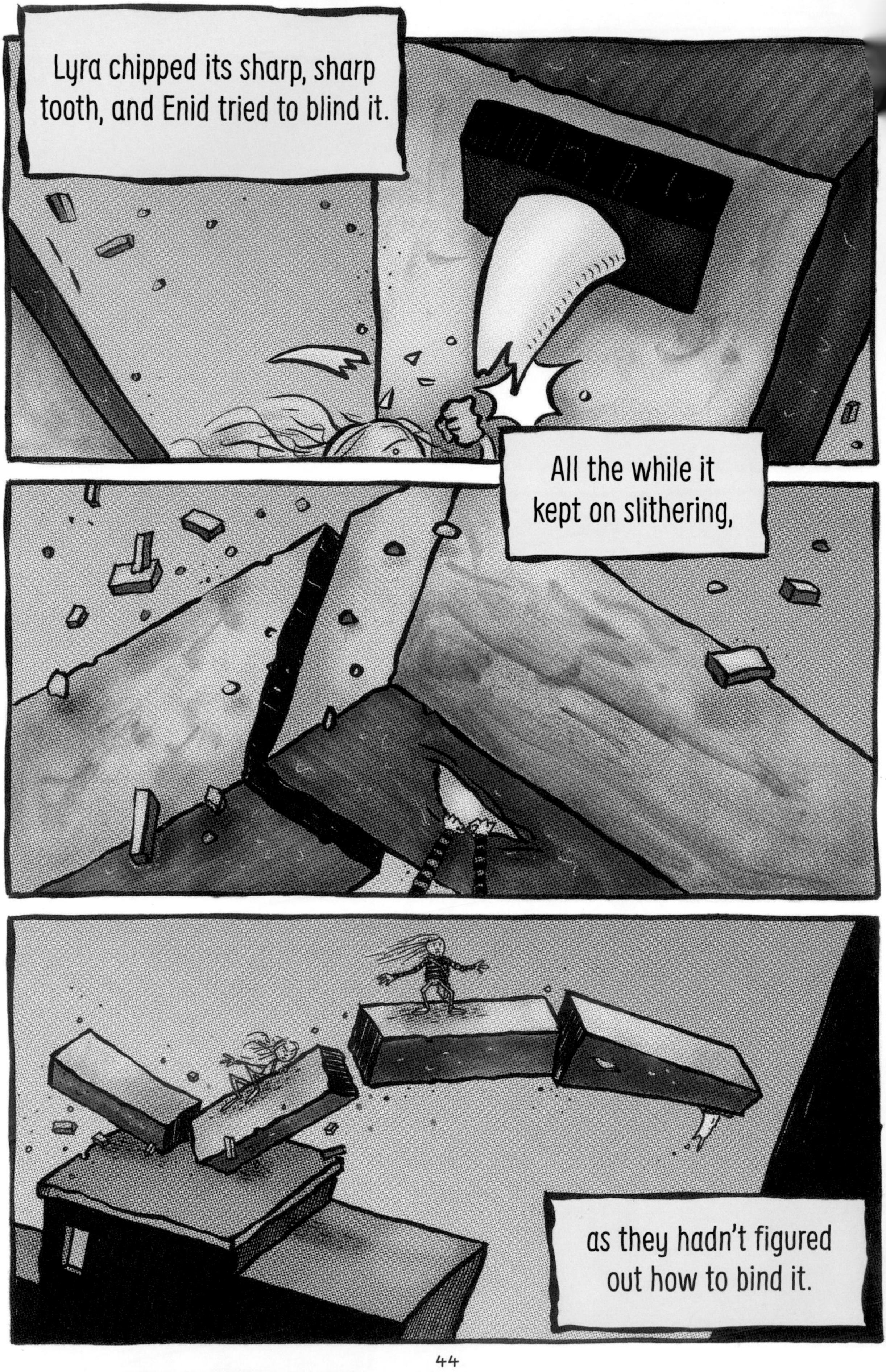

Lyra chipped its sharp, sharp tooth, and Enid tried to blind it.
All the while it kept on slithering,
as they hadn't figured out how to bind it.

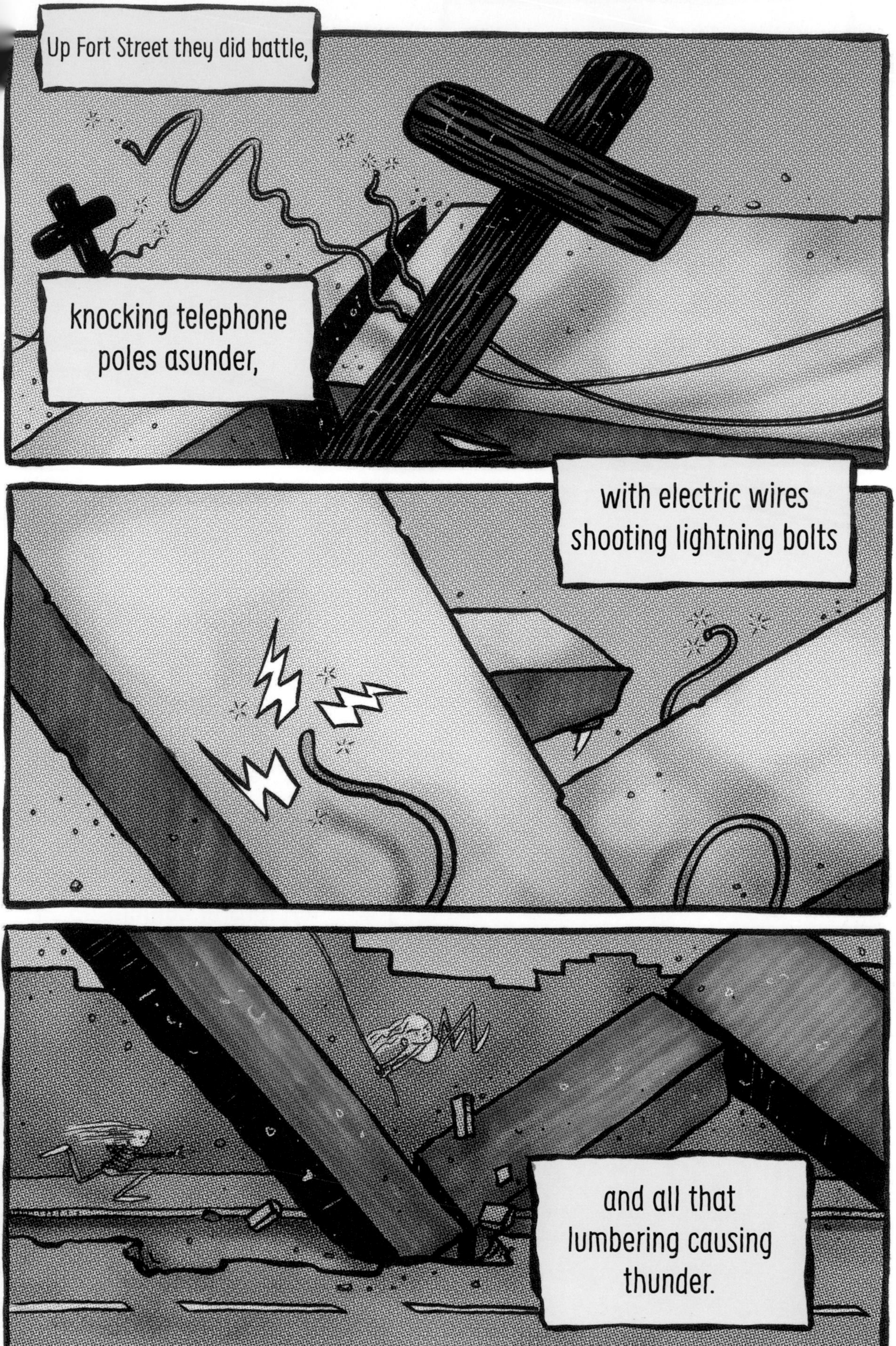
Up Fort Street they did battle,
knocking telephone poles asunder,
with electric wires shooting lightning bolts
and all that lumbering causing thunder.

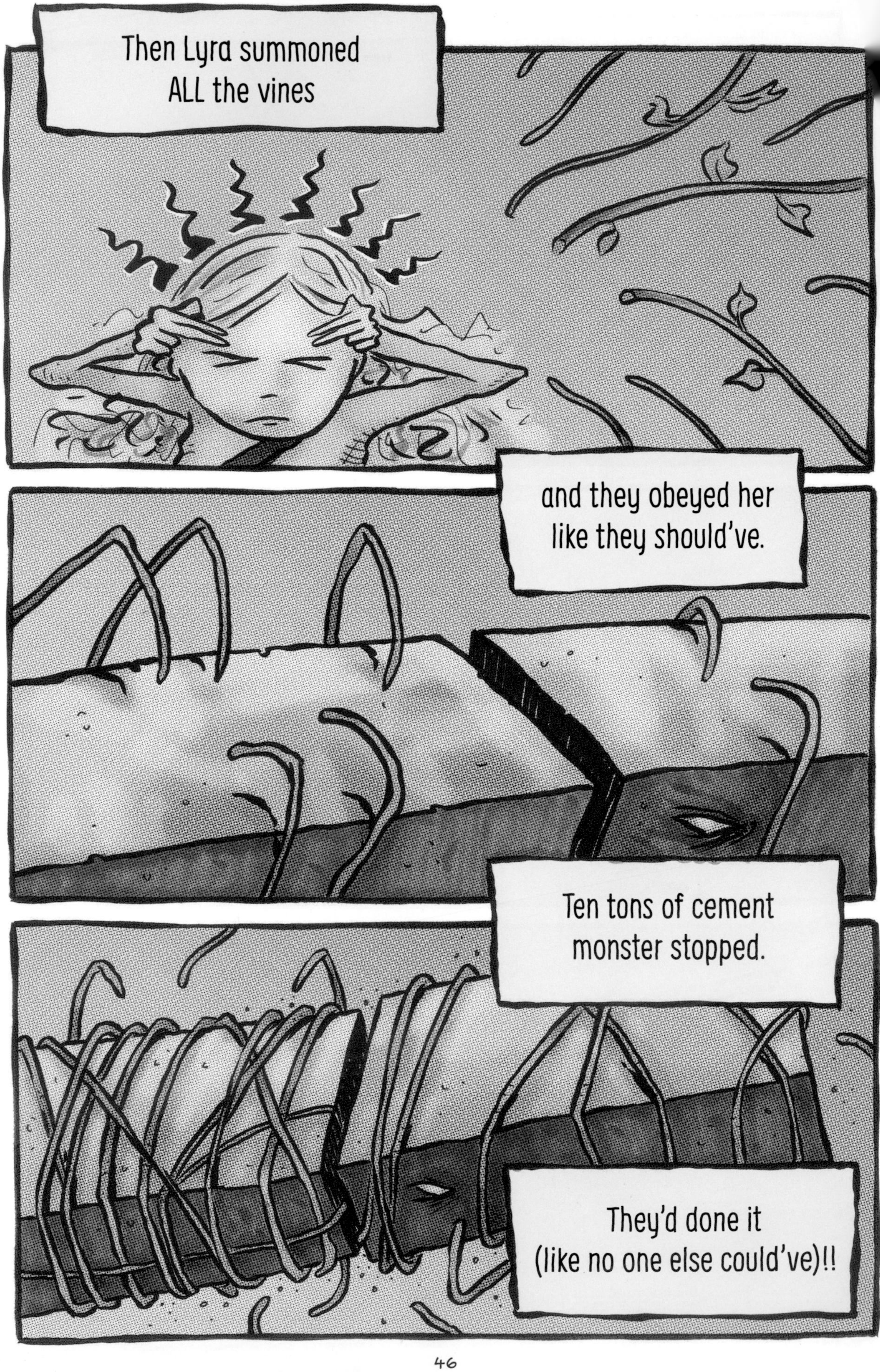
Then Lyra summoned ALL the vines
and they obeyed her like they should've.
Ten tons of cement monster stopped.
They'd done it (like no one else could've)!!

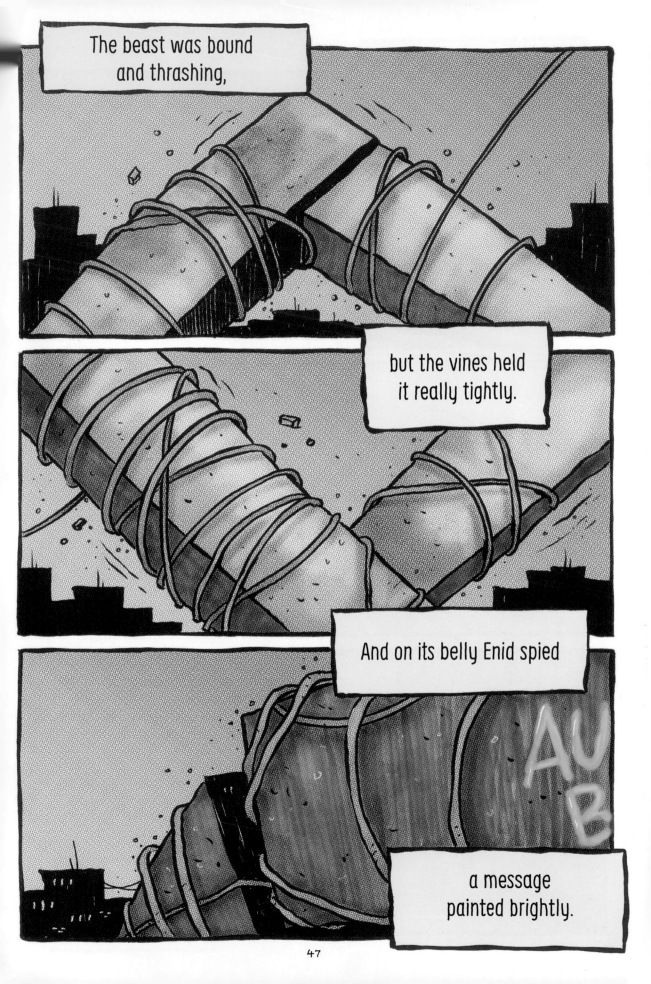

The beast was bound
and thrashing,

but the vines held
it really tightly.

And on its belly Enid spied

a message
painted brightly.

47

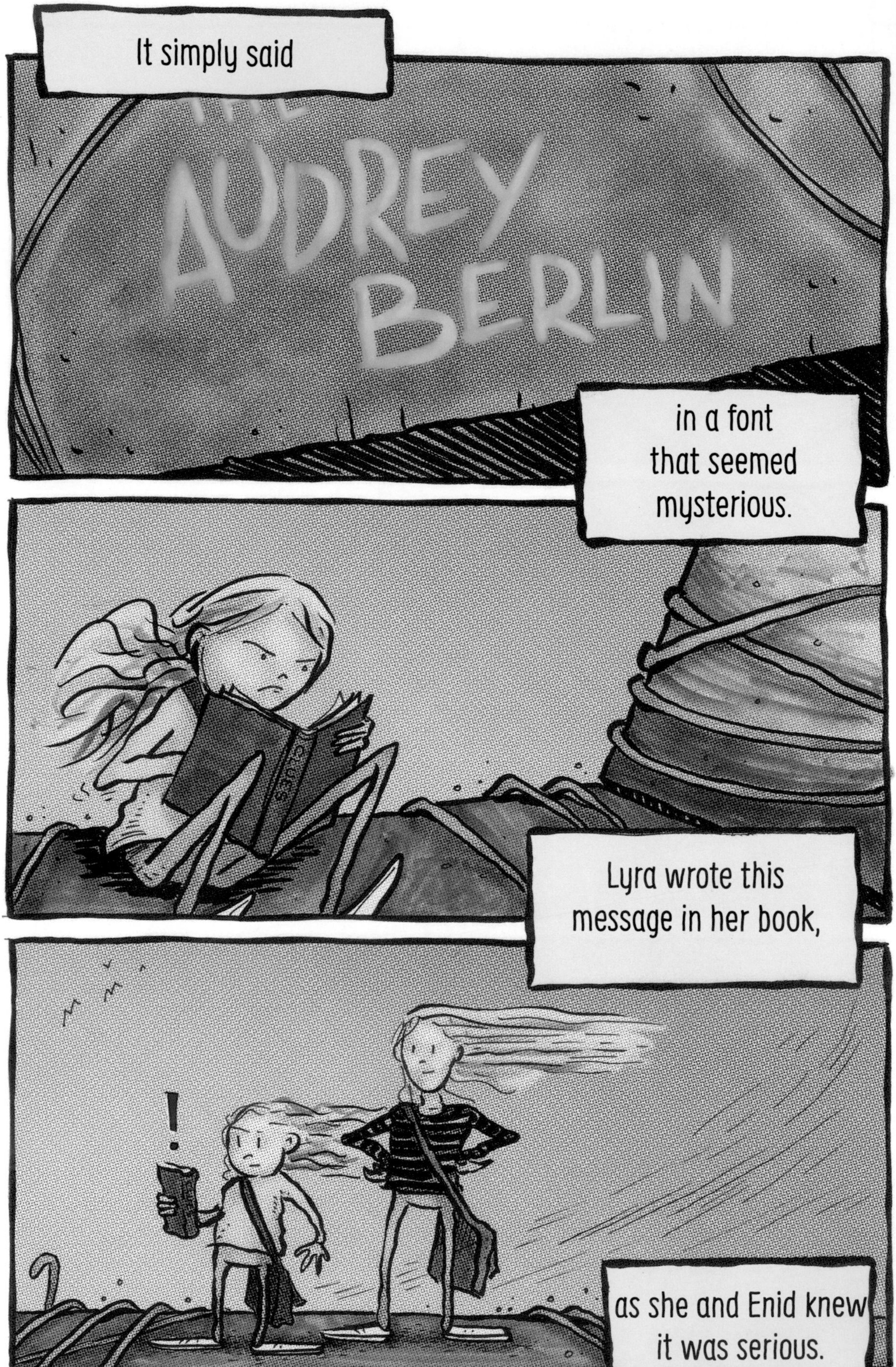
It simply said
AUDREY
BERLIN
in a font
that seemed
mysterious.
Lyra wrote this
message in her book,
as she and Enid knew
it was serious.

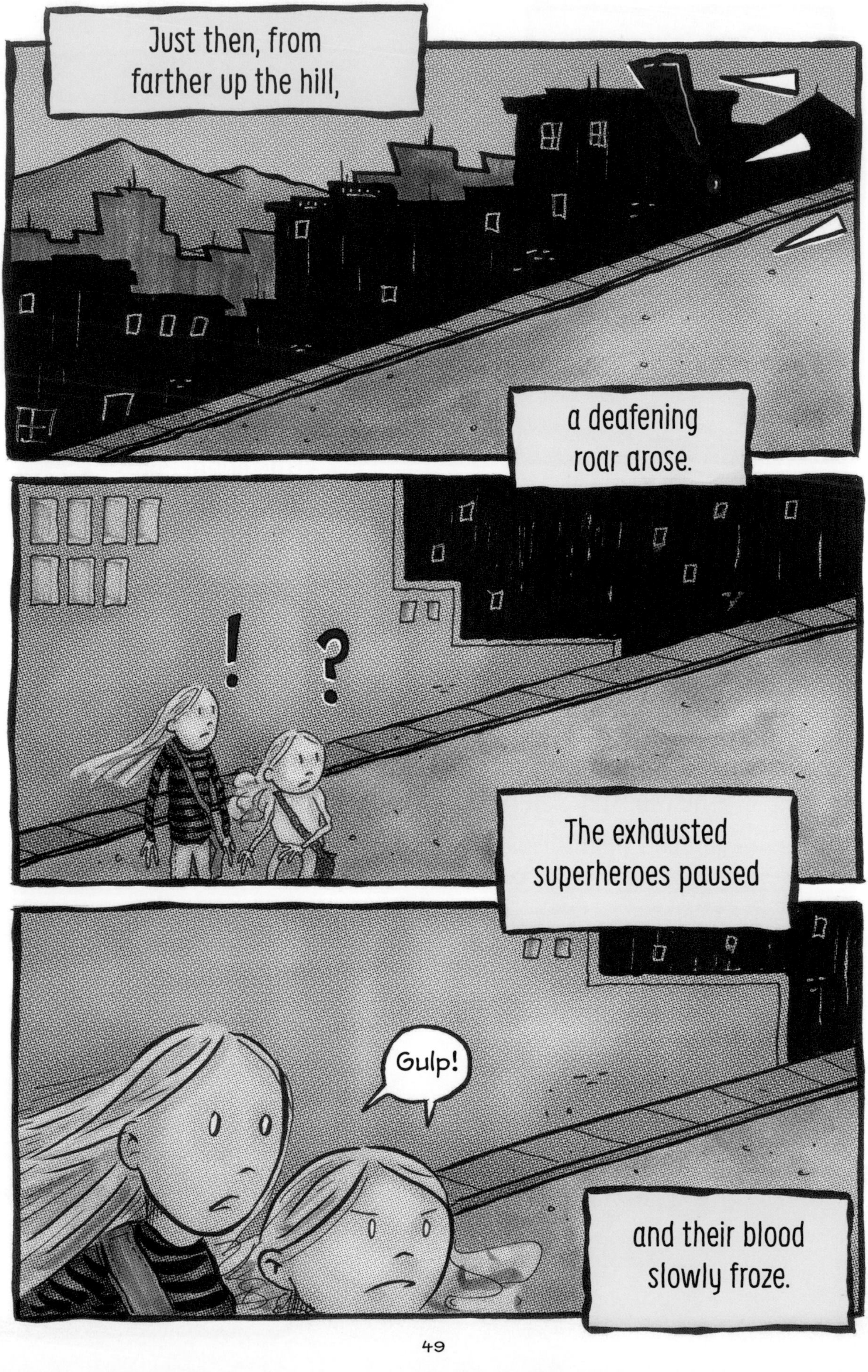
Just then, from farther up the hill,
a deafening roar arose.
!
?
The exhausted superheroes paused
Gulp!
and their blood slowly froze.

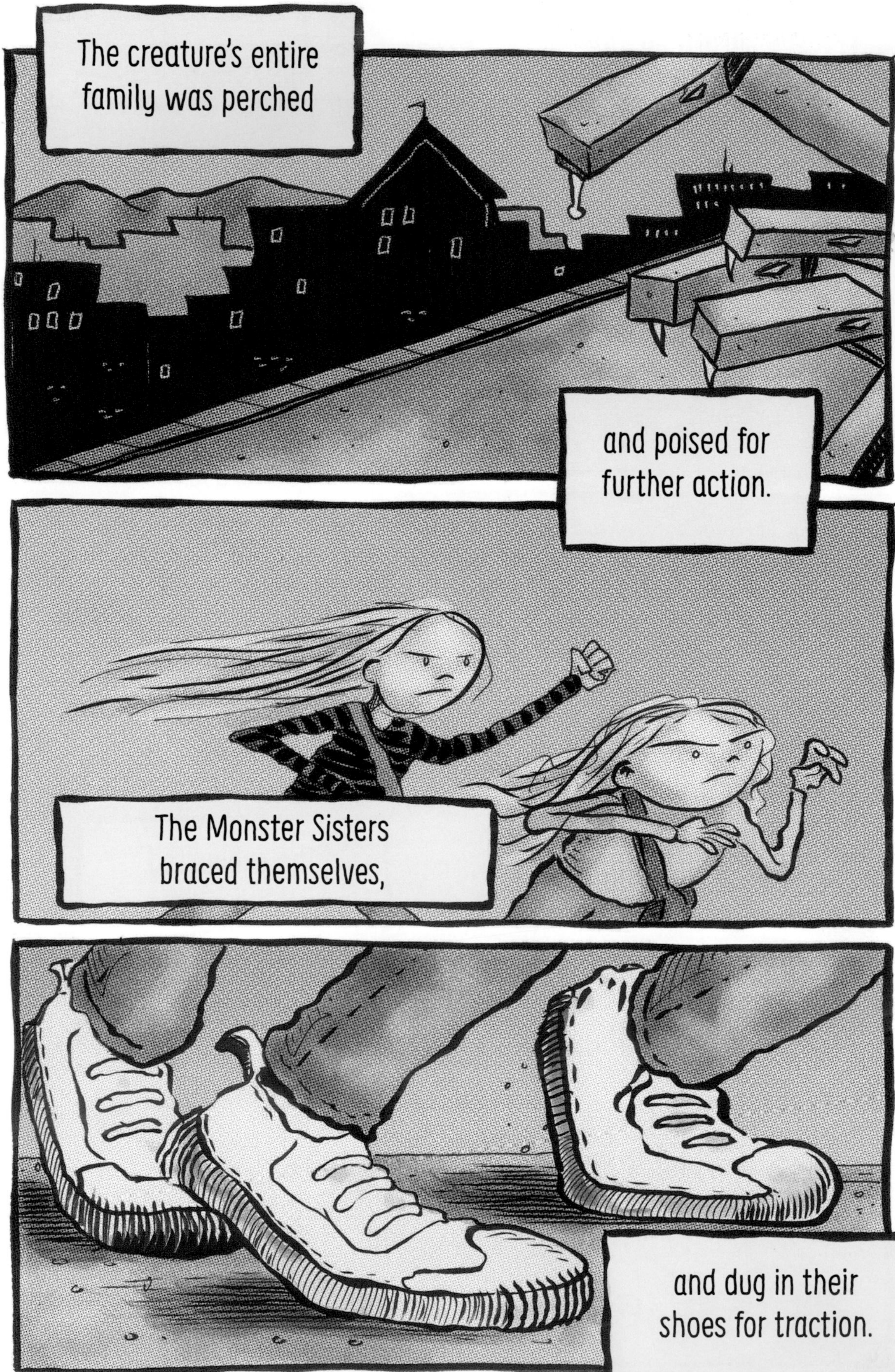
The creature's entire family was perched
and poised for further action.
The Monster Sisters braced themselves,
and dug in their shoes for traction.

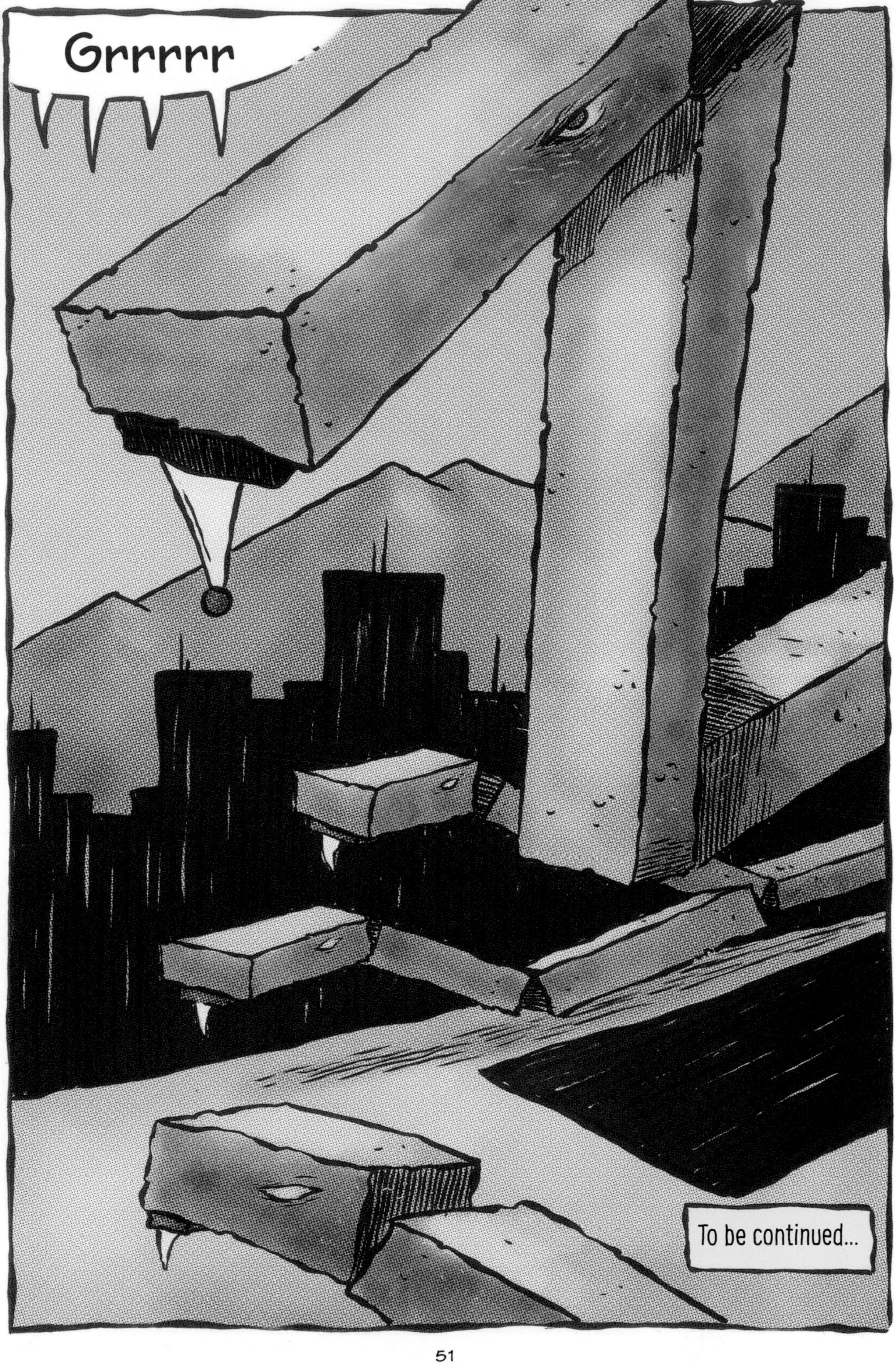
Grrrrr
To be continued...

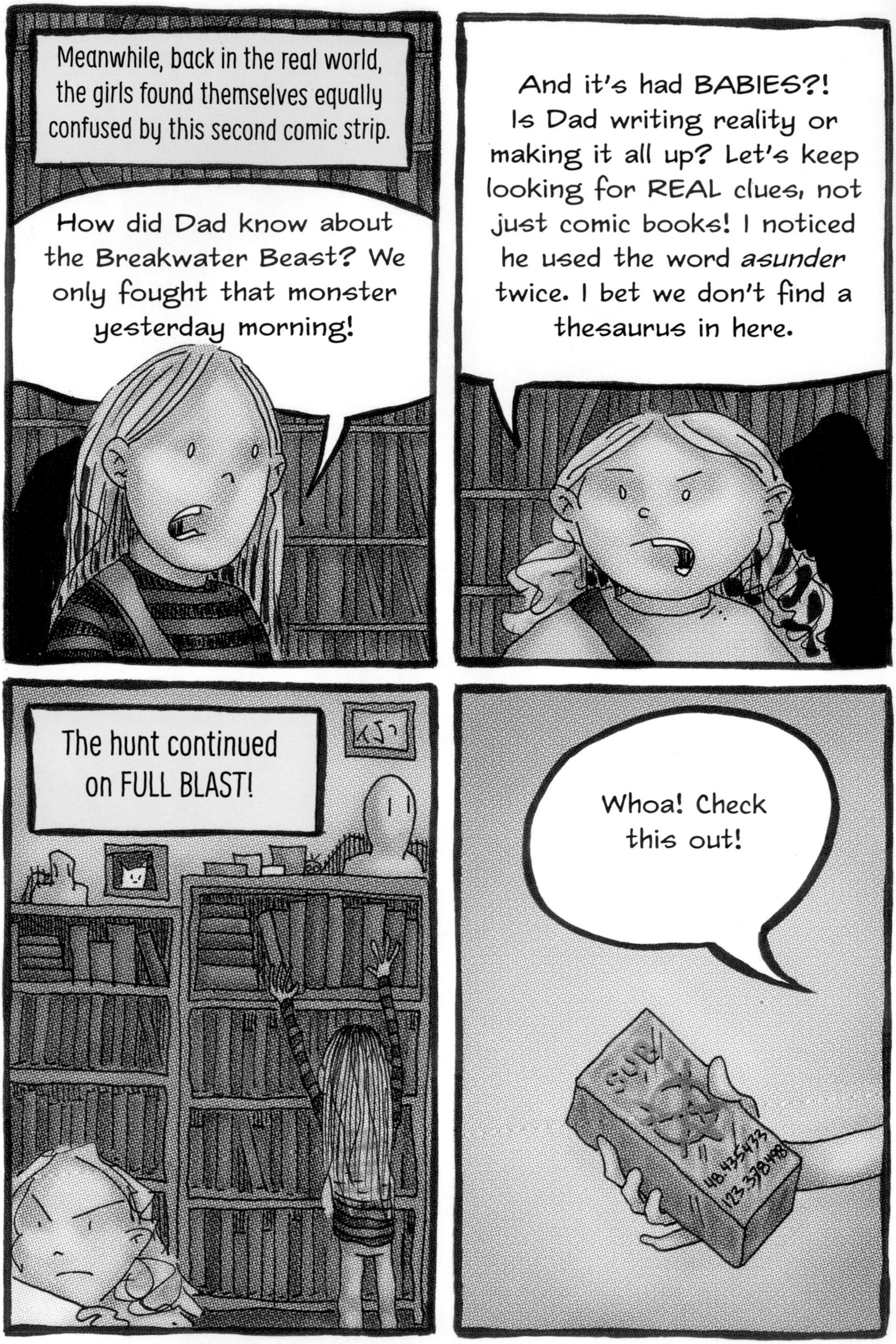
Meanwhile, back in the real world, the girls found themselves equally confused by this second comic strip.
How did Dad know about the Breakwater Beast? We only fought that monster yesterday morning!
And it's had BABIES?! Is Dad writing reality or making it all up? Let's keep looking for REAL clues, not just comic books! I noticed he used the word *asunder* twice. I bet we don't find a thesaurus in here.
The hunt continued on FULL BLAST!
Whoa! Check this out!
48.435433
123.378498

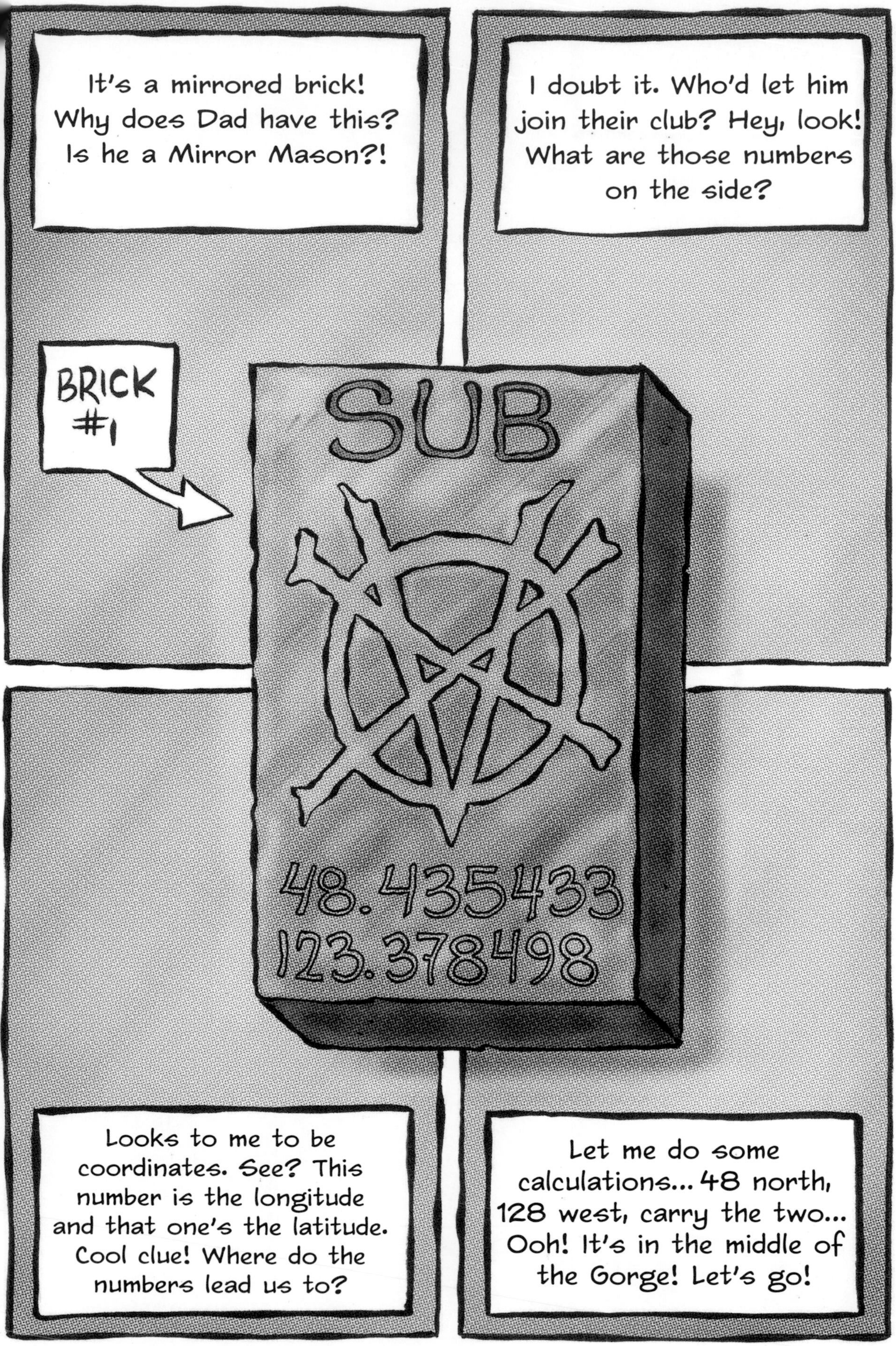
It's a mirrored brick! Why does Dad have this? Is he a Mirror Mason?!
I doubt it. Who'd let him join their club? Hey, look! What are those numbers on the side?
BRICK #1
SUB
48.435433
123.378498
Looks to me to be coordinates. See? This number is the longitude and that one's the latitude. Cool clue! Where do the numbers lead us to?
Let me do some calculations... 48 north, 128 west, carry the two... Ooh! It's in the middle of the Gorge! Let's go!

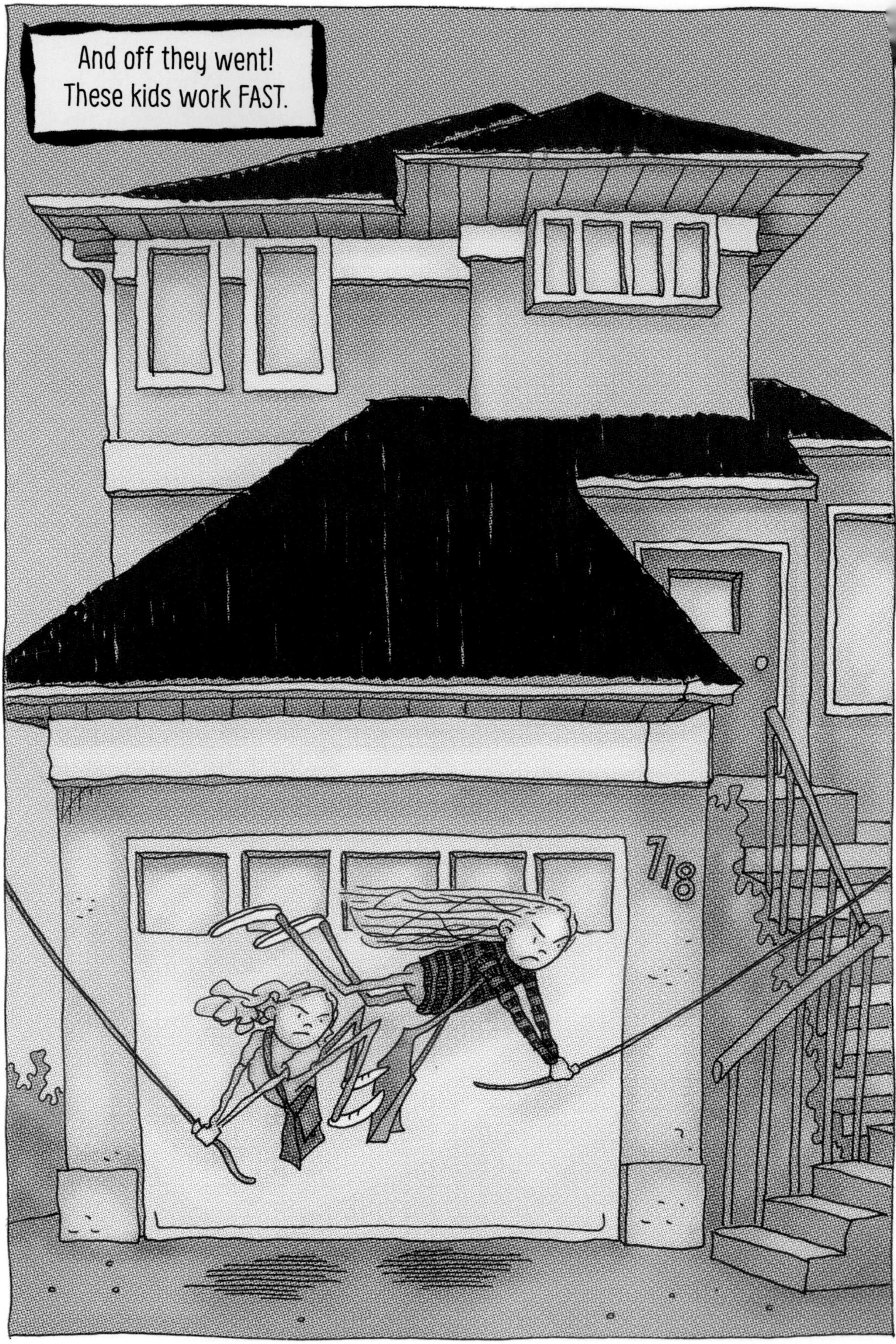
And off they went!
These kids work FAST.
718

CHAPTER THREE
BENEATH THE WATERS OF THE GORGE

The clue that the sisters have just found is a great one. If their calculations are correct (and I think they are), they're on their way to a waterway downtown that locals call "the Gorge." It's a narrow stretch of salt water that connects the Inner Harbour (where the Empress Hotel and legislative buildings are/were) and the tidal flats of Portage Inlet. There are thousands of years of history along the Gorge, as locals have fished, swum and lived along its banks since the last Ice Age receded and left the land etched into this beautiful passage. A streetcar crashed into the Gorge from the Bay Street Bridge back in 1896, and I think there may still be some sunken wreckage down there. I sure hope the girls stay safe. The coordinates are leading them to a spot just north of the Bay Street Bridge.

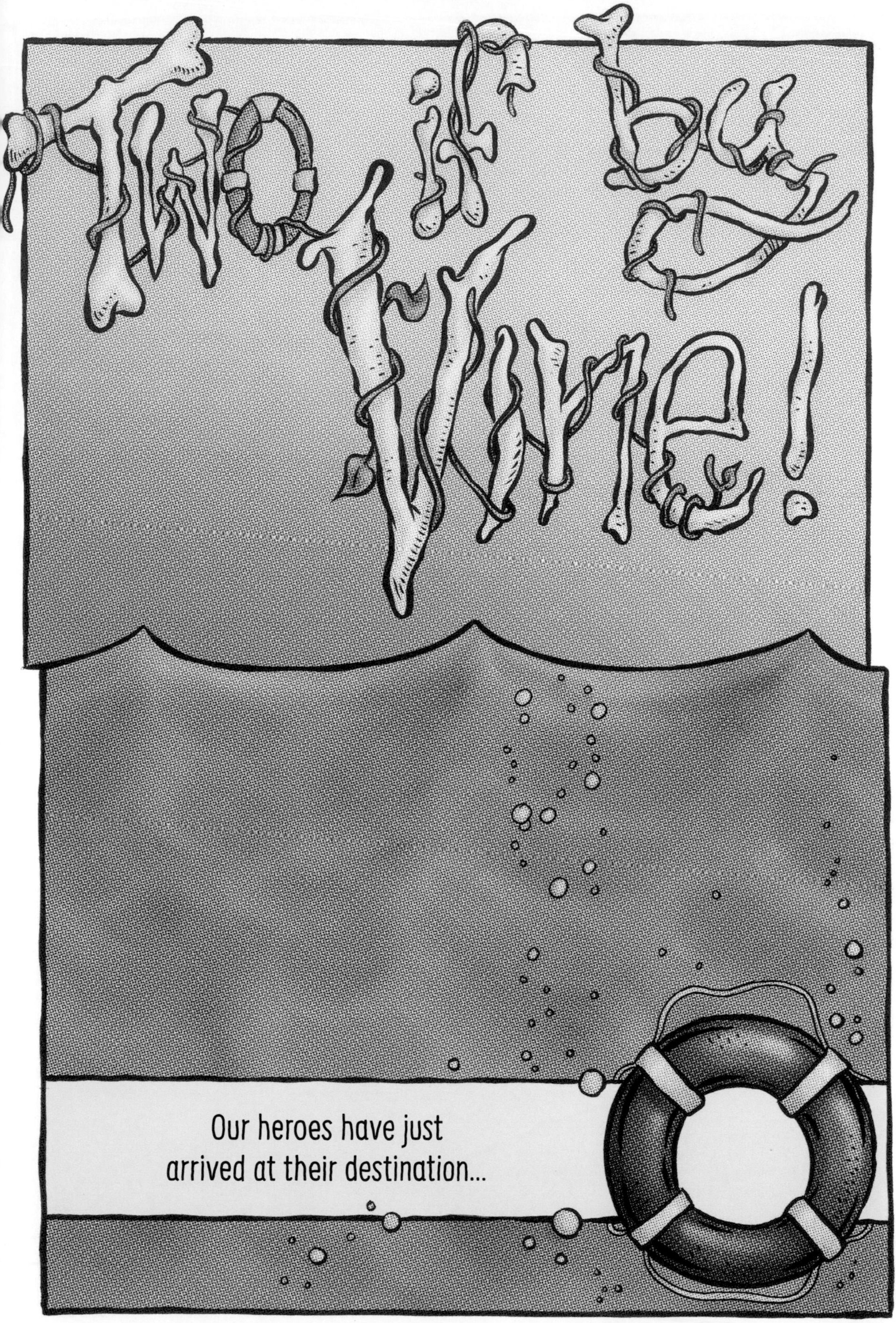
Two if by Vine!
Our heroes have just arrived at their destination...

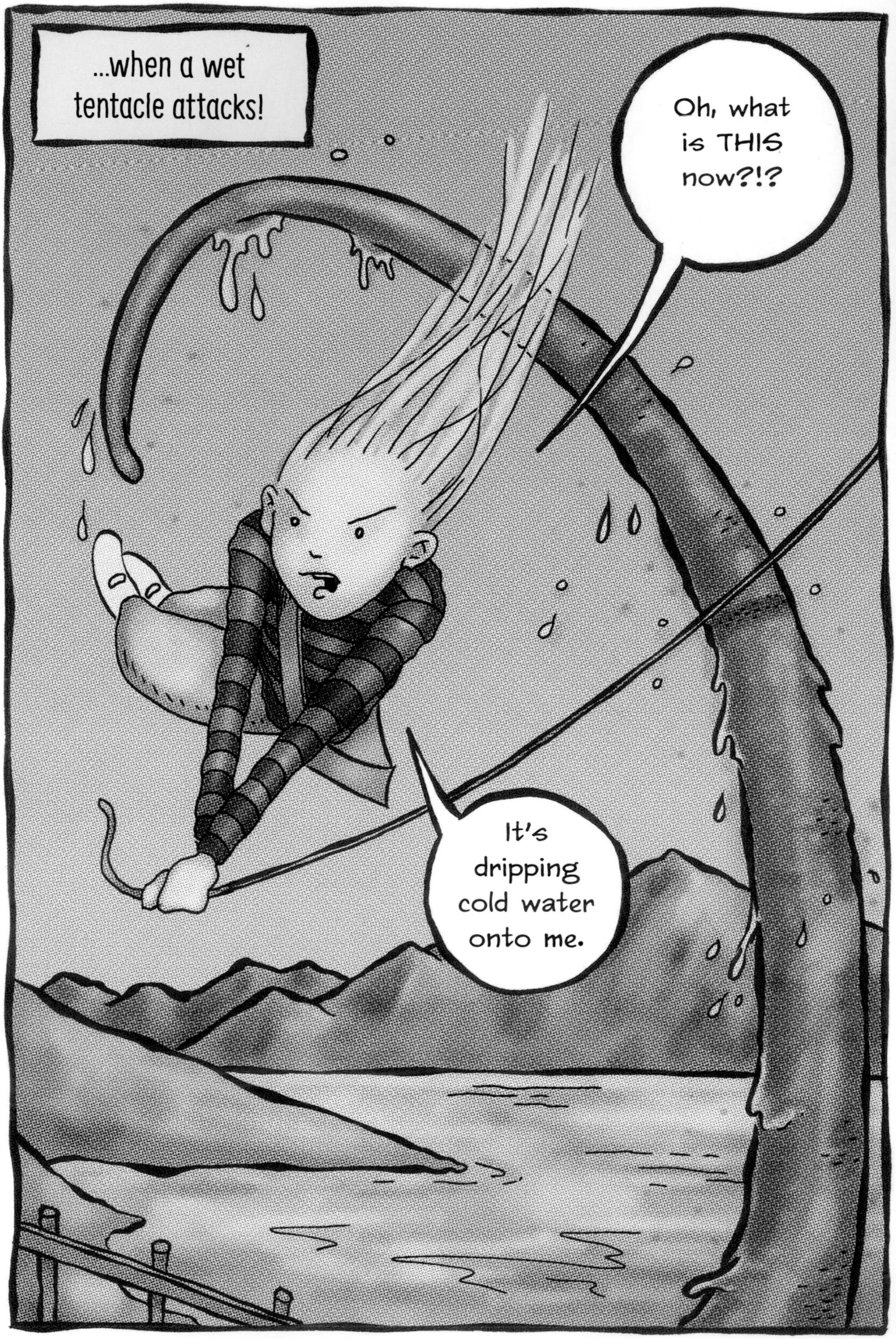
...when a wet tentacle attacks!
Oh, what is THIS now?!?
It's dripping cold water onto me.

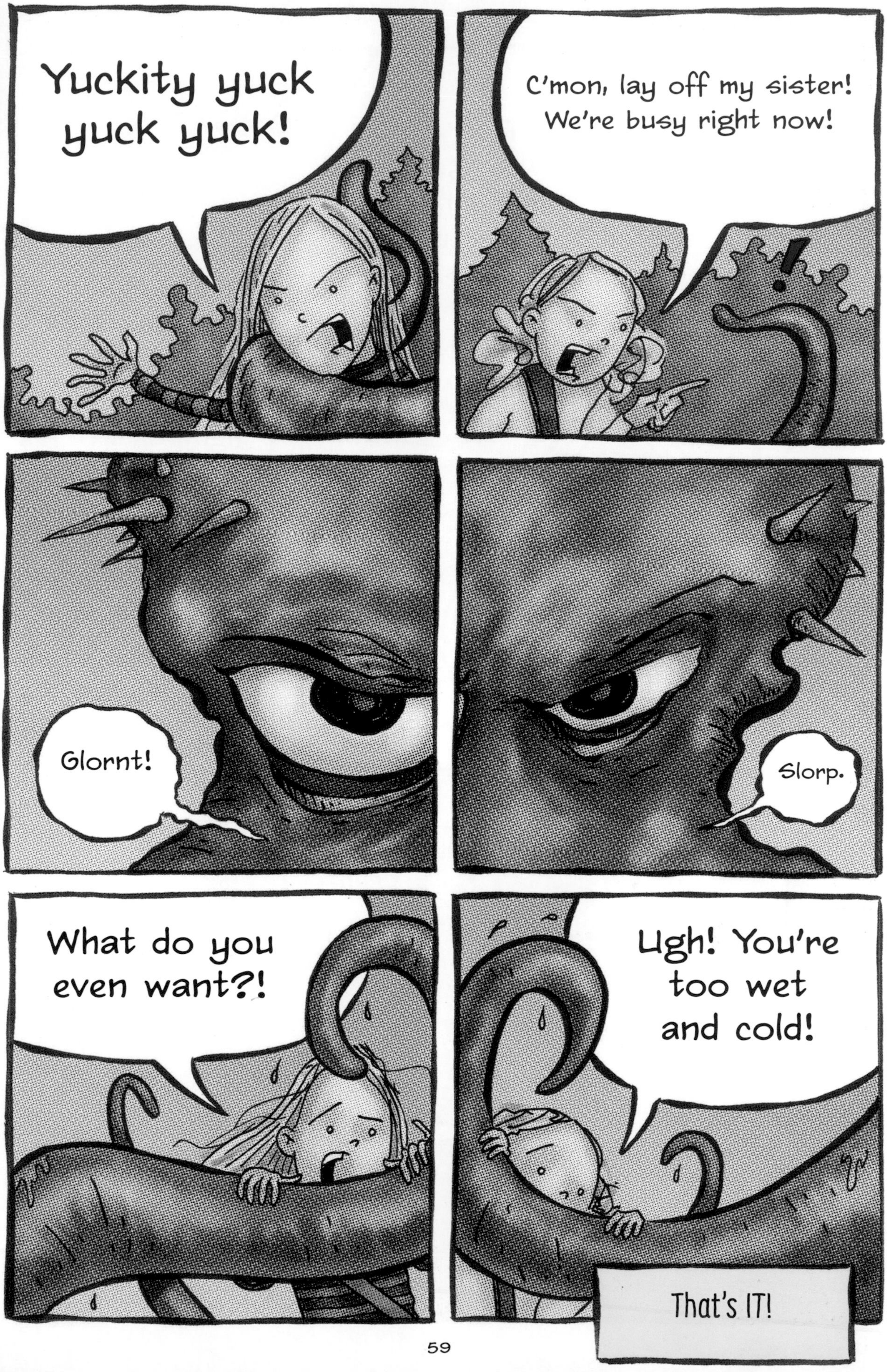

Yuckity yuck yuck yuck!
C'mon, lay off my sister! We're busy right now!
!
Glornt!
Slorp.
What do you even want?!
Ugh! You're too wet and cold!
That's IT!

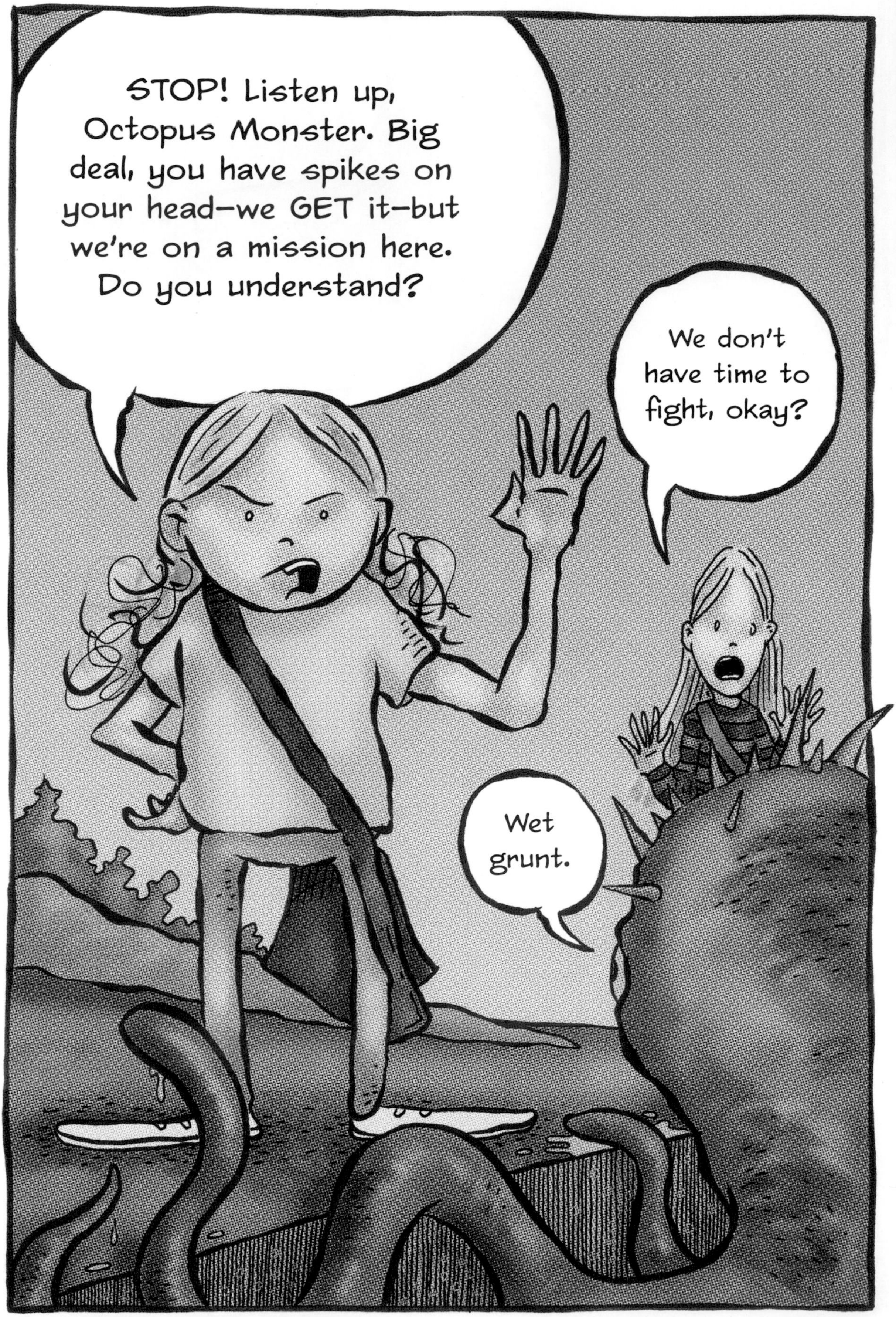
STOP! Listen up, Octopus Monster. Big deal, you have spikes on your head—we GET it—but we're on a mission here. Do you understand?
We don't have time to fight, okay?
Wet grunt.

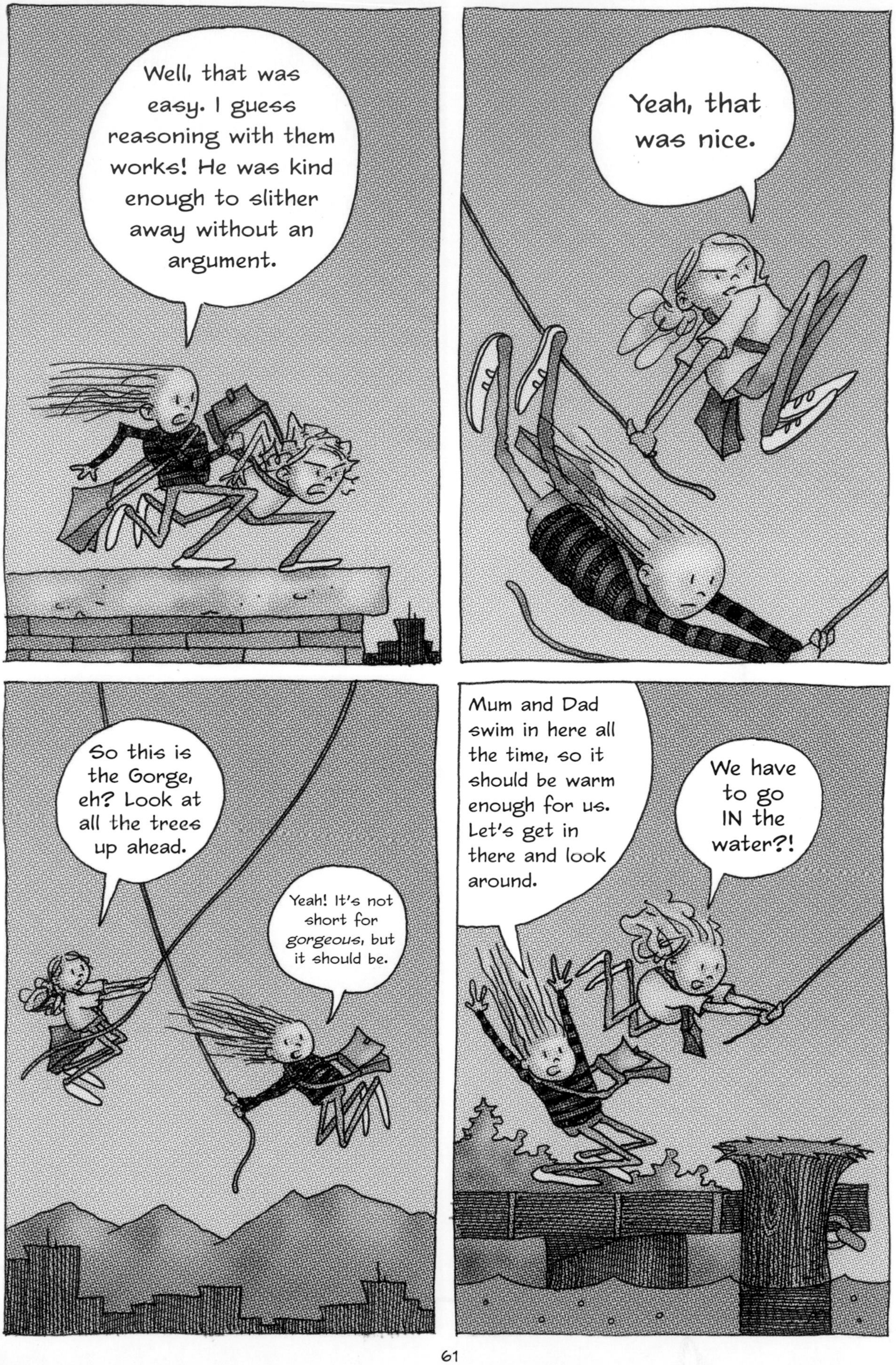
Well, that was easy. I guess reasoning with them works! He was kind enough to slither away without an argument.
Yeah, that was nice.
So this is the Gorge, eh? Look at all the trees up ahead.
Yeah! It's not short for *gorgeous*, but it should be.
Mum and Dad swim in here all the time, so it should be warm enough for us. Let's get in there and look around.
We have to go IN the water?!

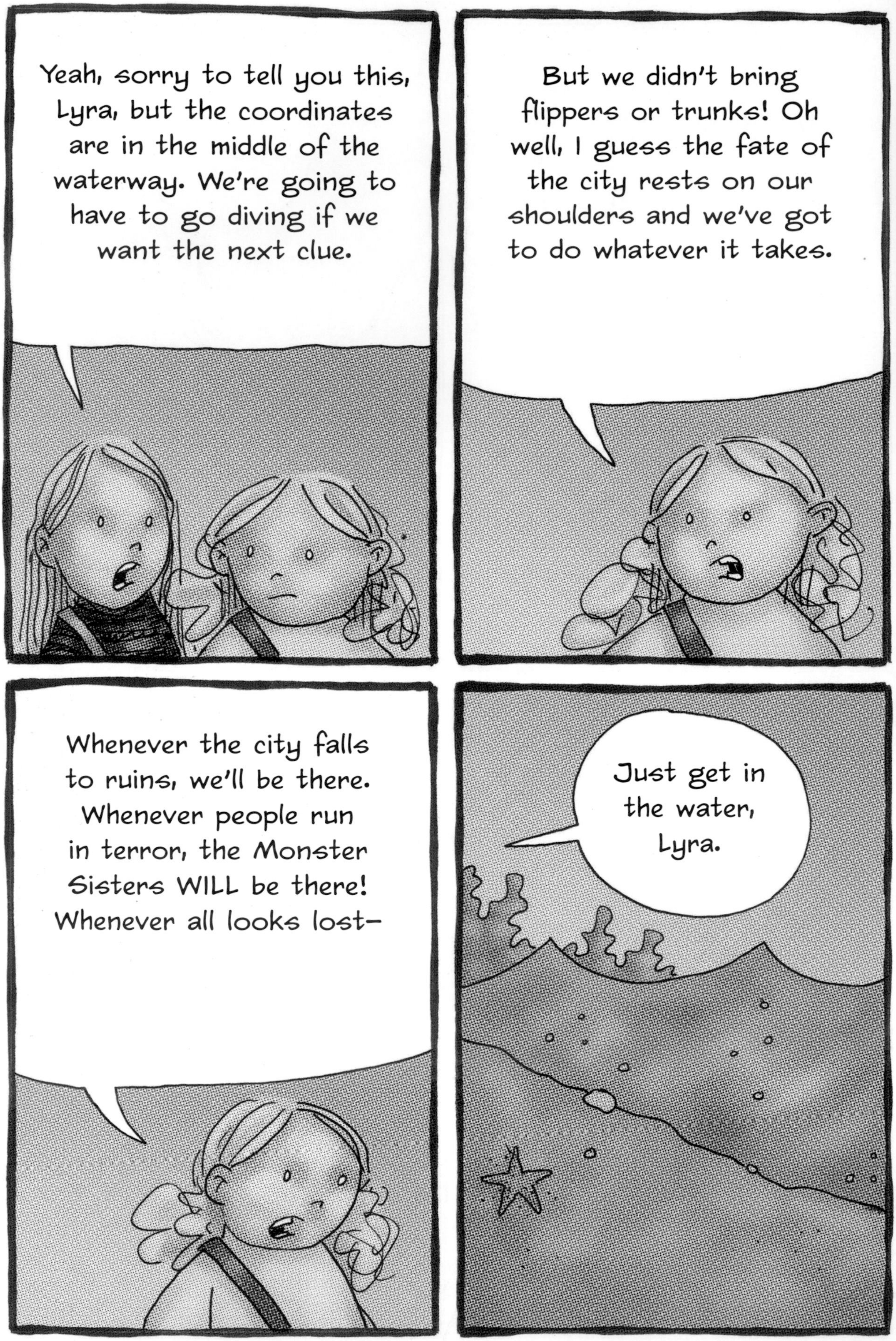
Yeah, sorry to tell you this, Lyra, but the coordinates are in the middle of the waterway. We're going to have to go diving if we want the next clue.
But we didn't bring flippers or trunks! Oh well, I guess the fate of the city rests on our shoulders and we've got to do whatever it takes.
Whenever the city falls to ruins, we'll be there. Whenever people run in terror, the Monster Sisters WILL be there! Whenever all looks lost–
Just get in the water, Lyra.

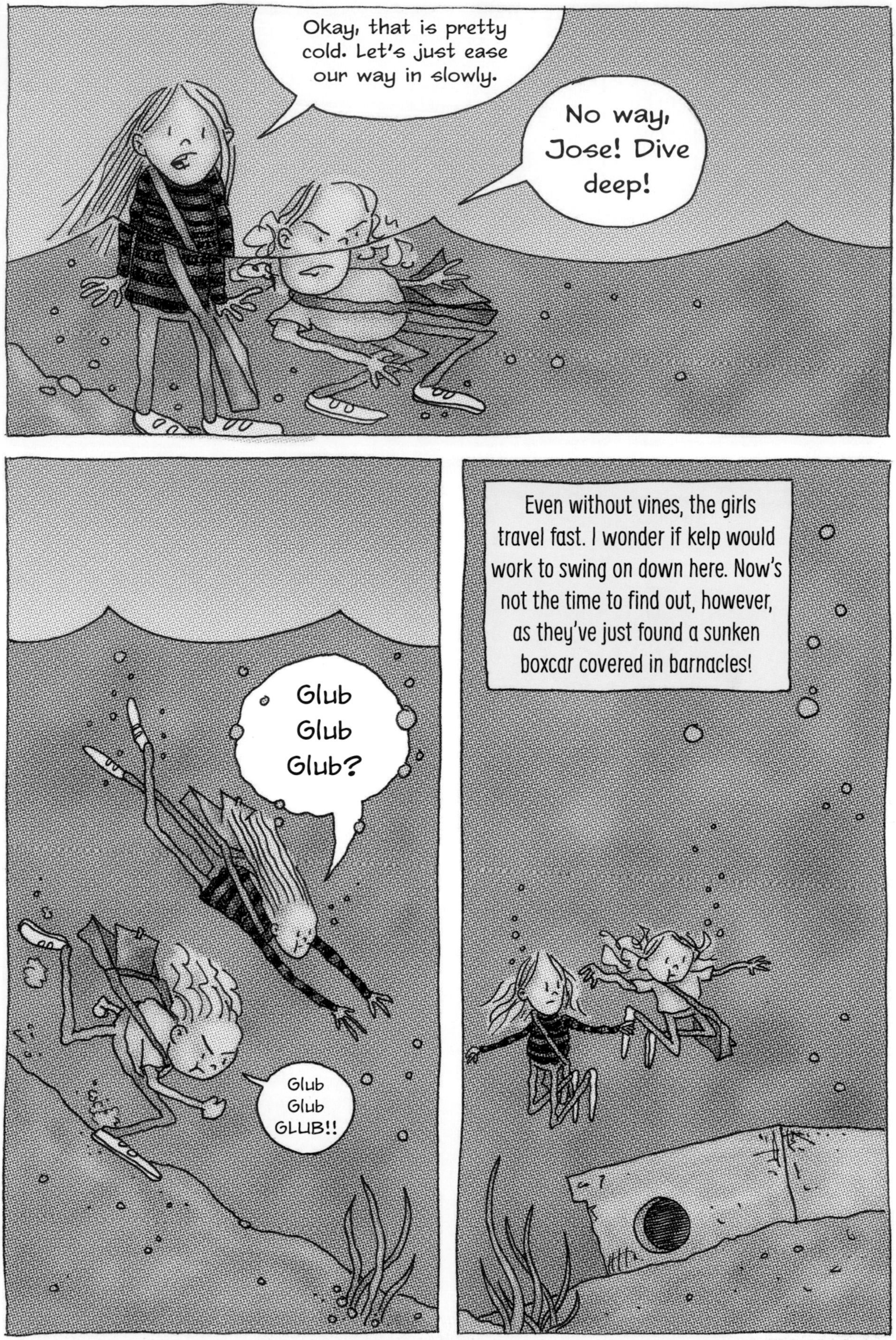
Okay, that is pretty cold. Let's just ease our way in slowly.
No way, Jose! Dive deep!
Glub Glub Glub?
Glub Glub GLUB!!
Even without vines, the girls travel fast. I wonder if kelp would work to swing on down here. Now's not the time to find out, however, as they've just found a sunken boxcar covered in barnacles!

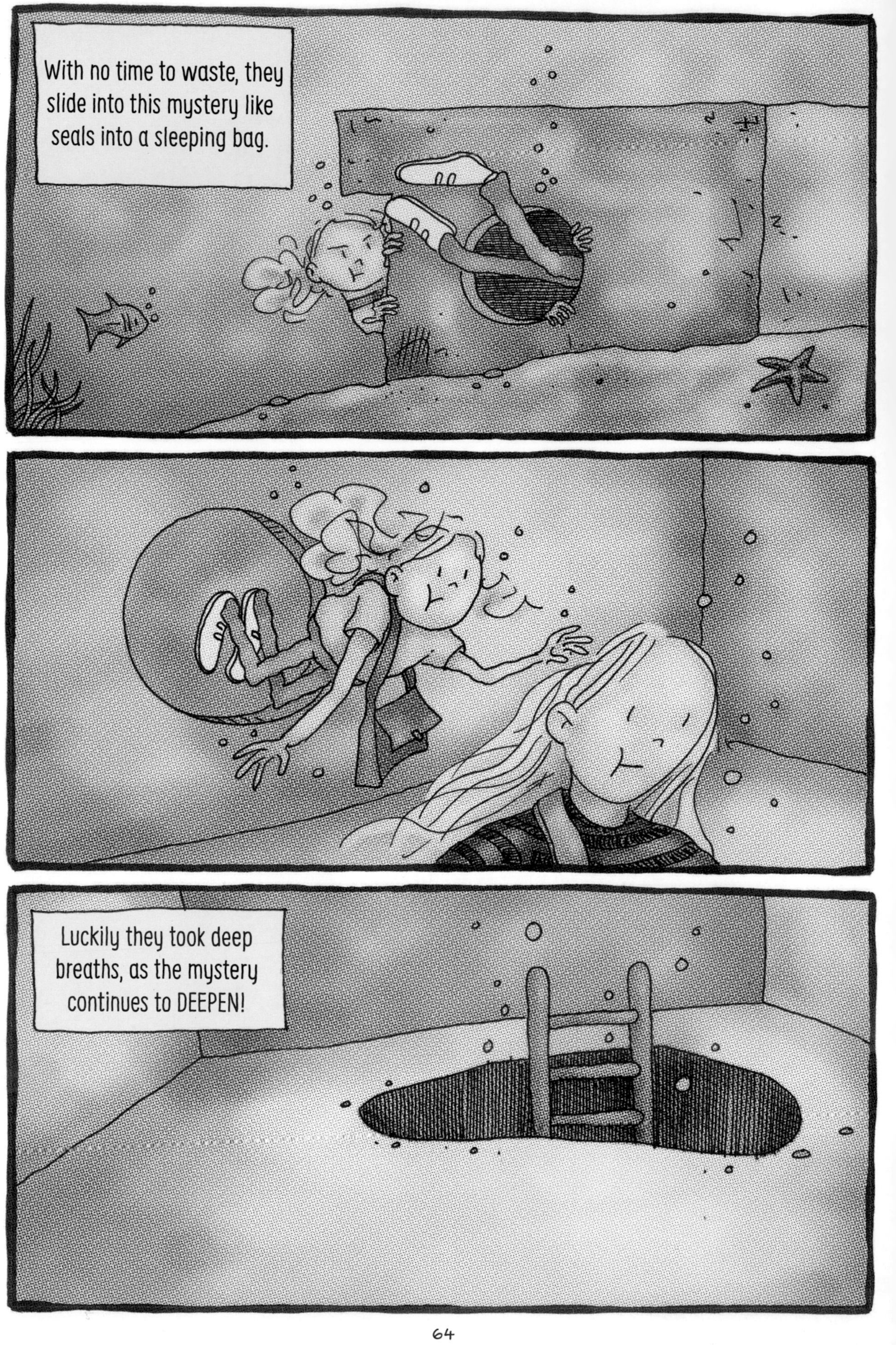
With no time to waste, they slide into this mystery like seals into a sleeping bag.
Luckily they took deep breaths, as the mystery continues to DEEPEN!

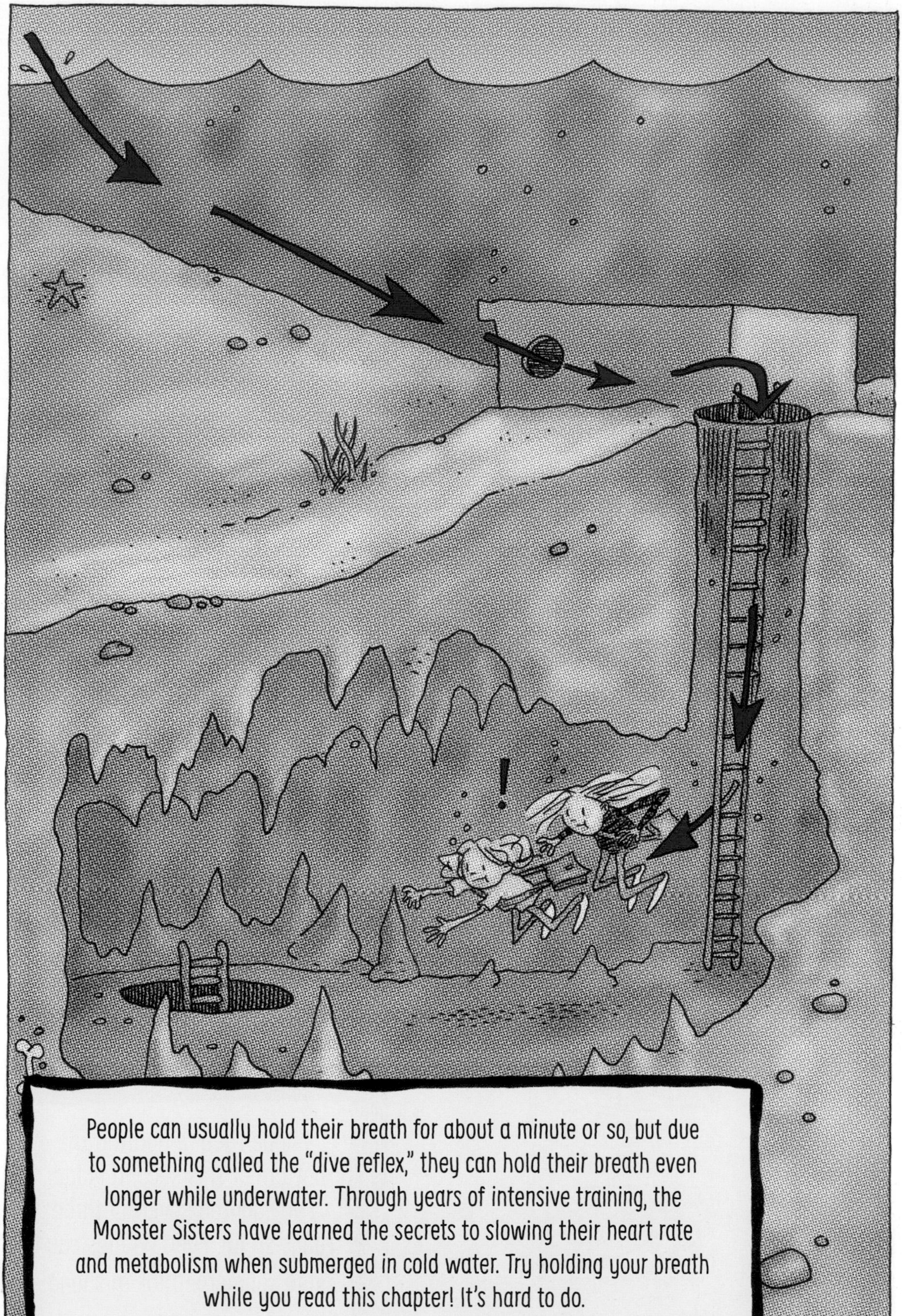
!
People can usually hold their breath for about a minute or so, but due to something called the "dive reflex," they can hold their breath even longer while underwater. Through years of intensive training, the Monster Sisters have learned the secrets to slowing their heart rate and metabolism when submerged in cold water. Try holding your breath while you read this chapter! It's hard to do.

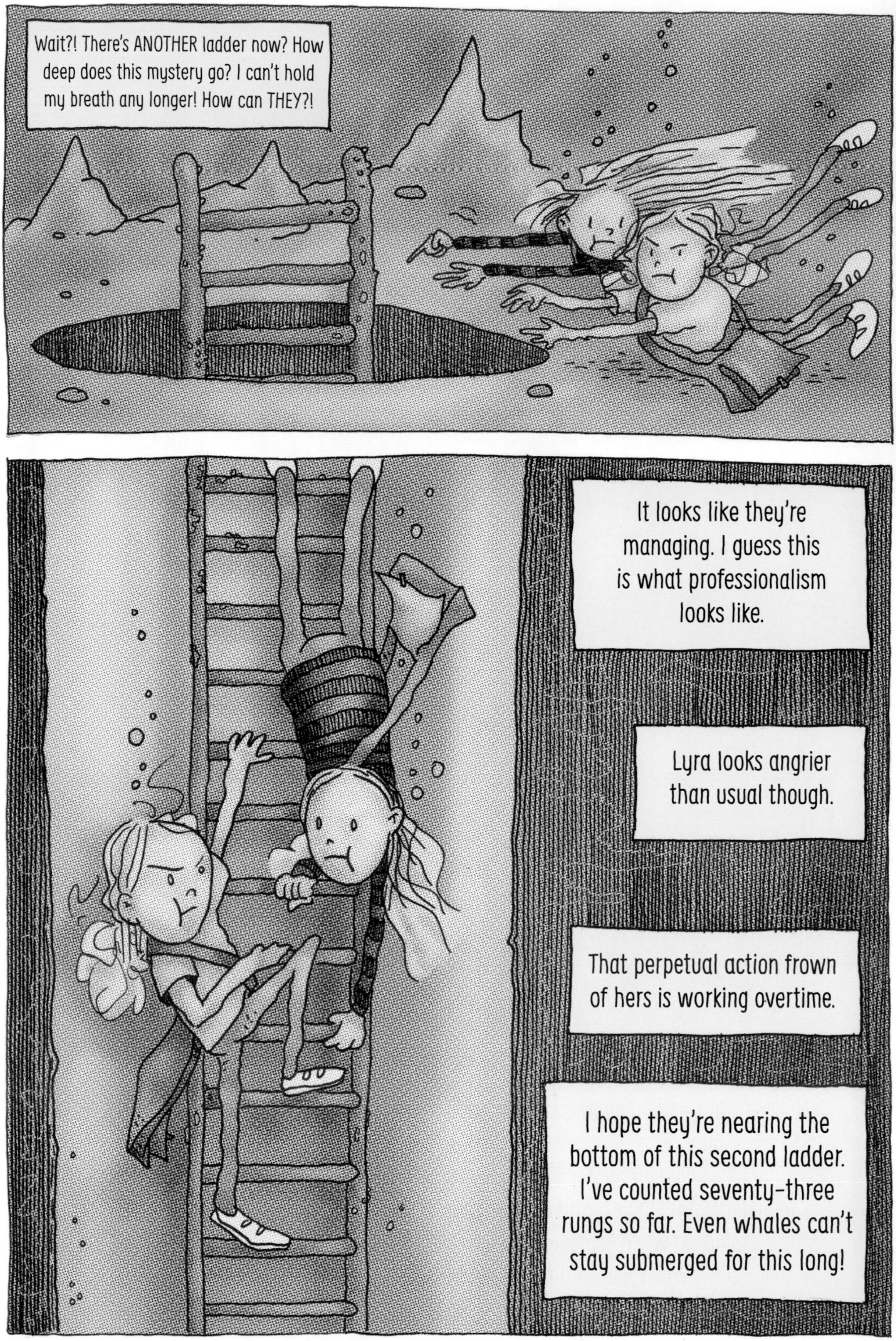
Wait?! There's ANOTHER ladder now? How deep does this mystery go? I can't hold my breath any longer! How can THEY?!
It looks like they're managing. I guess this is what professionalism looks like.
Lyra looks angrier than usual though.
That perpetual action frown of hers is working overtime.
I hope they're nearing the bottom of this second ladder. I've counted seventy-three rungs so far. Even whales can't stay submerged for this long!

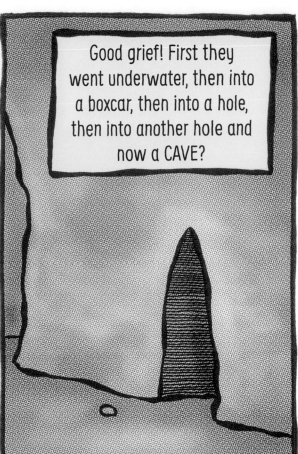

Good grief! First they went underwater, then into a boxcar, then into a hole, then into another hole and now a CAVE?

Girls! What are you doing? The farther you go, the farther it is to get back OUT!

I don't think they can hear me.

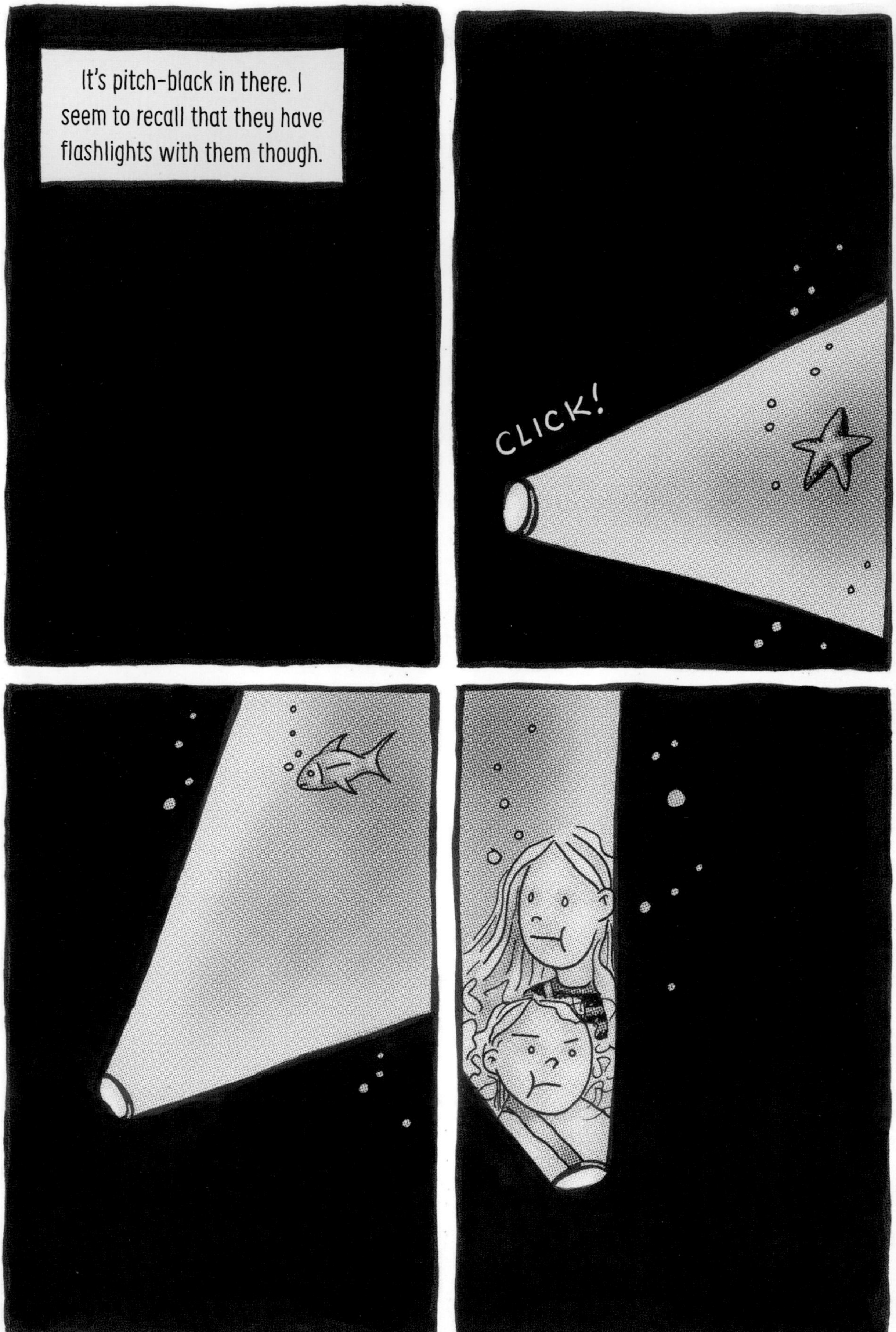
It's pitch-black in there. I seem to recall that they have flashlights with them though.
CLICK!

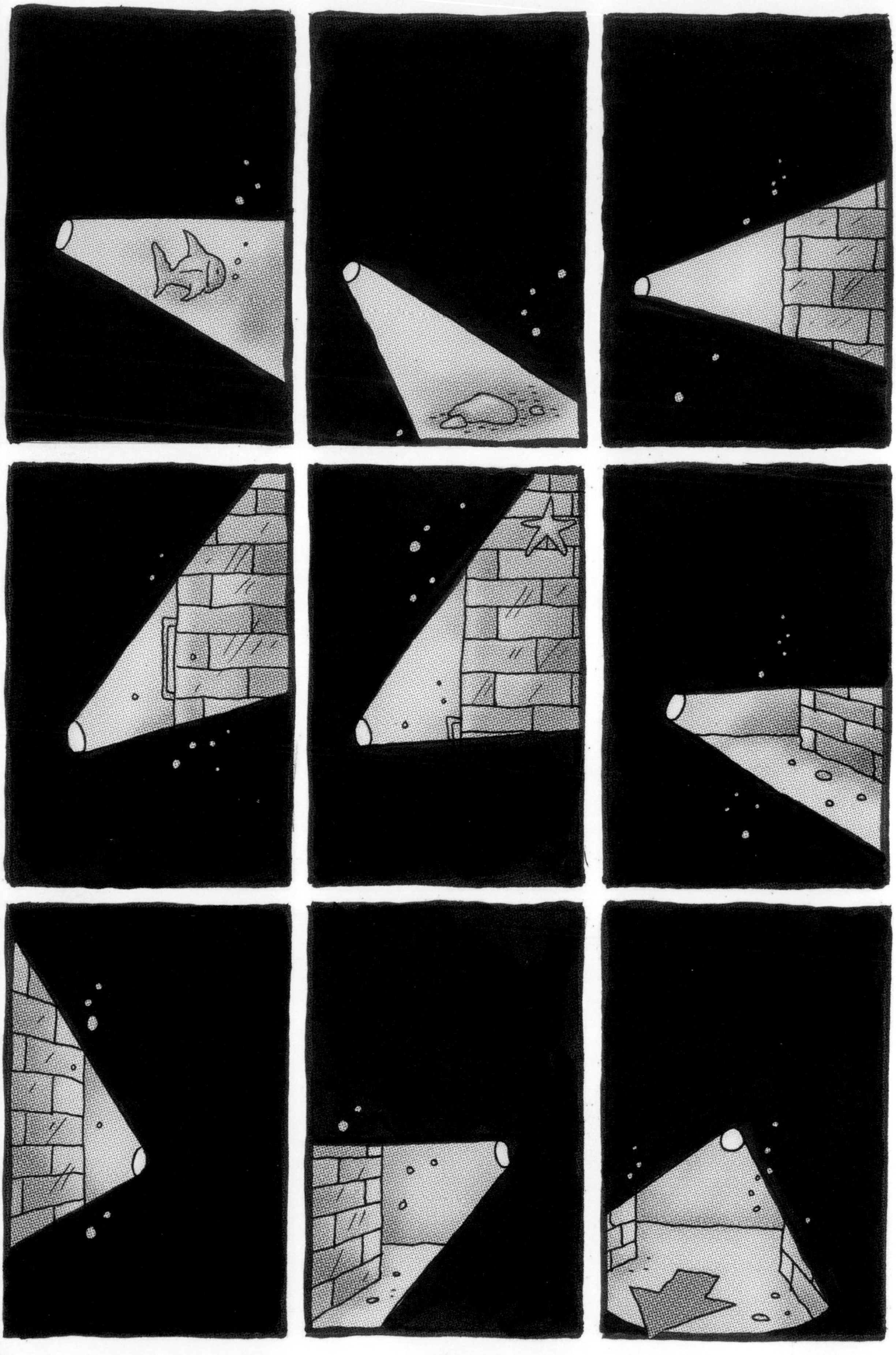

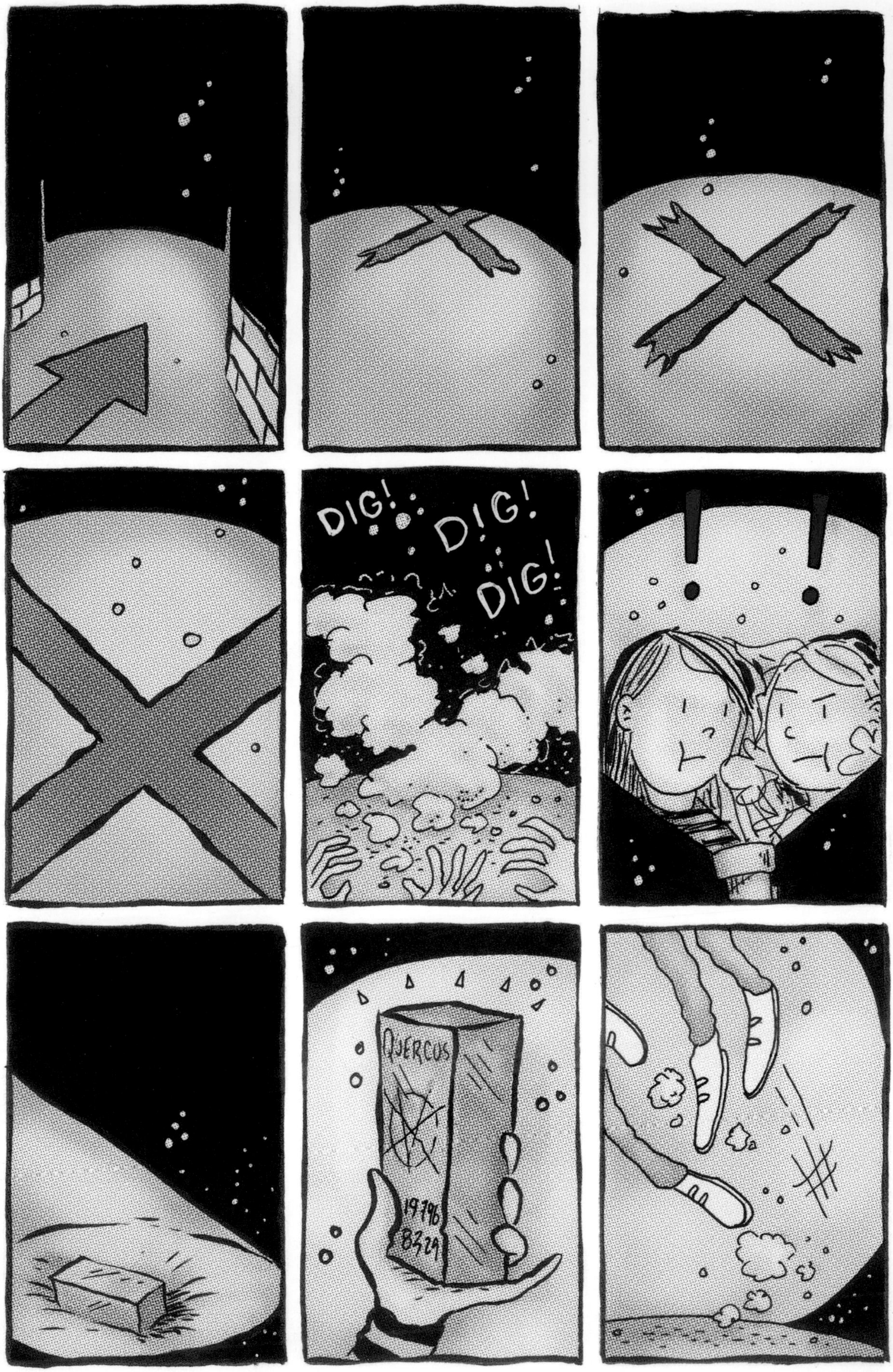
DIG! DIG! DIG!
QUERCUS
19796
8429

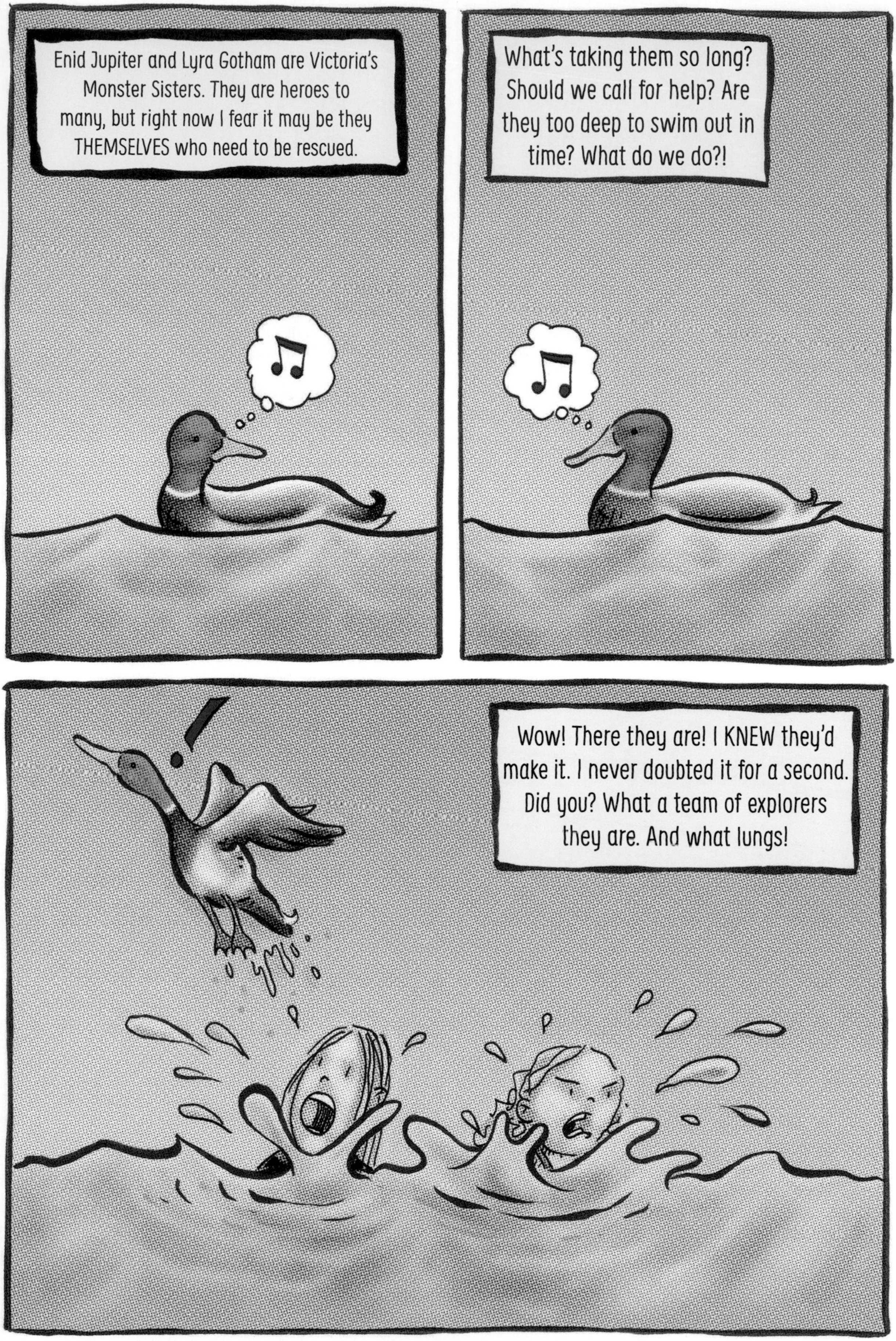
Enid Jupiter and Lyra Gotham are Victoria's Monster Sisters. They are heroes to many, but right now I fear it may be they THEMSELVES who need to be rescued.
What's taking them so long? Should we call for help? Are they too deep to swim out in time? What do we do?!
Wow! There they are! I KNEW they'd make it. I never doubted it for a second. Did you? What a team of explorers they are. And what lungs!

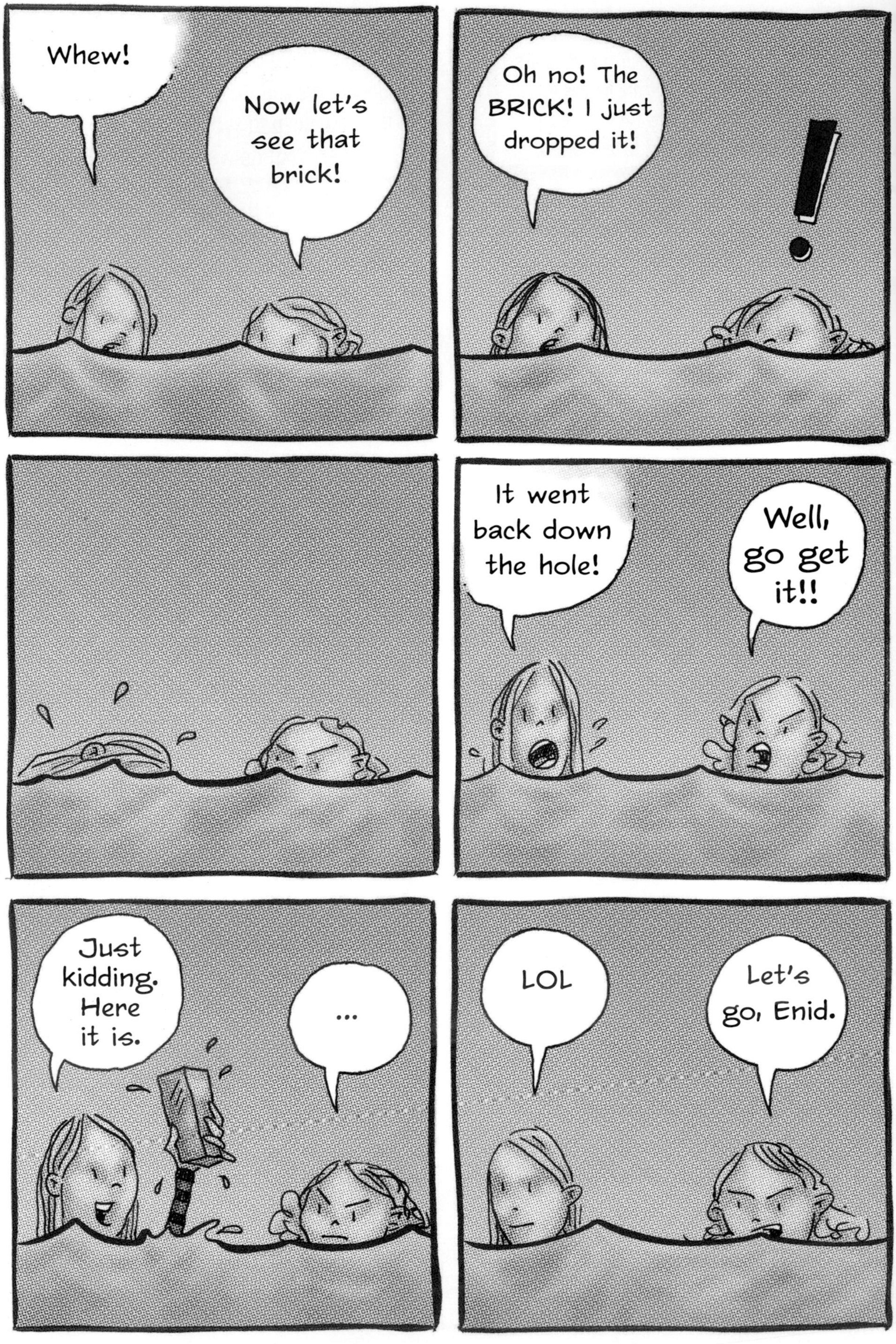
Whew!
Now let's see that brick!
Oh no! The BRICK! I just dropped it!
!
It went back down the hole!
Well, go get it!!
Just kidding. Here it is.
...
LOL
Let's go, Enid.

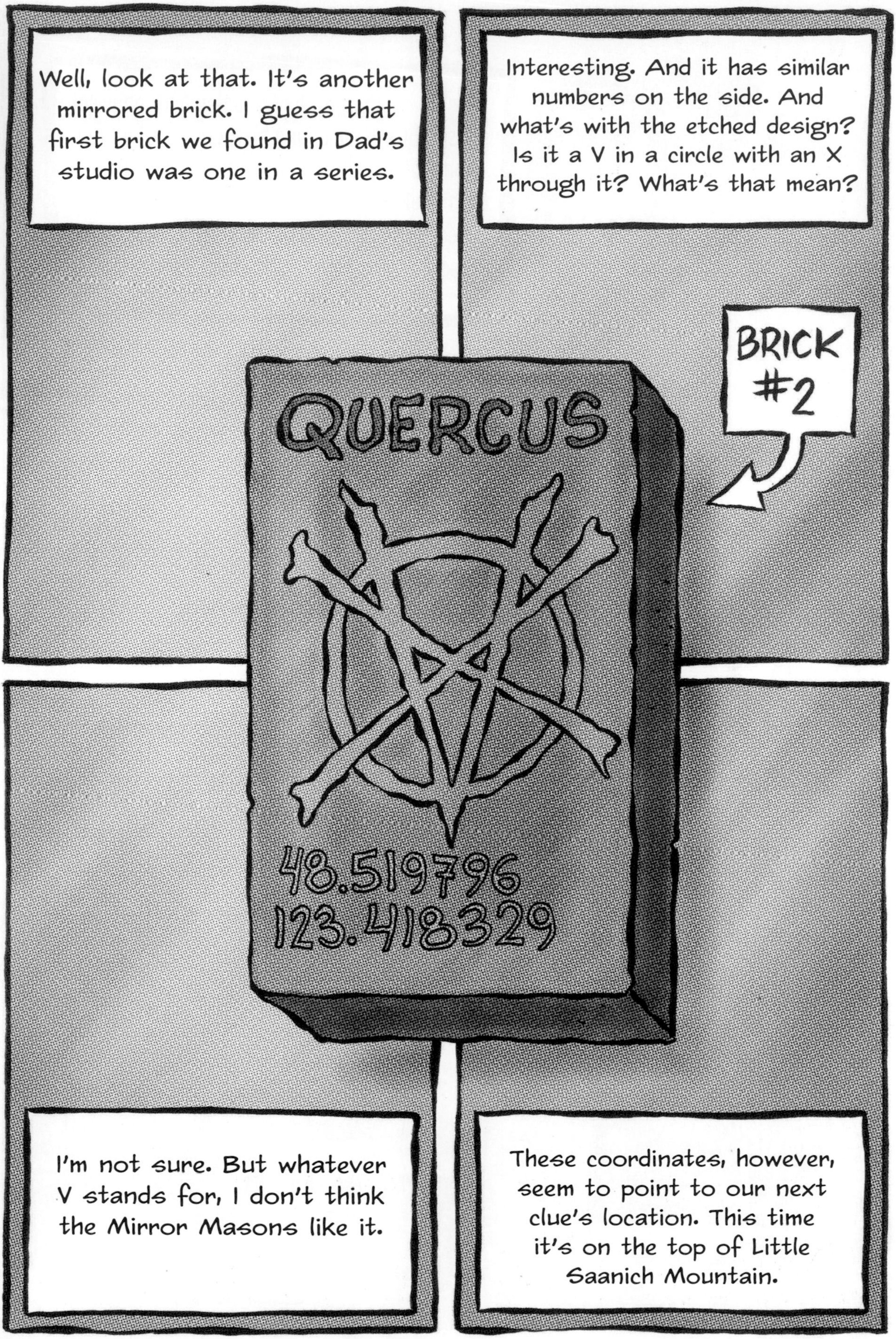

Well, look at that. It's another mirrored brick. I guess that first brick we found in Dad's studio was one in a series.
Interesting. And it has similar numbers on the side. And what's with the etched design? Is it a V in a circle with an X through it? What's that mean?
BRICK #2
QUERCUS
48.519796
123.418329
I'm not sure. But whatever V stands for, I don't think the Mirror Masons like it.
These coordinates, however, seem to point to our next clue's location. This time it's on the top of Little Saanich Mountain.

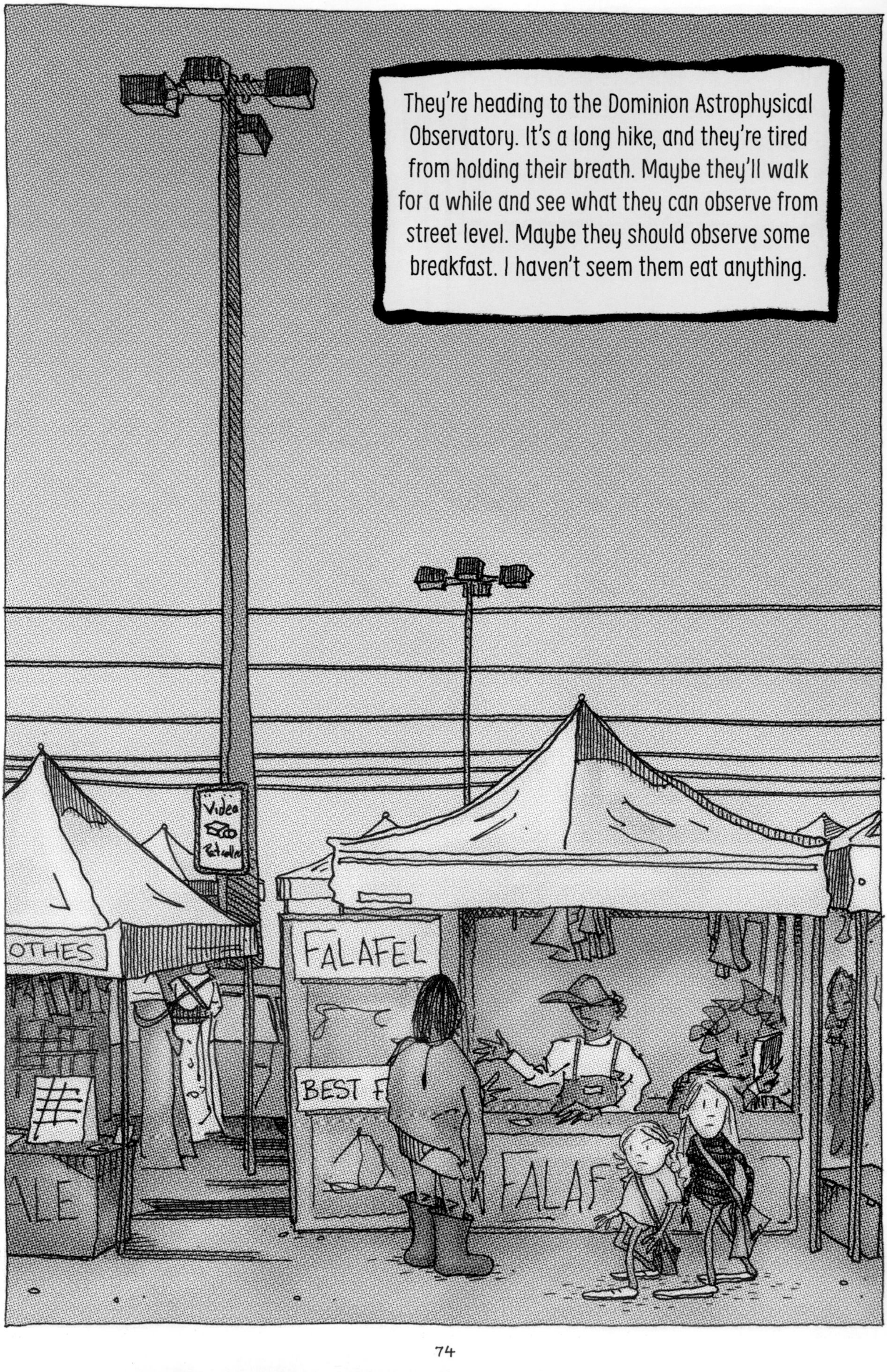
They're heading to the Dominion Astrophysical Observatory. It's a long hike, and they're tired from holding their breath. Maybe they'll walk for a while and see what they can observe from street level. Maybe they should observe some breakfast. I haven't seem them eat anything.
Video
OTHES
FALAFEL
BEST F
FALAF
LE

CHAPTER FOUR

OBSERVATORY LABORATORY

4

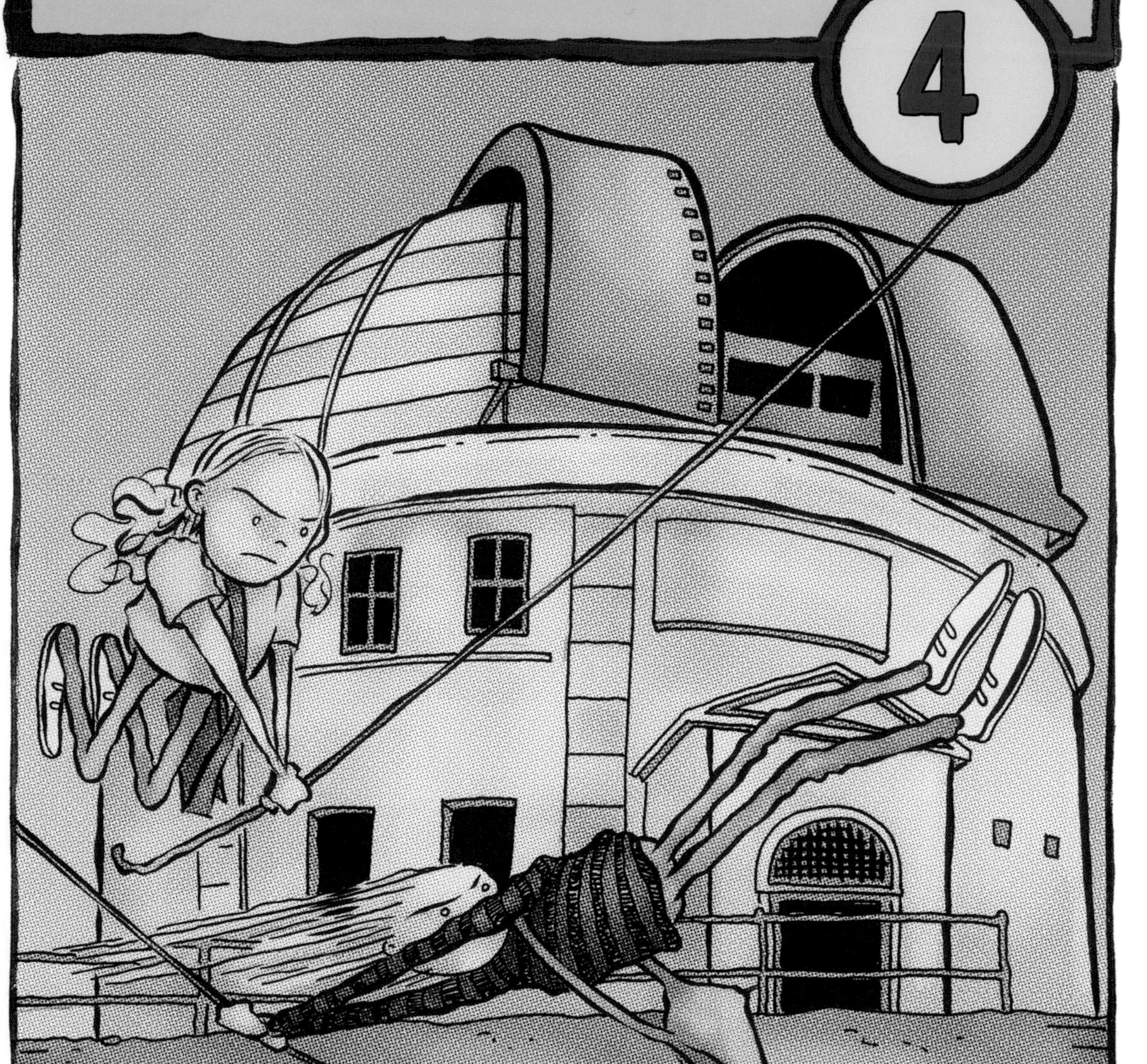

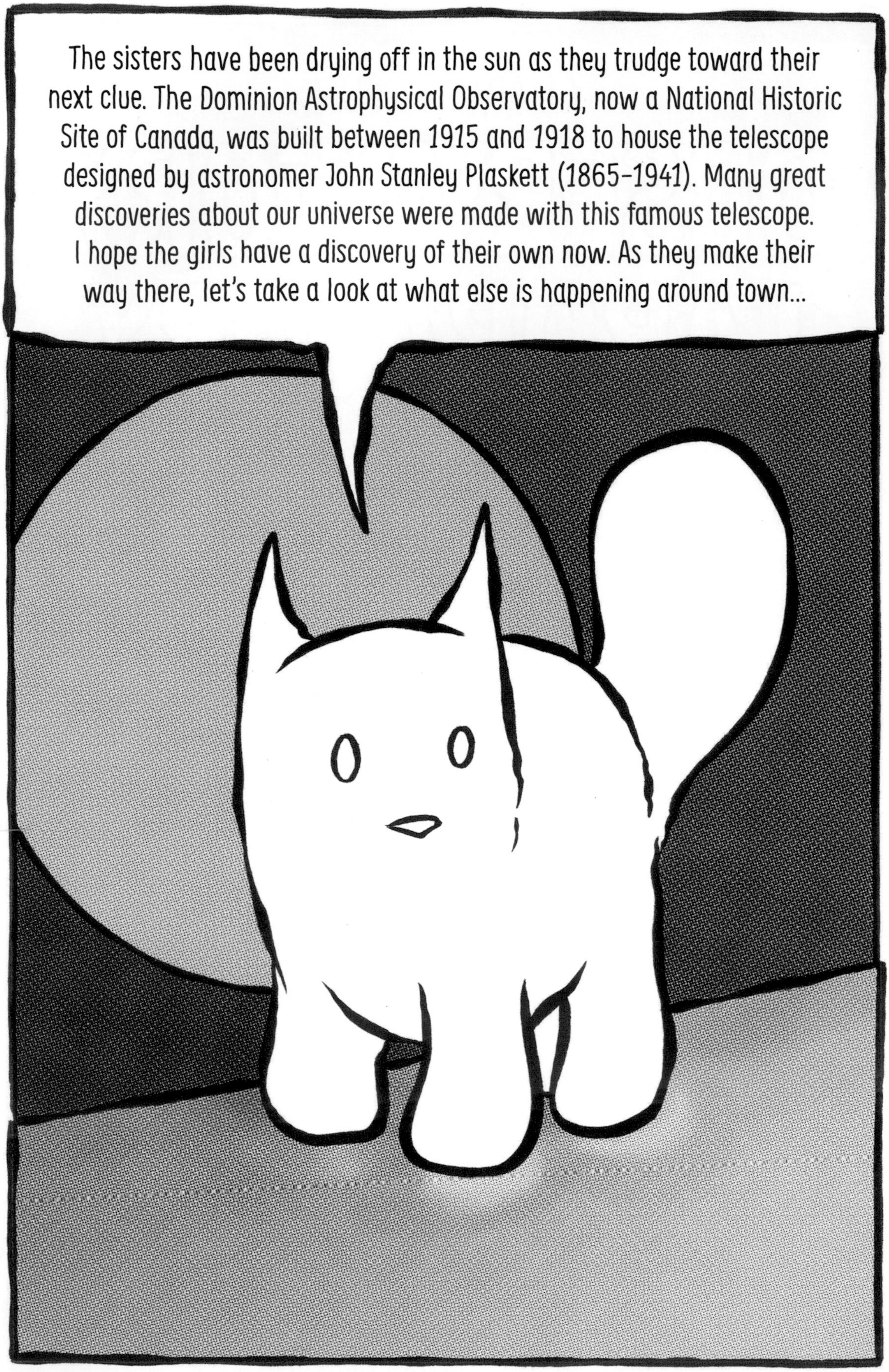
The sisters have been drying off in the sun as they trudge toward their next clue. The Dominion Astrophysical Observatory, now a National Historic Site of Canada, was built between 1915 and 1918 to house the telescope designed by astronomer John Stanley Plaskett (1865–1941). Many great discoveries about our universe were made with this famous telescope. I hope the girls have a discovery of their own now. As they make their way there, let's take a look at what else is happening around town...

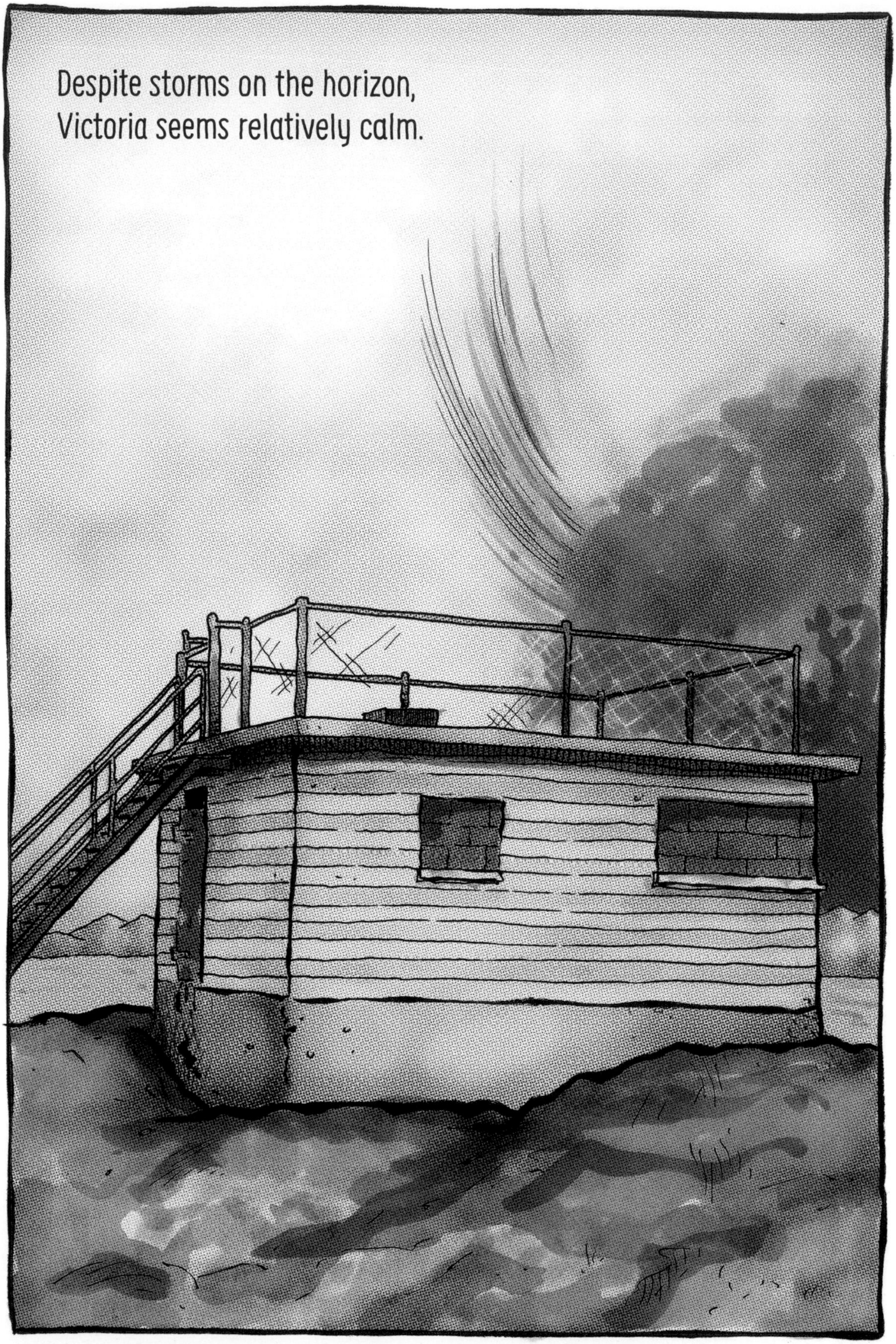
Despite storms on the horizon,
Victoria seems relatively calm.

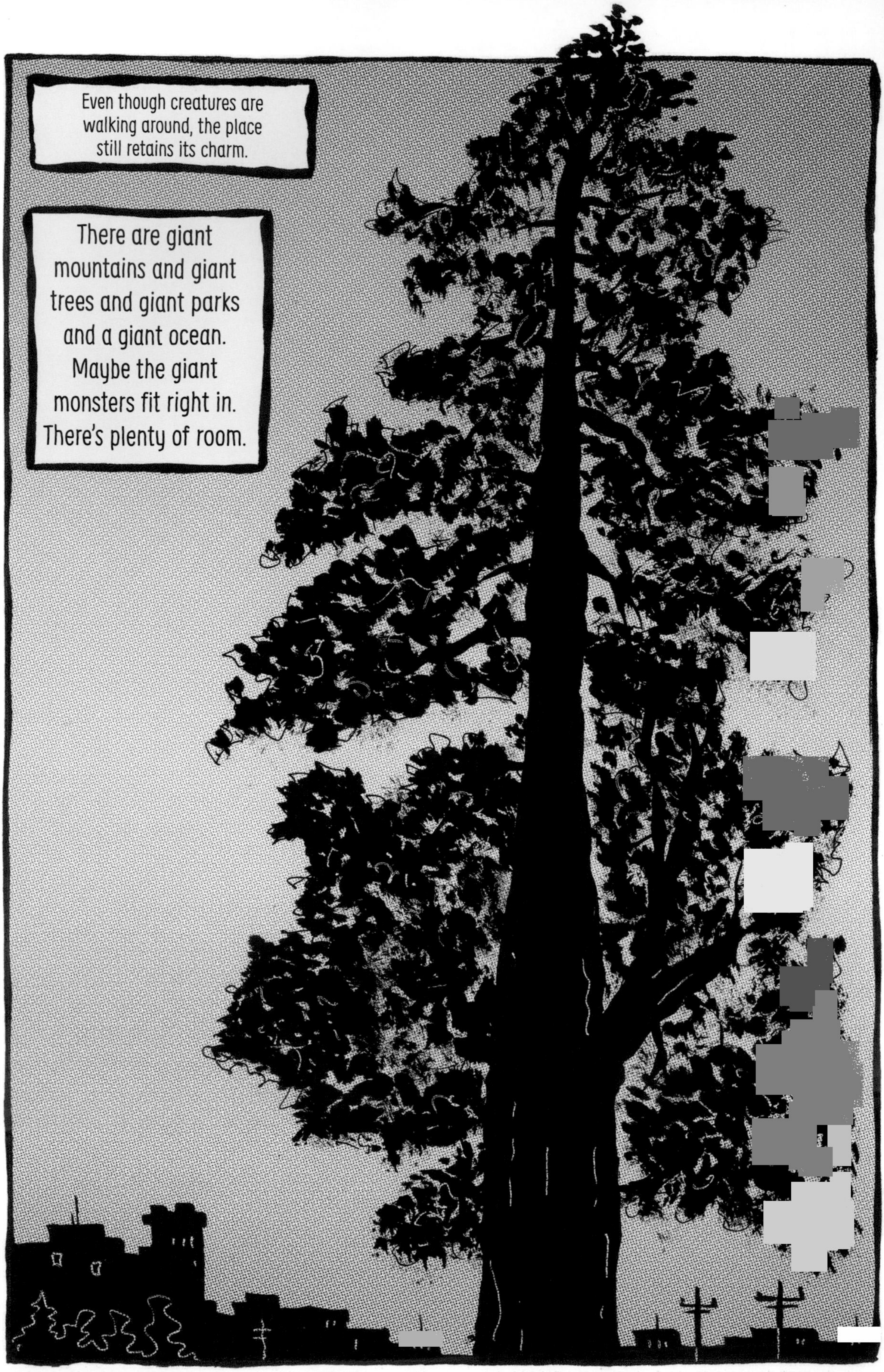
Even though creatures are walking around, the place still retains its charm.
There are giant mountains and giant trees and giant parks and a giant ocean. Maybe the giant monsters fit right in. There's plenty of room.

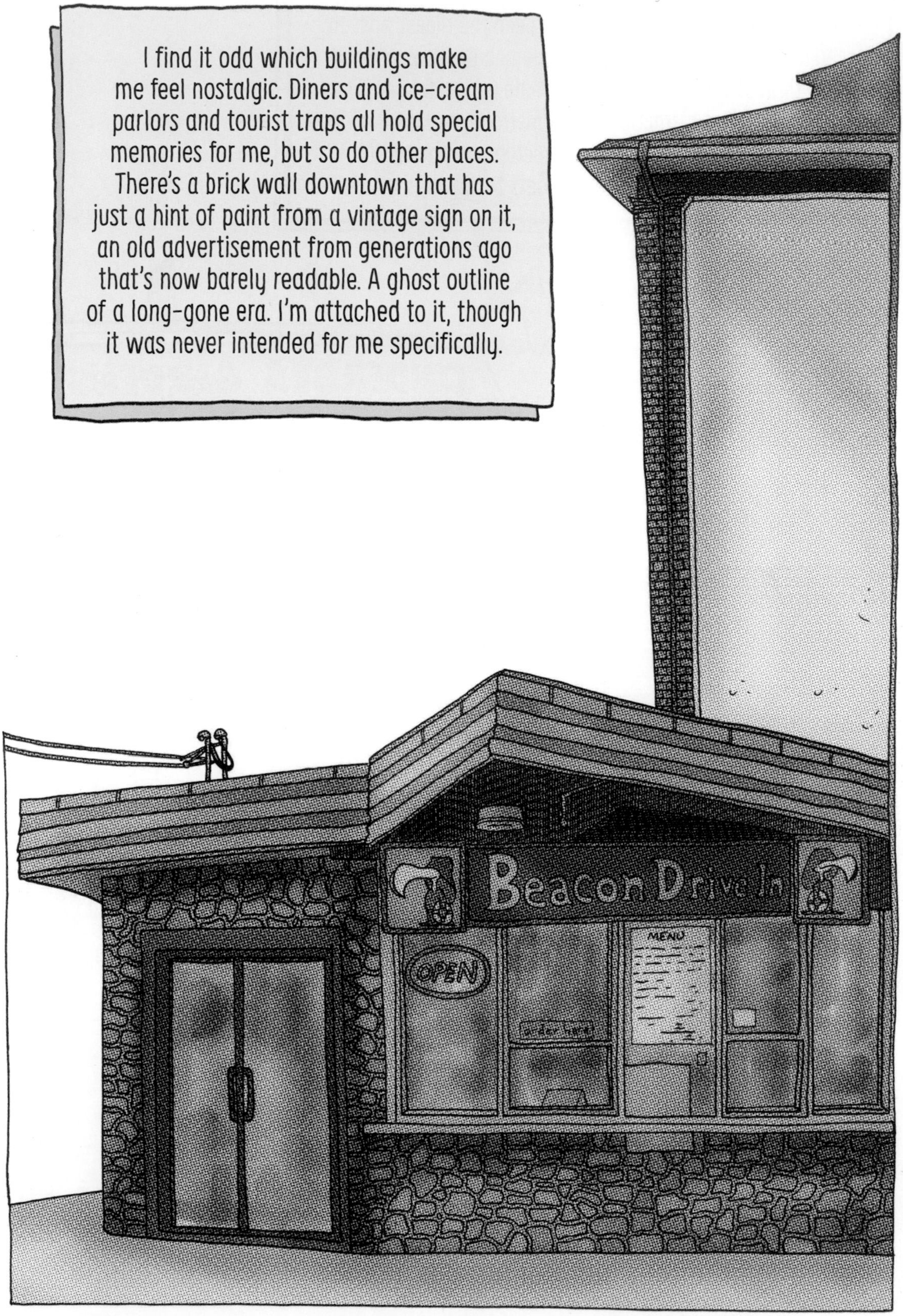
I find it odd which buildings make me feel nostalgic. Diners and ice-cream parlors and tourist traps all hold special memories for me, but so do other places. There's a brick wall downtown that has just a hint of paint from a vintage sign on it, an old advertisement from generations ago that's now barely readable. A ghost outline of a long-gone era. I'm attached to it, though it was never intended for me specifically.
Beacon Drive In
OPEN
MENU

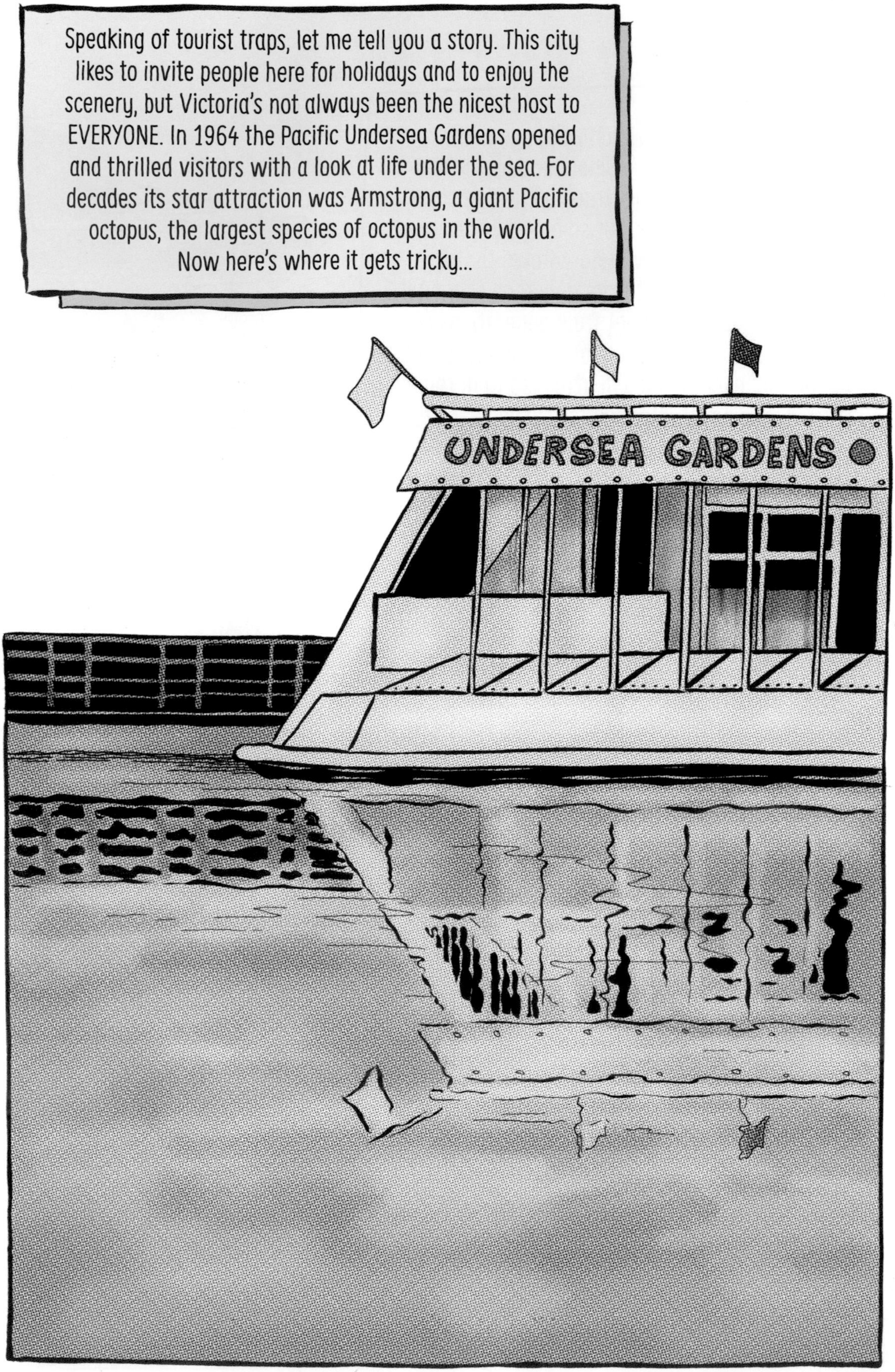
Speaking of tourist traps, let me tell you a story. This city likes to invite people here for holidays and to enjoy the scenery, but Victoria's not always been the nicest host to EVERYONE. In 1964 the Pacific Undersea Gardens opened and thrilled visitors with a look at life under the sea. For decades its star attraction was Armstrong, a giant Pacific octopus, the largest species of octopus in the world. Now here's where it gets tricky...
UNDERSEA GARDENS

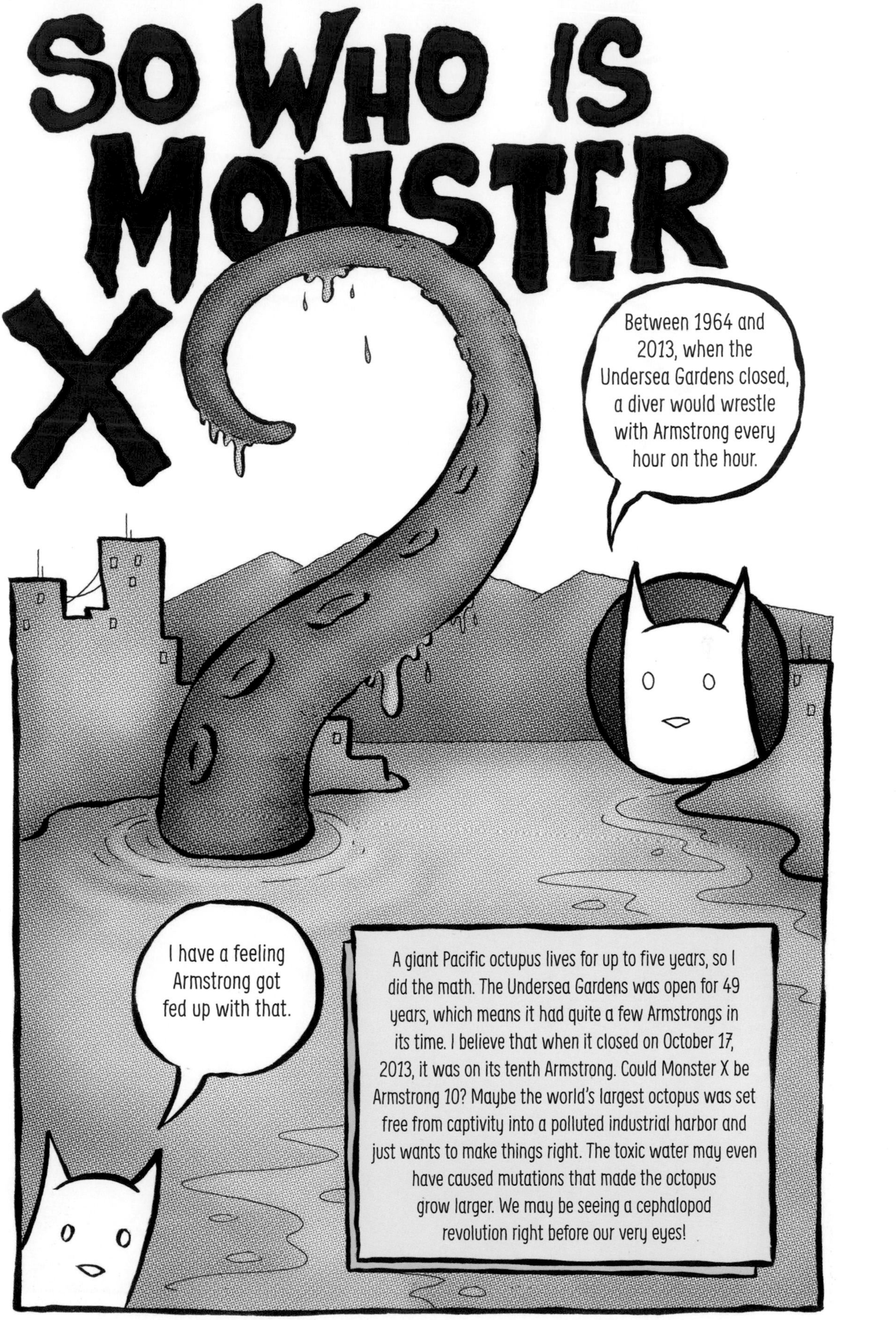
SO WHO IS MONSTER X?
Between 1964 and 2013, when the Undersea Gardens closed, a diver would wrestle with Armstrong every hour on the hour.
I have a feeling Armstrong got fed up with that.
A giant Pacific octopus lives for up to five years, so I did the math. The Undersea Gardens was open for 49 years, which means it had quite a few Armstrongs in its time. I believe that when it closed on October 17, 2013, it was on its tenth Armstrong. Could Monster X be Armstrong 10? Maybe the world's largest octopus was set free from captivity into a polluted industrial harbor and just wants to make things right. The toxic water may even have caused mutations that made the octopus grow larger. We may be seeing a cephalopod revolution right before our very eyes!

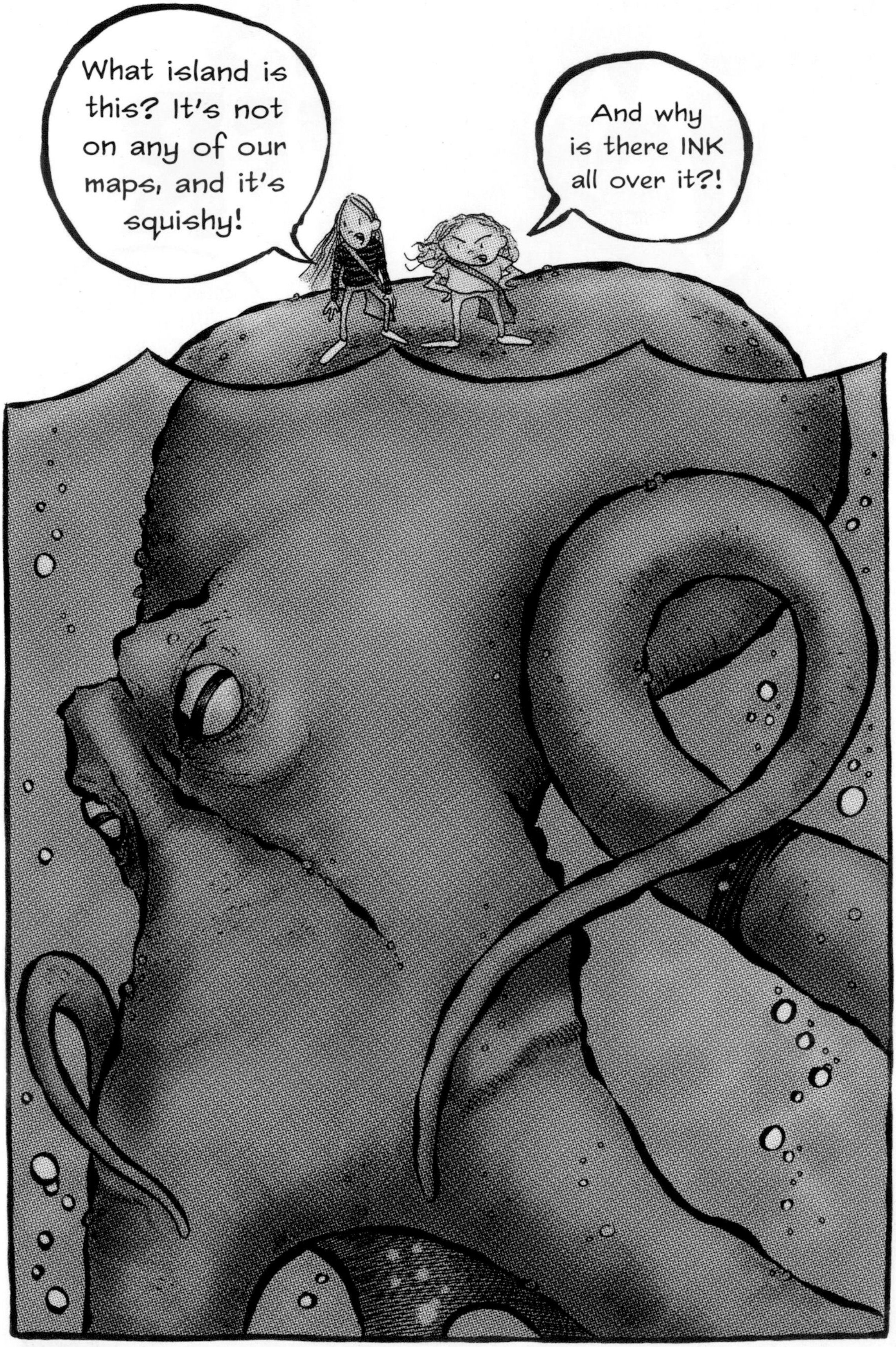
What island is this? It's not on any of our maps, and it's squishy!
And why is there INK all over it?!

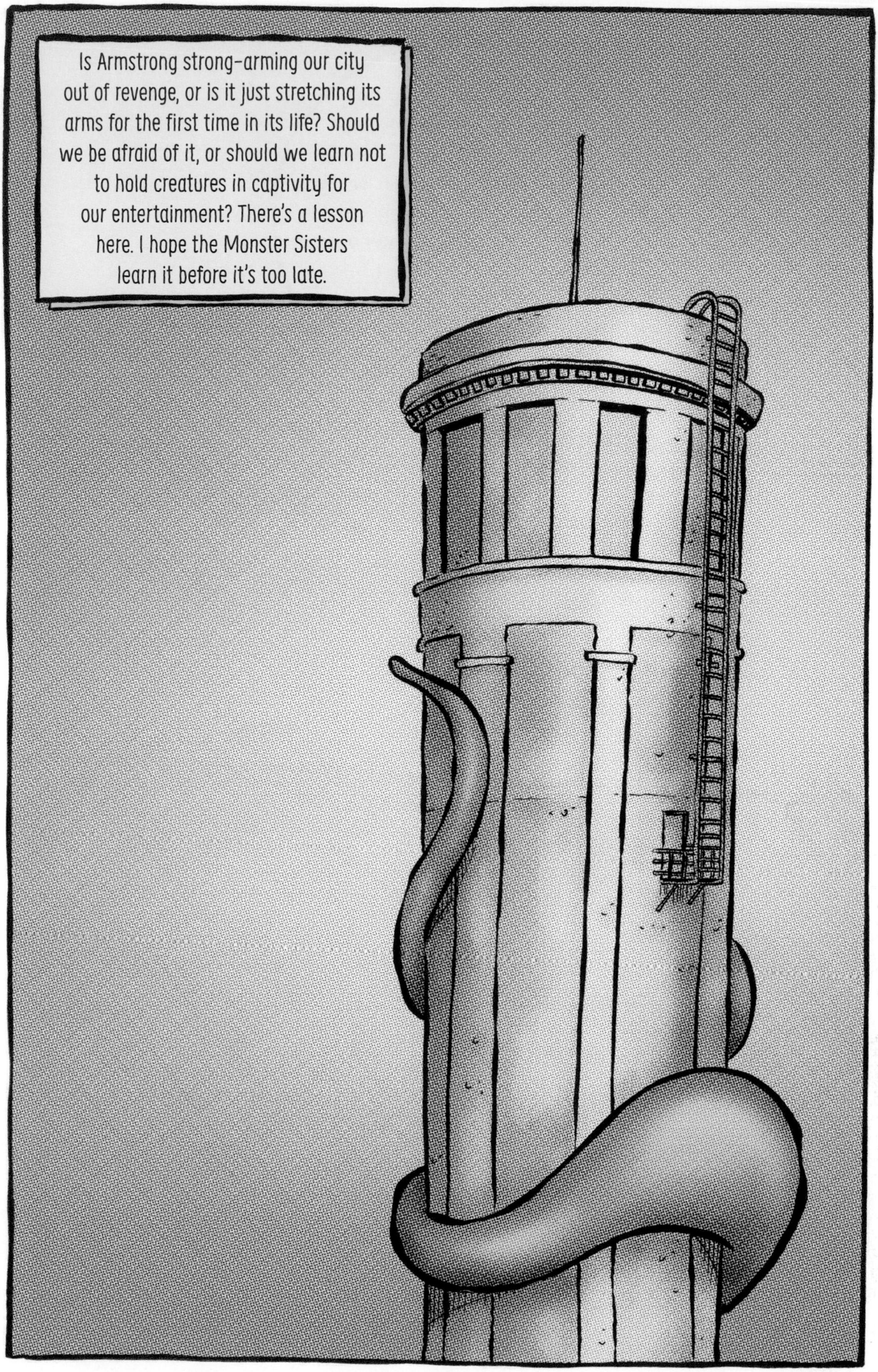
Is Armstrong strong-arming our city out of revenge, or is it just stretching its arms for the first time in its life? Should we be afraid of it, or should we learn not to hold creatures in captivity for our entertainment? There's a lesson here. I hope the Monster Sisters learn it before it's too late.

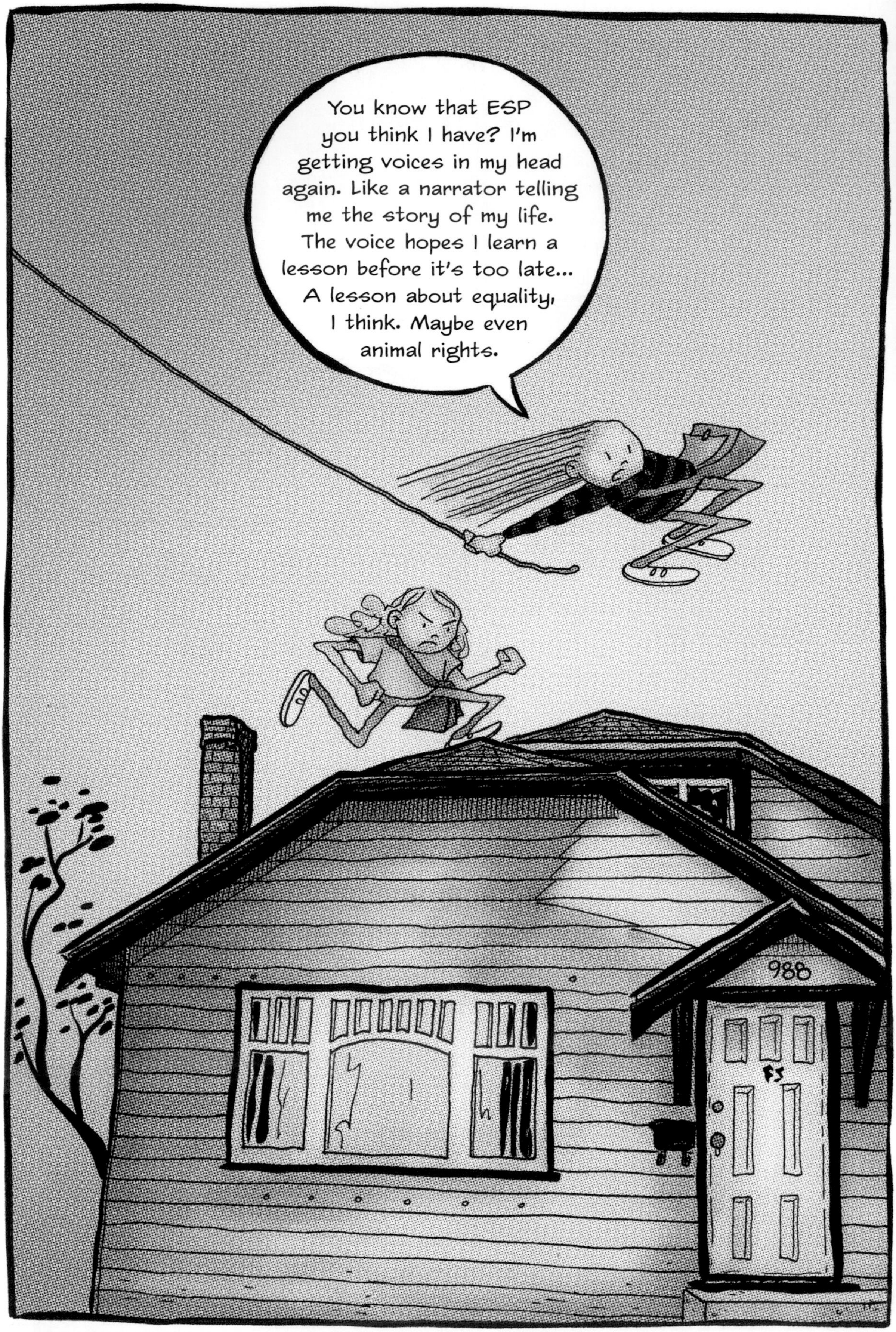
You know that ESP you think I have? I'm getting voices in my head again. Like a narrator telling me the story of my life. The voice hopes I learn a lesson before it's too late... A lesson about equality, I think. Maybe even animal rights.
988

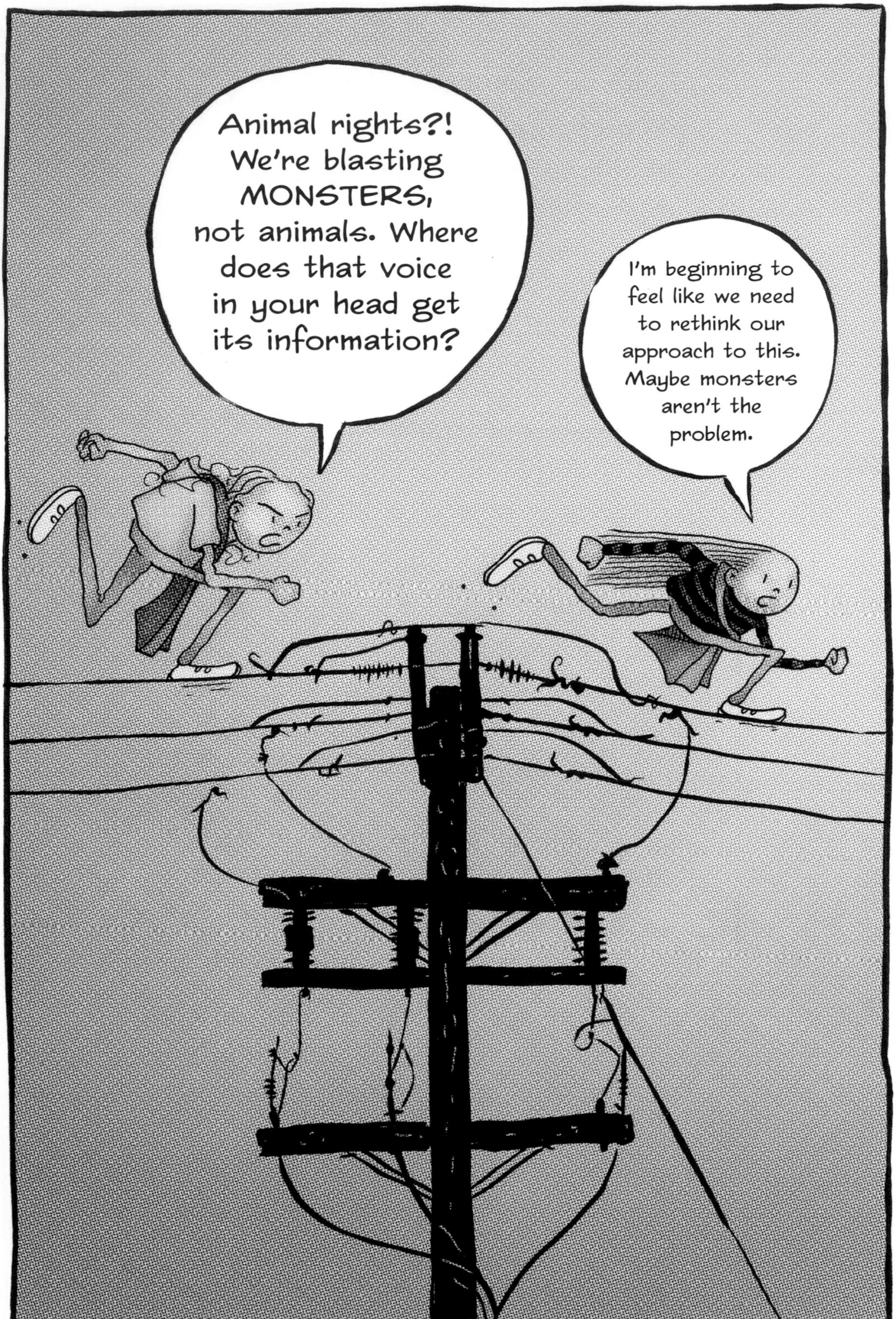
Animal rights?! We're blasting MONSTERS, not animals. Where does that voice in your head get its information?
I'm beginning to feel like we need to rethink our approach to this. Maybe monsters aren't the problem.

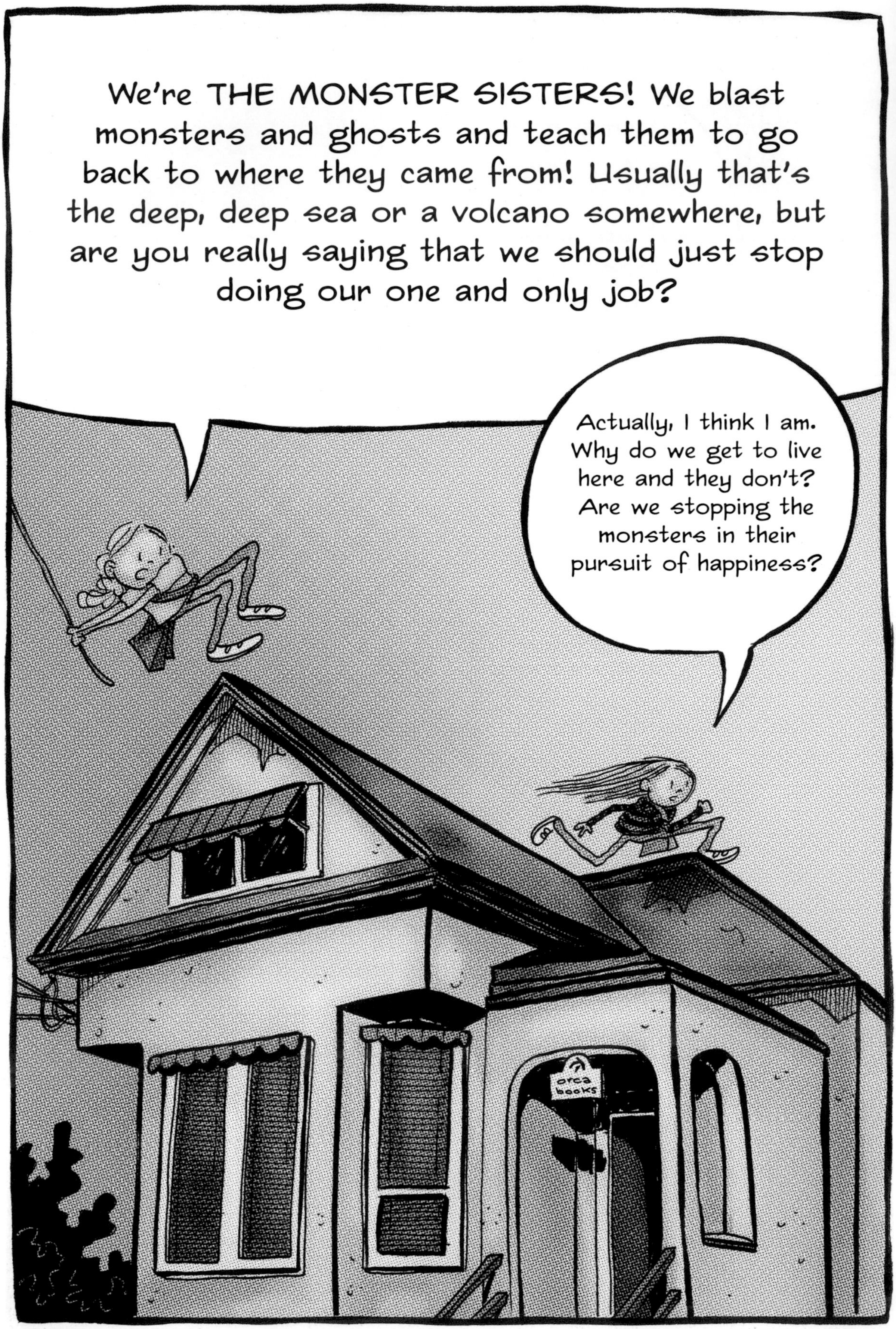
We're THE MONSTER SISTERS! We blast monsters and ghosts and teach them to go back to where they came from! Usually that's the deep, deep sea or a volcano somewhere, but are you really saying that we should just stop doing our one and only job?
Actually, I think I am. Why do we get to live here and they don't? Are we stopping the monsters in their pursuit of happiness?
orca books

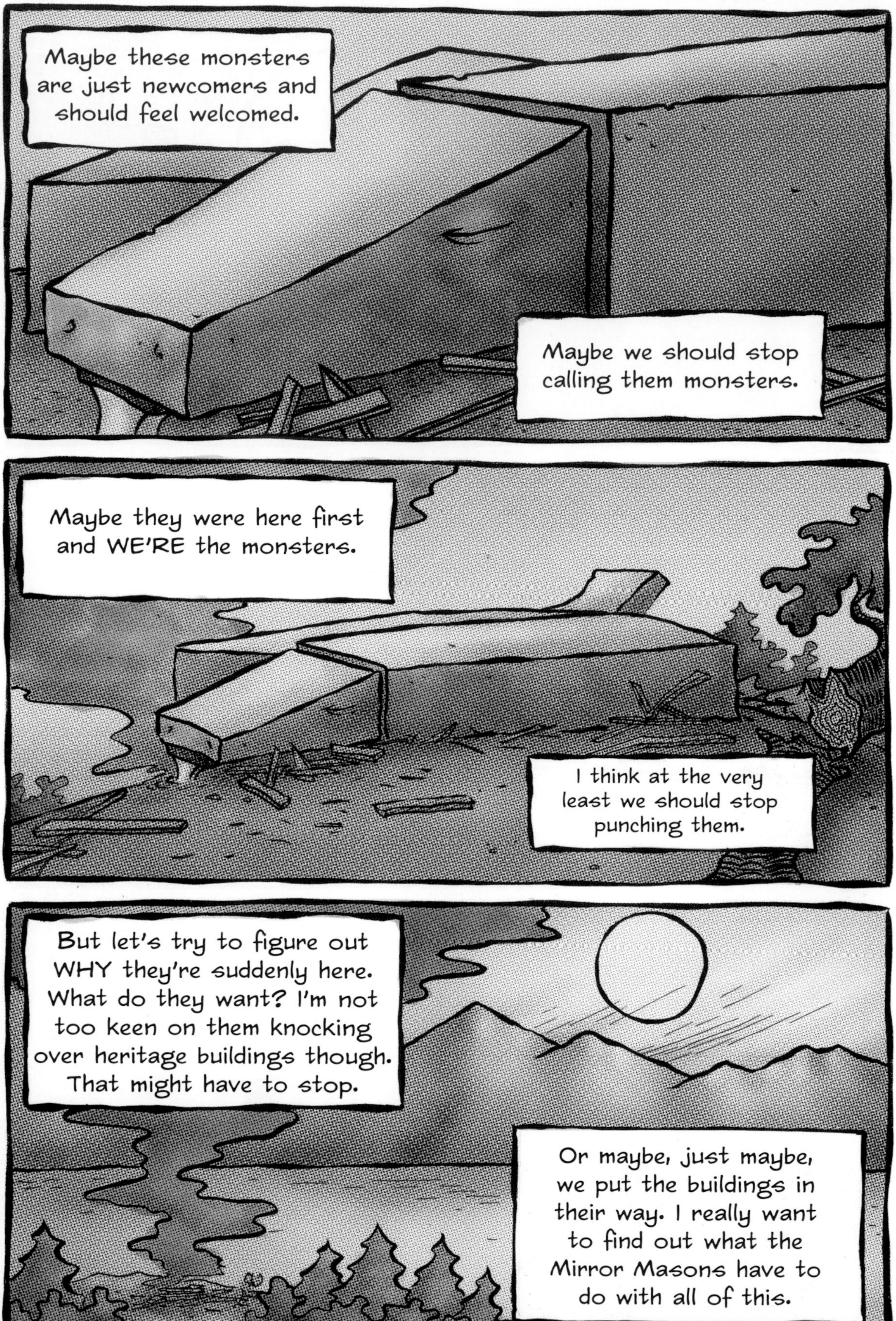
Maybe these monsters are just newcomers and should feel welcomed.
Maybe we should stop calling them monsters.
Maybe they were here first and WE'RE the monsters.
I think at the very least we should stop punching them.
But let's try to figure out WHY they're suddenly here. What do they want? I'm not too keen on them knocking over heritage buildings though. That might have to stop.
Or maybe, just maybe, we put the buildings in their way. I really want to find out what the Mirror Masons have to do with all of this.

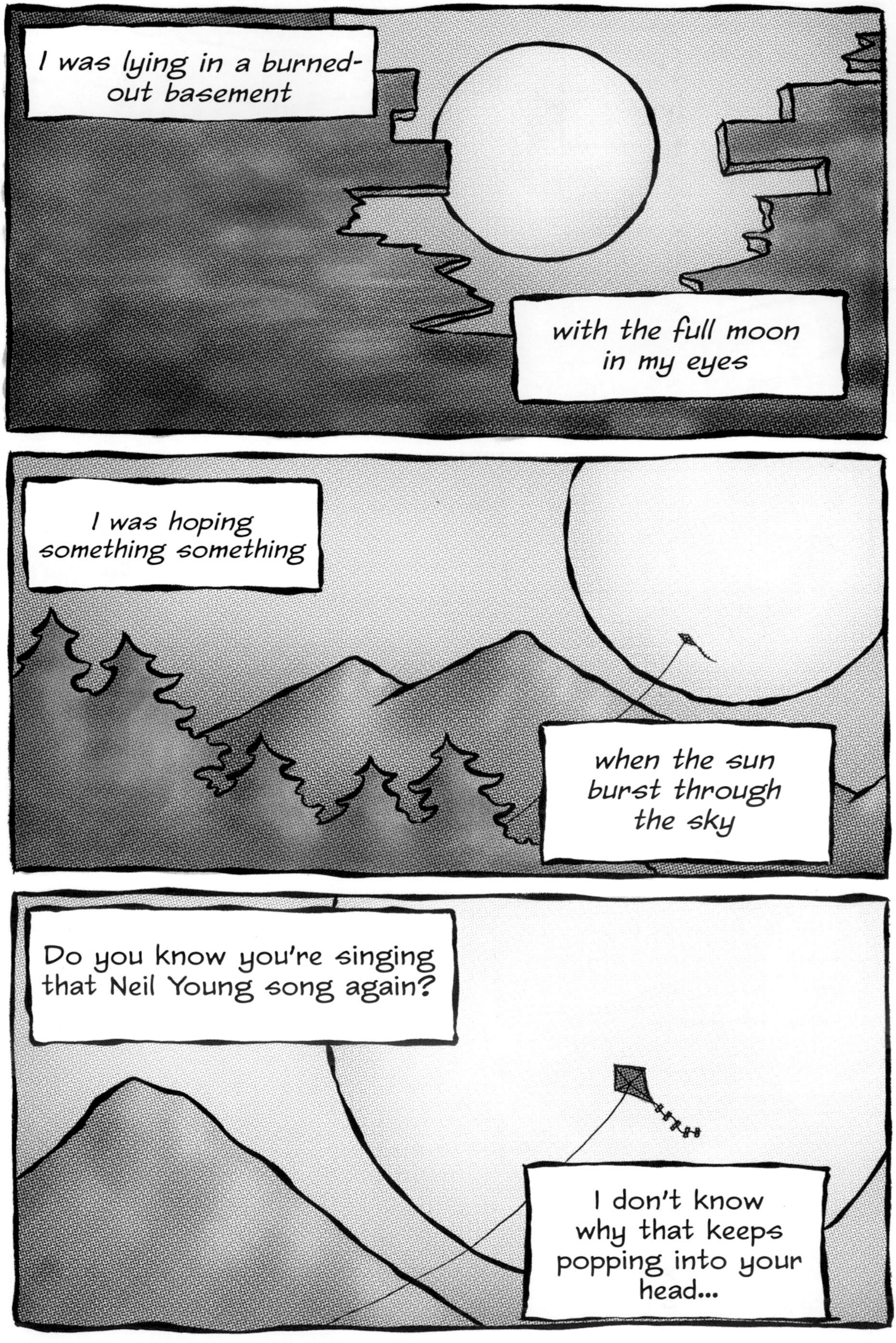
I was lying in a burned-out basement
with the full moon in my eyes
I was hoping something something
when the sun burst through the sky
Do you know you're singing that Neil Young song again?
I don't know why that keeps popping into your head...

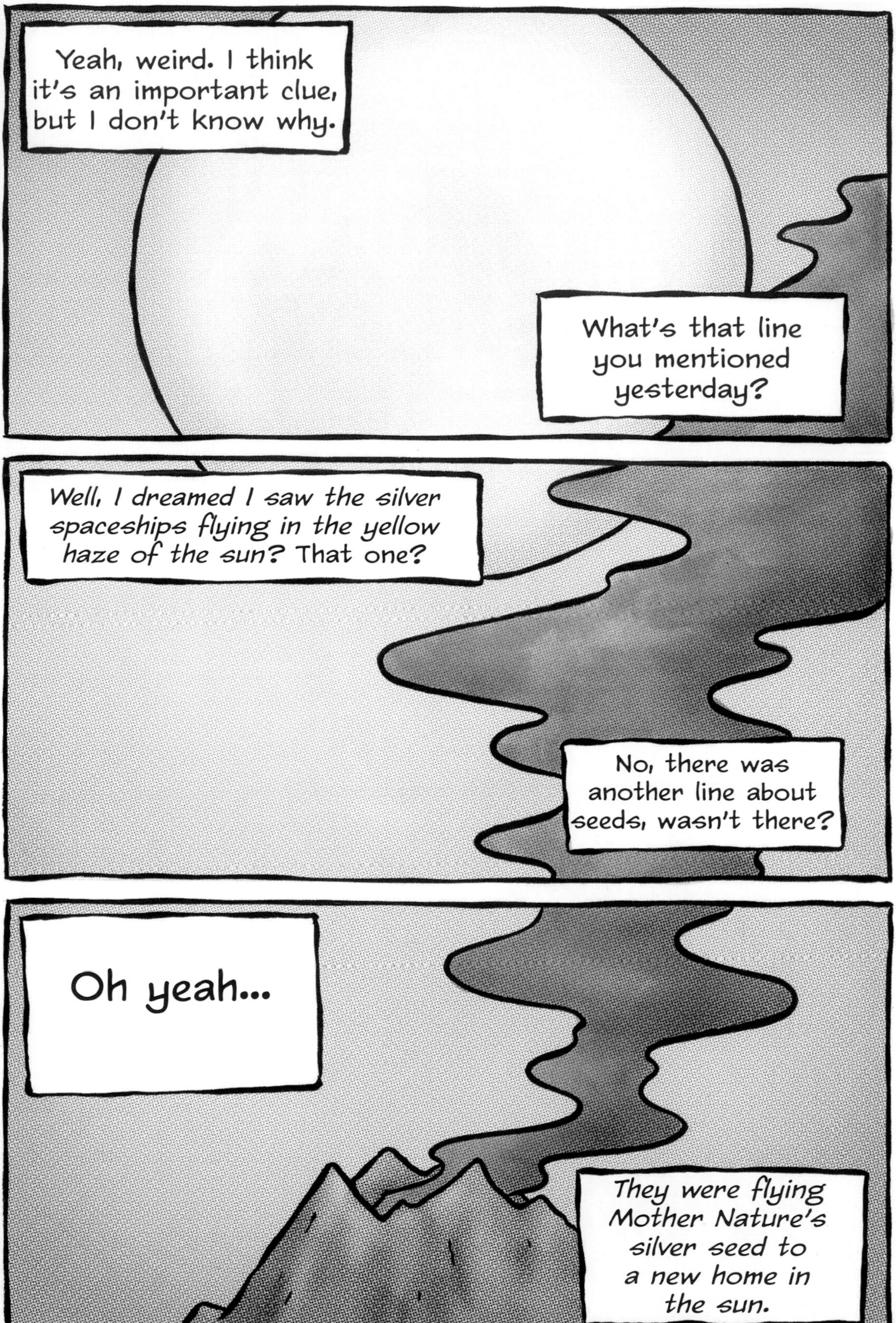
Yeah, weird. I think it's an important clue, but I don't know why.
What's that line you mentioned yesterday?
Well, I dreamed I saw the silver spaceships flying in the yellow haze of the sun? That one?
No, there was another line about seeds, wasn't there?
Oh yeah...
They were flying Mother Nature's silver seed to a new home in the sun.

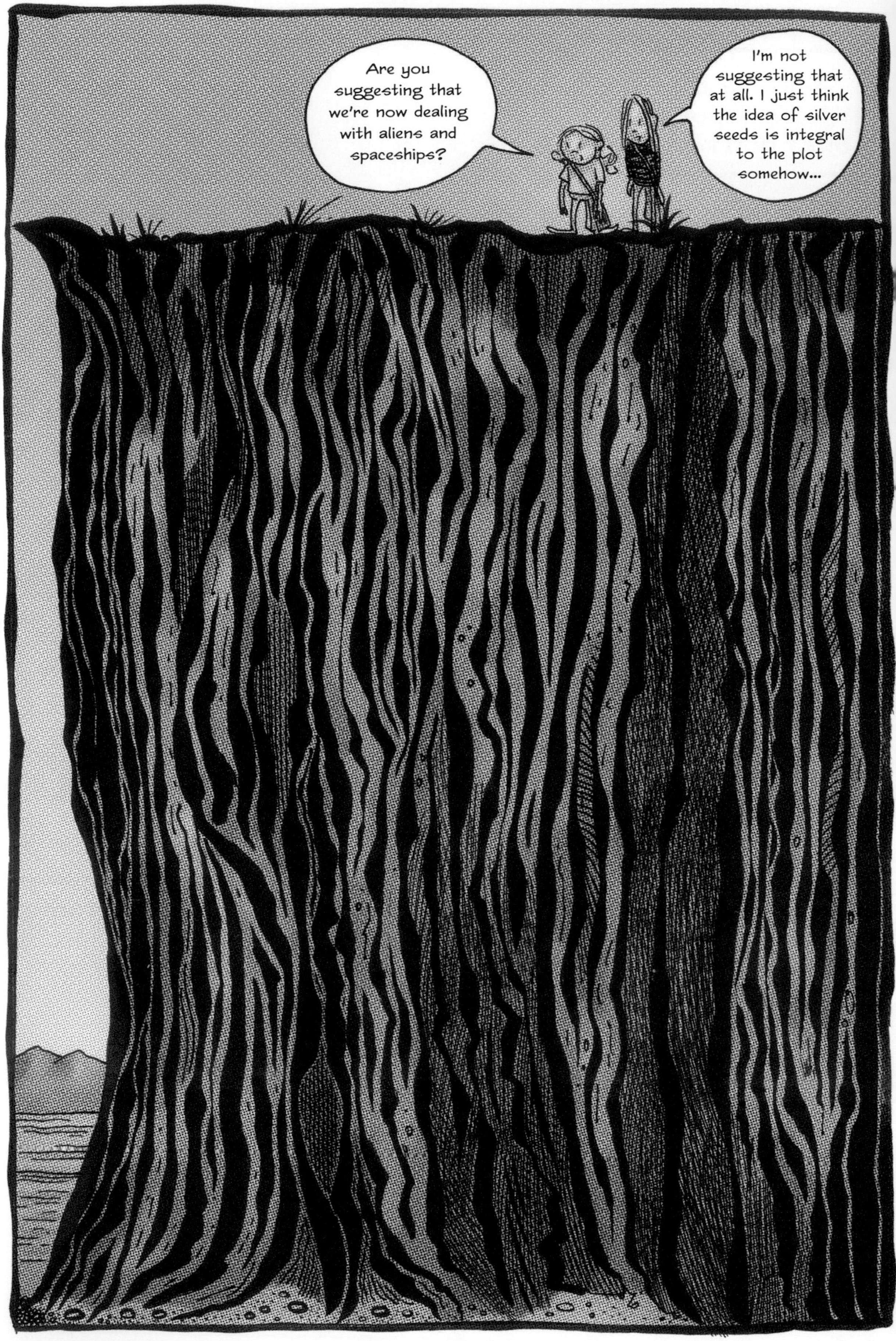
Are you suggesting that we're now dealing with aliens and spaceships?
I'm not suggesting that at all. I just think the idea of silver seeds is integral to the plot somehow...

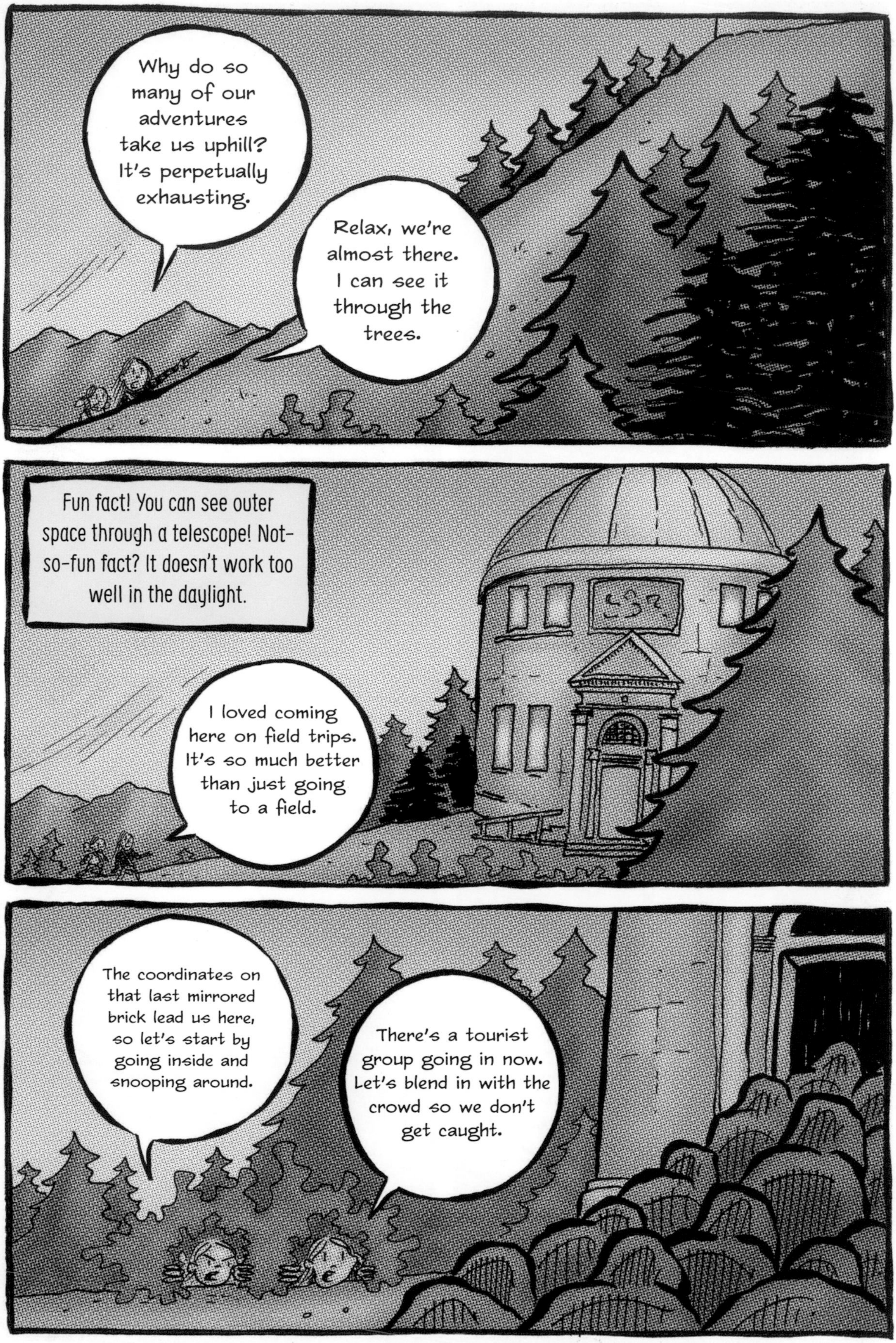

Why do so many of our adventures take us uphill? It's perpetually exhausting.
Relax, we're almost there. I can see it through the trees.
Fun fact! You can see outer space through a telescope! Not-so-fun fact? It doesn't work too well in the daylight.
I loved coming here on field trips. It's so much better than just going to a field.
The coordinates on that last mirrored brick lead us here, so let's start by going inside and snooping around.
There's a tourist group going in now. Let's blend in with the crowd so we don't get caught.

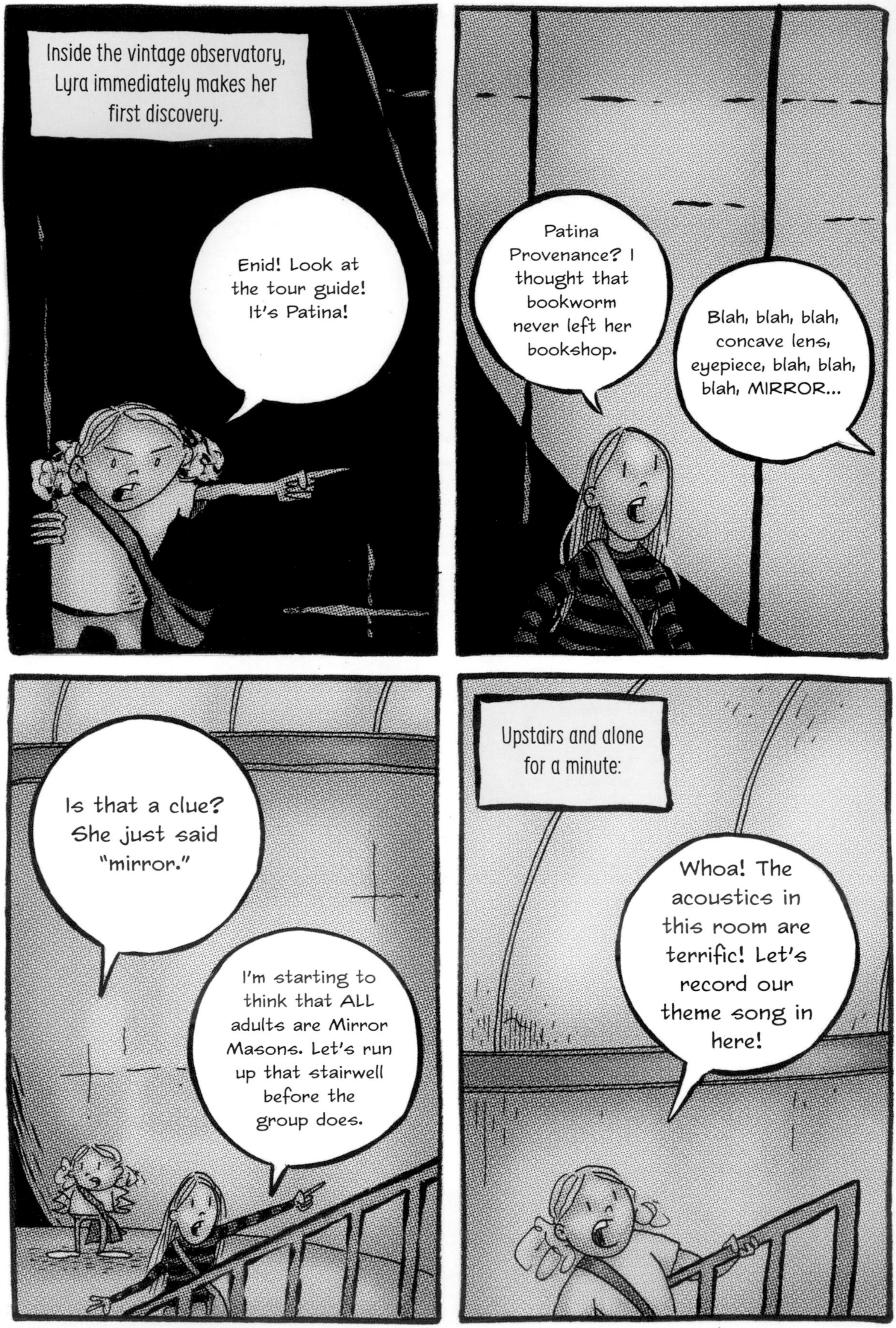

Inside the vintage observatory, Lyra immediately makes her first discovery.
Enid! Look at the tour guide! It's Patina!
Patina Provenance? I thought that bookworm never left her bookshop.
Blah, blah, blah, concave lens, eyepiece, blah, blah, blah, MIRROR...
Is that a clue? She just said "mirror."
I'm starting to think that ALL adults are Mirror Masons. Let's run up that stairwell before the group does.
Upstairs and alone for a minute:
Whoa! The acoustics in this room are terrific! Let's record our theme song in here!

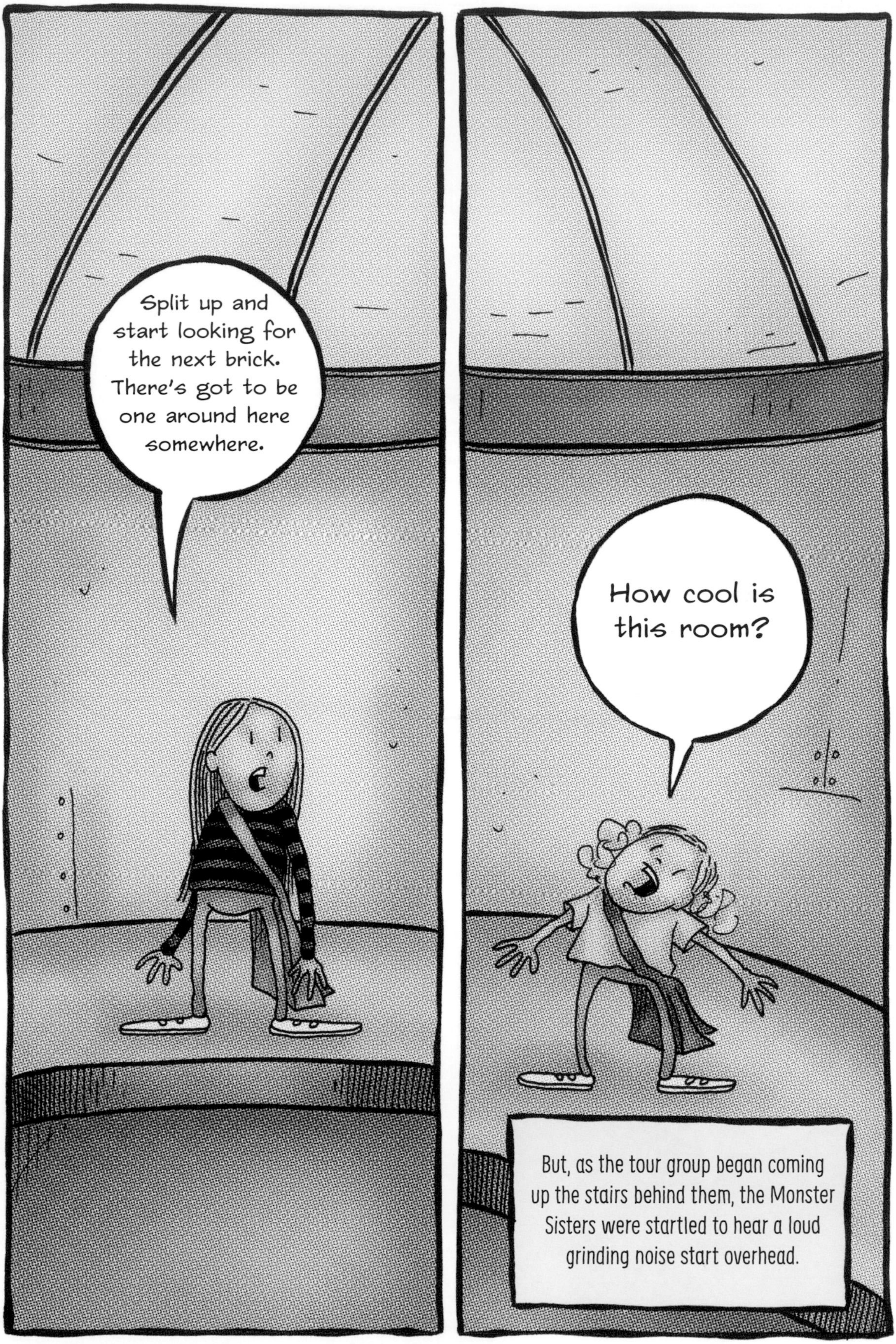
Split up and start looking for the next brick. There's got to be one around here somewhere.
How cool is this room?
But, as the tour group began coming up the stairs behind them, the Monster Sisters were startled to hear a loud grinding noise start overhead.

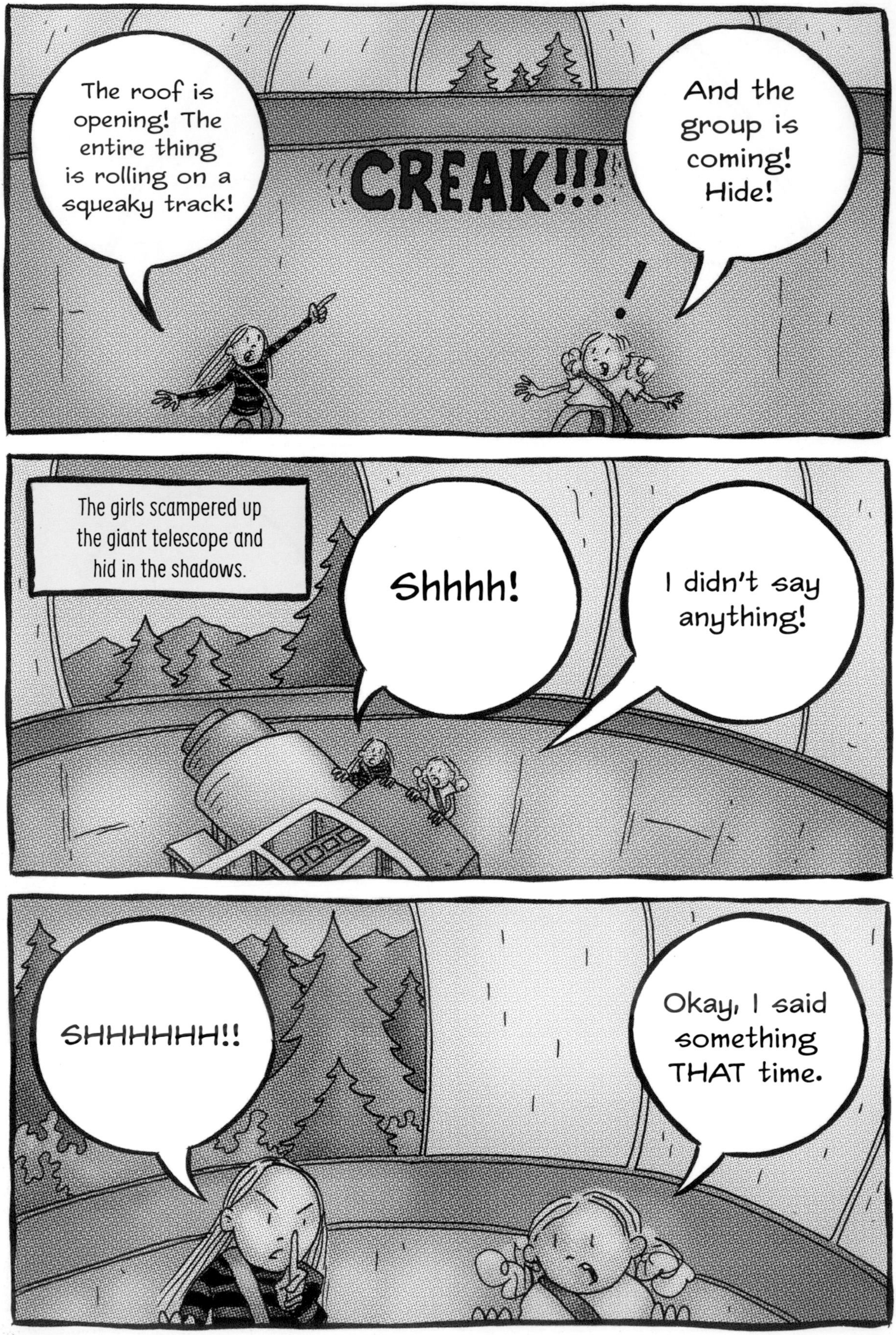
The roof is opening! The entire thing is rolling on a squeaky track!
CREAK!!!
And the group is coming! Hide!
!
The girls scampered up the giant telescope and hid in the shadows.
Shhhh!
I didn't say anything!
SHHHHHH!!
Okay, I said something THAT time.

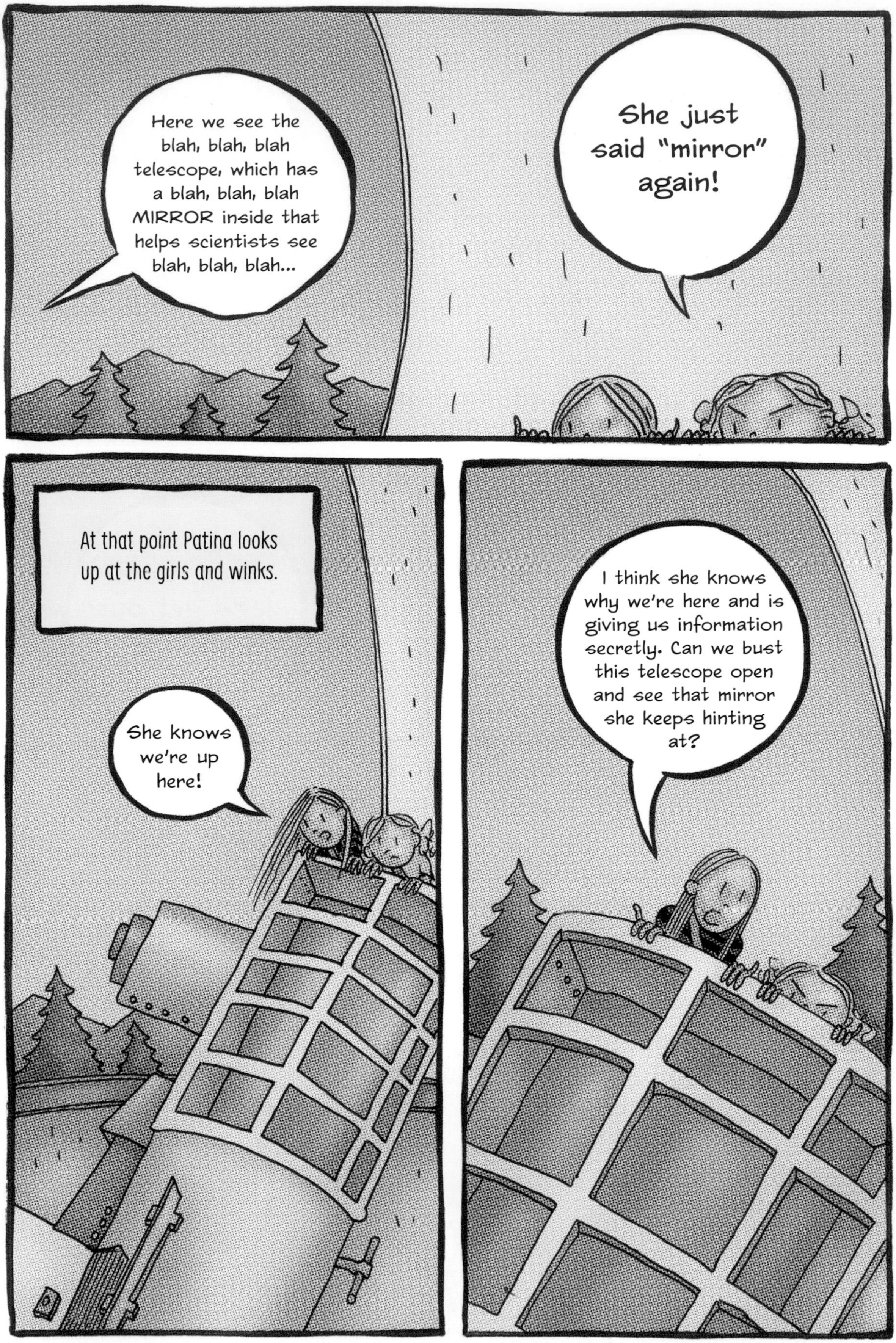
Here we see the blah, blah, blah telescope, which has a blah, blah, blah MIRROR inside that helps scientists see blah, blah, blah...
She just said "mirror" again!
At that point Patina looks up at the girls and winks.
She knows we're up here!
I think she knows why we're here and is giving us information secretly. Can we bust this telescope open and see that mirror she keeps hinting at?

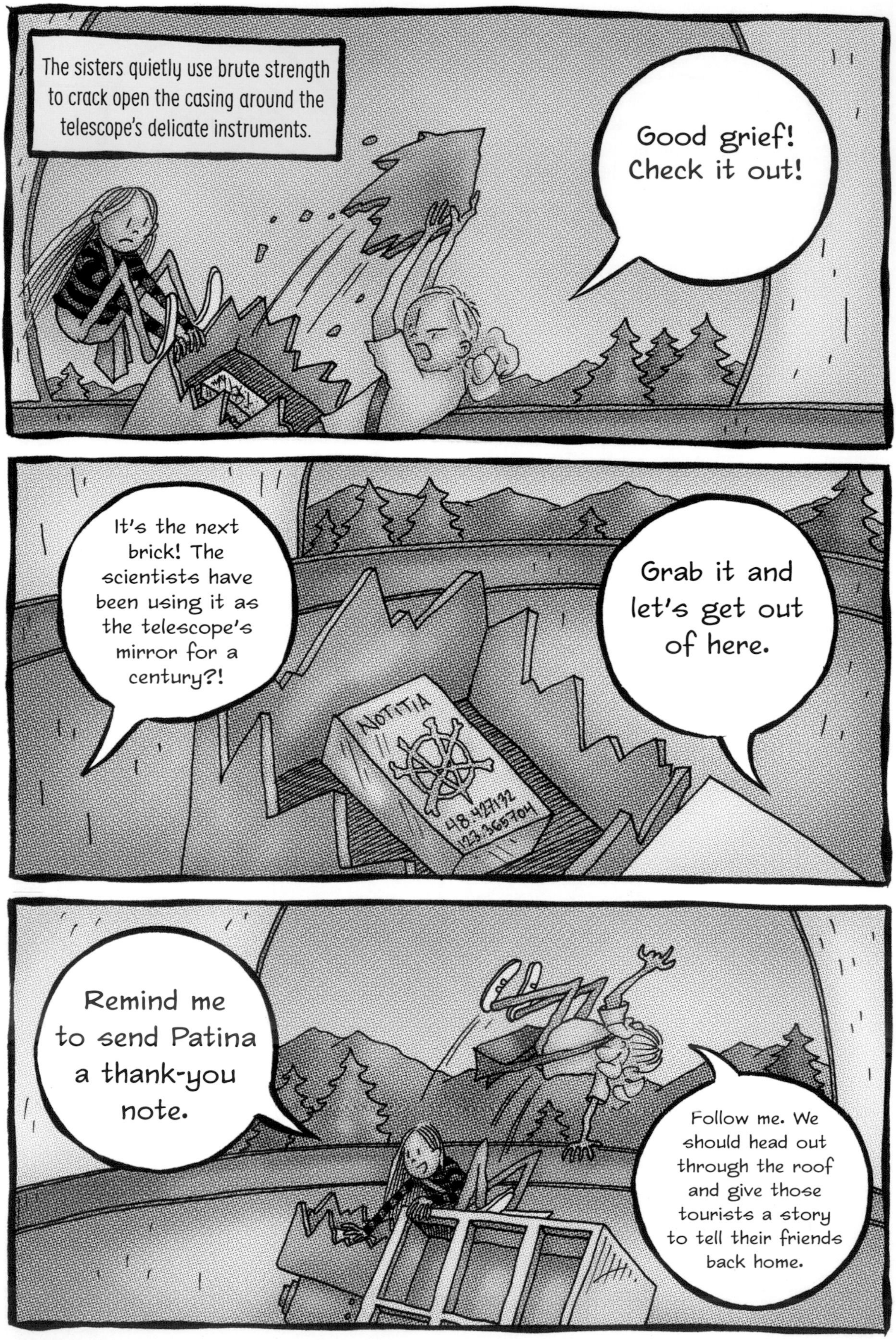
The sisters quietly use brute strength to crack open the casing around the telescope's delicate instruments.
Good grief! Check it out!
It's the next brick! The scientists have been using it as the telescope's mirror for a century?!
Grab it and let's get out of here.
NOTITIA
48 427132
123 365704
Remind me to send Patina a thank-you note.
Follow me. We should head out through the roof and give those tourists a story to tell their friends back home.

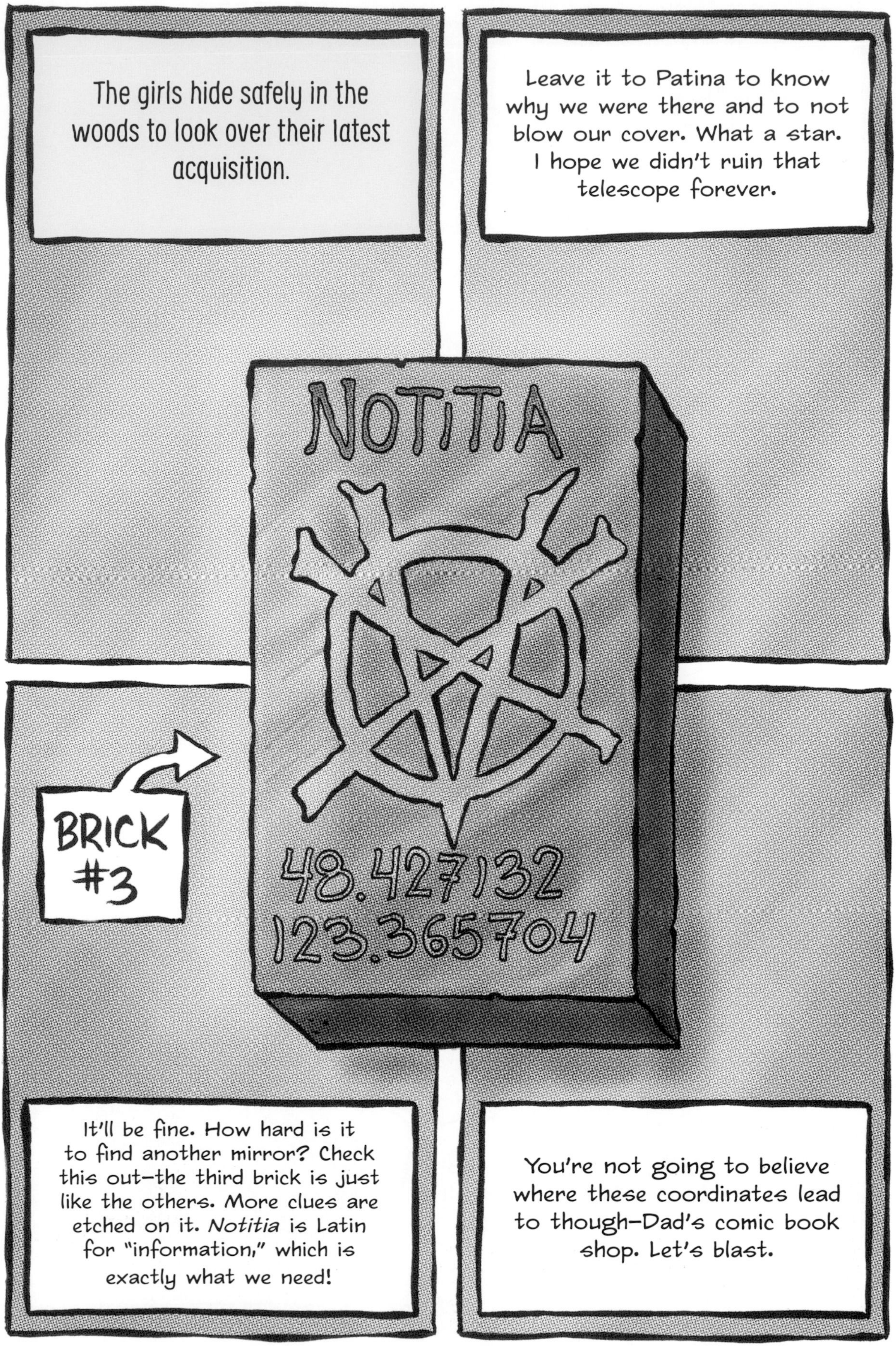

The girls hide safely in the woods to look over their latest acquisition.
Leave it to Patina to know why we were there and to not blow our cover. What a star. I hope we didn't ruin that telescope forever.
NOTITIA
48.427132
123.365704
BRICK #3
It'll be fine. How hard is it to find another mirror? Check this out—the third brick is just like the others. More clues are etched on it. *Notitia* is Latin for "information," which is exactly what we need!
You're not going to believe where these coordinates lead to though—Dad's comic book shop. Let's blast.

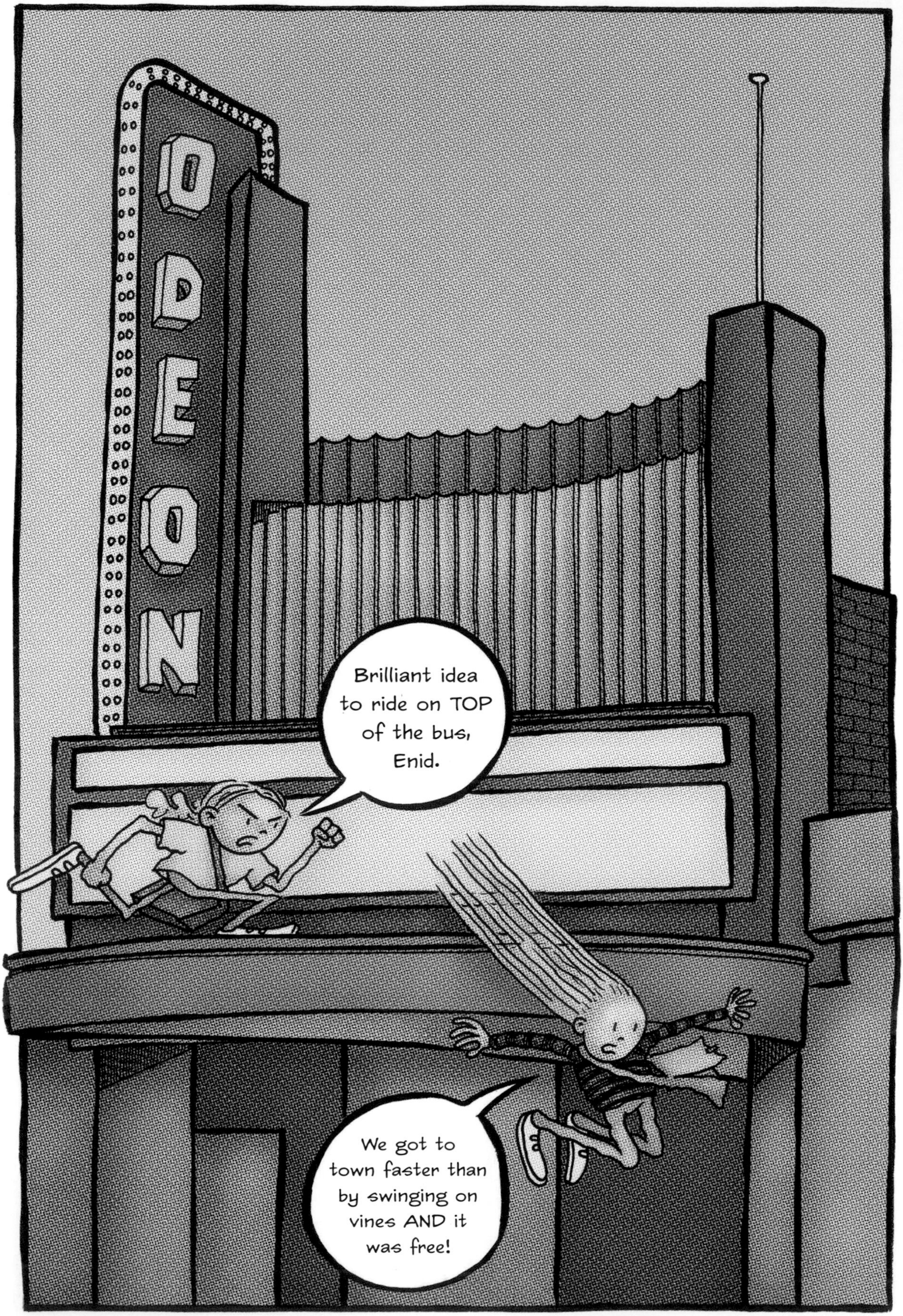
ODEON
Brilliant idea to ride on TOP of the bus, Enid.
We got to town faster than by swinging on vines AND it was free!

CHAPTER FIVE

THE COMIC BOOK SHOP

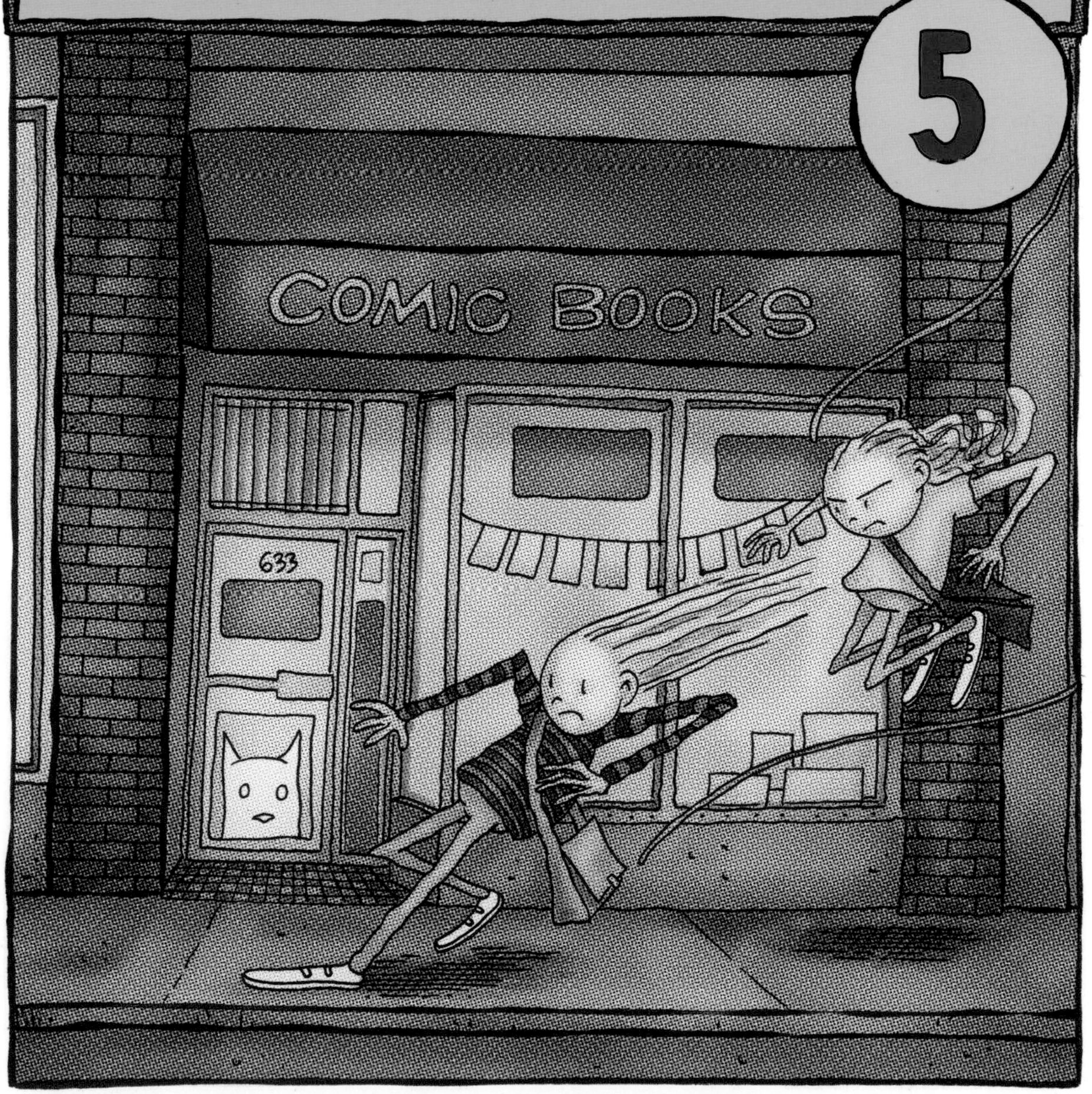
5
COMIC BOOKS
633

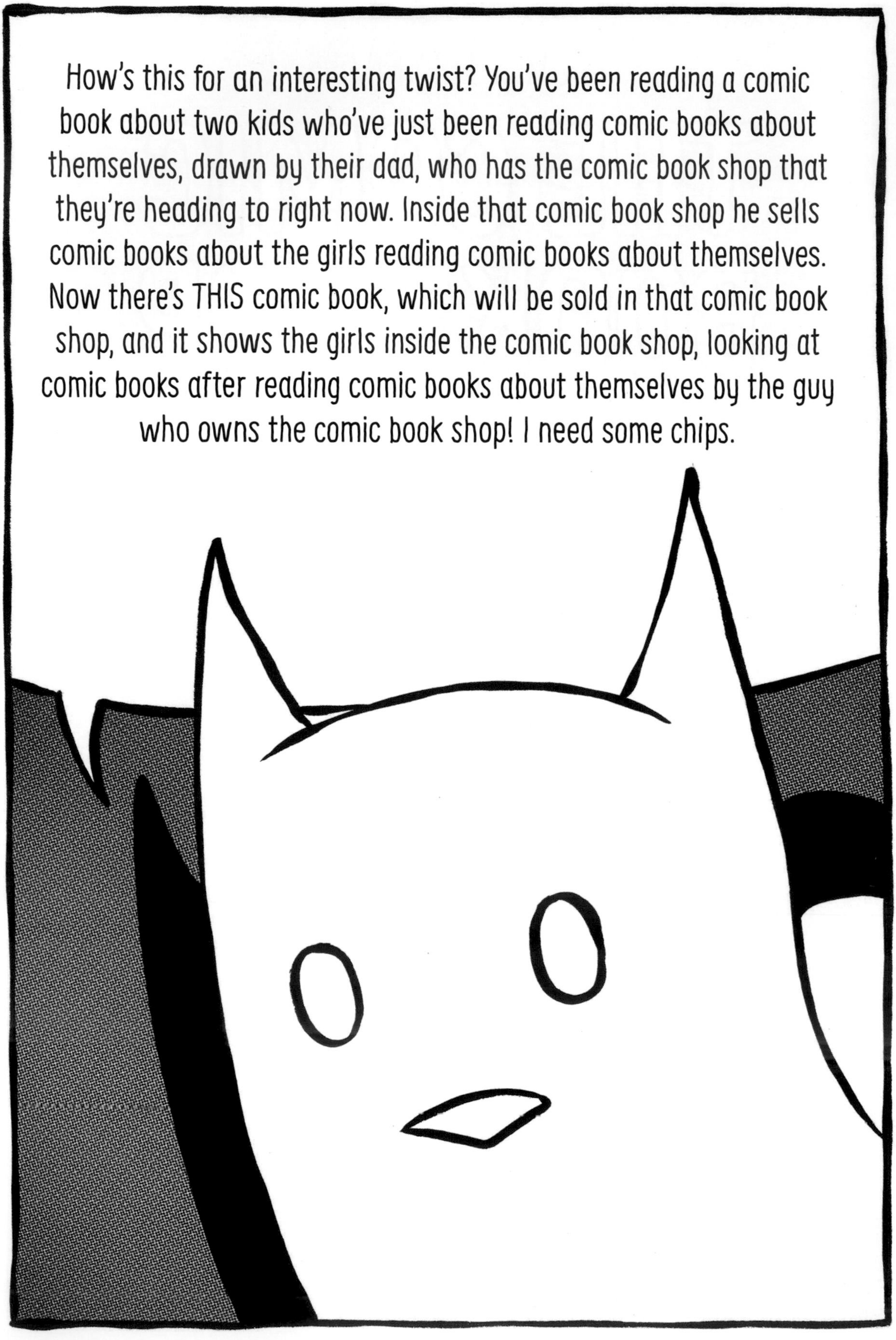
How's this for an interesting twist? You've been reading a comic book about two kids who've just been reading comic books about themselves, drawn by their dad, who has the comic book shop that they're heading to right now. Inside that comic book shop he sells comic books about the girls reading comic books about themselves. Now there's THIS comic book, which will be sold in that comic book shop, and it shows the girls inside the comic book shop, looking at comic books after reading comic books about themselves by the guy who owns the comic book shop! I need some chips.

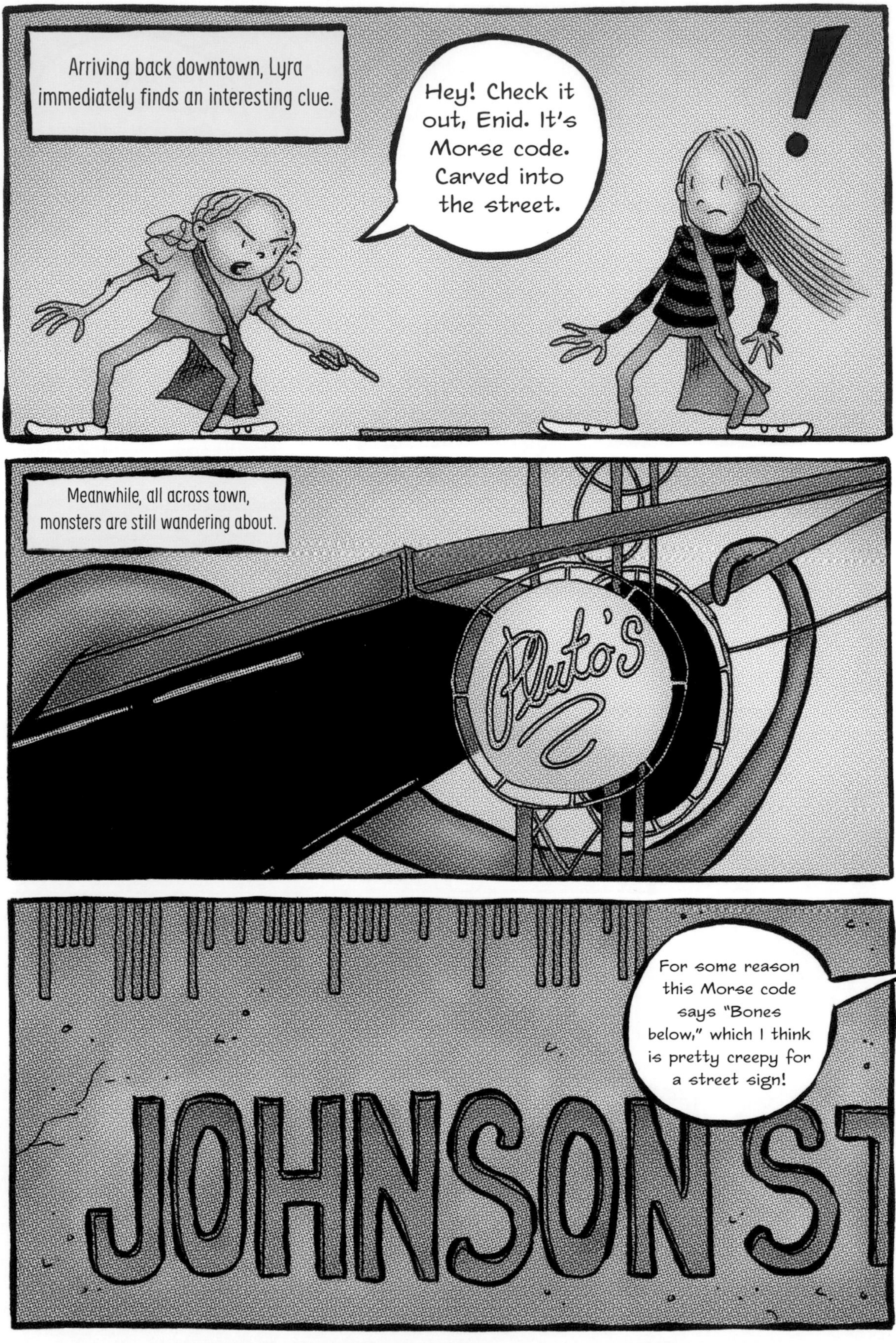
Arriving back downtown, Lyra immediately finds an interesting clue.
Hey! Check it out, Enid. It's Morse code. Carved into the street.
!
Meanwhile, all across town, monsters are still wandering about.
Pluto's
For some reason this Morse code says "Bones below," which I think is pretty creepy for a street sign!
JOHNSON ST

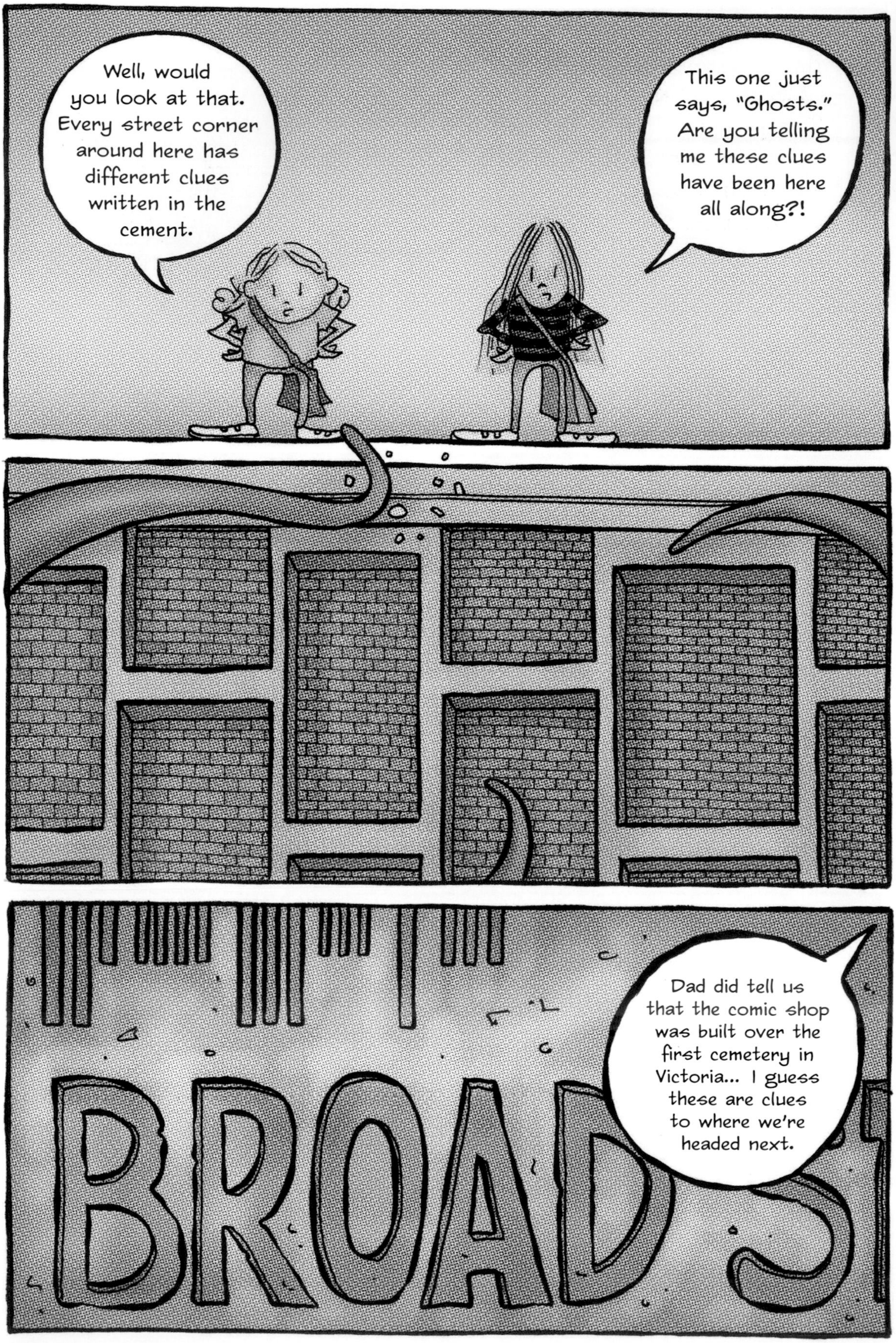
Well, would you look at that. Every street corner around here has different clues written in the cement.
This one just says, "Ghosts." Are you telling me these clues have been here all along?!
BROAD S
Dad did tell us that the comic shop was built over the first cemetery in Victoria... I guess these are clues to where we're headed next.

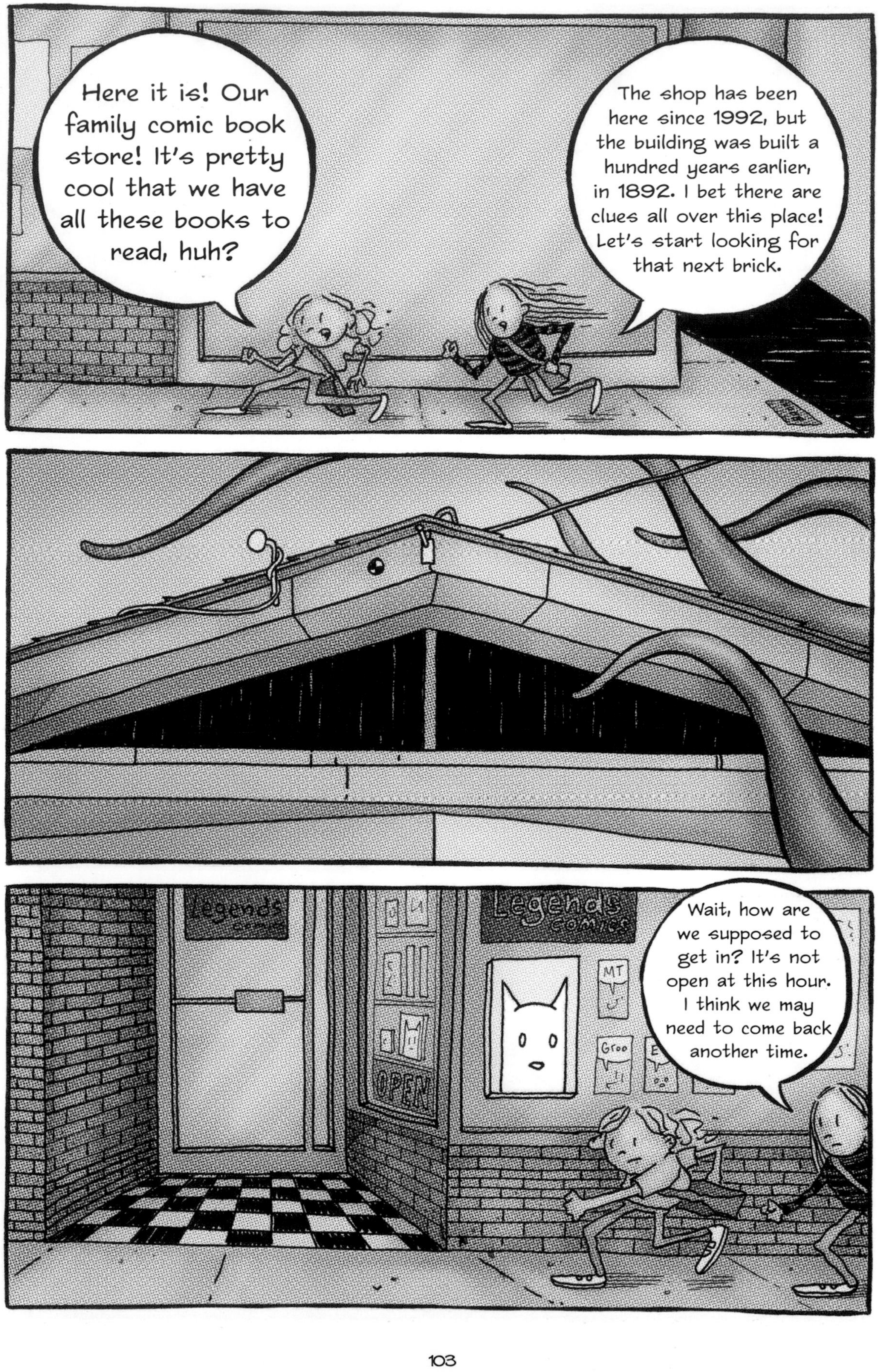
Here it is! Our family comic book store! It's pretty cool that we have all these books to read, huh?
The shop has been here since 1992, but the building was built a hundred years earlier, in 1892. I bet there are clues all over this place! Let's start looking for that next brick.
Legends Comics
OPEN
MT
Groo
Wait, how are we supposed to get in? It's not open at this hour. I think we may need to come back another time.

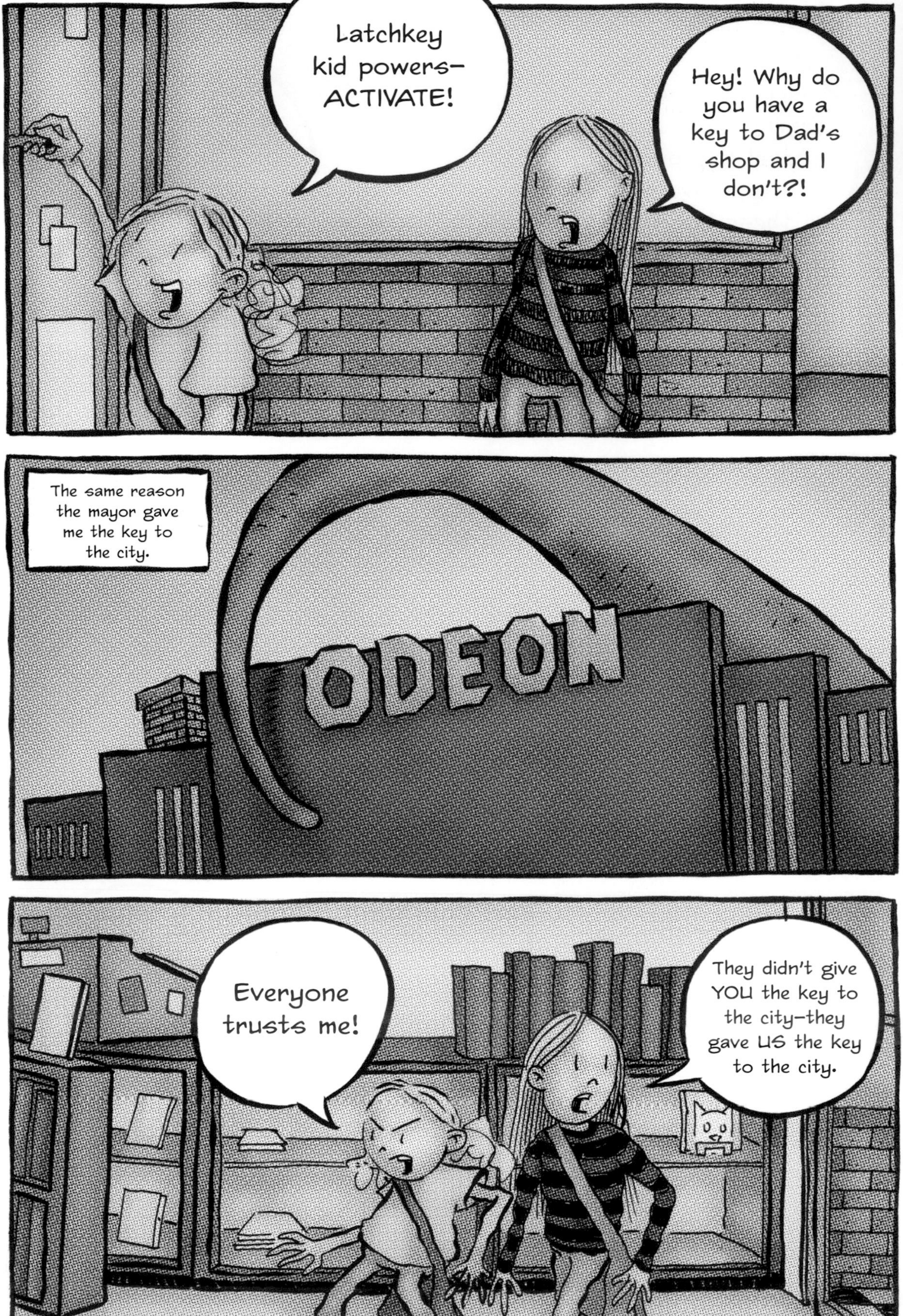

Latchkey kid powers–ACTIVATE!
Hey! Why do you have a key to Dad's shop and I don't?!
The same reason the mayor gave me the key to the city.
ODEON
Everyone trusts me!
They didn't give YOU the key to the city–they gave US the key to the city.

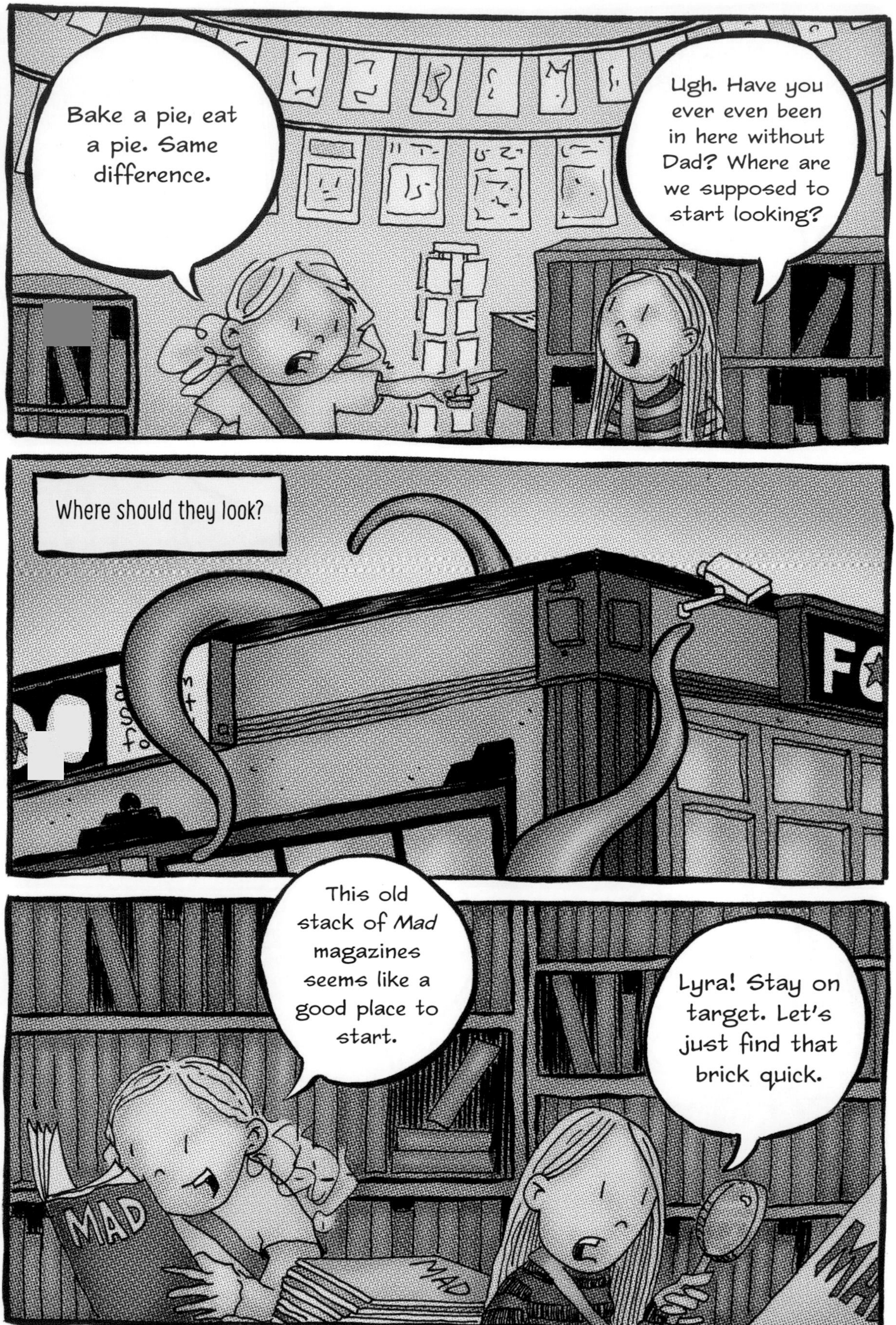

Bake a pie, eat a pie. Same difference.
Ugh. Have you ever even been in here without Dad? Where are we supposed to start looking?
Where should they look?
This old stack of *Mad* magazines seems like a good place to start.
Lyra! Stay on target. Let's just find that brick quick.
MAD
MAD

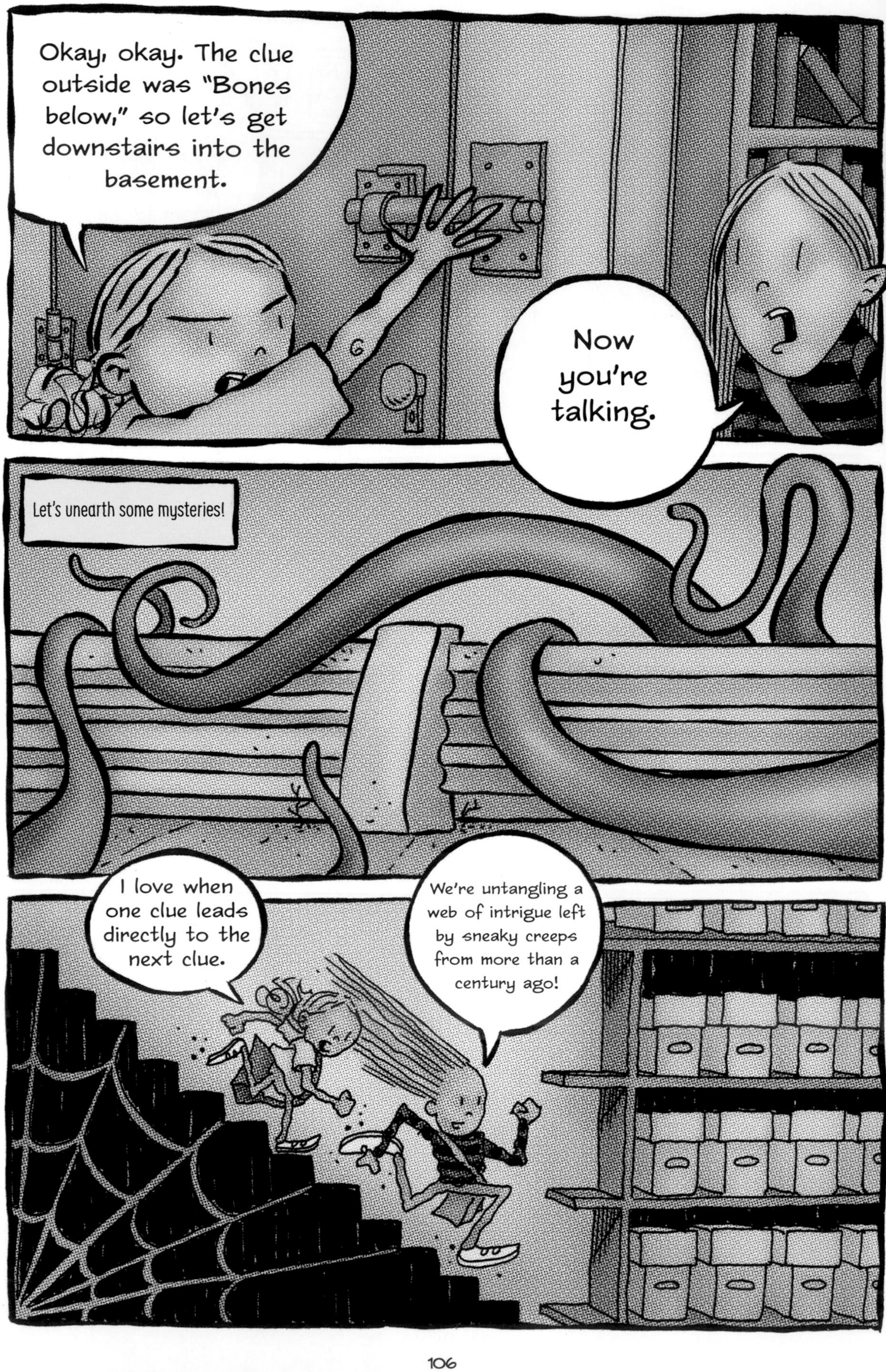
Okay, okay. The clue outside was "Bones below," so let's get downstairs into the basement.
Now you're talking.
Let's unearth some mysteries!
I love when one clue leads directly to the next clue.
We're untangling a web of intrigue left by sneaky creeps from more than a century ago!

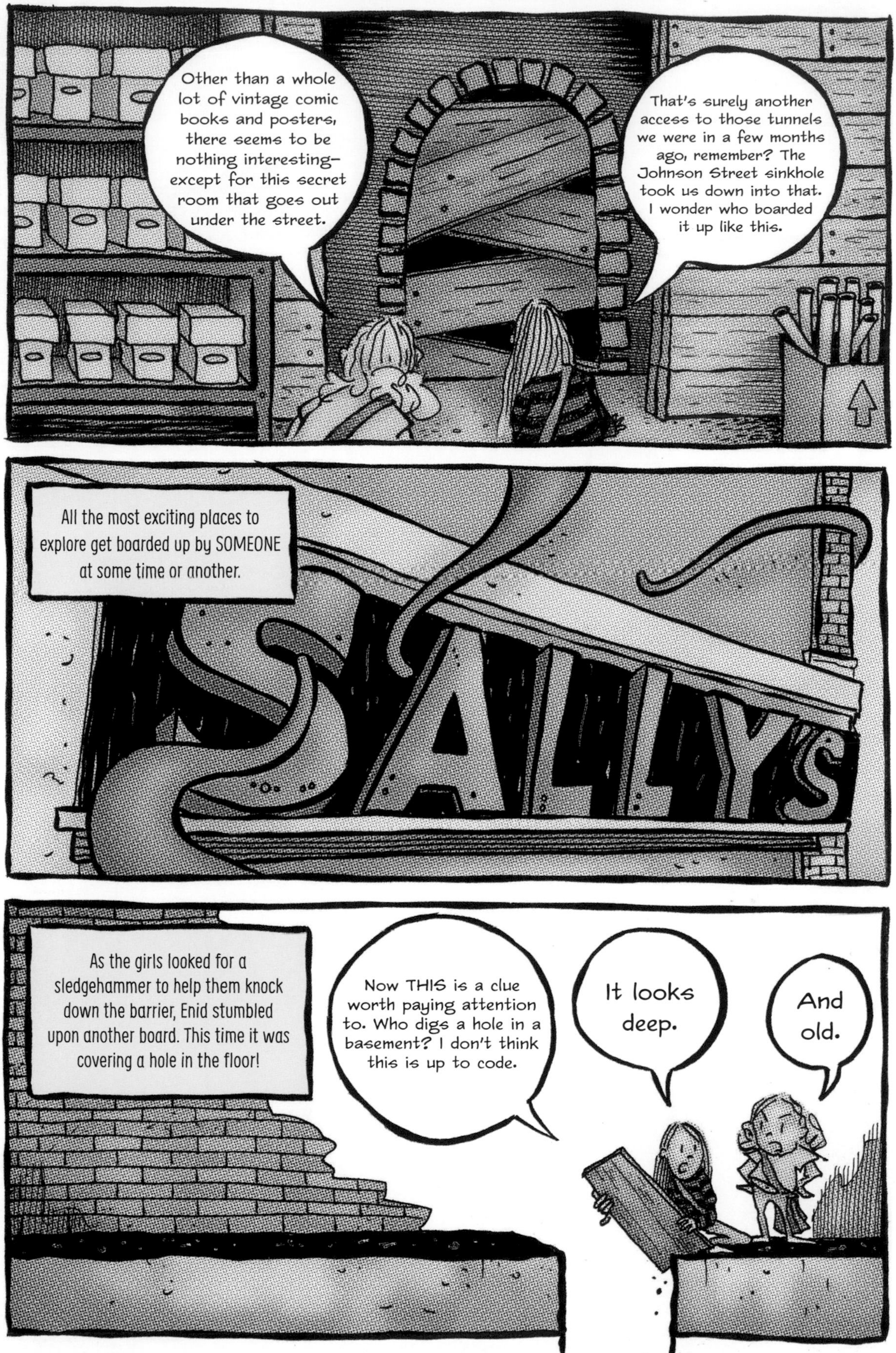
Other than a whole lot of vintage comic books and posters, there seems to be nothing interesting—except for this secret room that goes out under the street.
That's surely another access to those tunnels we were in a few months ago, remember? The Johnson Street sinkhole took us down into that. I wonder who boarded it up like this.
All the most exciting places to explore get boarded up by SOMEONE at some time or another.
SALLY'S
As the girls looked for a sledgehammer to help them knock down the barrier, Enid stumbled upon another board. This time it was covering a hole in the floor!
Now THIS is a clue worth paying attention to. Who digs a hole in a basement? I don't think this is up to code.
It looks deep.
And old.

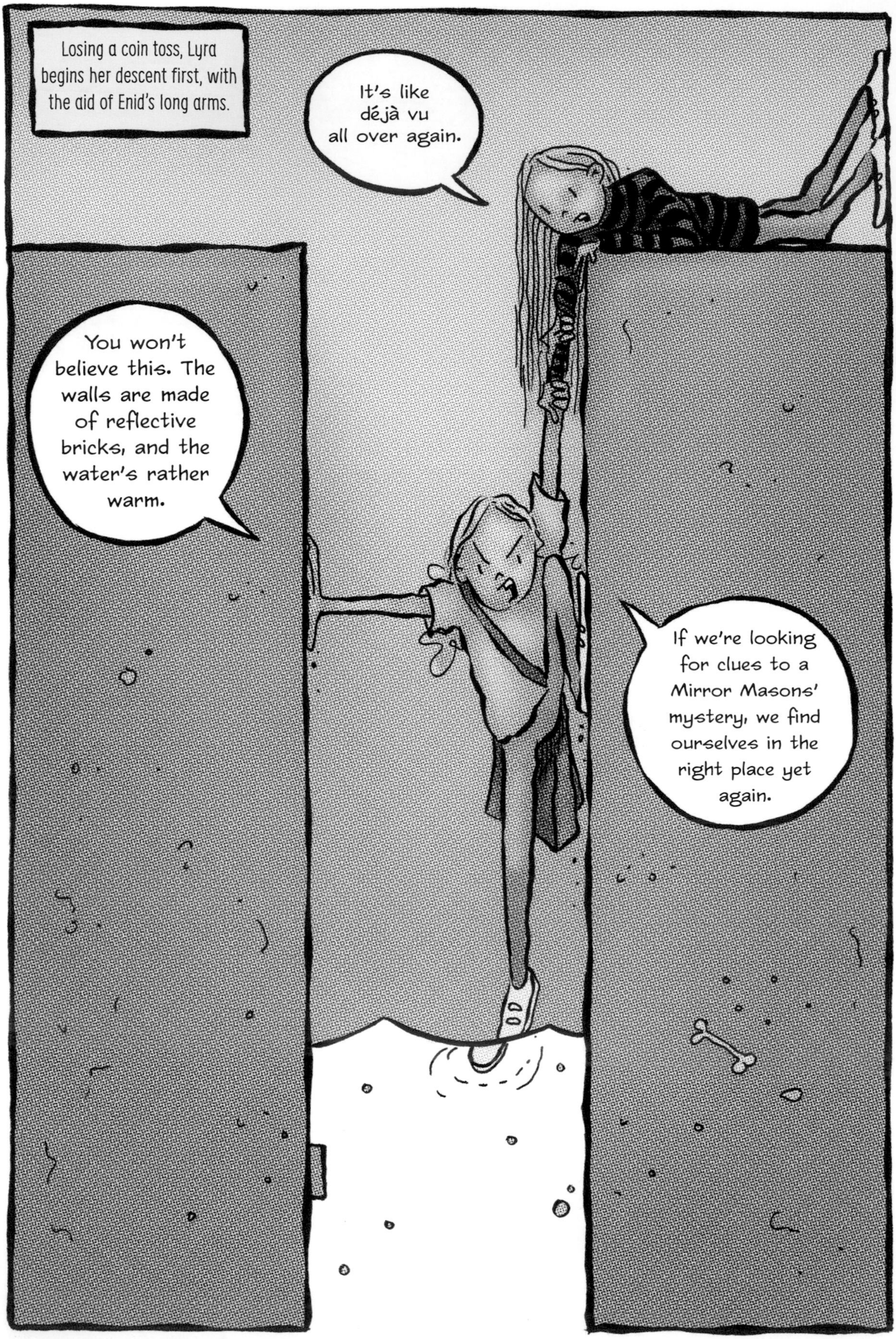
Losing a coin toss, Lyra begins her descent first, with the aid of Enid's long arms.
It's like déjà vu all over again.
You won't believe this. The walls are made of reflective bricks, and the water's rather warm.
If we're looking for clues to a Mirror Masons' mystery, we find ourselves in the right place yet again.

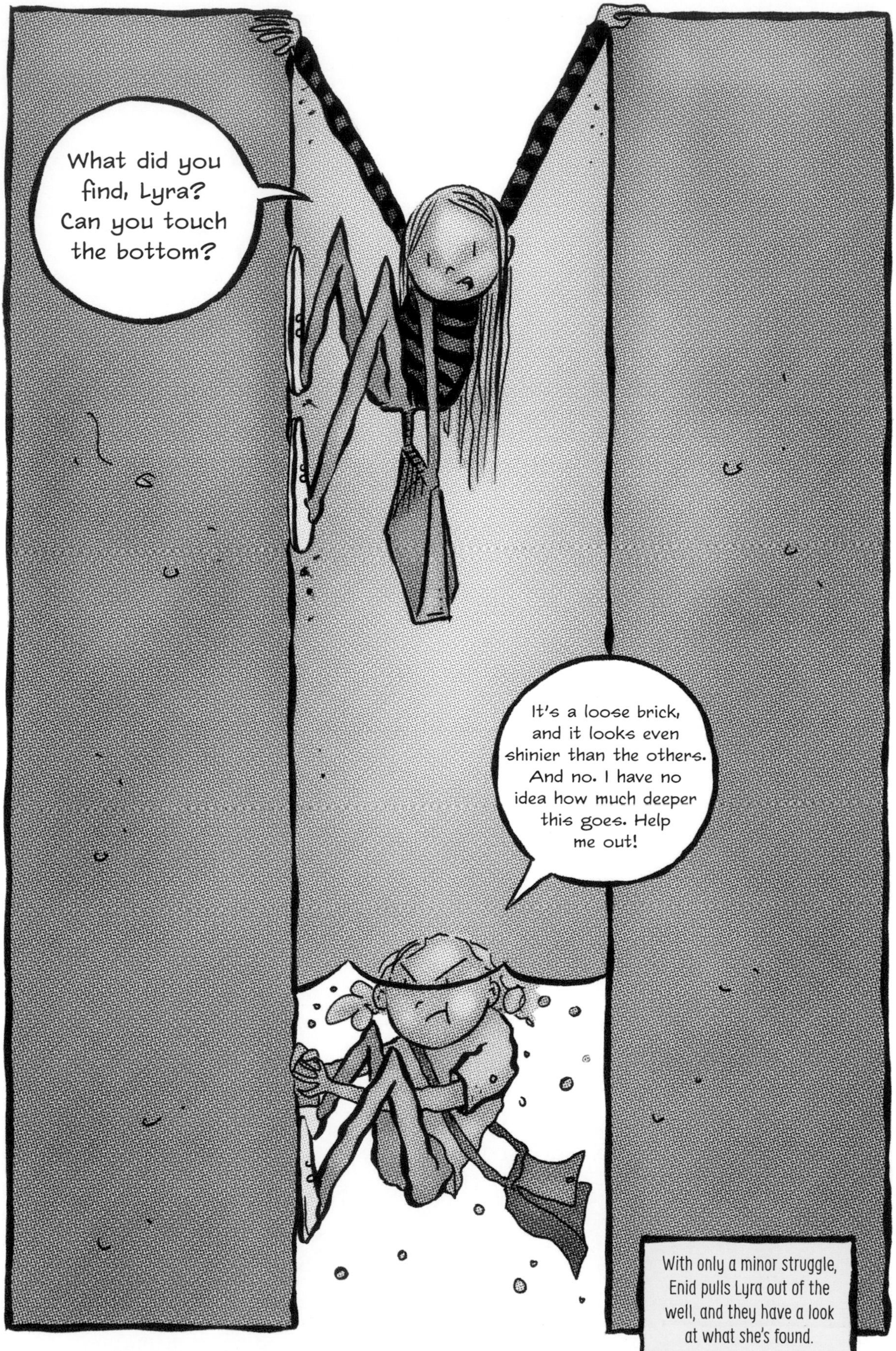
What did you find, Lyra? Can you touch the bottom?
It's a loose brick, and it looks even shinier than the others. And no. I have no idea how much deeper this goes. Help me out!
With only a minor struggle, Enid pulls Lyra out of the well, and they have a look at what she's found.

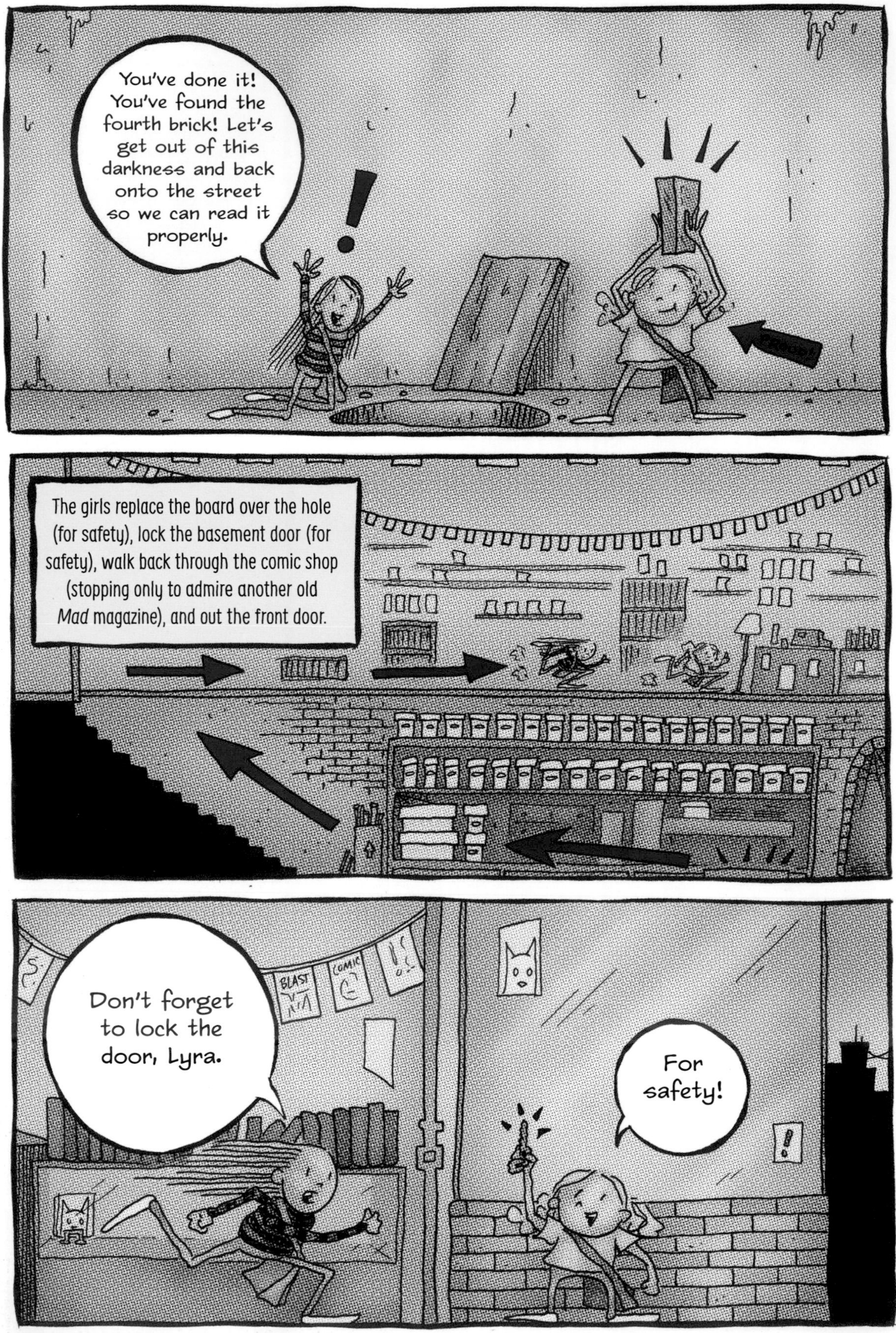
You've done it! You've found the fourth brick! Let's get out of this darkness and back onto the street so we can read it properly.
The girls replace the board over the hole (for safety), lock the basement door (for safety), walk back through the comic shop (stopping only to admire another old *Mad* magazine), and out the front door.
BLAST
COMIC
Don't forget to lock the door, Lyra.
For safety!

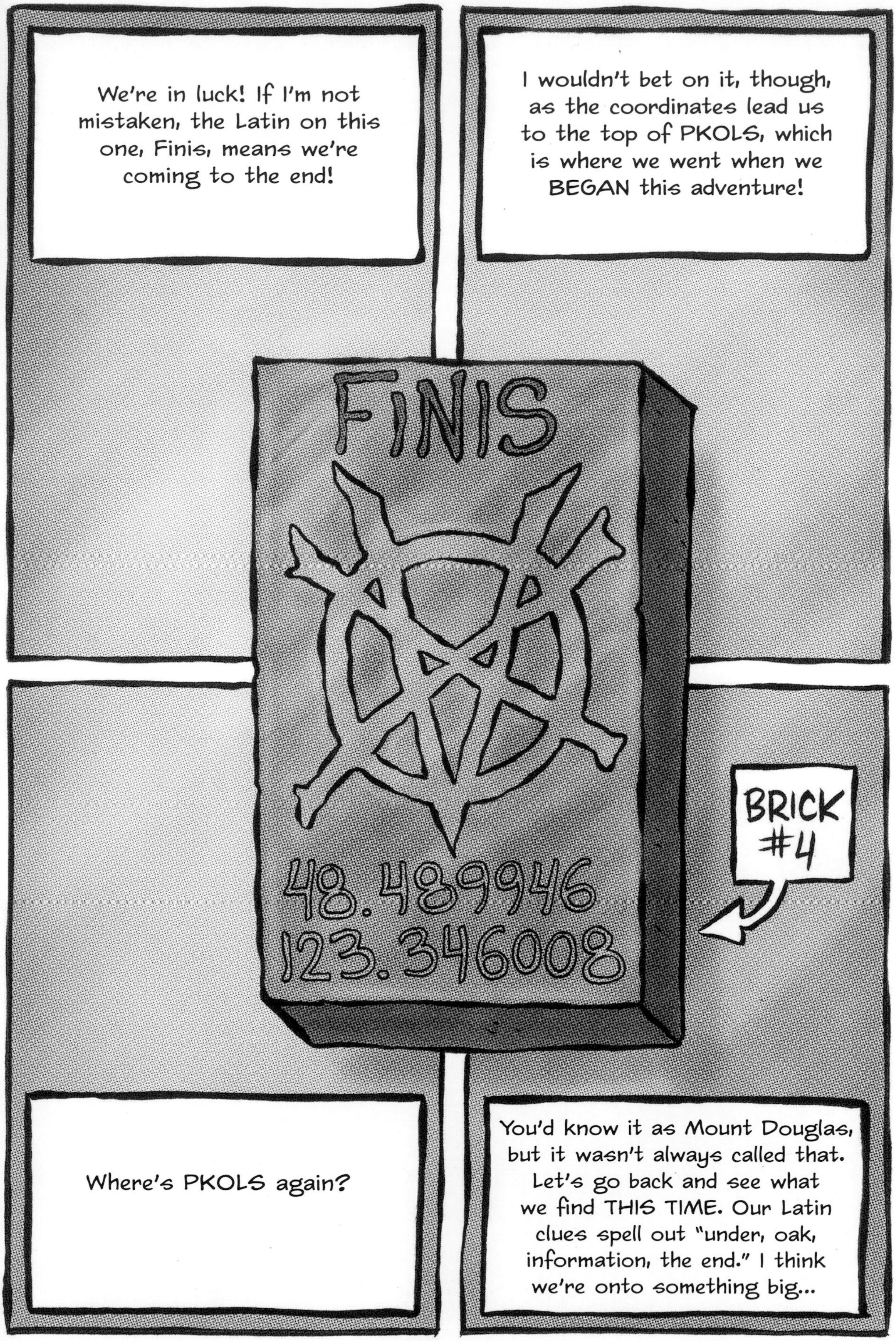
We're in luck! If I'm not mistaken, the Latin on this one, Finis, means we're coming to the end!
I wouldn't bet on it, though, as the coordinates lead us to the top of PKOLS, which is where we went when we BEGAN this adventure!
FINIS
48.489946
123.346008
BRICK #4
Where's PKOLS again?
You'd know it as Mount Douglas, but it wasn't always called that. Let's go back and see what we find THIS TIME. Our Latin clues spell out "under, oak, information, the end." I think we're onto something big...

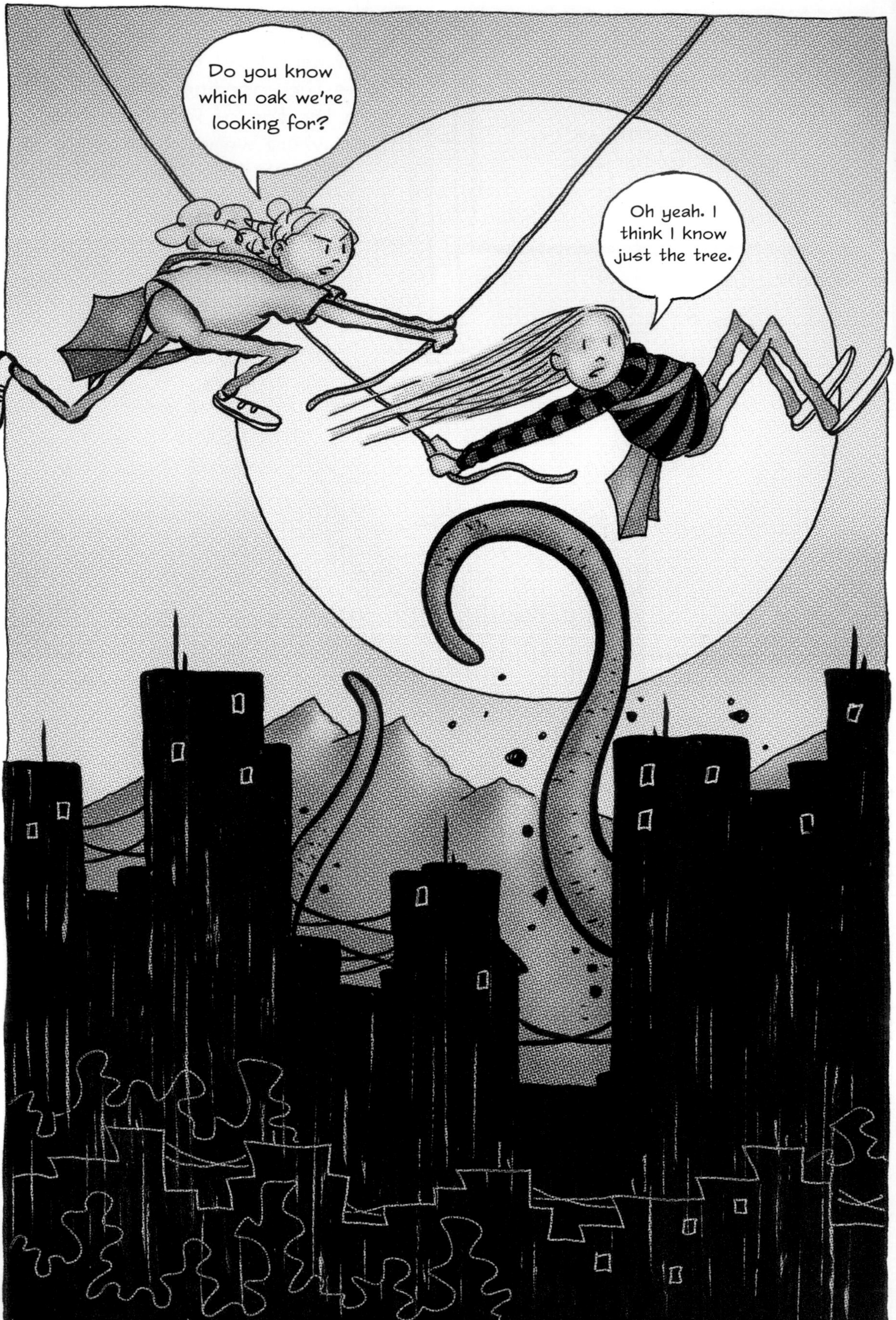
Do you know which oak we're looking for?
Oh yeah. I think I know just the tree.

CHAPTER SIX

ANSWERS FROM WITHIN A DARKENED CAVE

6

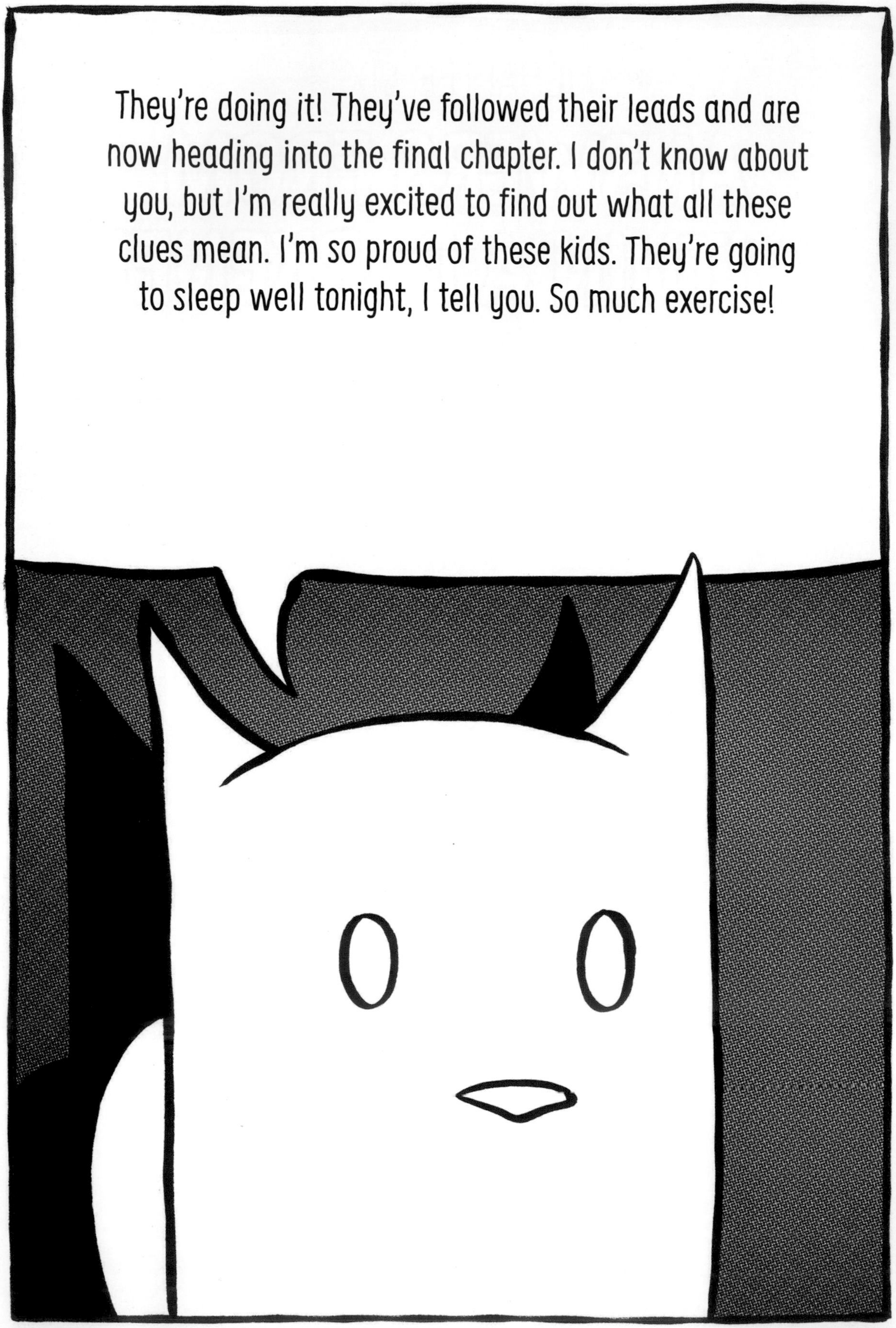
They're doing it! They've followed their leads and are now heading into the final chapter. I don't know about you, but I'm really excited to find out what all these clues mean. I'm so proud of these kids. They're going to sleep well tonight, I tell you. So much exercise!

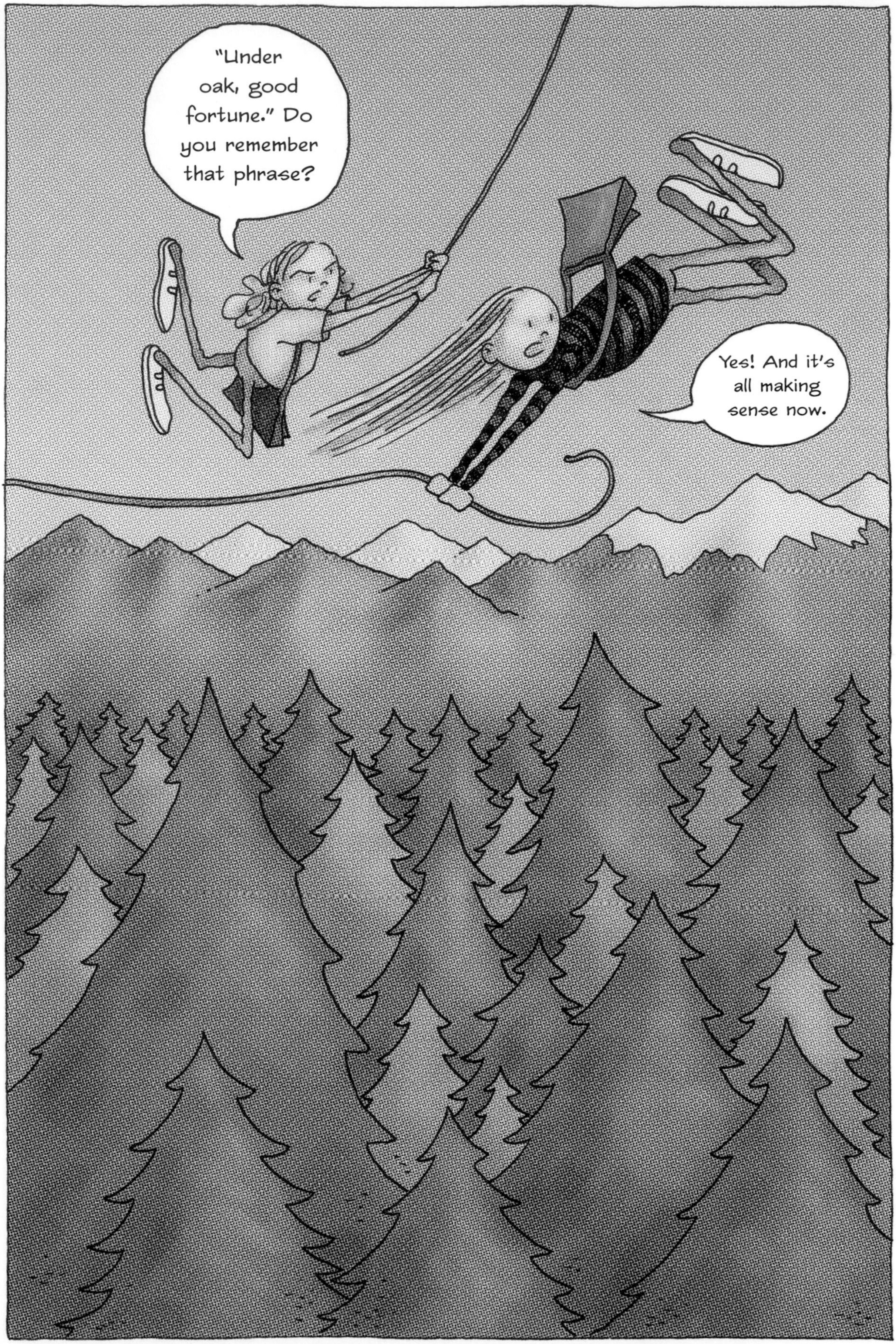
"Under oak, good fortune." Do you remember that phrase?
Yes! And it's all making sense now.

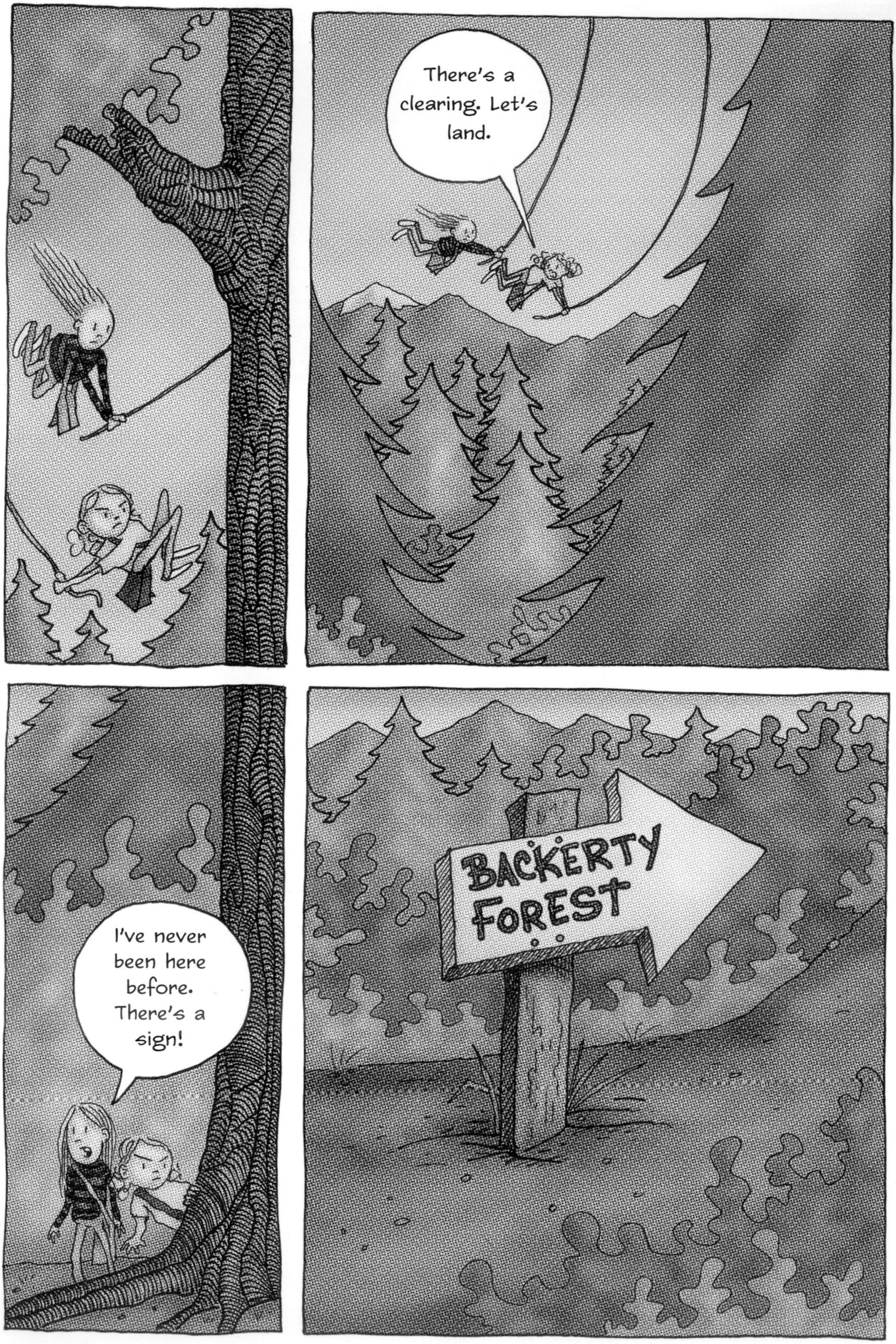
There's a clearing. Let's land.
I've never been here before. There's a sign!
BACKERTY FOREST

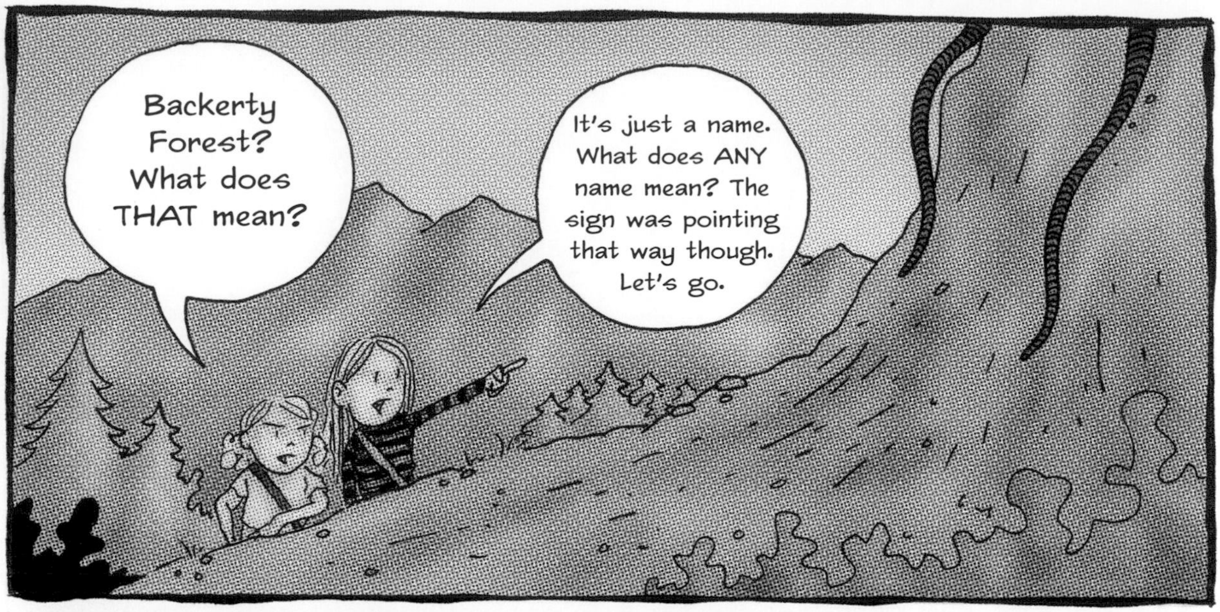
Backerty Forest? What does THAT mean?
It's just a name. What does ANY name mean? The sign was pointing that way though. Let's go.

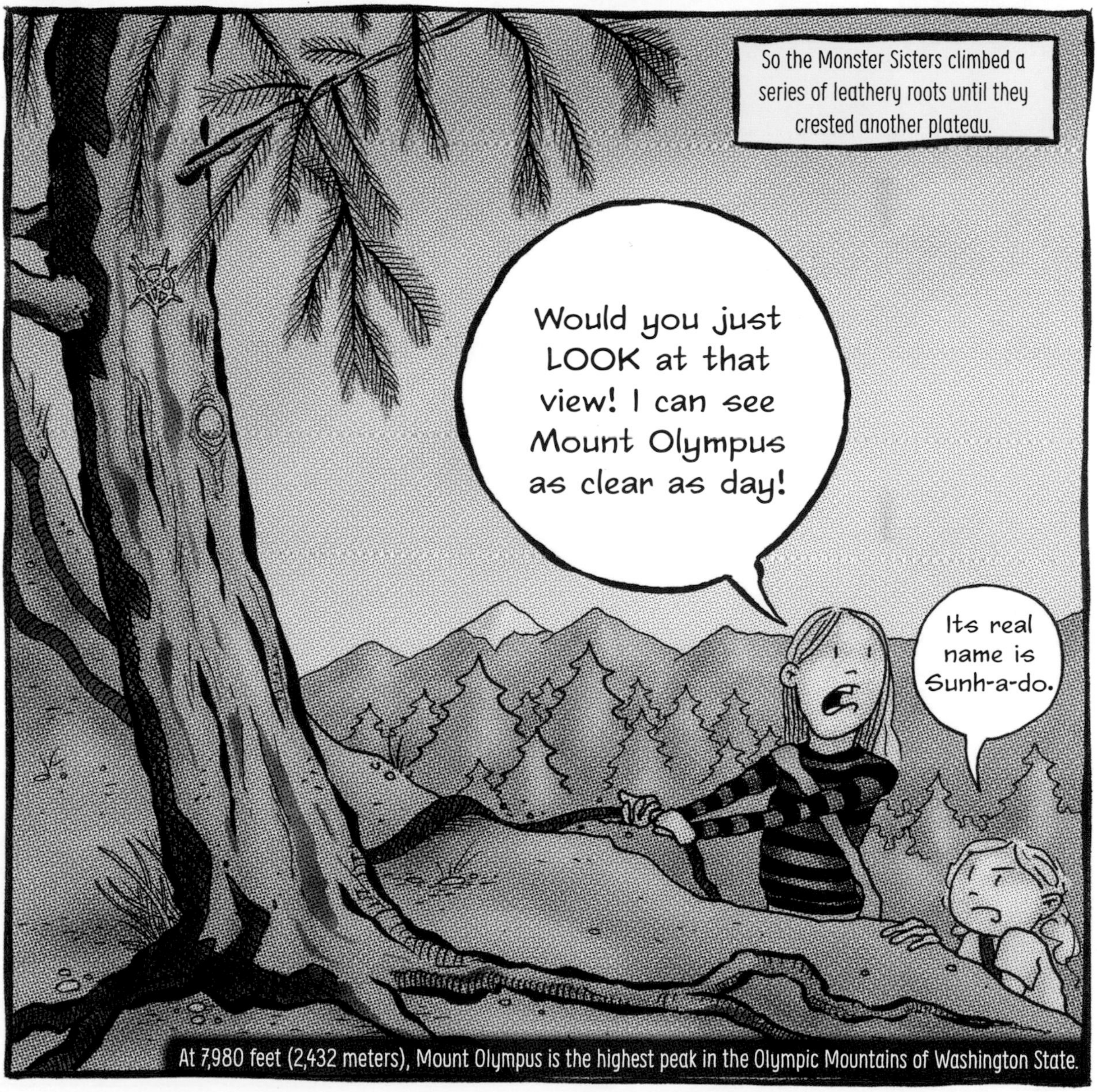
So the Monster Sisters climbed a series of leathery roots until they crested another plateau.
Would you just LOOK at that view! I can see Mount Olympus as clear as day!
Its real name is Sunh-a-do.
At 7,980 feet (2,432 meters), Mount Olympus is the highest peak in the Olympic Mountains of Washington State.

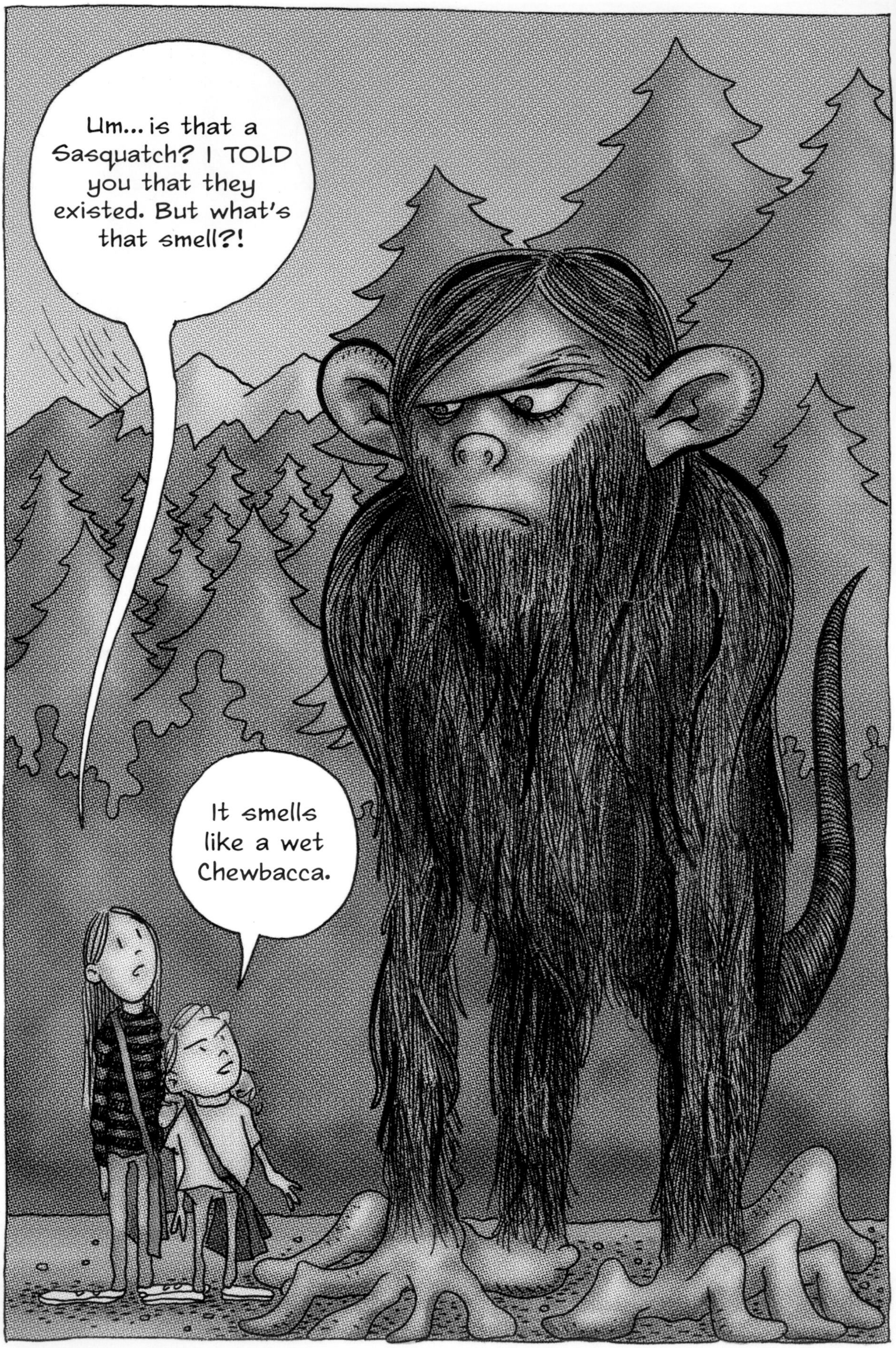
Um... is that a Sasquatch? I TOLD you that they existed. But what's that smell?!
It smells like a wet Chewbacca.

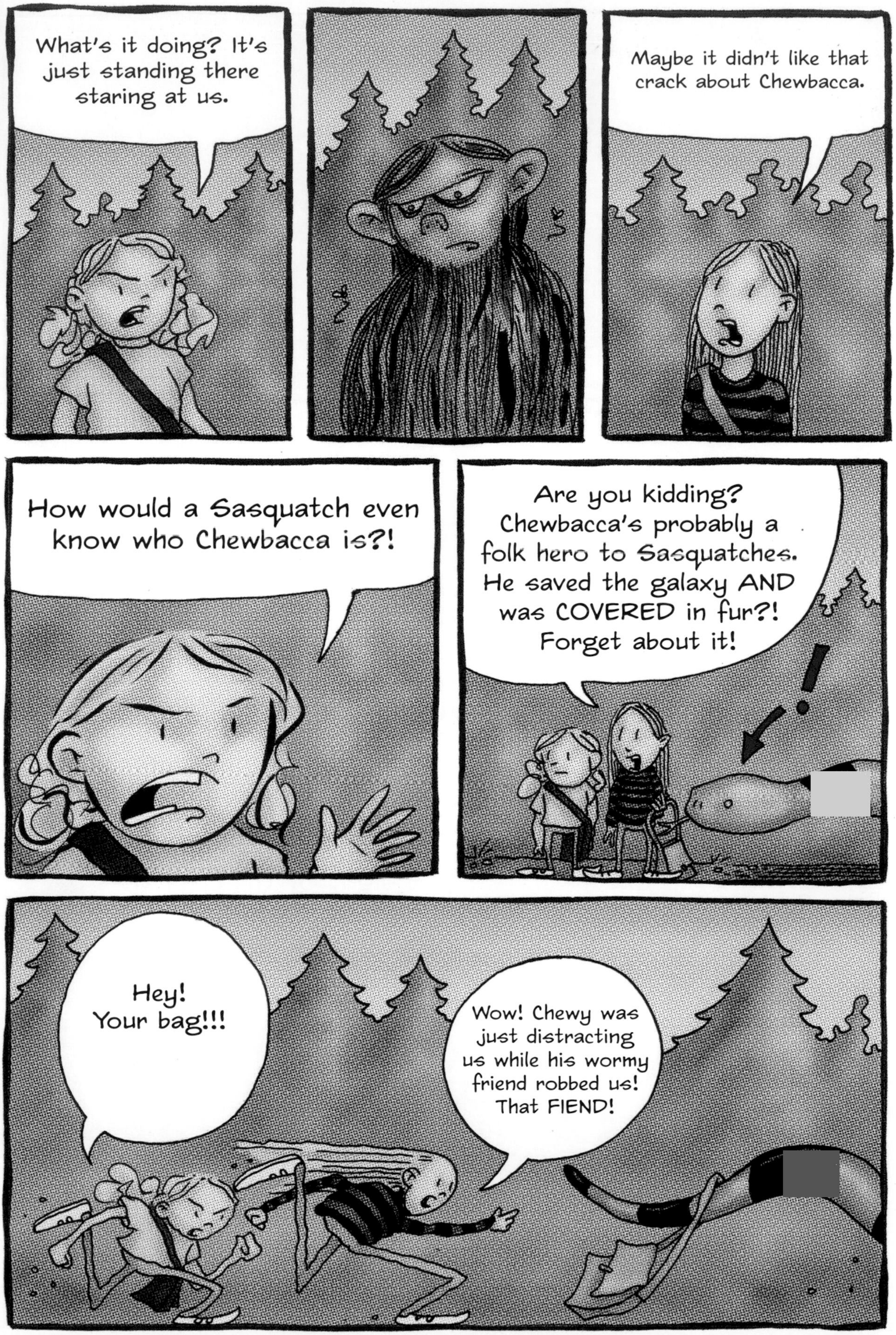
What's it doing? It's just standing there staring at us.
Maybe it didn't like that crack about Chewbacca.
How would a Sasquatch even know who Chewbacca is?!
Are you kidding? Chewbacca's probably a folk hero to Sasquatches. He saved the galaxy AND was COVERED in fur?! Forget about it!
!
Hey! Your bag!!!
Wow! Chewy was just distracting us while his wormy friend robbed us! That FIEND!

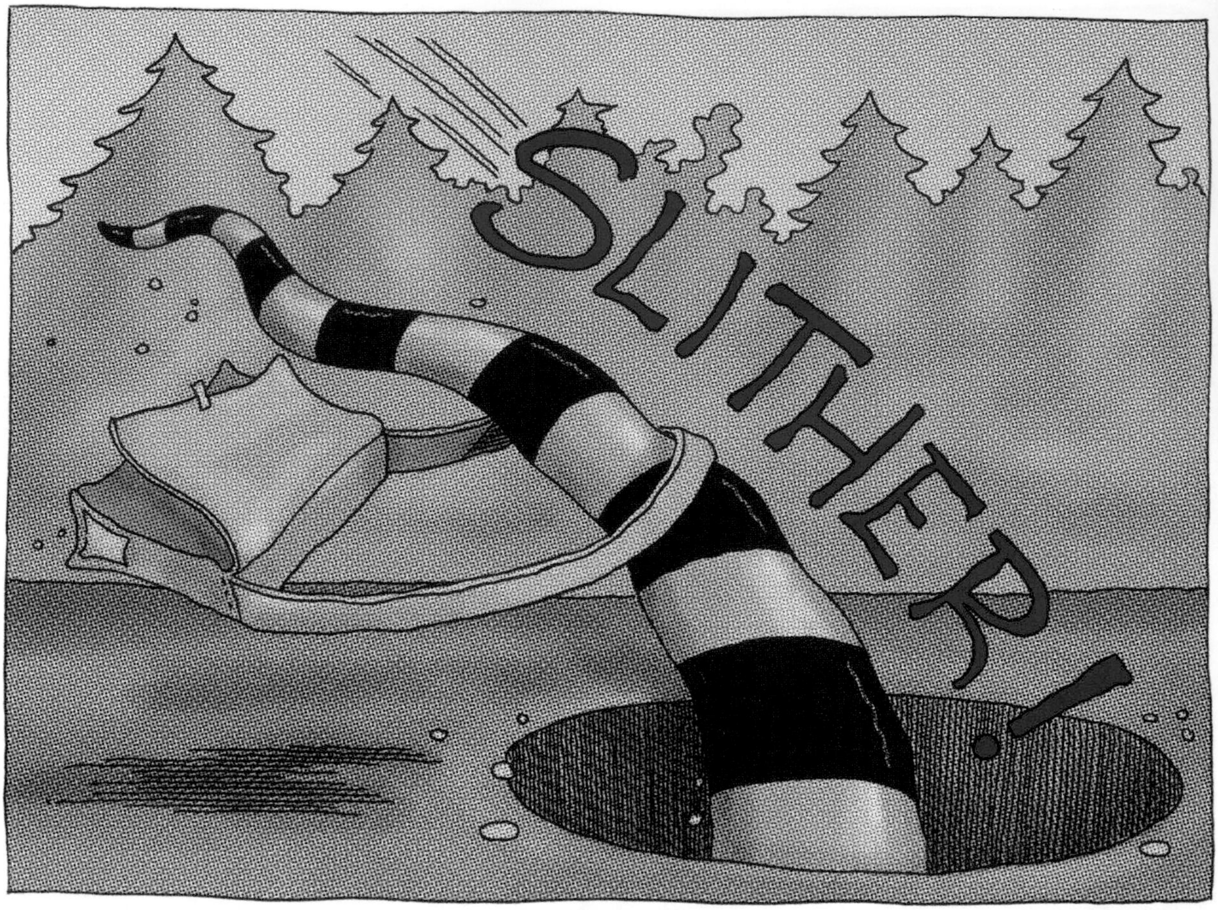
SLITHER!

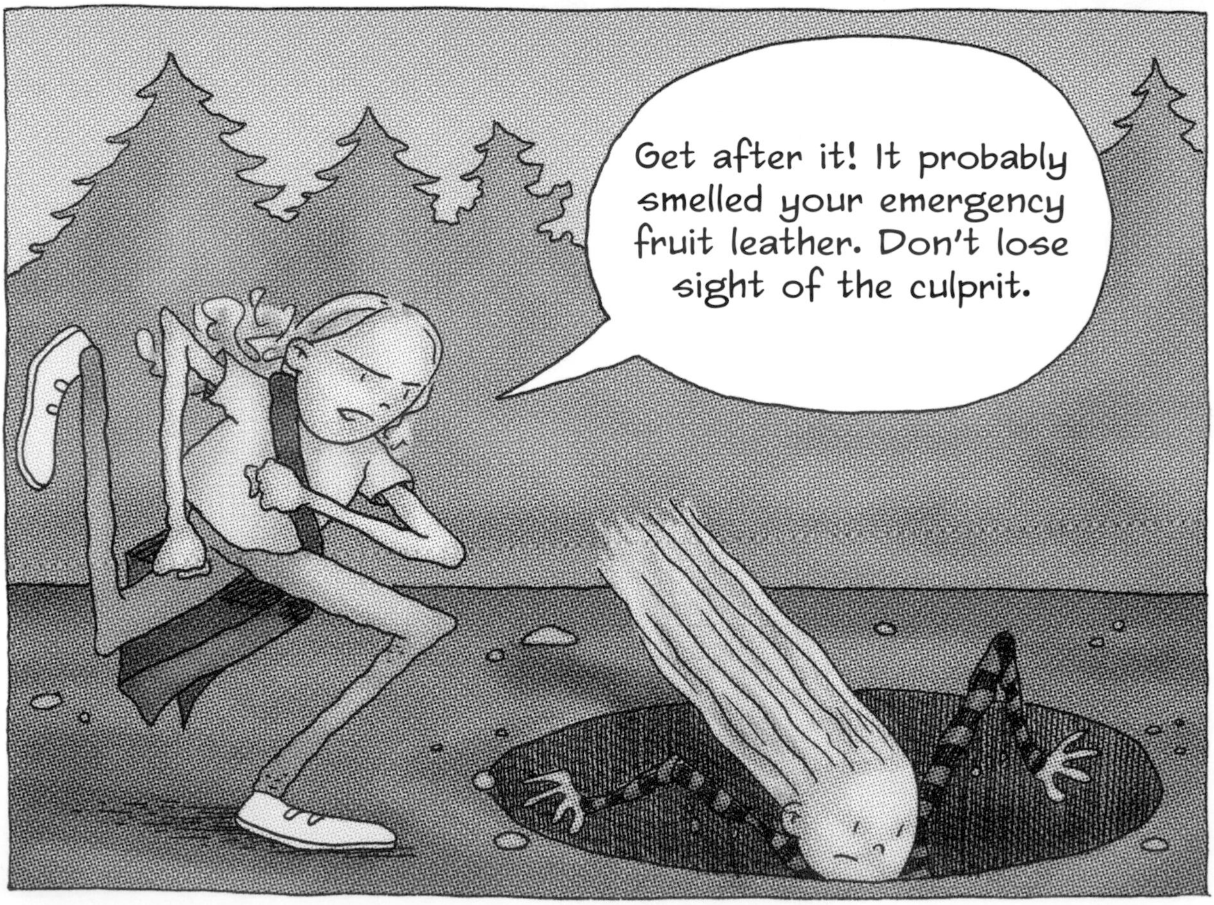
Get after it! It probably smelled your emergency fruit leather. Don't lose sight of the culprit.

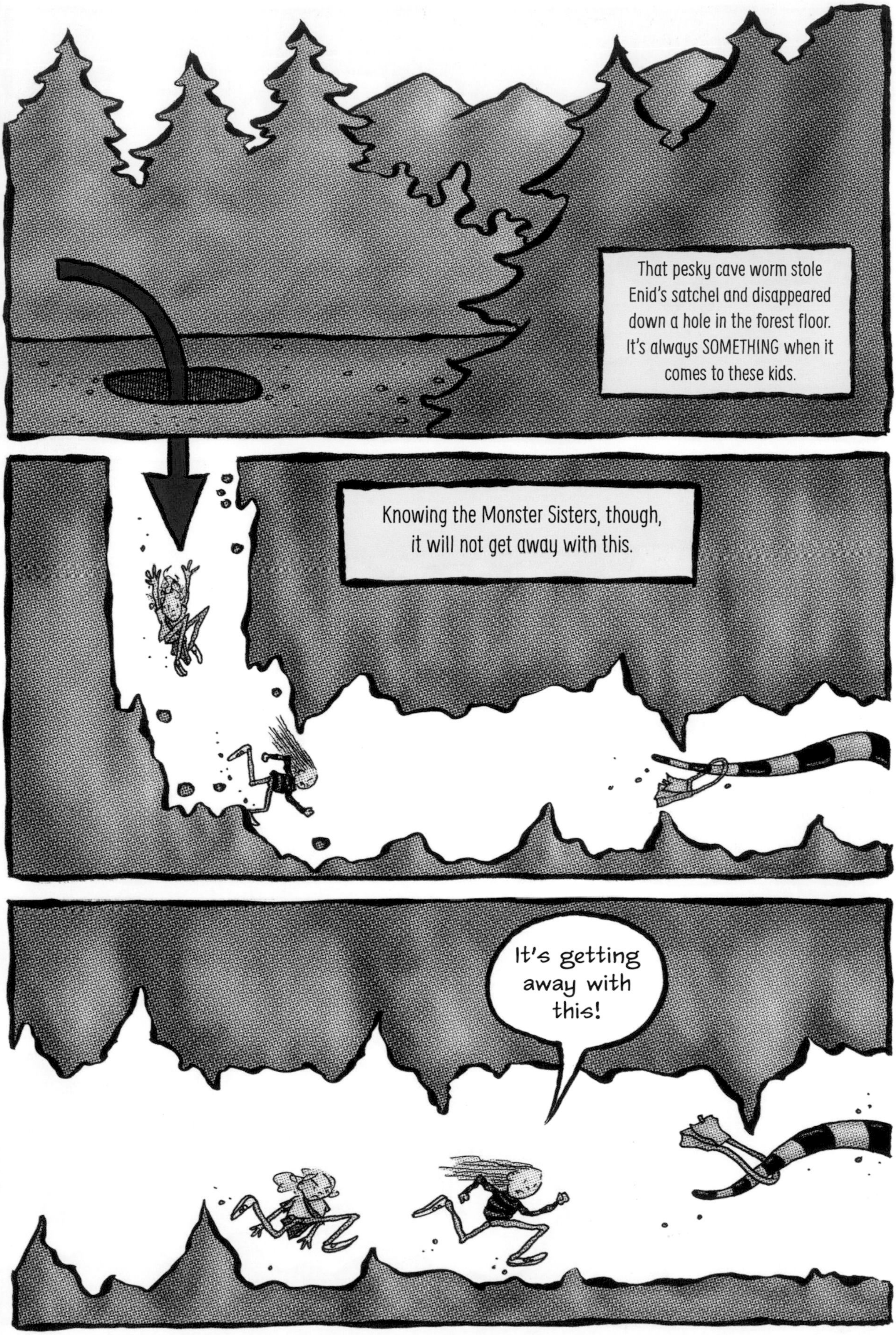
That pesky cave worm stole Enid's satchel and disappeared down a hole in the forest floor. It's always SOMETHING when it comes to these kids.
Knowing the Monster Sisters, though, it will not get away with this.
It's getting away with this!

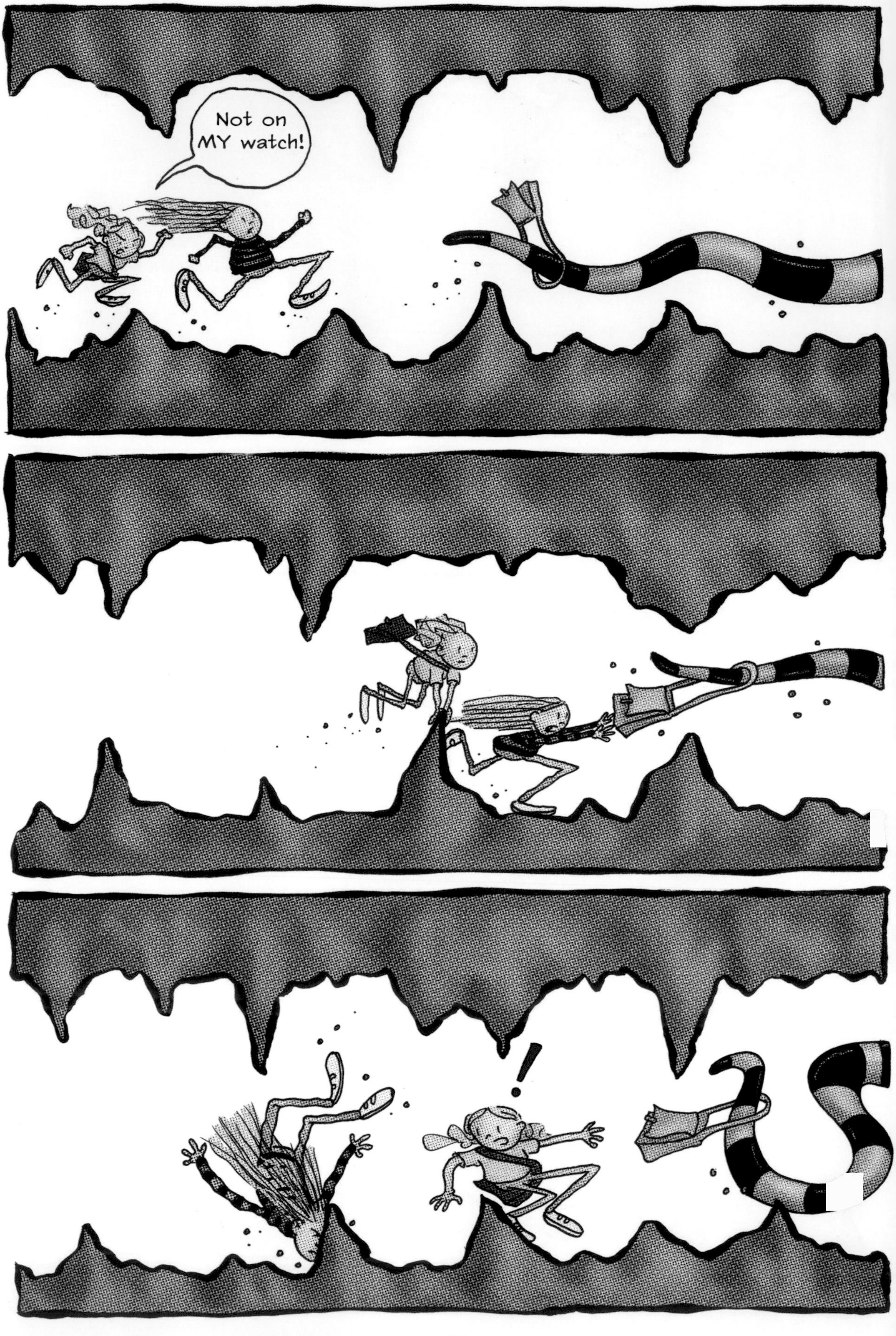
Not on MY watch!
!

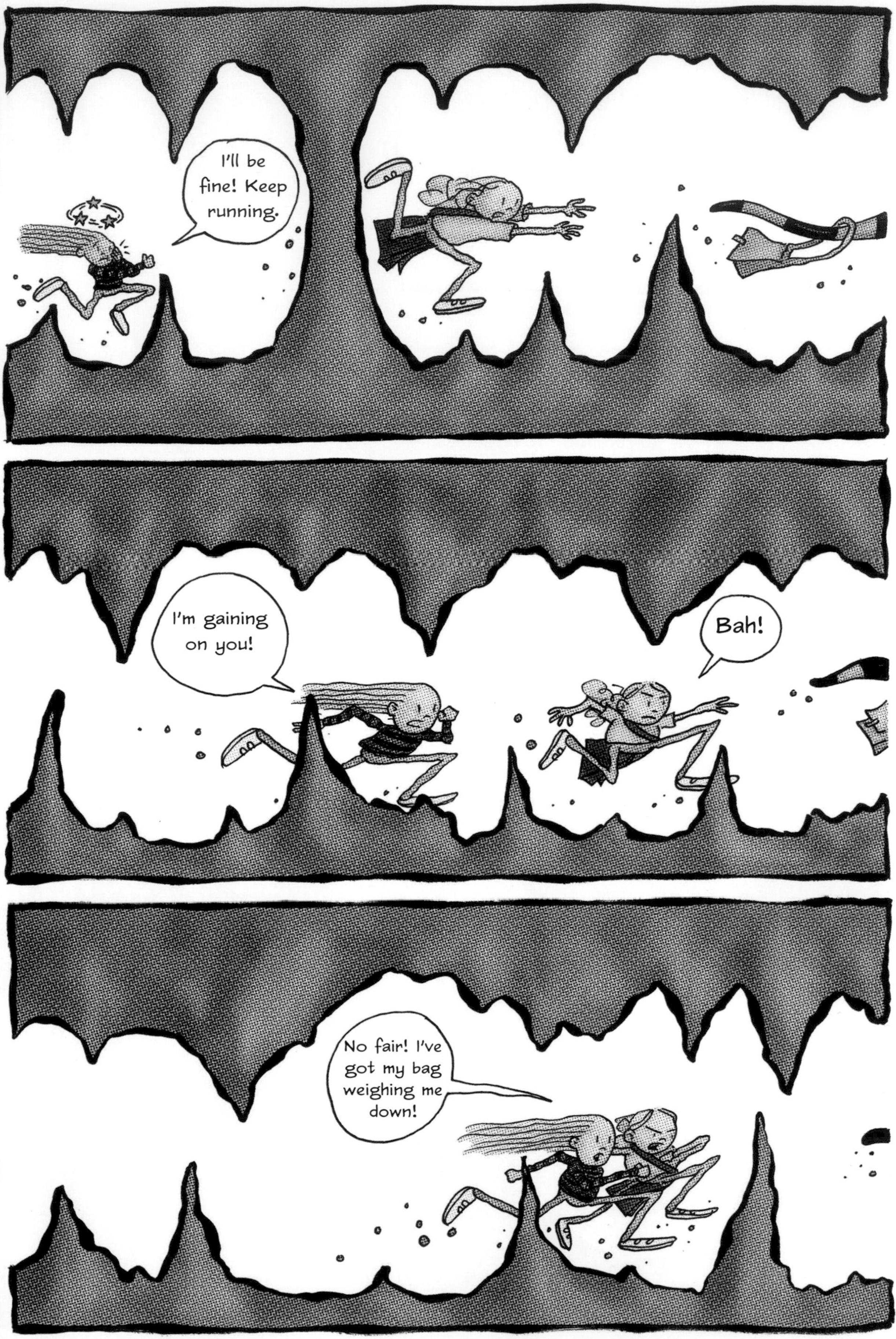
I'll be fine! Keep running.
I'm gaining on you!
Bah!
No fair! I've got my bag weighing me down!

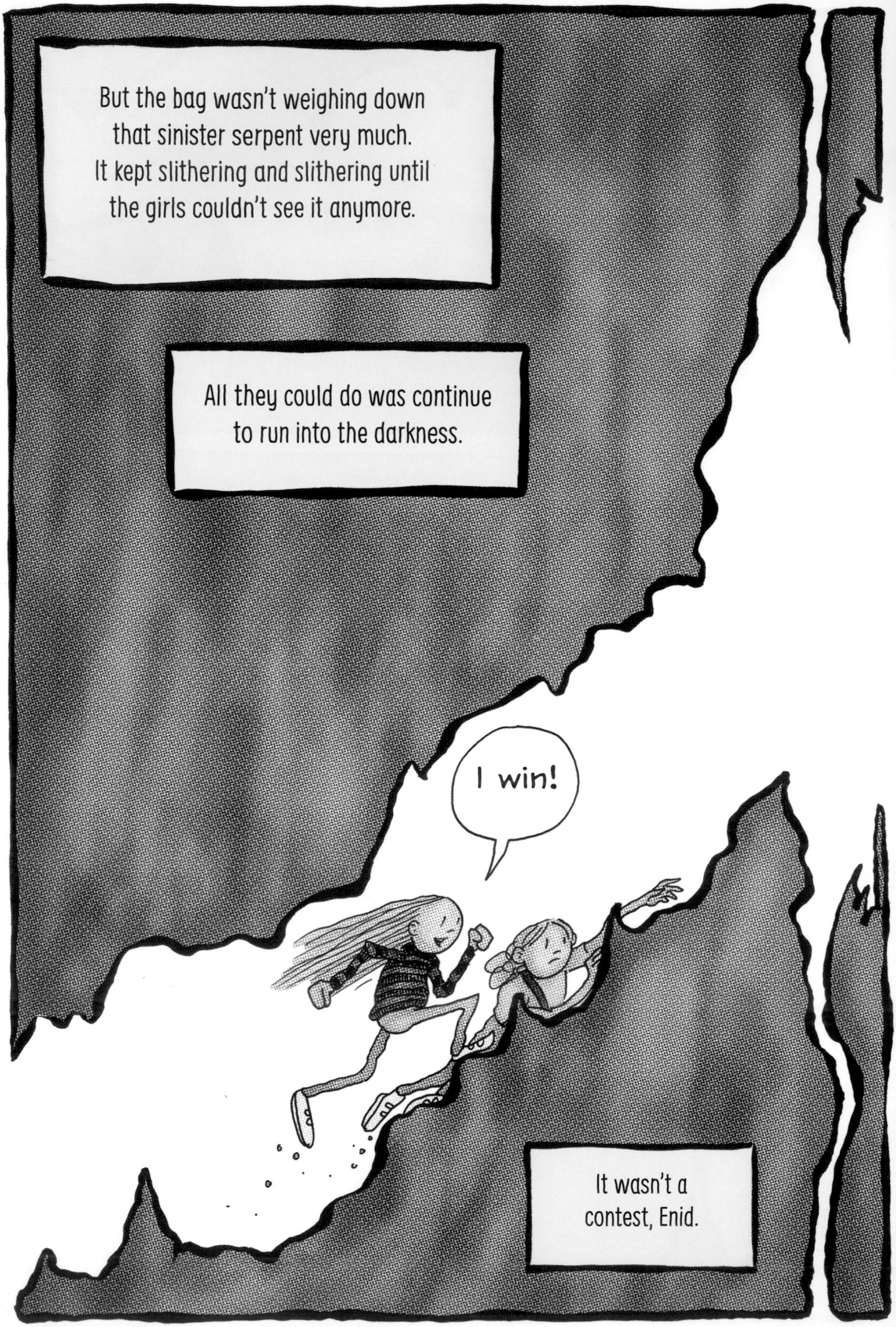
But the bag wasn't weighing down that sinister serpent very much. It kept slithering and slithering until the girls couldn't see it anymore.
All they could do was continue to run into the darkness.
I win!
It wasn't a contest, Enid.

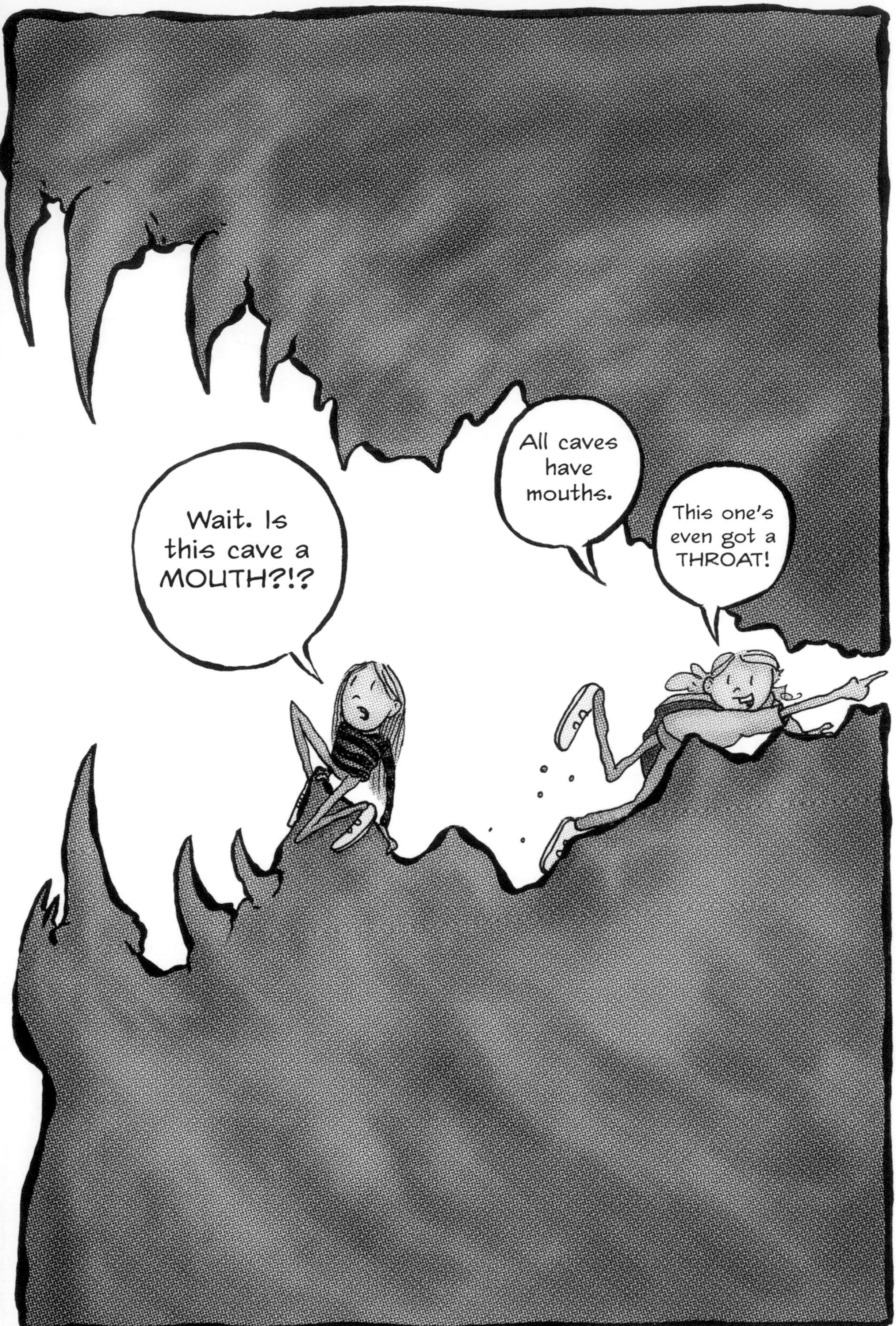
Wait. Is this cave a MOUTH?!?
All caves have mouths.
This one's even got a THROAT!

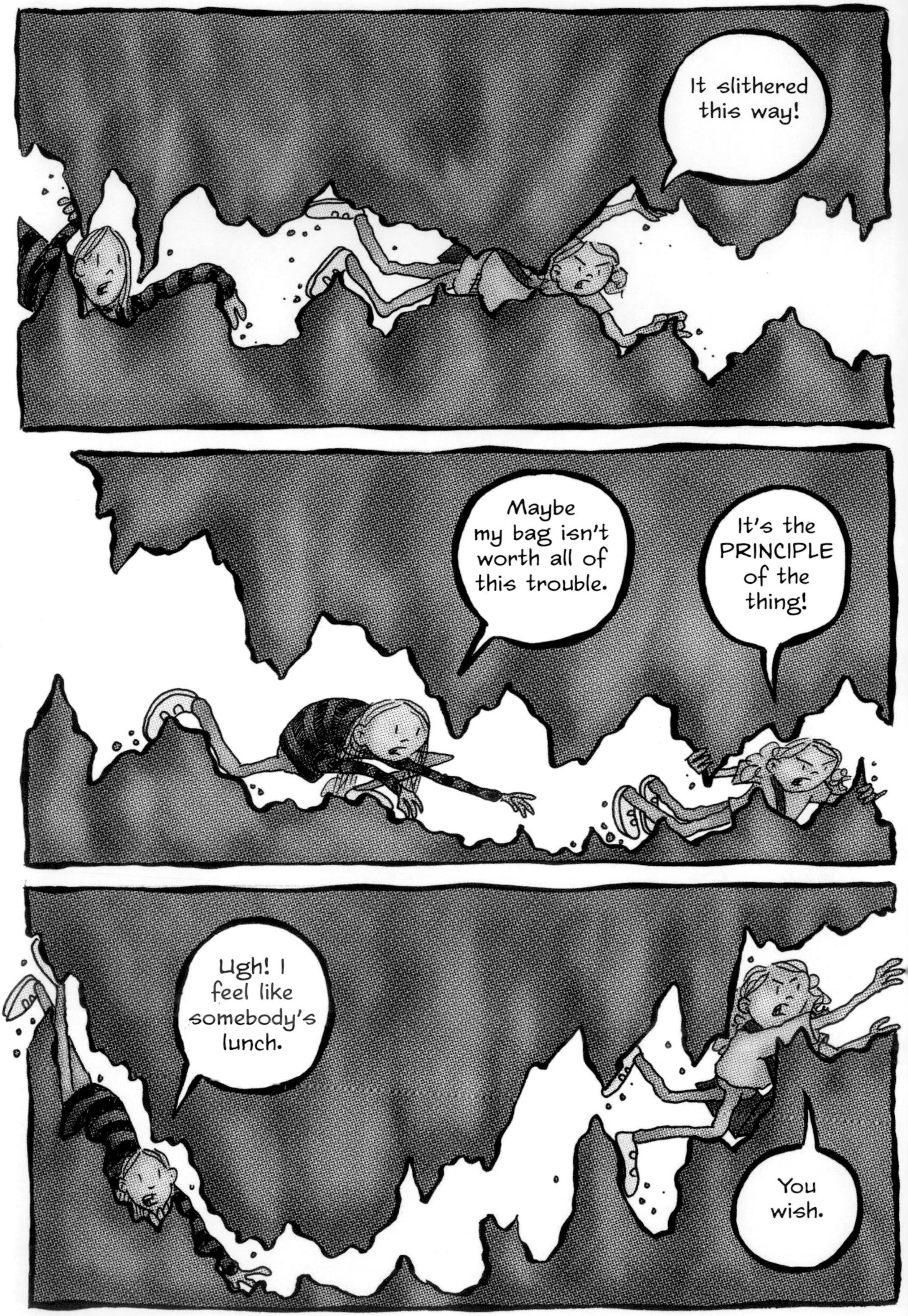
It slithered this way!
Maybe my bag isn't worth all of this trouble.
It's the PRINCIPLE of the thing!
Ugh! I feel like somebody's lunch.
You wish.

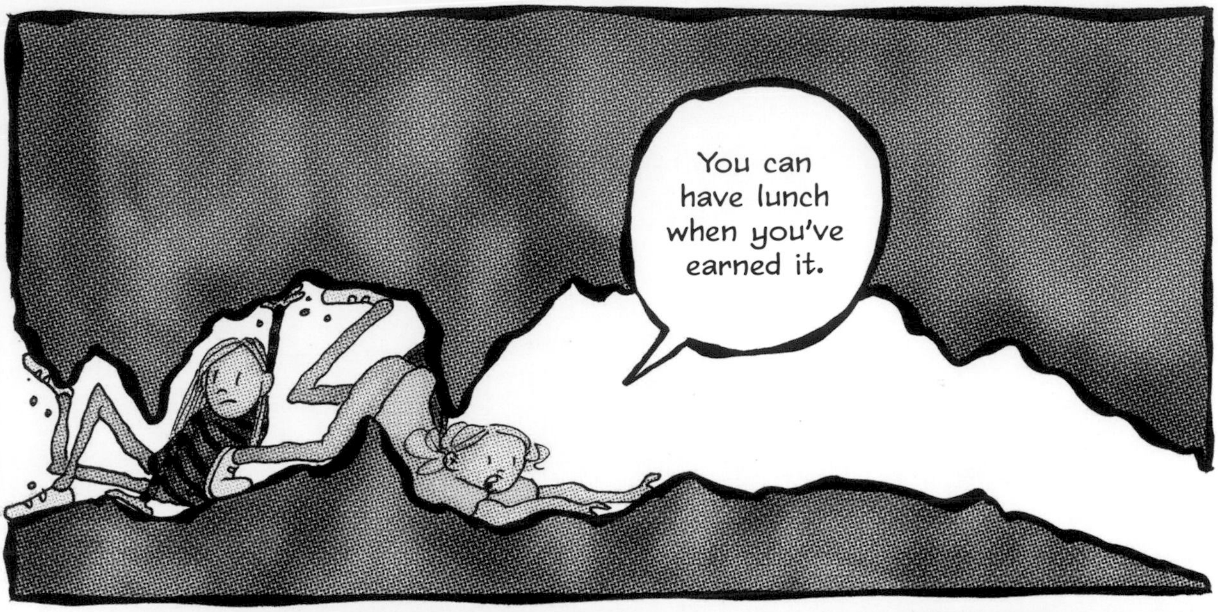
You can have lunch when you've earned it.

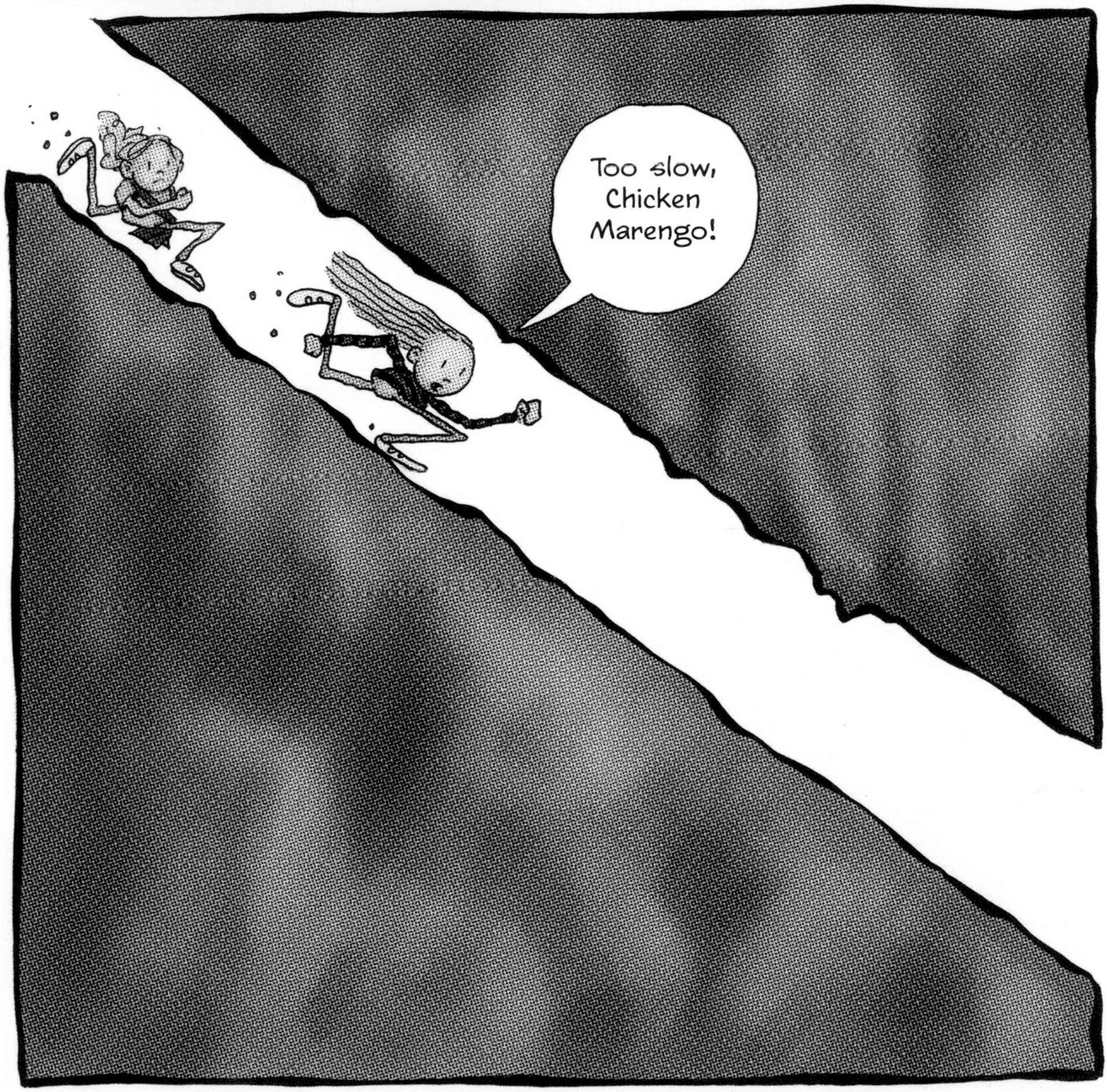
Too slow, Chicken Marengo!

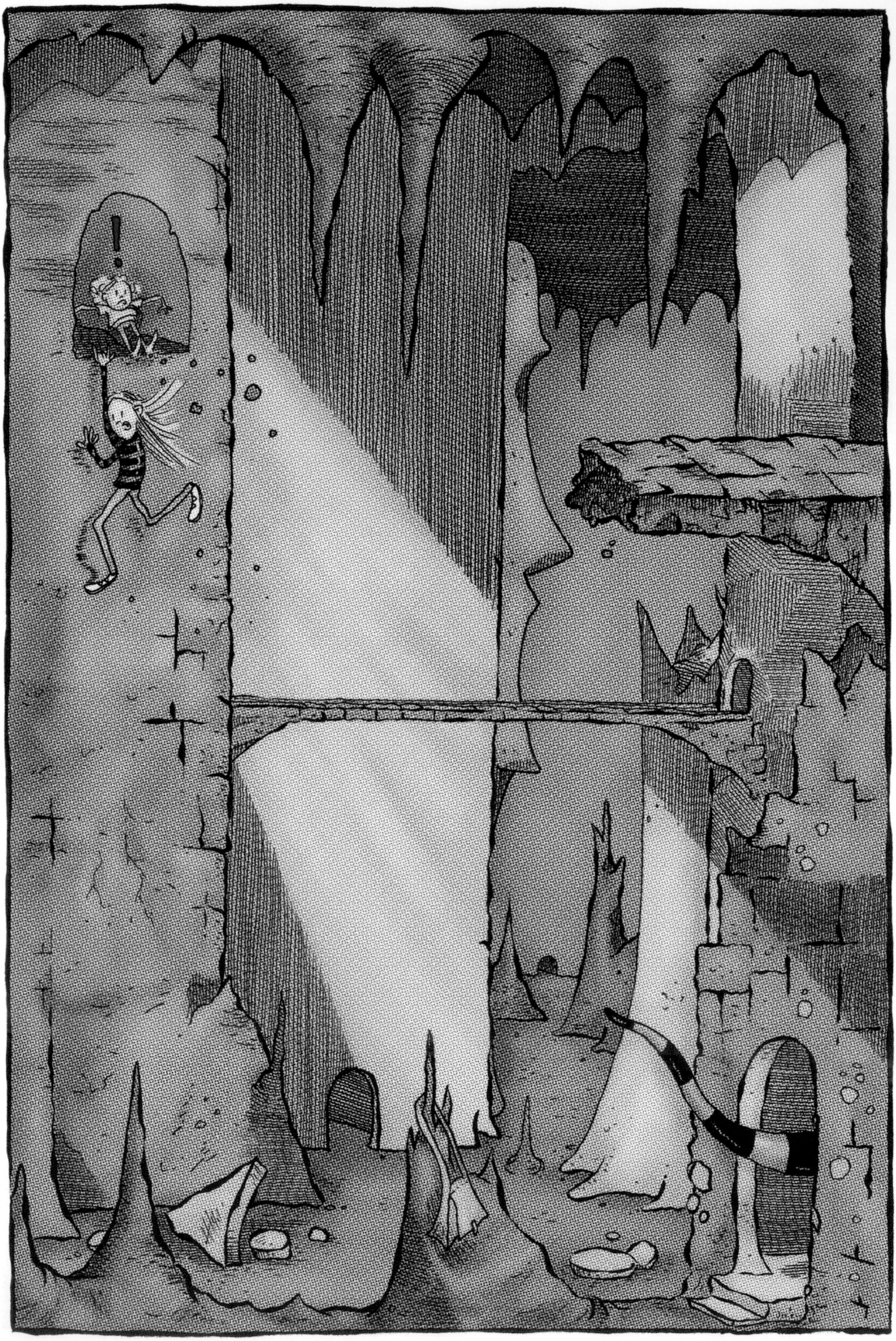
!

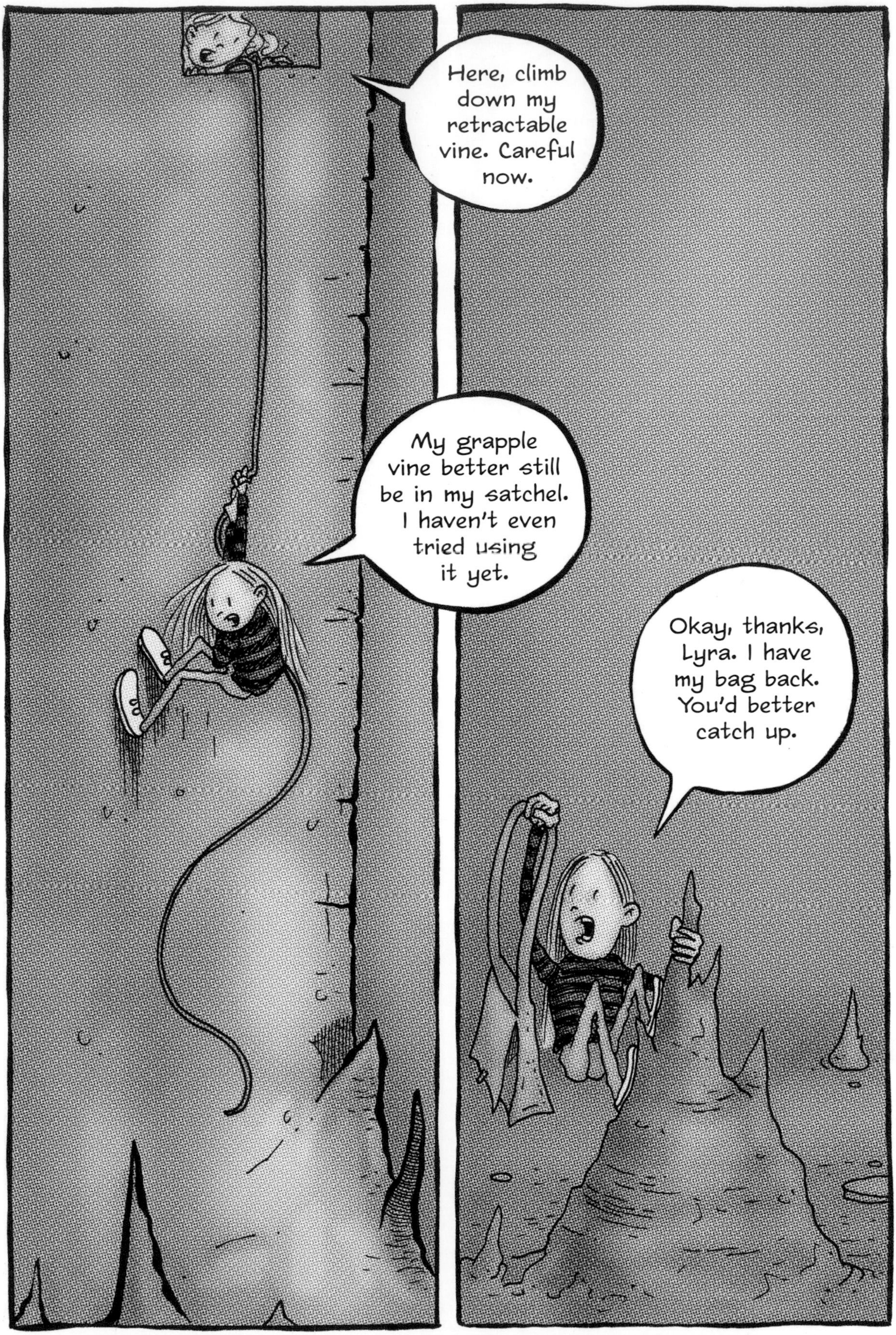
Here, climb down my retractable vine. Careful now.
My grapple vine better still be in my satchel. I haven't even tried using it yet.
Okay, thanks, Lyra. I have my bag back. You'd better catch up.

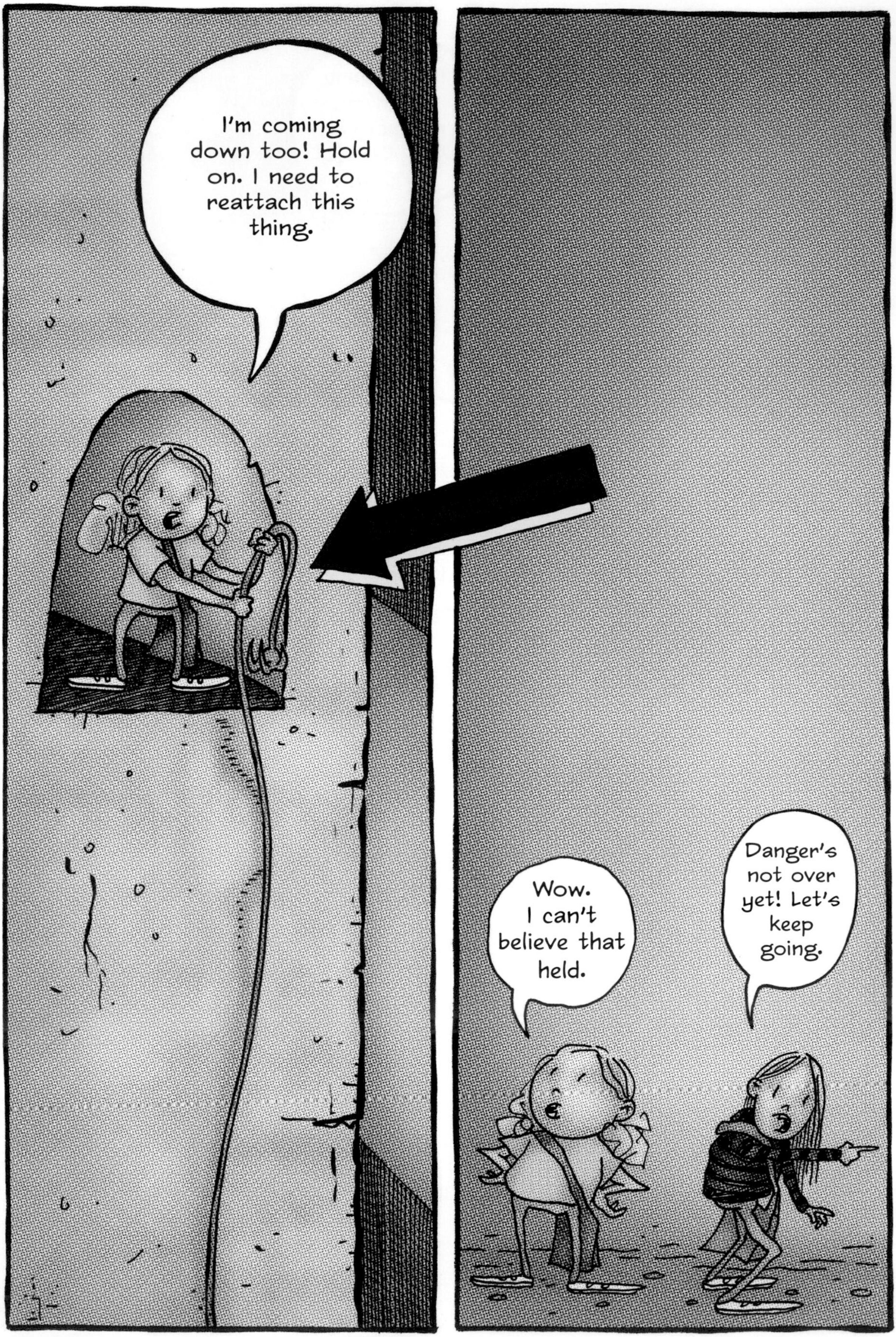

I'm coming down too! Hold on. I need to reattach this thing.
Wow. I can't believe that held.
Danger's not over yet! Let's keep going.

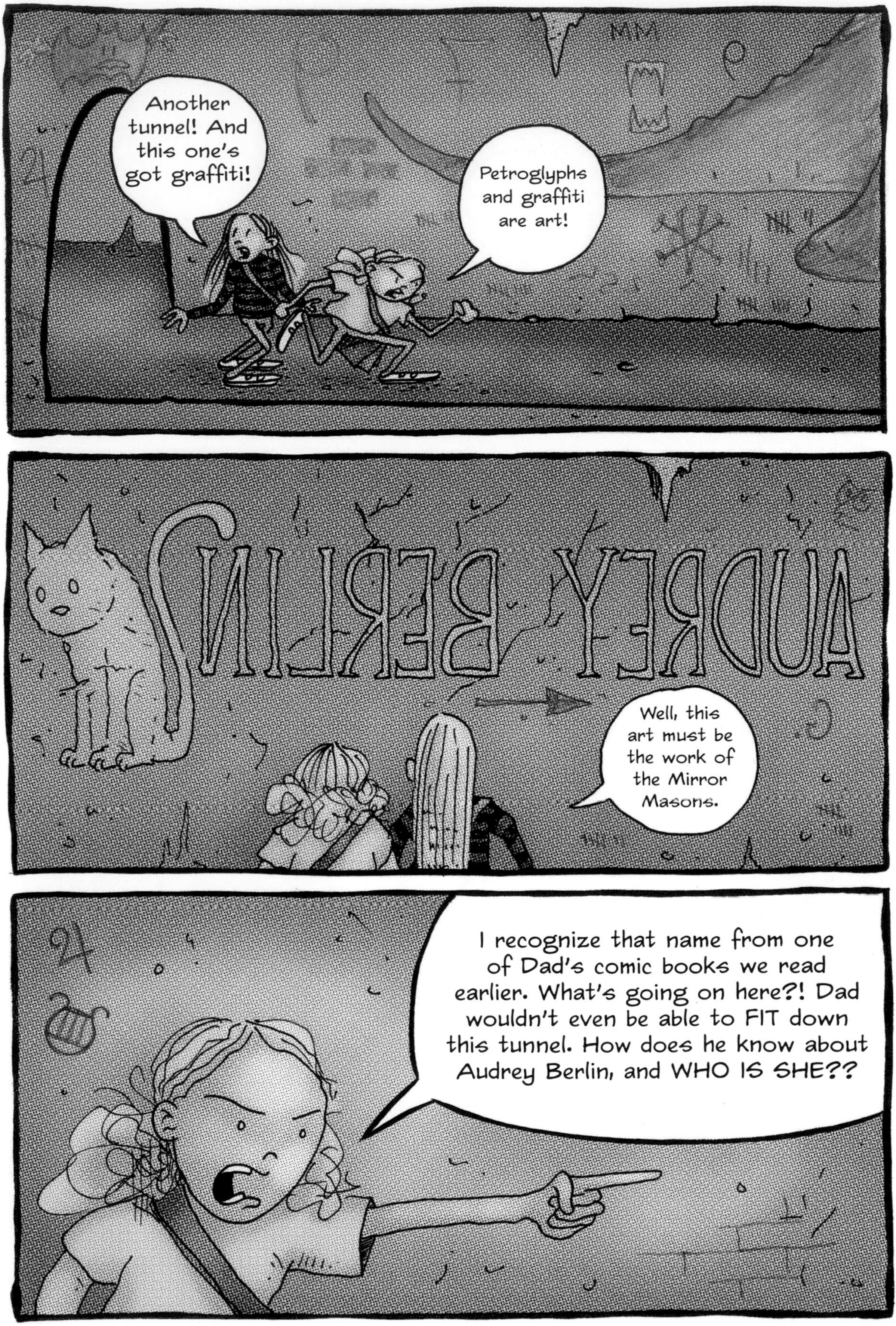
Another tunnel! And this one's got graffiti!
Petroglyphs and graffiti are art!
AUDREY BERLIN
Well, this art must be the work of the Mirror Masons.
I recognize that name from one of Dad's comic books we read earlier. What's going on here?! Dad wouldn't even be able to FIT down this tunnel. How does he know about Audrey Berlin, and WHO IS SHE??

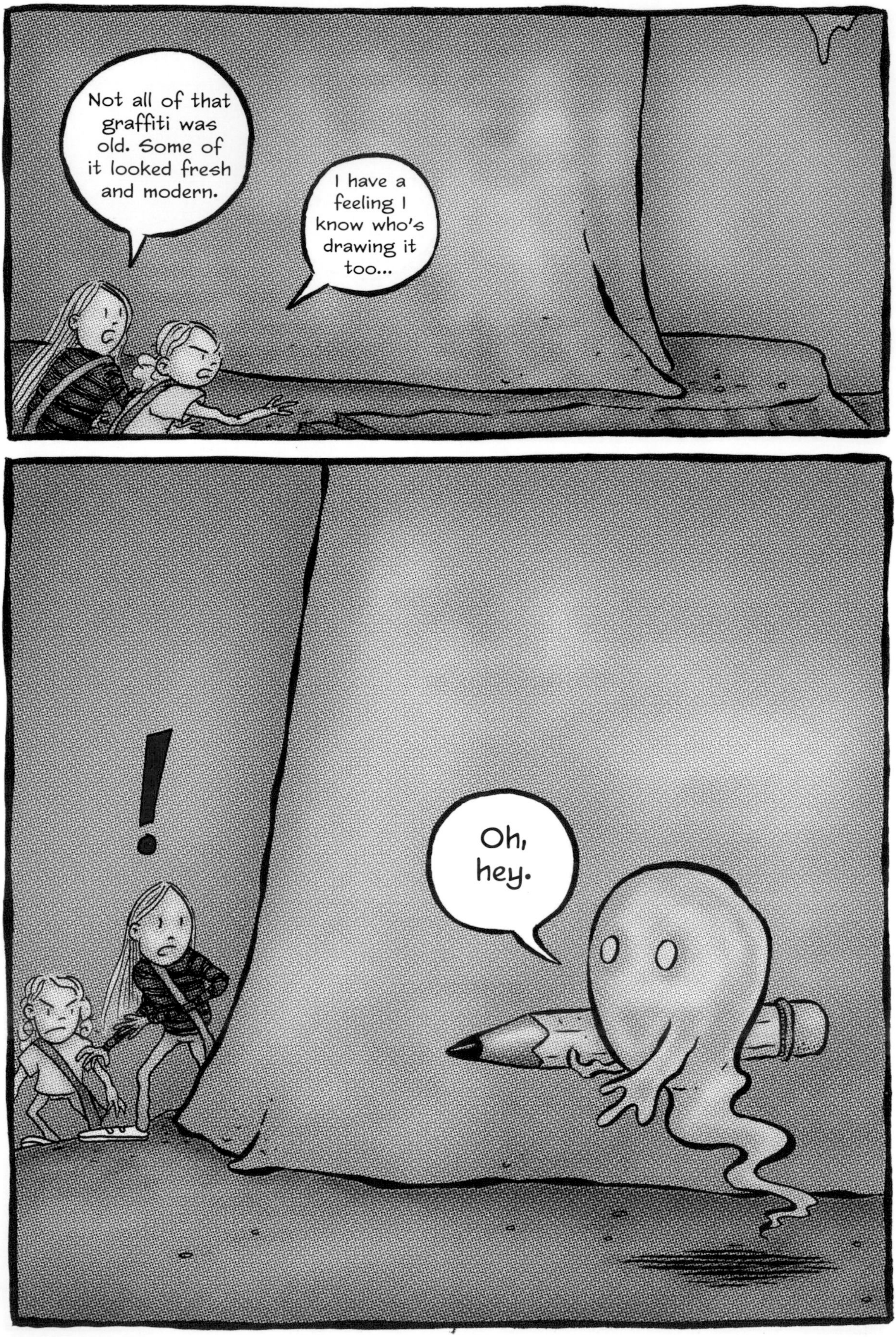

Not all of that graffiti was old. Some of it looked fresh and modern.
I have a feeling I know who's drawing it too...
!
Oh, hey.

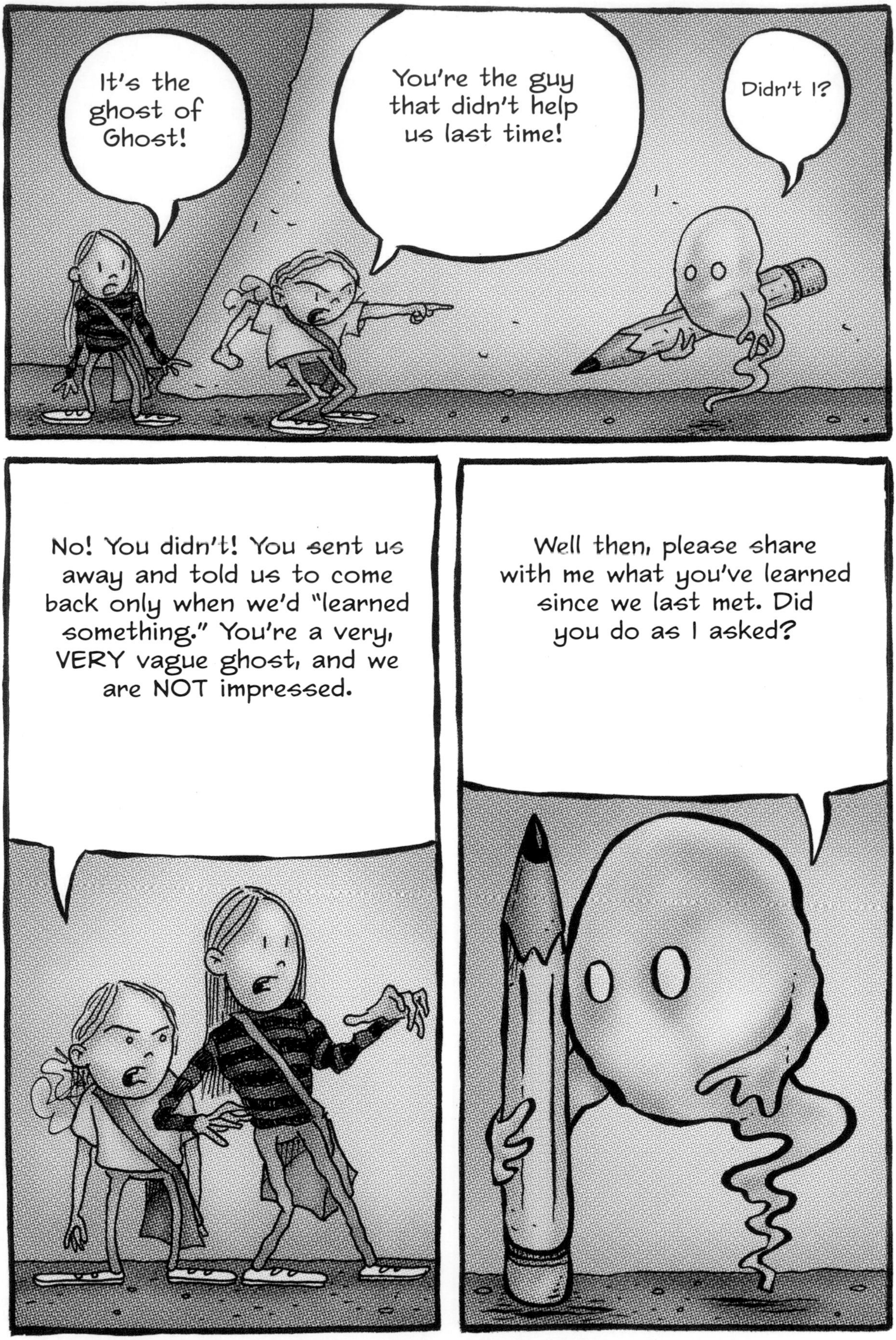

It's the ghost of Ghost!
You're the guy that didn't help us last time!
Didn't I?
No! You didn't! You sent us away and told us to come back only when we'd "learned something." You're a very, VERY vague ghost, and we are NOT impressed.
Well then, please share with me what you've learned since we last met. Did you do as I asked?

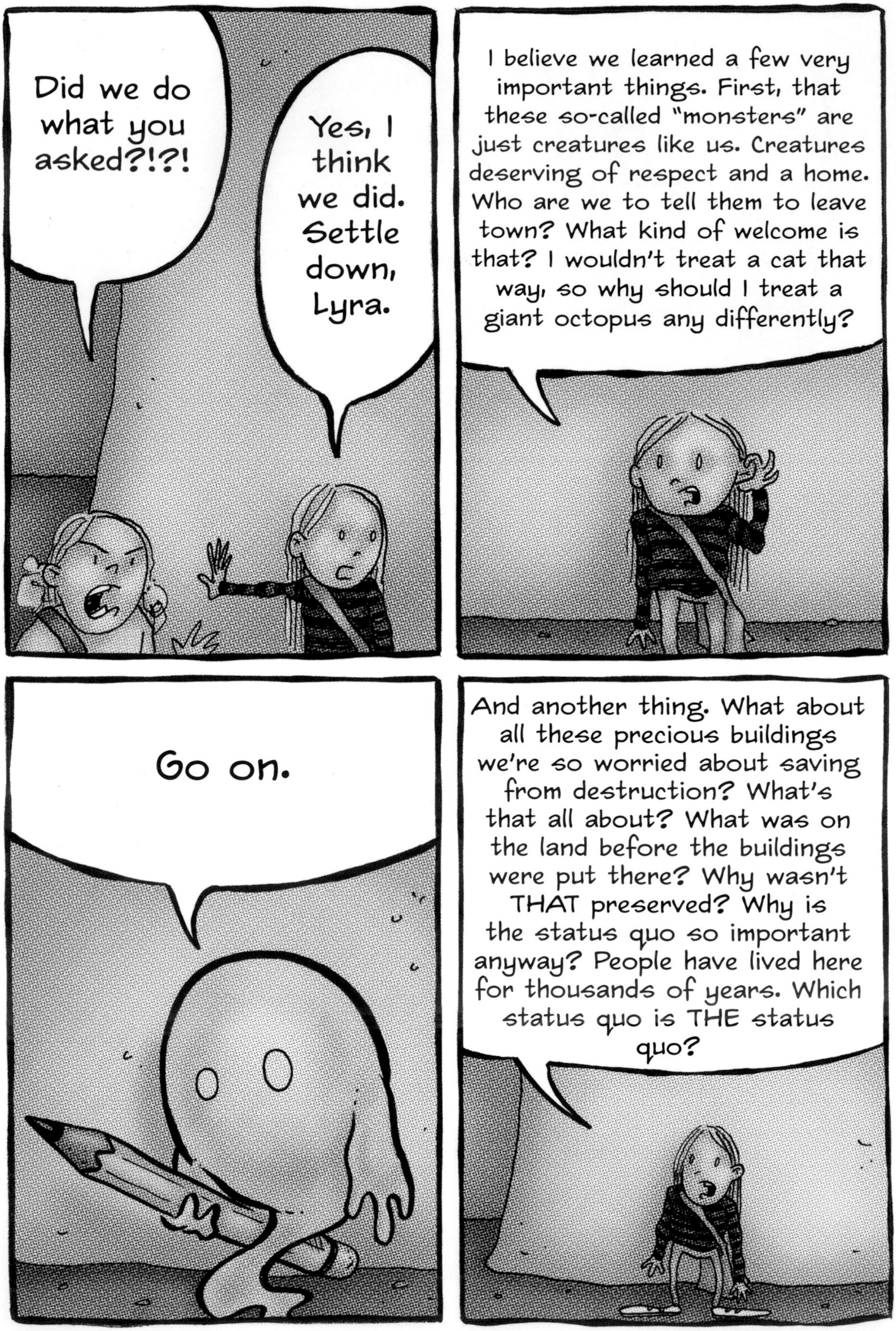
Did we do what you asked?!?!
Yes, I think we did. Settle down, Lyra.
I believe we learned a few very important things. First, that these so-called "monsters" are just creatures like us. Creatures deserving of respect and a home. Who are we to tell them to leave town? What kind of welcome is that? I wouldn't treat a cat that way, so why should I treat a giant octopus any differently?
Go on.
And another thing. What about all these precious buildings we're so worried about saving from destruction? What's that all about? What was on the land before the buildings were put there? Why wasn't THAT preserved? Why is the status quo so important anyway? People have lived here for thousands of years. Which status quo is THE status quo?

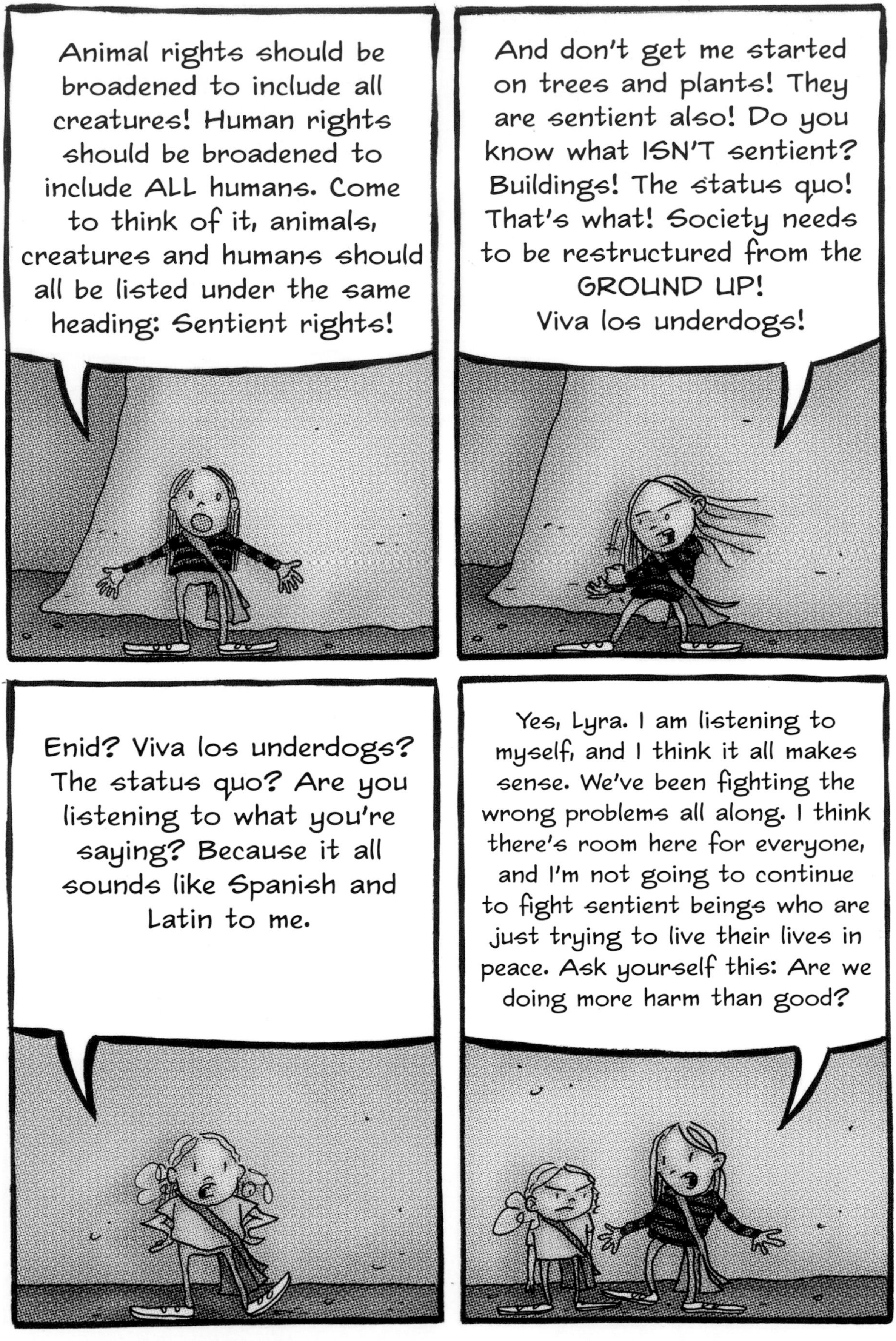
Animal rights should be broadened to include all creatures! Human rights should be broadened to include ALL humans. Come to think of it, animals, creatures and humans should all be listed under the same heading: Sentient rights!
And don't get me started on trees and plants! They are sentient also! Do you know what ISN'T sentient? Buildings! The status quo! That's what! Society needs to be restructured from the GROUND UP! Viva los underdogs!
Enid? Viva los underdogs? The status quo? Are you listening to what you're saying? Because it all sounds like Spanish and Latin to me.
Yes, Lyra. I am listening to myself, and I think it all makes sense. We've been fighting the wrong problems all along. I think there's room here for everyone, and I'm not going to continue to fight sentient beings who are just trying to live their lives in peace. Ask yourself this: Are we doing more harm than good?

Very good, Monster Sisters. You have indeed returned with a better understanding of what is actually going on out there.

Yes, previous citizens of this land have returned, and new denizens are arriving daily. Yes, they are causing discomfort to the status quo, but does the status quo not deserve to be uncomfortable now and then?

You may fear your land is being taken from you, but your land was taken from somebody else once, and their land was taken from the animals once, and the animals took it from the sea, and the sea took it from the creatures who are back to continue the cycle.

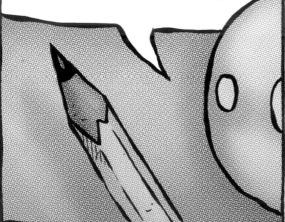

You're alive. Right now you both are alive and well. What else do you need? Live your lives and stop clinging to a future you can't control. You'll find that very liberating.

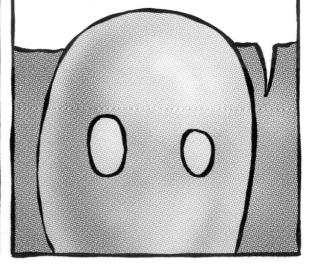

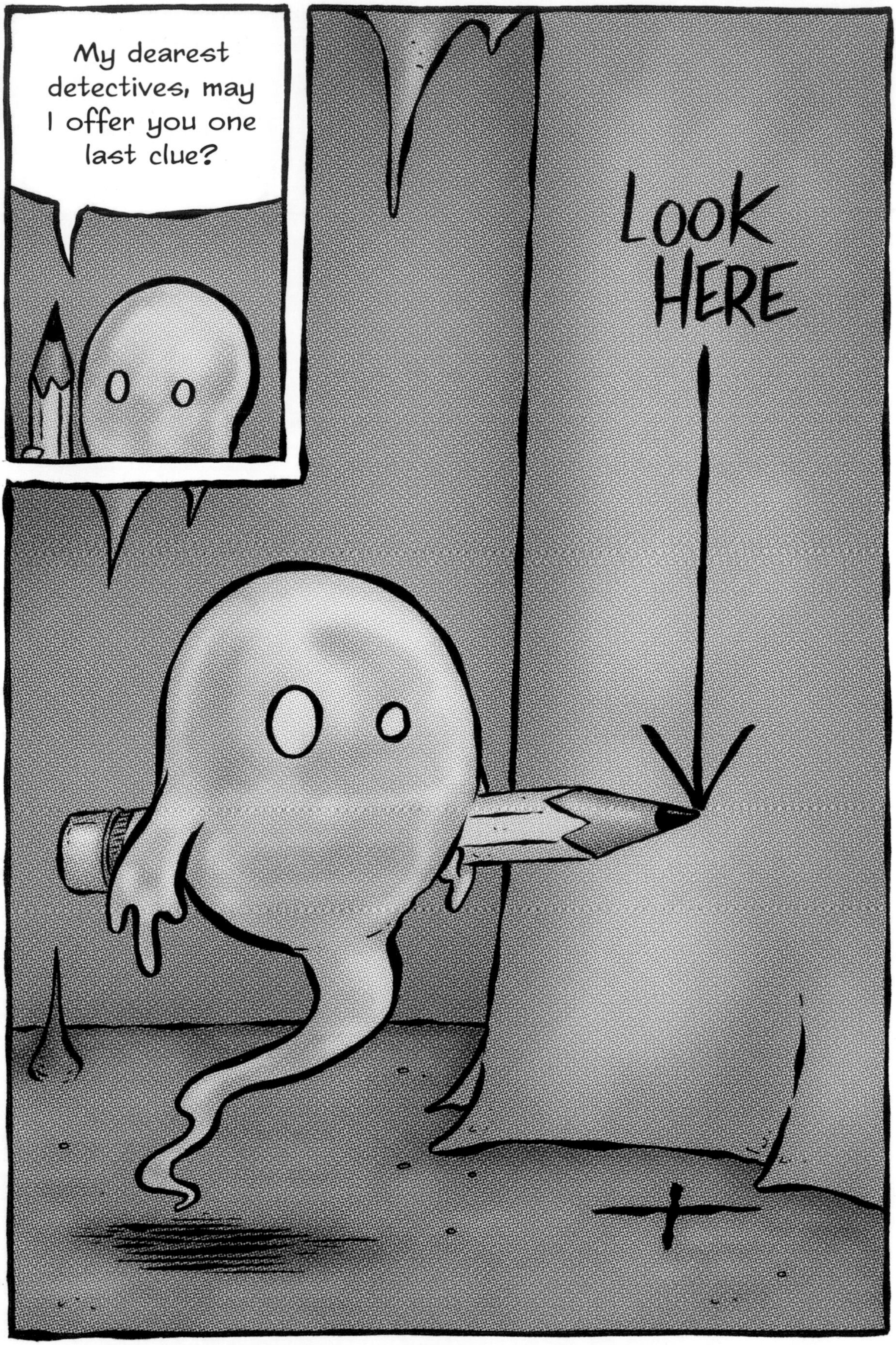
My dearest detectives, may I offer you one last clue?
LOOK HERE

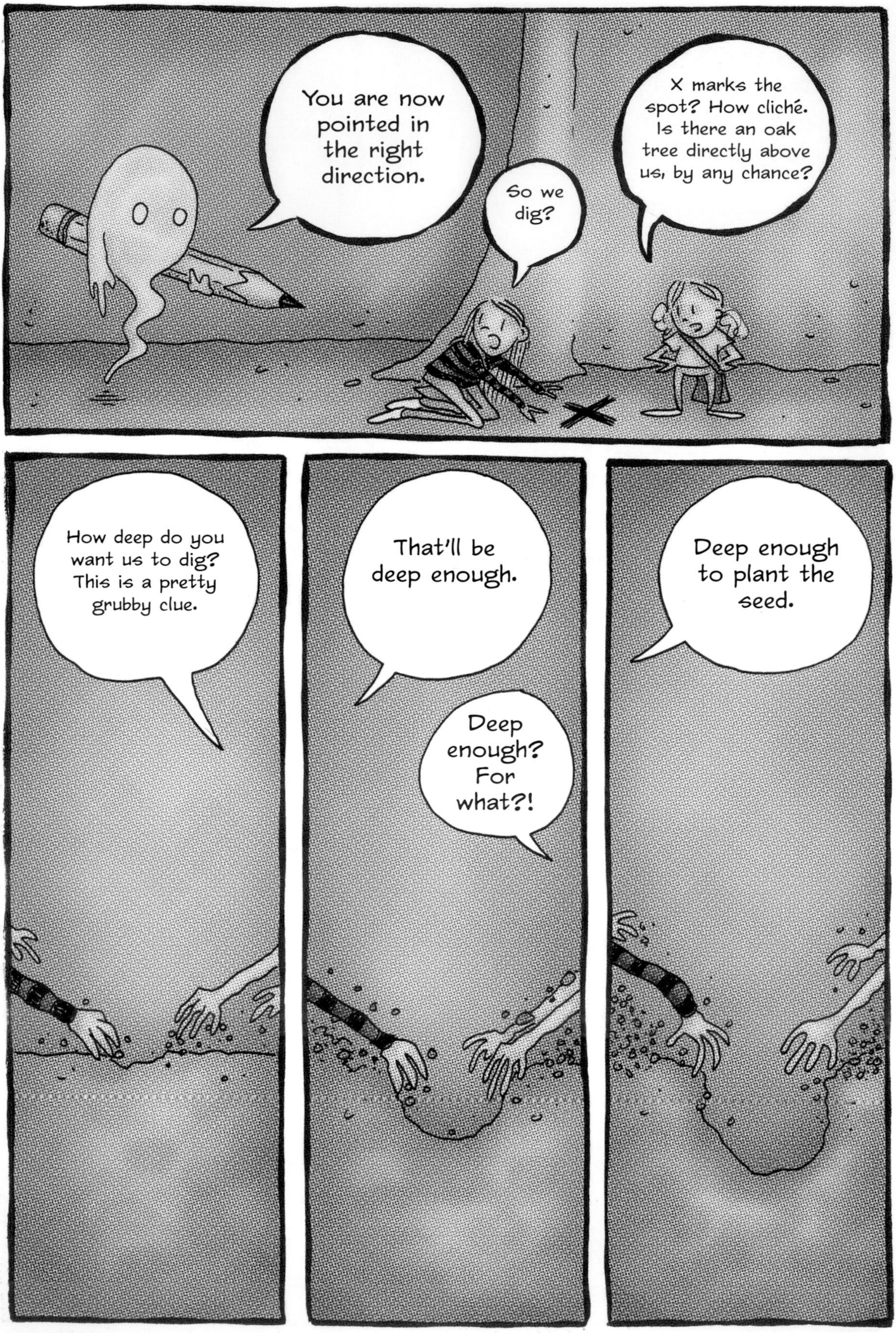
You are now pointed in the right direction.
So we dig?
X marks the spot? How cliché. Is there an oak tree directly above us, by any chance?
How deep do you want us to dig? This is a pretty grubby clue.
That'll be deep enough.
Deep enough? For what?!
Deep enough to plant the seed.

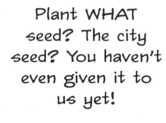

Plant WHAT seed? The city seed? You haven't even given it to us yet!

Yes. You've had the seeds with you the whole time.

You have the seeds with you.

Hole time.

...

...

What?

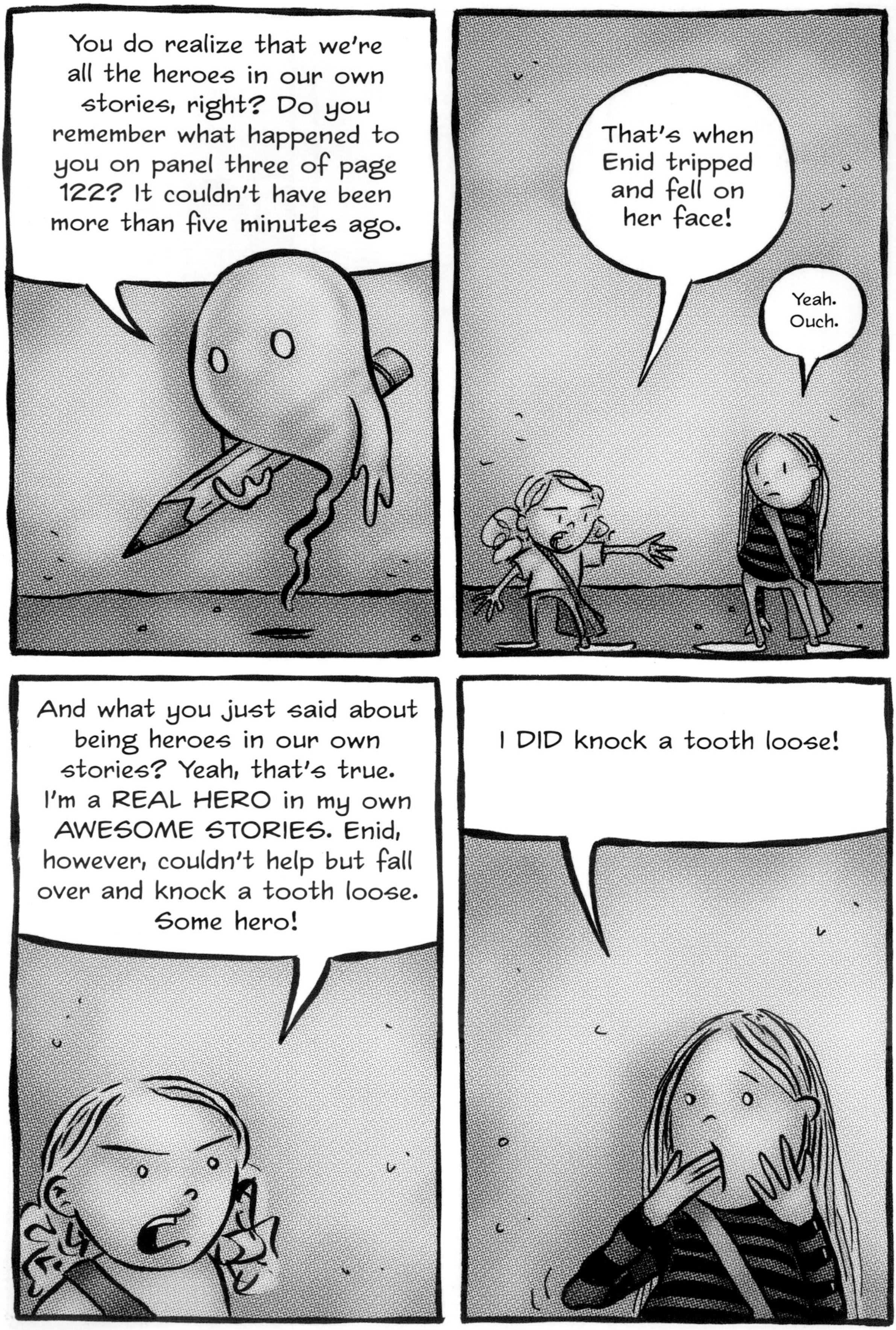

You do realize that we're all the heroes in our own stories, right? Do you remember what happened to you on panel three of page 122? It couldn't have been more than five minutes ago.
That's when Enid tripped and fell on her face!
Yeah. Ouch.
And what you just said about being heroes in our own stories? Yeah, that's true. I'm a REAL HERO in my own AWESOME STORIES. Enid, however, couldn't help but fall over and knock a tooth loose. Some hero!
I DID knock a tooth loose!

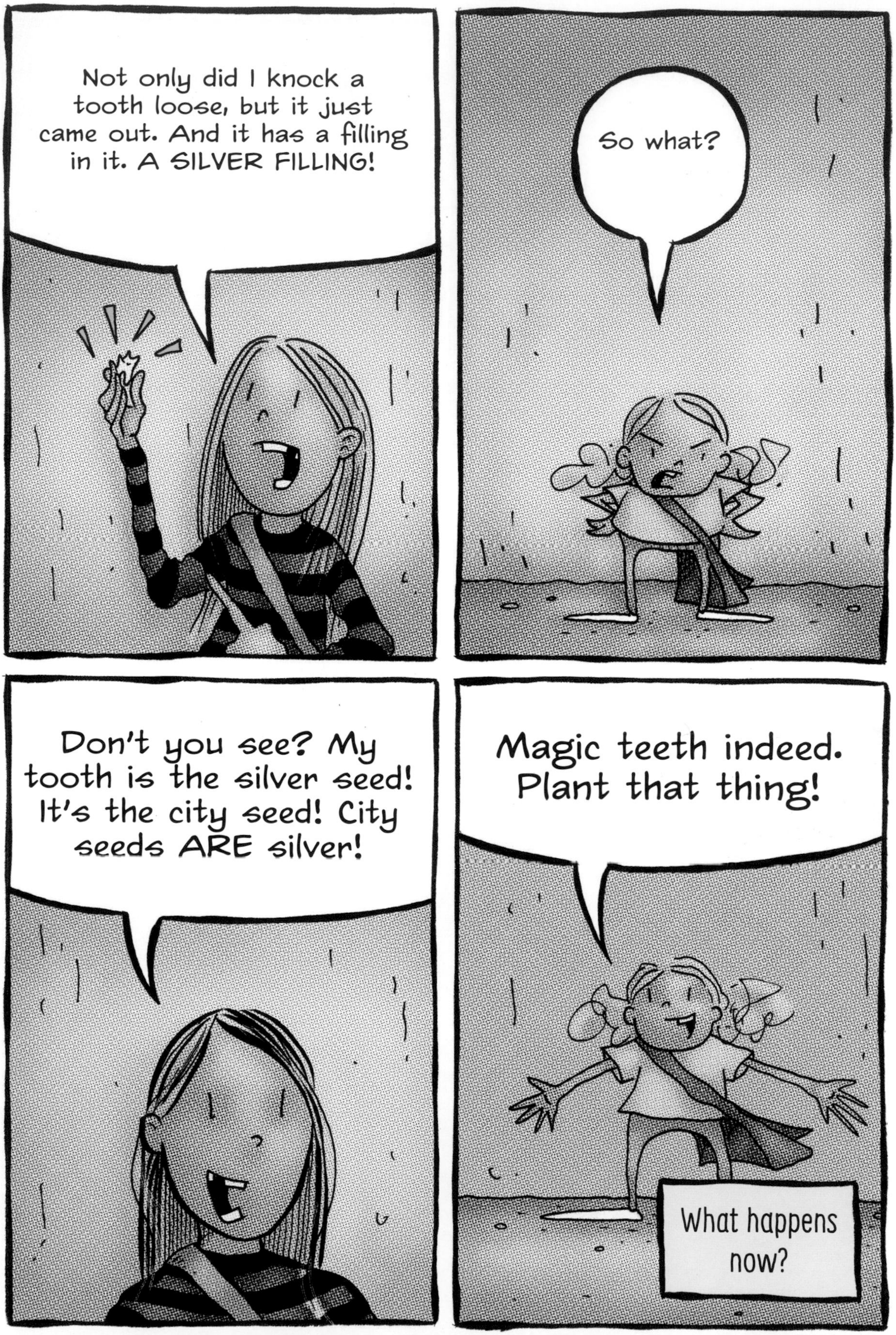
Not only did I knock a tooth loose, but it just came out. And it has a filling in it. A SILVER FILLING!
So what?
Don't you see? My tooth is the silver seed! It's the city seed! City seeds ARE silver!
Magic teeth indeed. Plant that thing!
What happens now?

(RUMBLING ENSUES)

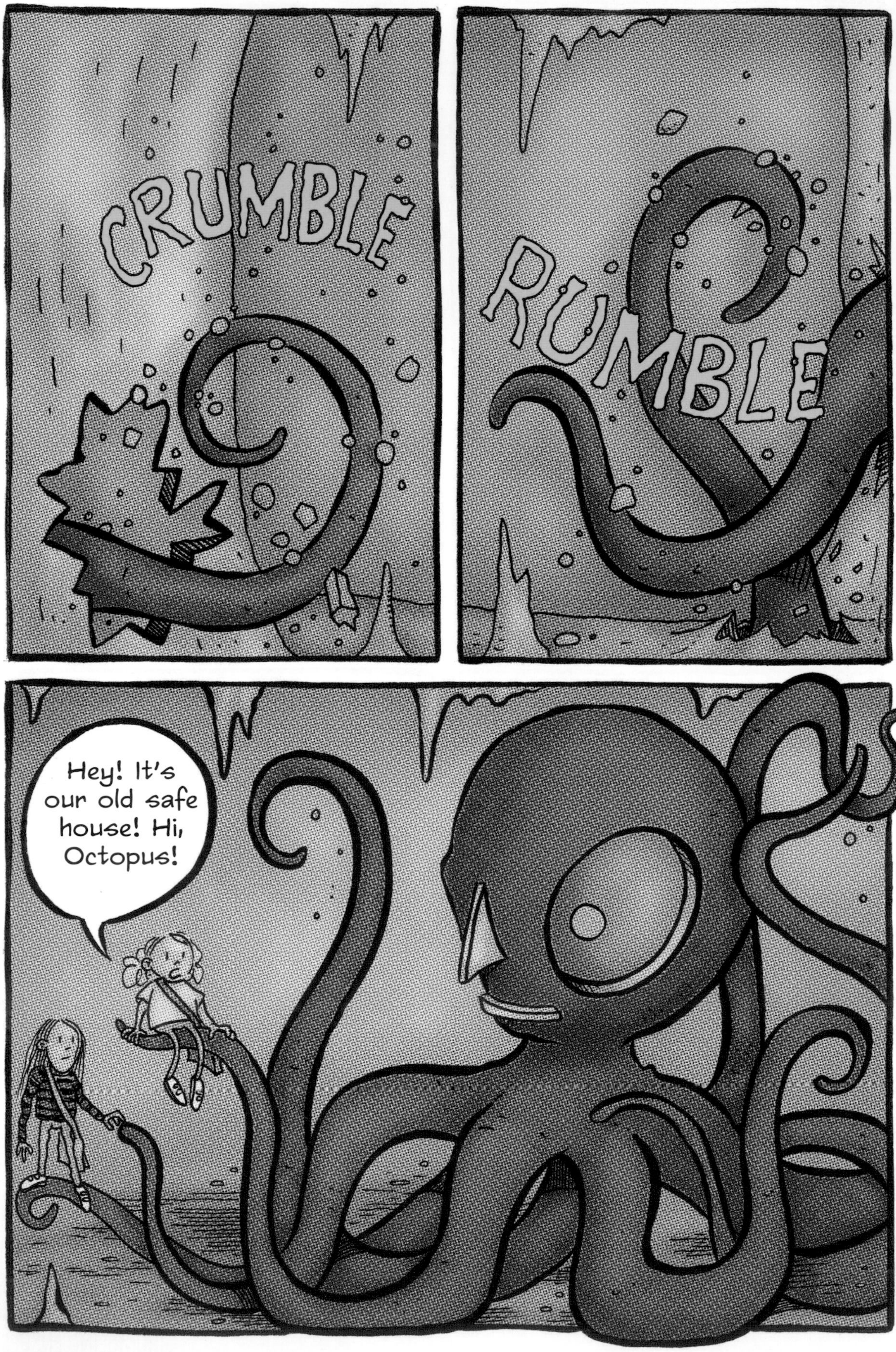
CRUMBLE
RUMBLE
Hey! It's our old safe house! Hi, Octopus!

Hi, girls. Thanks for dropping by. I trust you didn't have any trouble finding the place.

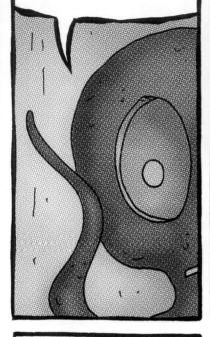

Were you expecting us? Did you know the Mirror Masons left a very complicated trail leading us here?

I know they TRIED to leave a trail leading here, but they never got past the waiting room themselves.

That room with all the graffiti? Ha! We got farther because of the magic teeth, right?

That's right. You did it. You used teamwork and ingenuity, and you made it.

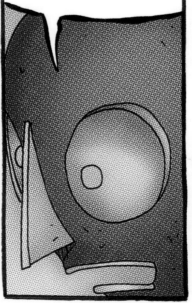

Is there treasure? What do we win? We'll gladly accept treasure.

The treasure is knowledge. I can tell you a story as your reward.

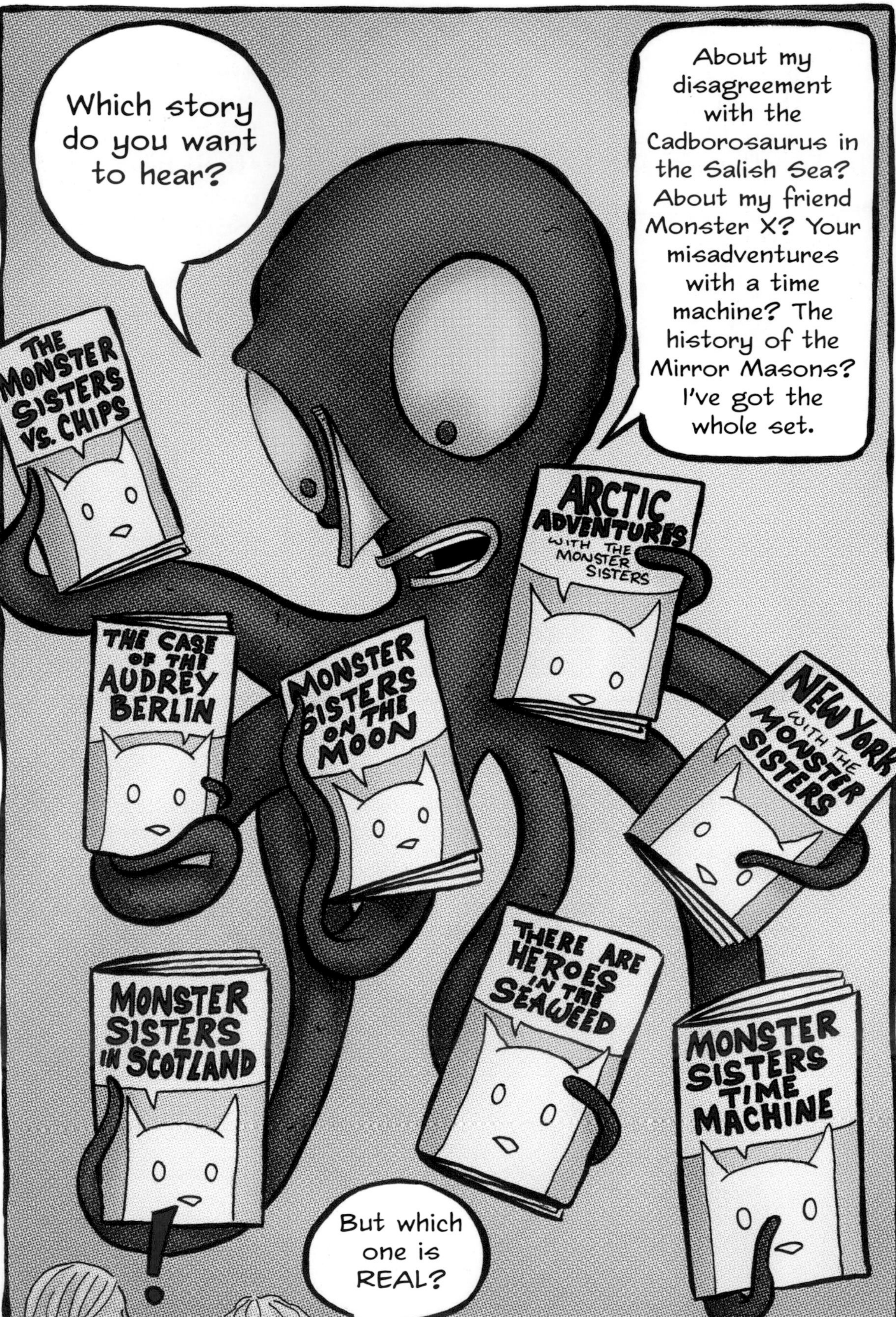
Which story do you want to hear?
About my disagreement with the Cadborosaurus in the Salish Sea? About my friend Monster X? Your misadventures with a time machine? The history of the Mirror Masons? I've got the whole set.
THE MONSTER SISTERS VS. CHIPS
ARCTIC ADVENTURES WITH THE MONSTER SISTERS
THE CASE OF THE AUDREY BERLIN
MONSTER SISTERS ON THE MOON
NEW YORK WITH THE MONSTER SISTERS
MONSTER SISTERS IN SCOTLAND
THERE ARE HEROES IN THE SEAWEED
MONSTER SISTERS TIME MACHINE
!
But which one is REAL?

Which one is real? They're ALL real. Your stories are as real to someone else as their stories are to you, don't forget. When it comes right down to it, nothing else matters except stories.

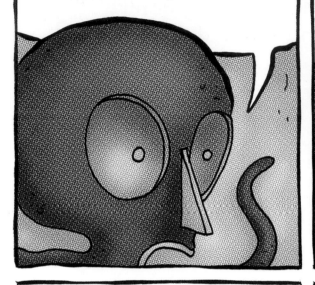

This cave and these comics are part of the history of this city, which is always growing and changing and adapting to new challenges. It's not always about YOU. Remember that. Some of these stories are, but most of them aren't.

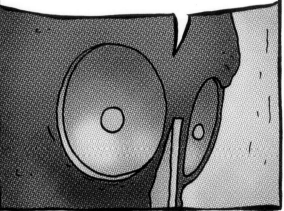

The secret the Mirror Masons are so closely guarding is this: It's not about you. Art holds a mirror up to society, but our heads keep getting in the way when we look into that mirror.

We're so busy focusing on ourselves that we block our own view. Step aside and enjoy the scenery that expands out behind you in all directions. The reflections show the vast beauty all around us, but we need to know enough to step back a bit to let everything else fit in.

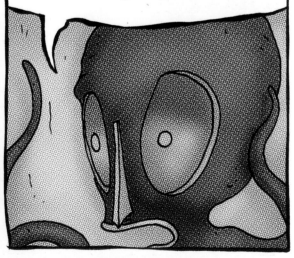

This is your city as much as it is theirs. The monsters aren't out to take your city so much as trying to make room for themselves. Can you live with that? Will you allow the city to evolve and adapt? Are you willing to choose your battles? If they don't belong here, then neither do you.

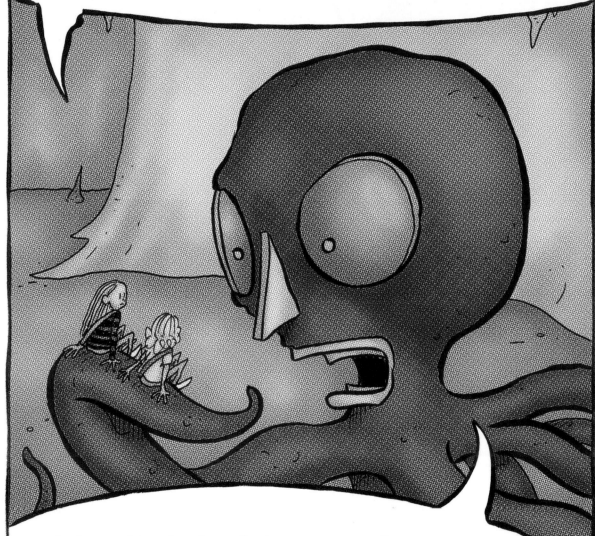

We have hundreds of thousands of stories here. These are just some of them. Ours is a city of artists and poets and musicians, and where else than among these misfits can other misfits fit?

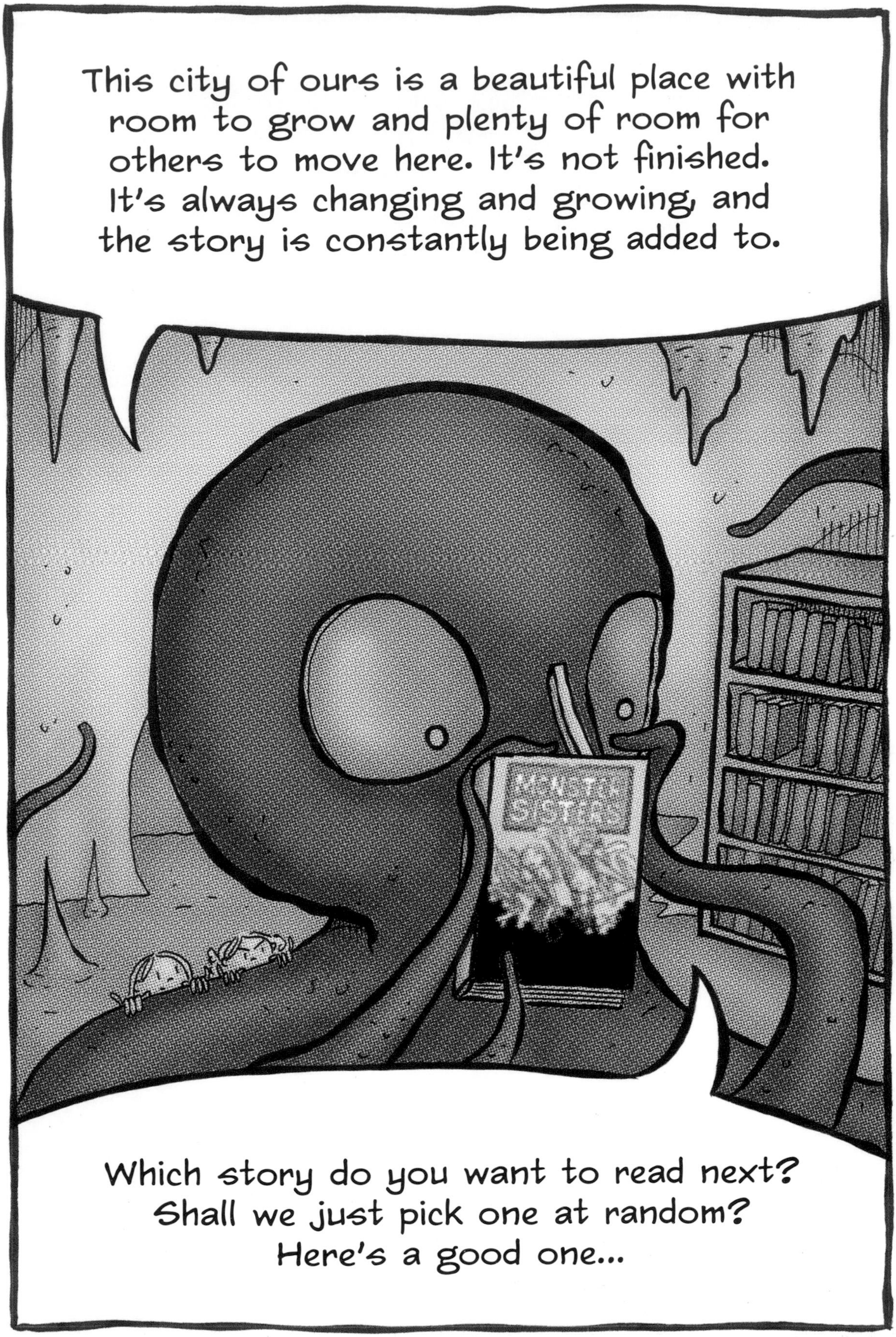
This city of ours is a beautiful place with room to grow and plenty of room for others to move here. It's not finished. It's always changing and growing, and the story is constantly being added to.
MONSTER SISTERS
Which story do you want to read next? Shall we just pick one at random? Here's a good one...

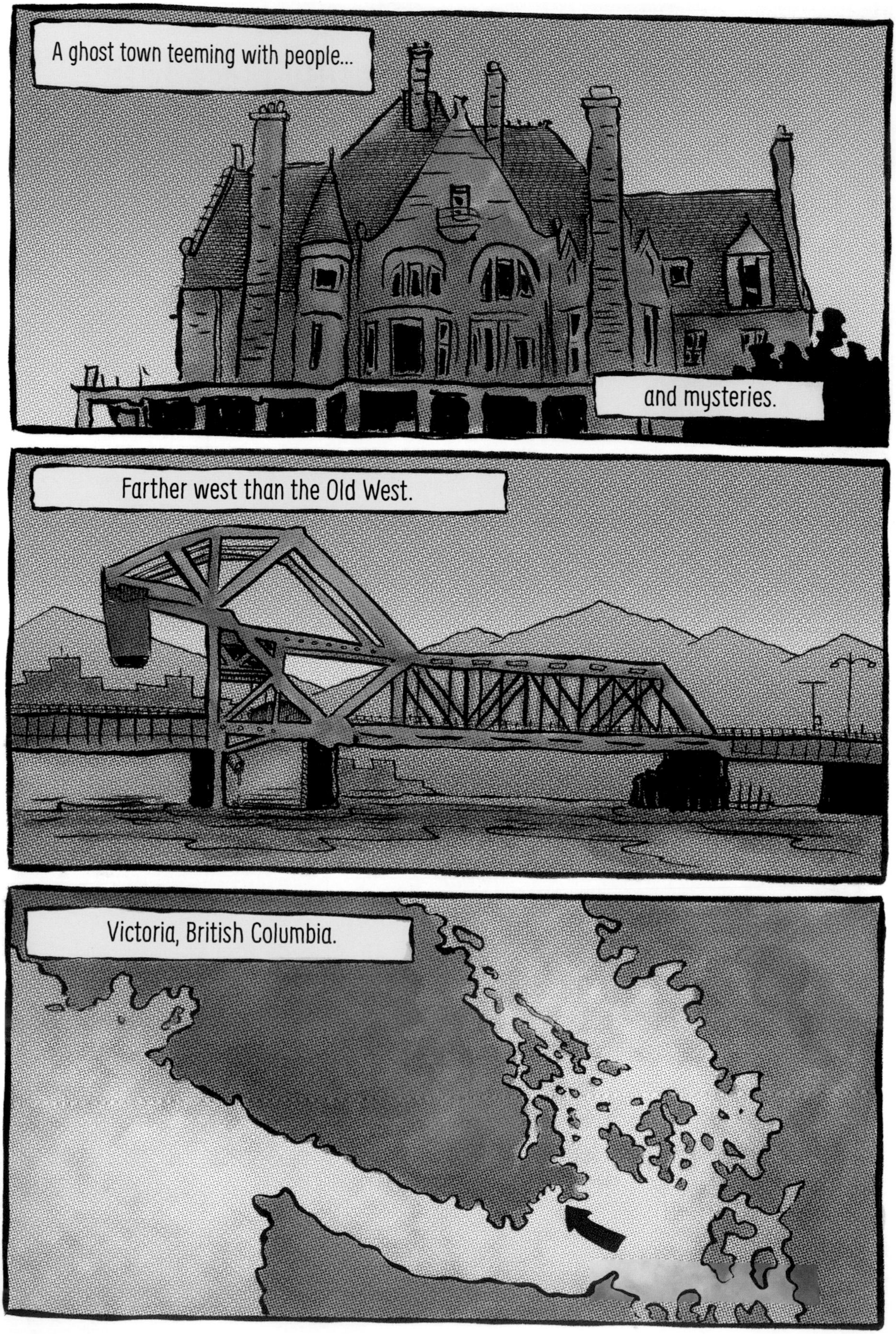
A ghost town teeming with people...
and mysteries.
Farther west than the Old West.
Victoria, British Columbia.

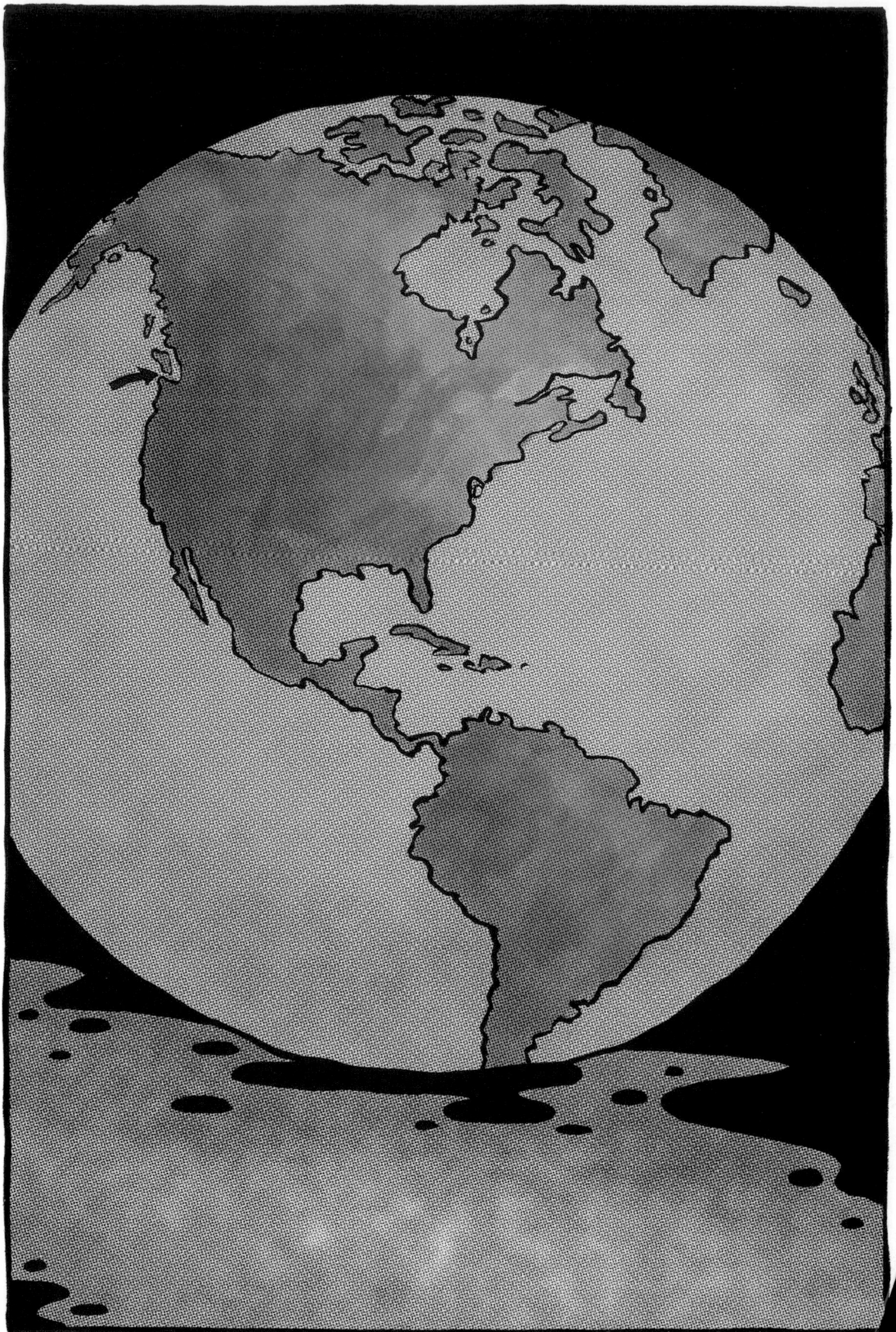

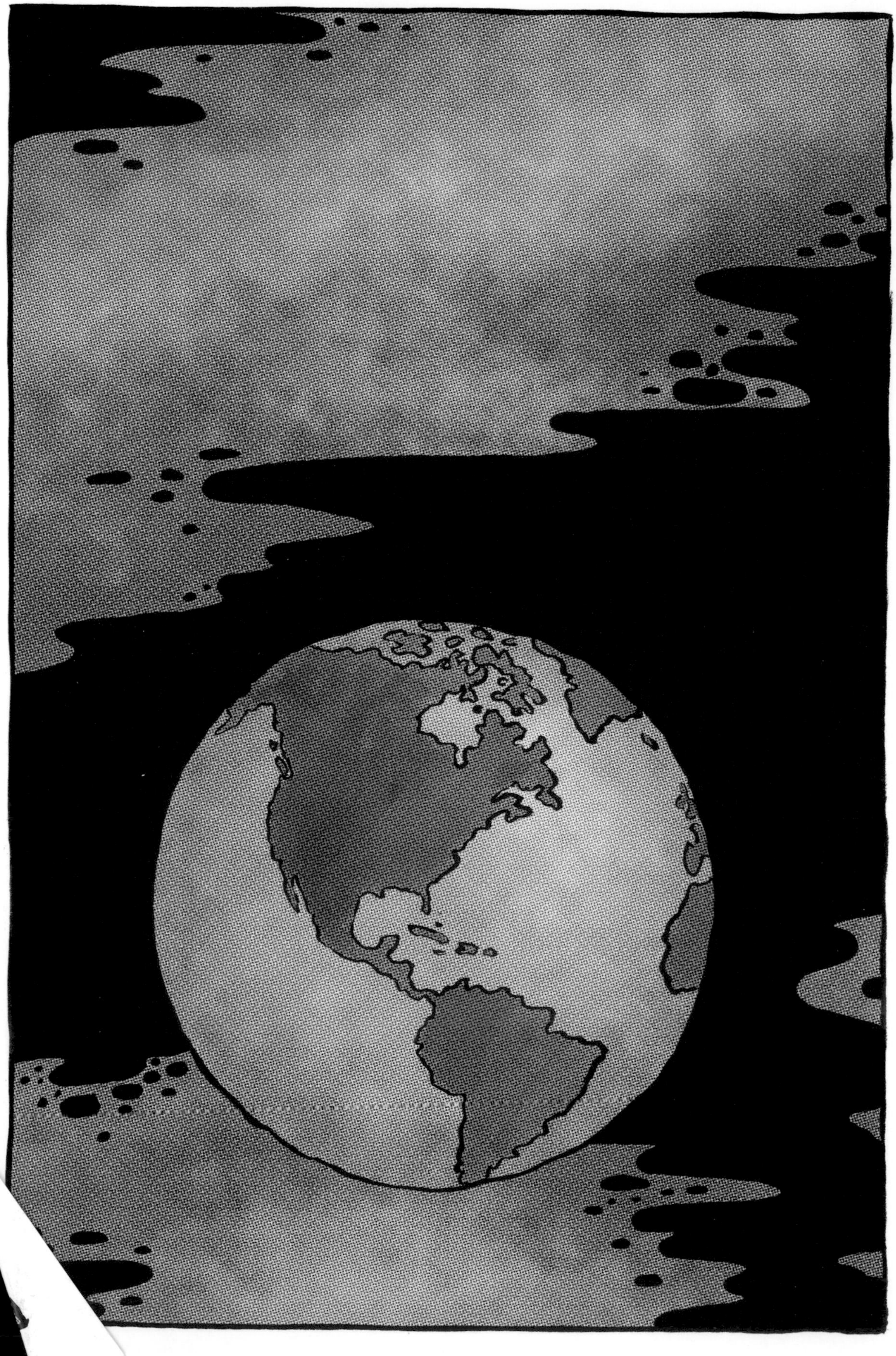

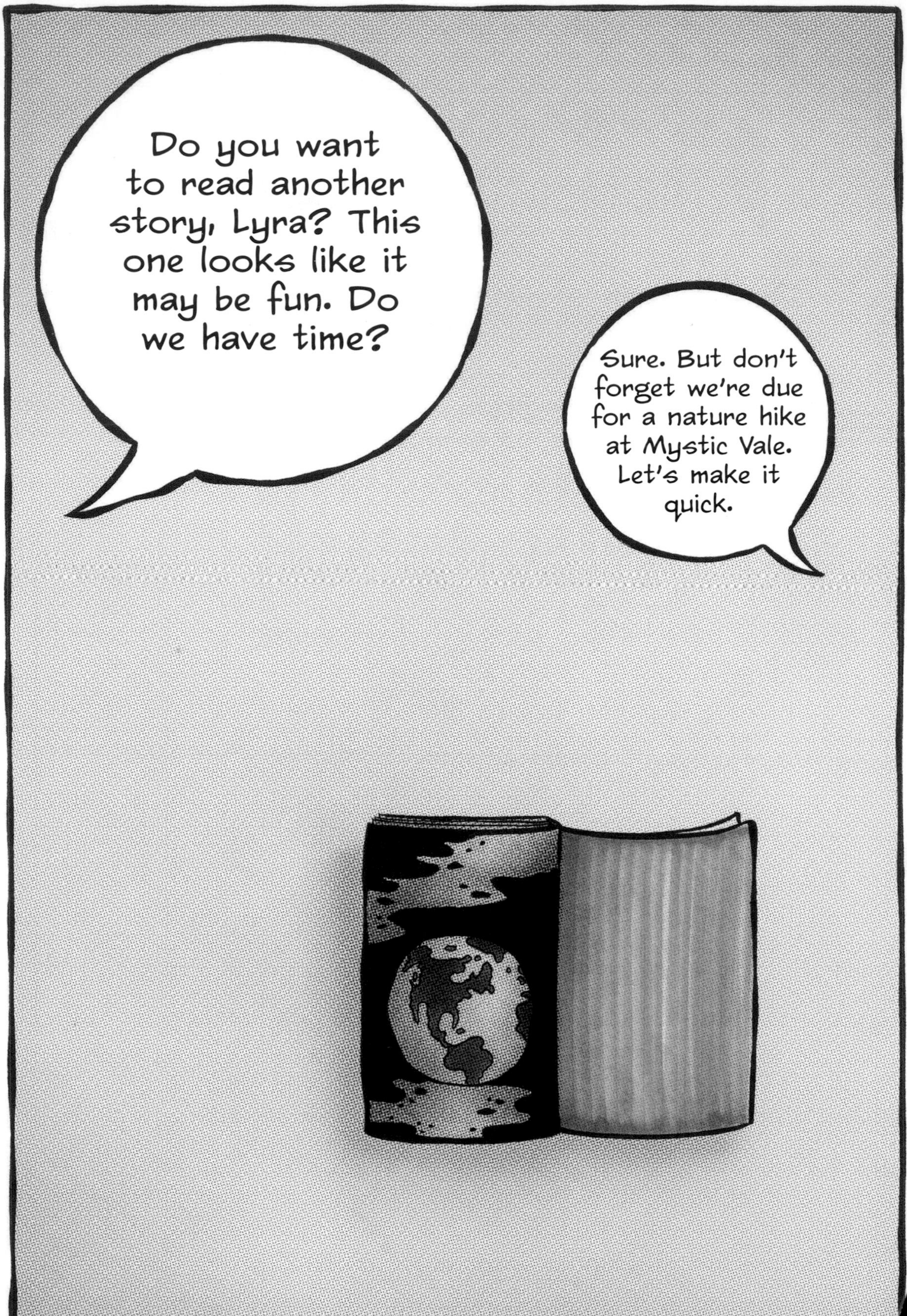
Do you want to read another story, Lyra? This one looks like it may be fun. Do we have time?
Sure. But don't forget we're due for a nature hike at Mystic Vale. Let's make it quick.

Go back to the beginning with
The Monster Sisters Book One

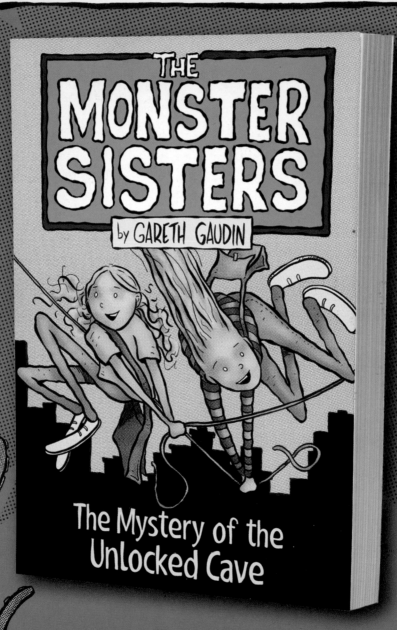

"The Monster Sisters are
rabble-rousing, smart-talking kids."
—School Library Journal